The dead soldi quite recently.
Probably a small raiding party behind or a dedicated group of guerillas with some particular object in view.

Hammond walked from the hut and laid the rifles on the ground. There was blood on his hands and shirt. He said in a flat voice, 'Anything else?'

Trewin stared at him fixedly. He wanted to explain, to sympathise, but the words held back. 'We'll get some real daylight in a moment, Sub. Then we can signal the ship from up here, right?' He raised his voice, 'Do you read me?'

Hammond nodded dully.

'Good. Now post the men around the clearing. We don't want to get jumped ourselves.'

He pulled the revolver from his holster and turned it over in his hands. The touch of the warm metal was not reassuring. It just seemed to bring the nightmare a little closer.

Also in Arrow by Douglas Reeman

Douglas Reeman

THE PRIDE AND THE ANGUISH

ARROW BOOKS

Arrow Books Limited
17-21 Conway Street, London W1P 6JD

An imprint of the Hutchinson Publishing Group

London Melbourne Sydney Auckland
Johannesburg and agencies throughout
the world

First published by Hutchinson 1968

Arrow edition 1970

Reprinted 1970, 1973, 1974, 1976, 1979 and 1983

Made and printed in Great Britain
by The Anchor Press Ltd
Tiptree, Essex

ISBN 0 09 907940 2

Contents

Author's Note

The invasion and lightning defeat of Singapore—the 'Gibraltar of the Far East'—was a catastrophe and a disgrace, but like most military disasters there were shades of glory, too. Looking back over the twenty-six years since those tragic days it is perhaps significant that the courage and desperate determination of the few overshadow the craven incompetence and foolish optimism of the many.

Today, the true weight and meaning of that defeat are still showing themselves, for with the fall of Singapore an enduring and respected link between East and West was broken. It has never been, and may never be, repaired.

The reasons for the swift success of the Japanese invasion have been stated many times. The ill-founded belief that an enemy would attack by sea and never through the Malayan jungles. The confidence in naval and air power, which because of other commitments and crushing losses, as well as short-sighted planning, were not available when they were most needed.

But there were other reasons of a more personal nature, for which there was no quick solution. While far-off Europe had endured two years of anguish and war, Singapore had retained a remote, colonial existence, where segregation was the rule rather than the exception, and the bravery and value of fighting men were not considered until too late.

When the blow fell, morale crumbled with it, because danger, like affluence, cannot be shared unequally.

D.R.

I
The Flagship

The midday sun blazed relentlessly across Singapore's wide naval anchorage so that the lines of moored warships and auxiliaries seemed pinned to the sea's flat, glittering surface like models. Around and between the grey hulls there was an aimless but constant movement of other, stranger craft. Sampans and water-taxis, and tall weathered junks, reminders of another way of life which lay behind the haze-shrouded hills and the gleaming white buildings which crowded the waterfront.

The slow-moving taxi ground into bottom gear and climbed up a straight road away from the anchorage, its wheels spewing out yellow dust across the ever-changing procession of Malays, Chinese and Indians which grudgingly parted to allow the taxi through, and then closed ranks immediately in a seemingly endless throng of humanity.

The Sikh driver swung the wheel and jerked the taxi to a halt. 'This is the place, sir.' He stared incuriously at the square white building with its marine sentry and neat Malay policeman and reached out to open the door for his passenger.

Lieutenant Ralph Trewin winced as he stepped on to the road and felt the sun smash across his shoulders like an open furnace. He saw the helmeted marine watching him cautiously, and beneath his unblinking scrutiny he felt suddenly unclean and crumpled. He was wearing the same uniform in which he had stepped aboard the big troopship at Liverpool, and that too seemed to add to his sense of unreality. It was like part of the England he had left behind. The England of 1941, grey and grimly united at the end of a long summer of disasters and defeats.

He turned and shaded his eyes to peer down at the shimmering anchorage where some sturdy tugs were already nudging same troopship into the fairway ready for the next trip. Out here, in the sunshine, surrounded by life and colour of another world, she looked alien, a reminder of the war Trewin had left behind. She was an old Shaw Savill liner, her tall sides shining in dazzle paint and streaked with rust and red lead from her new and harder usage. Trewin watched her backing between two anchored cruisers and then thrust her from his thoughts. That part of it was over. The long weeks in convoy, with each thrust of the screws carrying him further and further from the life and death he had come to understand so well. Even the stopping places seemed vague and distorted now. Through the Bay, with its high-crested rollers and the nerve-jarring crash of a torpedo in the night as a lagging freighter fell victim to one of the shadowing U-boats. Gibraltar, and a day of gaiety, the strange sights of well-lit shops, crowded streets, but hardly a woman to be seen. On and on, with ships joining and leaving the convoy like busy tradesmen. Freetown, where the battered little corvettes had handed over to an escort of lean destroyers. Simonstown, and, after a night of heavy drinking, on across the empty vastness of the Indian Ocean to Trincomalee, where the trooper had taken on another mass of soldiers en route for the final destination, Singapore.

Trewin paid the driver and turned hastily away as the taxi roared back down the hill, tooting noisily as it cleaved through the endless throng of people.

Trewin returned the marine's salute and walked through the gateway. There was a well-watered square of lawn upon which stood a painted signboard. It stated: 'Rear-Admiral, East Coast Patrols'. Beside it was a smaller board which said: 'Tennis tournament tonight!'

He strode along a neat gravel drive, his uniform clinging to his body like another skin, his throat dry and craving for a drink. He still did not know what he was doing here. He had left England with a handful of other naval personnel, his orders clear and concise. He was to take command of an armed patrol launch, one of several which were being sent to Singapore to help in the work of preventing infiltration by saboteurs and arms-smugglers. But within a few minutes of the troopship's arrival he had been seized by a harassed lieutenant from naval headquarters and had been ordered here instead.

When he had pressed the officer for further details he had snapped, 'Your launch never arrived, old boy. Nor did any of the others. The ship bringing them was torpedoed two days out of the U.K.' He had smiled vaguely. 'Curiously enough, their engines got here right on time in another ship.' He had gone off, shaking his head, without a further word.

A marine orderly stepped from the shade and asked, 'You'll be Mr. Trewin, sir?' His eye strayed to the wavy gold lace on his sleeve and his lips puckered slightly. 'If you'll come this way, sir?'

Trewin followed the orderly through a long, cool corridor, past offices which for the most part seemed deserted and silent. He had not failed to note the expression on the marine's face. In point of fact, Trewin had already noticed how few reservists there seemed to be in Singapore. Like the war, they seemed apart and far away.

The marine opened a door and said curtly, 'If you'll wait here.'

Trewin walked to the window of the small waiting room and stared down across the square of green grass. He could see a few groups of white-uniformed officers walking away from the main building as if some silent signal had driven them from their hidden offices.

Another door opened, and a tall, tanned lieutenant in white drill, gestured with a sheaf of papers. 'In here, please.' He waited until Trewin had followed him into the larger office and then said impatiently. 'You're a bit late, Trewin, so I'll make it short.' He leafed through some more papers and added, 'You know about the change of orders, of course?'

'Only what I was told in the trooper. Does that mean I'll be going back to England now?'

The lieutenant stared at him. 'Good Lord, no!' He glanced

at his watch. 'You've been passed on to us. A lot of our people have been sent away to other ships. We're getting a bit thin on the ground out here.' He looked over Trewin's creased uniform. 'Still, I expect you'll settle in all right.' He handed Trewin a sealed envelope. 'You've to report aboard the *Porcupine* immediately. It's all in the envelope, old boy.' He reached under his desk and picked up a tennis racket. 'Now I must dash. I've got to get in some practice.'

Trewin stood his ground, feeling the tired anger throbbing behind his eyes like an old wound. 'What is the *Porcupine*? And what am I supposed to do?'

The lieutenant glared. 'You're to take over as first lieutenant.' He walked deliberately to the door. 'I'd have thought that as a reservist you'd have jumped at the job!'

Trewin had been carrying his raincoat across his shoulder, and very deliberately he let it fall across his arm. He saw the lieutenant's eye fall to the ribbon of the Distinguished Service Cross which had been hidden beneath the raincoat and then said calmly, 'Thank you for telling me. Now don't let me detain you from your, er, duties.' He walked past the officer and out into the sunlight.

The marine orderly was waiting for him. 'I've laid on a car, sir. It'll take you straight down to the flagship right away.'

Trewin turned guardedly. *'Flagship?'*

The marine nodded gravely. 'Oh yes, sir. The *Porcupine* is the flagship of the squadron.'

Trewin was still smarting from the lieutenant's rudeness and his own cheap revenge. 'That'll make a change!'

He waited as the marine went to call the car's driver and then stared at himself in a tall mirror beside the entrance. Even if he had been dressed in a crisp drill uniform he guessed that he would never match the other officer's smartness. There was something rebellious, even wild, about himself, he thought vaguely. The grey eyes which stared back at him from the mirror were steady enough, but there was something else too. Hurt perhaps?

He was tall and well proportioned, but any smartness gained

by the strong shoulders and the easy stance was lost immediately in the dark, unruly hair which curled up around the edges of his cap.

Almost nervously he moved his left shoulder and tried to gauge whether the stab of pain was really from his wounds or from their memories. He closed his mind to them immediately. They were behind him. This was now.

He saw the driver watching from the doorway. '*Porcupine, sir?*'

Trewin hitched his raincoat across his shoulder and picked up his case. He nodded firmly. '*Porcupine,*' he said.

*   *   *

The little harbour launch wended its way casually between the busy traffic of native craft and service boats, a defiant plume of blue smoke trailing from its funnel. Trewin, the sole passenger, stood in the cockpit his arms resting on the canopy, his cap pulled forward to shield his eyes from the glare as he watched the anchored ships sliding past. How different they all seemed from those he had left behind, he thought. They looked clean and graceful, well painted and ready for an inspection. Taut awnings shaded their quarterdecks, and more than once he saw a raised telescope watching his slow progress.

Again he felt his mind drawn back to his last ship. Actually she could hardly be described as a ship. A Fairmile armed motor launch with a three-pounder, a couple of machine-guns and a crew of sixteen men. But she had been his command, and they had gone through a great deal together. It was easy to think back and see things more clearly than at the time. But Trewin was equally sure that commanding M.L. No. 99 was the first positive thing he had achieved in all his twenty-eight years of life.

They had been a happy little company in spite of the world around them. Doing any small job thrown their way, from escorting convoys to humping stores. From fighting off air attacks to open combat with E-boats in the Channel. They had wallowed amidst the pain and misery of Dunkirk, and when based at Harwich Trewin had learned to feel his way between the unlighted sandbars until he could do it blindfolded. Then with England alone against a victorious Germany he had been ordered to the Mediterranean, where with his companions he had watched the same pattern of retreats, the blind optimism of leaders made stale by the mentality of a peacetime service. On to Greece to help with yet one more withdrawal. More gasping, bitter soldiers to be pulled from the water under air attack, their eyes fixed with relief and emotion on the little, scarred M.L. which waited for them in spite of everything. The army had fallen back on Crete, and that was when M.L. 99's luck ended.

Crammed with retreating troops Trewin's boat had been one of the last to leave. Hard wear and little maintenance had fouled the engines, and while the mechanics worked desperately in the tiny engine room Trewin and his men had watched the bare, bright sky and waited.

He had counted seven aircraft. But there might have been more. Like diving gulls the planes had swooped over the motionless craft, the air tearing apart with the sounds of their guns, the scream and crash of high explosive. The boat had caught fire and almost immediately had started to capsize.

Trewin had stayed afloat for eleven hours, supported by his lifejacket, his soul only just hanging on to life. It had been like a mad dream. A nightmare which he shared without really seeming to belong to it. He had heard his men crying and drowning. Had felt the savage ache of his flayed shoulder where the blazing fuel had sent him like a torch into the water. When a minesweeper had found them there had been only six alive. The others stayed with their comrades, bobbing in their lifejackets or floating face down in the sea amidst a few slivers of charred timber.

Perhaps that was really why he had been sent to Singapore. Maybe he had said or done something in the hospital which had ruled him unfit for further combat? Trewin stared with sudden anger at the moored warships. They reminded him of the lieutenant at the naval headquarters he had just left. Sleek and untried. What the hell did they know about war?

The harbour launch puffed round a big transport and headed towards the Malayan shoreline. In the far distance Trewin could see the big causeway which linked the mainland with Singapore Island and the lush green foliage of Johore Bahru abeam of the launch. He stared round with surprise. The last of the big ships were falling astern. Nothing lay across the launch's bows but a line of small, antiquated river gunboats. Trewin had seen pictures of them in the past, in the days when such little ships kept order and showed the flag along the miles of China's great rivers and waterways. With the Japanese playing havoc in China most of these gunboats had, of course, been withdrawn and sent either to Singapore or Hong Kong. A few had even managed to find their way to the Mediterranean to join the rest of that mixed assortment of craft which supplied and protected the flanks of the desert armies.

Now, in the unwinking sunlight, beneath their awnings, the little ships looked for all the world like a line of Thames houseboats, or the old Mississippi river steamers. There were five of them moored in a single line, the largest one being anchored nearest to the causeway.

Trewin craned his head to look down at the boat's coxswain, a bearded seaman with tattooed arms. 'Where are we heading now?'

The coxswain showed his strong teeth. 'There she is, sir!' He raised one arm and swung the brass wheel with the other. 'At the head of the trot.' He barked an order and the launch started to lose way. 'The gunboat *Porcupine!*' He grinned broadly. 'Flagship of the East Coast Patrols!'

Trewin stared at the approaching vessel. Now he could see the name in gilt across her flat stern where the white ensign hung motionless above the clear water. She was about two hundred feet along, and being designed for shallow-draught work had most of her accommodation above the maindeck. There was a square, businesslike bridge, abaft which the main cabin section ran almost the full length of the deck. She had a single funnel, tall and thin, and two tapering masts which added to the first impression of past grandeur. Even her grey paint could not mask this effect. The paint was not the hasty, dull affair Trewin had come to recognise in home waters, but shone like polished glass, so that as the launch turned towards the varnished accommodation ladder he could pick out his own reflection.

The coxswain said, 'Trim little ship, ain't she, sir? Wouldn't mind a billet in 'er meself.' He snarled suddenly at the Chinese bowman, and as the launch nudged against the gangway he added, 'I believe the discipline's a bit sharp, sir.' He gave Trewin a hard stare and then dropped his eyes to his wavy stripes. 'If you'll pardon the liberty, sir?'

Trewin nodded. 'Thanks. I'll bear it in mind!'

He climbed up the short ladder and stepped on to the shaded sidedeck, saluting as he did so.

A very young sub-lieutenant in shirt and shorts saluted him in return and said, 'Lieutenant Trewin, sir?'

'Yes. I understand I am to take over as number one from . . .'

The young officer darted a quick glance at the idling launch and then sighed as it moved clear. 'Oh yes, we had a signal about you. Your predecessor has already gone, I'm afraid.' He pulled his mind away from the heavy launch and the obvious threat to the paintwork and said, 'Welcome aboard. I'm Hammond. Colin Hammond.'

He had a brusque, clipped way of speaking, but Trewin thought it was due more to nervousness than anything deeper. Hammond had an open, pleasant face with a rather sensitive mouth, and was at a guess about twenty.

Trewin glanced slowly around him, noting the spotless decks, the neatly flaked lines and the general air of disciplined perfection. Rather like a millionaire's yacht, he thought.

'And what do you do, Sub?'

Hammond tucked his telescope under his arm. 'I was doing an interpreter's course out here, so they sent me aboard as boarding officer and general dogsbody.' He smiled, so that he looked suddenly defenceless. 'Shall I show you around first, Number One? Or would you rather go to your quarters?'

Trewin started. It was strange being addressed as Number One after having a command of his own. 'A quick inspection, I think.'

They fell in step and walked along the port sidedeck. Hammond said at length. 'The captain's ashore, but left instructions that you were to stay on call for his return.' He added, 'How's England, sir?'

Trewin glanced sideways at him. Hammond could have been asking about the North Pole. Perhaps Singapore's impregnable fortress did that to people.

'Fighting,' he said flatly.

They walked on to the forecastle and stopped beside a four-inch gun. Hammond seemed cautious. 'This is "A" gun. We have another four-inch aft on the battery deck.' He pointed up beyond the bridge. 'That's back there.' He saw Trewin's smile and coloured. 'I'm sorry, Number One, but I'm not trying to play the "old soldier".'

Trewin nodded. 'That's all right, Sub. Keep talking. Otherwise I'll think I'm dreaming.'

Hammond led the way up a ladder through the quiet, orderly wheelhouse and on to the open bridge. From there Trewin could see the ship's top or battery deck and the other gun. There were also a pair of businesslike Oerlikons behind the funnel, and a squat, unknown shape shrouded in a canopy.

Hammond saw his gaze and said hastily. 'Three point seven howitzer.' He added awkwardly, 'For lobbing shells at shore positions, I believe. Though that was before my time.'

'Before anyone's time, I would think.' Trewin felt the heat across his neck and walked along the open deck until he could look down on her blunt stern.

The young sub-lieutenant said, 'Apart from the officers we have sixty ship's company. Half British, half Chinese. The latter are mostly engine-room and ordinary seamen.'

Trewin stared at him. 'But what do we *do*?'

'Oh, patrols.' Hammond was vague. 'We sail up the east

coast of Malaya. Three hundred miles. Two days up and two days down. We can get right inshore and keep an eye on things.'

He did not explain what 'things' were, nor did Trewin pursue the point. He had been told enough for a start, he decided.

Porcupine was something out of the past. As he looked around the neat, even prim exterior he felt the same edge of alarm which had stayed with him after Dunkirk and Crete.

They climbed down to the maindeck and he saw the ship's bell hanging from a beautifully polished dolphin. On it was inscribed: 'H.M.S. *Porcupine*, 1937'. So she was not really old. It was just her role which had been left behind when the Germans had marched into Poland. Maybe even before that.

He looked astern at the other gunboats. 'Are they all like this?'

Hammond shrugged. 'Most of them are older, of course. *Prawn* and *Shrike* were built in World War One, *Squalus* and *Grayling* 1924, and *Beaver* is our sister ship.'

Trewin turned away. Even their names were odd.

'Now this is the wardroom, Number One.' Hammond pushed open a screen door and they stepped into a large, rectangular room immediately below the bridge. It was panelled in dark wood, and, after an M.L., luxurious.

There was the usual small-ship clutter of furniture, magazine racks, and a stand of rifles and pistols below the vessel's crest on one bulkhead. It was, of course, a porcupine, with the motto '*Usque ad Finem*' in gold lettering below.

Trewin breathed out slowly. '*Touch me not!*'

Hammond watched him. 'Would you like lunch now? I'm the only one aboard and I've had mine.'

Almost to himself Trewin repeated, 'Touch me not!' Then he said wearily, 'No thanks. I want a shower and a change out of these clothes.'

Hammond touched a bell push and a wizened Chinese messman with a thin, goatlike beard pattered in from the pantry.

Hammond said offhandedly, 'This is Ching, our *makeelearn*. He can also show you your quarters. The cabin is next door, actually. He can also fix you up with better tropical rig than you can get in the U.K.'

Trewin had a sudden picture of London. The criss-cross of searchlights, the brittle cheerfulness of a city under bombardment. 'That's very reassuring, Sub.' He looked past the unwinking Chinese messman. 'Who are the other officers, by the way?'

Hammond seemed relieved to change the subject. 'There's Lieutenant Mallory, the navigating officer. He's an Australian.' He looked uncomfortable again. 'He's a reservist. Used to be in the Merchant Service.' He hurried on. 'And Mr. Tweedie, the gunner. He's been in the Navy since he was a boy.'

Trewin thought, I can imagine! He said, 'Thank you for the tour. I'll take myself to my cabin now.'

When Ching had closed the door behind him Trewin stood for several minutes by the square, shuttered scuttle staring out unseeingly at the anchored gunboats. He thought he heard the mournful hoot of the trooper's siren and imagined her butting back to England and reality.

Then he sat down on the neat bunk and looked at the small, comfortable cabin. His clothes had been unpacked and his bathrobe hung behind the door as if he had always been here. Almost savagely he threw off his clothes and glared at himself in a bulkhead mirror.

'Welcome to the flagship!' He heard the hiss of a shower adjoining the cabin and imagined the aged Ching waiting to tend his needs. His mouth turned upward in a rueful smile. 'Touch me not! That was *all* I needed!'

*　　　*　　　*

Trewin returned from his shower and stood breathing deeply below the deckhead fan. He saw with amazement that during his absence Ching had re-entered his cabin and had laid out a shirt and shorts on the bunk, with his white shoes standing on the small carpet beneath at an angle of forty-five degrees.

He towelled his unruly hair vigorously and felt some of the

strain leaving his body. Dropping the towel on the deck he jerked open a drawer and carefully unwrapped an untouched bottle of whisky. He had procured it aboard the troopship and had intended to save this luxury for commissioning his new command. He smiled grimly and poured a generous helping into a glass on the neat chest of drawers. It was unlikely that he would get a command of his own again for a long, long time, he thought. Maybe never. So he would just drink to himself.

The whisky tasted like fire on his empty stomach but he downed the glass in one swallow.

There was a tap at the door, and without thinking Trewin said. 'Come in.'

Sub-Lieutenant Hammond stepped over the coaming and stopped dead, his face colouring as he saw his new first lieutenant standing naked below the fan, a glass gripped in one hand.

Trewin had been so used to the crowded informality of a small M.L. that for a few seconds he was unaware of the young officer's embarrassment. Then he grinned and turned to gather up his bathrobe. As he slipped it over his shoulders he caught sight of Hammond's face in the bulkhead mirror and felt his stomach contract with something like shame.

Hammond blurted out, 'My God, Number One! Your *back*!' He shrugged helplessly 'What on earth happened?'

Trewin turned away. 'Forget it!' Angrily he poured another drink, feeling Hammond's eyes following every movement. 'Well? What did you want to tell me?'

Hammond pulled himself together. 'Just had a signal. The captain's coming offshore. He'll be aboard in ten minutes.' He ran his fingers through his fair hair. 'He'll want to see you at the gangway.'

'All right.' Trewin held his breath as the neat spirit explored his stomach and wished that Hammond would go away. Just one moment off guard, just one stupid bit of carelessness, and he was right back where he was before the shower.

He heard the door close and Hammond's footsteps retreating

down the passageway, and then with slow deliberation Trewin pulled on his shirt and shorts and sat down heavily on the bunk. Would he always be ashamed of his scalded body? How much longer could this ridiculous thing last? When there was so much to worry about and remember. With a frown he picked up his cap and let himself out of the cabin.

As he walked aft along the narrow sidedeck he noticed that the whole ship seemed to have come alive since he had climbed aboard just two hours earlier. It was strange to see Chinese faces beneath British caps and to hear the unfamiliar chatter of their voices.

There were British ratings, too, well tanned and healthy looking, who watched him pass and tried to catch his eye. Trewin ignored them. There would be time enough to get to know the men behind the faces, he thought. All the time in the world if Hammond's sketchy description of the *Porcupine*'s duties was to be believed. Chugging up and down the Malayan coast. Back and forth, back and forth. God, he thought savagely, what they could do with all these men at home, or in the Mediterranean!

He found Hammond beside the gangway, his telescope trained on a fast-moving motor boat. He said, 'Here he comes.' He glanced at a tall, bearded seaman. 'Man the side, Jardine!' To Trewin he added quickly, 'The captain always likes to see the gangway properly manned.' He sounded nervous.

Trewin stood aside as the boatswain's mates moistened their pipes on their lips, and a small Chinese rating pulled on a pair of white gloves and stood at the foot of the ladder. Trewin felt dazed. It was more like the quarterdeck of a battleship than a minute gunboat!

He watched narrowly as the small motor boat turned in a sharp arc and dashed smartly to the gangway. A boathook gleamed in the bright sunlight, and as the screw surged astern the boat sighed to a halt with the foot of the ladder exactly opposite the cockpit.

Trewin saw Hammond watching him expectantly and raised his hand in salute. The side party sprang to attention, and as the pipes trilled in salute the *Porcupine*'s captain stepped briskly on to the deck.

Commander Greville Corbett was slight in build and incredibly neat. He was dressed from top to toe in impeccable white drill, and wore a line of bright decorations as well as a sword which he now carried against his thigh like a pointer. It was hard to guess his age, and in the shade of his oak-leaved cap his face was entirely devoid of expression. But Trewin's attention was immediately drawn to his eyes. They were blue. Not the colour of the sea or the sky, but bright and pale like two polished stones. Even now they were moving swiftly around the motionless side party as if completely independent of the neat, rigid frame which carried them.

The captain said, 'You must be Lieutenant Trewin.' He did not wait for a reply, nor did he relax, but added sharply, 'The forrard awning is *slack*, Hammond!' The eyes paused on the sub-lieutenant's face. 'There is also a smudge on the hull below "A" gun.' The sword scabbard tapped the deck. 'I will not have the native seamen throwing their gash over the side! Deal with it at once!'

Hammond saluted and stuttered, 'Yes, sir! I told the chief bosun's mate to check the awning earlier . . .'

Corbett's mouth opened and closed in crisp, precise movements. '*You* are the officer-of-the-day, not the chief bosun's mate! So try not to cover your neglect in excuses!' He watched the wretched Hammond hurry away and then remarked calmly, 'Come with me, Trewin.'

Trewin followed the other man along the deck and up the ladder to the bridge. From behind he could see that Corbett's hair was grey beneath his cap but his figure and movements were as fresh as young Hammond's.

Corbett walked swiftly through the deserted chartroom and threw open the door of his day cabin. Without speaking he unclipped his medals and laid them on a desk and then removed his sword. Then he pressed a small bell and stared unwinking at the other door.

A small Chinese appeared as if by magic, and Trewin had

the crazy idea that he spent his whole life lurking behind that door just waiting for such a summons.

Corbett removed his cap and handed it to the steward. He said, 'Coffee.' Nothing else.

Trewin stared at the back of Corbett's neat head, feeling suddenly untidy and awkward in spite of his shower and fresh shirt. Then with a start he realised that Corbett's pale eyes were watching him from a bulkhead mirror.

The captain said, 'Well, if you are to be my first lieutenant, Trewin, you must certainly start by clamping down on slackness.' Then he turned, his tanned features relaxed and composed. 'I have just been with the admiral. I can't watch things here *all* the time.'

Coffee was brought and poured in complete silence, then as the messman departed Corbett sat behind the desk and opened a folder of signals. He said, 'I'll just get up to date. You sit and enjoy the coffee.'

Trewin sat. For a moment longer he watched Corbett's inclined head as he leafed slowly through the pile of signals, then he turned his attention to the cabin, as if to glean some other impressions of this extraordinary man.

It was a very spacious cabin indeed. High up on the superstructure it somehow managed to stay cool and shaded, and both furniture and fittings were in perfect order. There was a bookcase near Trewin's chair full of expensive, leather-bound books. Most of them seemed to be concerned with the lives of famous admirals, Rodney, Nelson and many more, and there were several outdated ones on astral navigation.

On the desk he could see a framed photograph of an unsmiling woman with fair hair and another of a small boy holding a rubber duck. The woman looked much younger than Corbett, Trewin decided. Without his cap Corbett seemed less jaunty, and he put his age at about forty-five. Yet he was only a commander? That was odd. Especially when at home every regular officer was being promoted at a fantastic speed as more and more half-trained reservists poured into the Navy to man

23

the growing ranks of ships and to fill the gaps left by an equally growing casualty list.

Corbett closed the folder with a snap. 'Damn fools!' He picked up his coffee and added offhandedly. 'You'll find things a bit different out here, Trewin.' His eyes fastened on Trewin's shoulder straps. 'You'll have to work twice as hard to catch up. This is a crack squadron. I intend it should stay so.'

He seemed to dismiss the subject and leaned back in his chair. Then he said, 'I understand you were a journalist before you joined up?'

Trewin thought of the dingy East End newspaper office with its staff of five reporters. 'That's right, sir.' What else could he say? It had been just one more milestone on his search for himself.

'Yet you were born in Dorset?' Corbett put his head on one side. 'So why did you go to work in London?'

Trewin stared at him. 'I felt like it, sir.'

'Quite so.' Corbett pursed his lips. 'You may wonder why I attach so much importance to the backgrounds of my officers, eh? Well, as I said, this is a crack squadron. And now that we can expect a slow stream of reserve officers it is necessary to investigate certain matters.' He gave what might have been a smile. 'Before this war you could gauge an officer by his attainment and rank. Nothing more was necessary.' He shrugged. 'Now we cannot be so sure.' He ignored Trewin's growing anger and continued coolly, 'And you are married.'

'She's dead, sir!' Trewin felt the throb of pain as he said the words. 'In an air raid.' He looked away from the pale eyes. 'It's not as quiet as this in London!'

Corbett shuffled some papers. 'And it is our duty to see that it remains quiet, as you put it.' He added, 'I am sorry about your wife.' Had Trewin been watching he would have seen Corbett's eyes stray to the framed photograph with something like sadness.

Then he said in a crisper tone, 'But still, you were in the R.N.V.R. before the war began, and you have had some experience of combat, it seems. So if you work hard at your duties

I see no reason why you should not make a success of your appointment.'

Trewin watched him dully. Then he replied quietly, 'There are sixty men aboard this ship, sir. And there are three hundred miles of coastline to patrol. I think I can manage that well enough.'

Corbett eyed him for several seconds as if making up his mind about something. 'I never take things on trust, Trewin. Time will tell me what I want to know about every man aboard this ship, do you understand?'

Trewin stood up. 'Is that all, sir?'

Corbett seemed to ponder. 'For the present. We sail tomorrow morning at 0700. By then I hope you will have made yourself familiar with my standing orders and with the heads of departments. Tomorrow you will take the ship to sea.' He smiled slightly. 'Just to get the feel of things.' He waited until Trewin had reached the door. 'One thing, Trewin. When I come aboard in the afternoon I do not want the gangway smelling of whisky. We have a crew which half consists of *native* seamen. Just remember that in future!' He stared down at his desk. 'You may go now.'

Trewin did not remember reaching his cabin, but found himself standing in front of that same mirror his eyes blazing with anger. He said aloud, 'The pompous, bloody bastard!' Then deliberately he opened his drawer and took out the bottle.

2
Toy Fleet

Lieutenant Ralph Trewin climbed on to the open bridge and glanced upwards at the masthead pendant. It hung quite limp, and although it was still early morning he guessed it was going to be another scorching day. He crossed the bridge and stared over the screen at the ship's broad forecastle. A faint cloud of vapour hung above the capstan, and he could see the anchor party moving busily around the cable and young Hammond right in the bows beside the jackstaff. It was all the usual excitement of getting a ship under way, he thought. It never left you, no matter what ship it happened to be. He swallowed hard, feeling the taste of coffee and the remains of a hasty breakfast.

There had been only one other officer at the wardroom table. Mr. Archibald Tweedie, the warrant gunner. He was a thickset, even squat little man with a brick-red complexion which had defied all the efforts of the sun to produce a tan. To Trewin he seemed typical. A hardcore gunner who had worked his way up through every rank on the lower deck to finally attain the thin gold stripe of his trade. Trewin knew from early experience that such men usually resented the quick commissions of the wartime reservists. He could sympathise to begin with, but as time wore on he found such attitudes tiresome and irritating. Tweedie, it seemed, was no exception. He had been formal and withdrawn throughout breakfast, and had spent most of the time reading a pile of newly arrived letters which lay beside his plate. Trewin had seen that the big, spidery handwriting which covered each sheet of paper made up very few words, yet Tweedie read each page as slowly as if he were studying the Bible.

Hammond had told Trewin earlier that the gunner was paying for a new bungalow in Southsea to which he had hoped to retire. The war had stopped all that and Tweedie had been sent to the Far East immediately after the first shots had been fired. Now apparently he relied on his wife's letters to keep him informed, not about her wellbeing, but of all the recent progress to bungalow and garden.

He had a tight, tapered mouth, and Trewin guessed that he probably suffered from stomach trouble. When the ship was in harbour and he was not required for duty, Tweedie just disappeared. Nobody knew where he went, and no one, it seemed, cared very much either.

Trewin forgot the morose gunner as a voice-pipe intoned, 'Steam on capstan, sir!'

He recognised the voice as belonging to the chief E.R.A., Nimmo, whom he had met the previous evening when exploring the engine room. *Porcupine* did not warrant a commissioned engineer, but Nimmo's square, competent face left Trewin in no doubt that the ship's power department was in excellent hands.

'Very good, Chief.' He looked round the bridge as a loud-speaker blared. 'Special sea dutymen to your stations! Stand by for leaving harbour!'

He loosened his shirt, feeling suddenly tense. All at once it was new and different again. He heard the clatter of running feet on ladders and sidedecks and saw the white-clad seamen scampering below the bridge as if their lives depended on it. Others appeared on the bridge, and below in the wheelhouse he heard C.P.O. Unwin, the coxswain, testing the wheel and speaking severely to one of the telegraphsmen.

There was a step behind him and Trewin turned to face a tall, lanky lieutenant who was carrying a folded chart under one arm. His shoulder straps showed that he was a reservist, and before Trewin could speak he said easily, 'I'm Ted Mallory, navigating officer.' He held out his free hand and raised one eyebrow. 'How are you doing?'

Trewin grinned. Mallory was the sort of man you either took

27

to immediately or disliked on sight. He had dark, steady eyes and deep lines around his mouth which gave him a sort of permanent derisive smile. He was very tanned and his cheeks were covered with tiny pockmarks, mementoes from some childhood acne.

'Glad to meet you.' Trewin looked across at one of the anchored gunboats. She too had steam up, and he could see the white caps of her officers along the bridge screen. 'We're sailing in company then?'

Mallory clipped the chart on to the bridge table and laid his ruler and dividers on top. 'Sure. We often do.' He smiled. 'A proper toy fleet, this is!' He glanced at his watch and became very serious. 'I was ashore till this morning, otherwise I'd have had a quiet word.' He screwed up his eyes and added, 'You seem a nice bloke, so I'd better warn you.' He waved his hand across the bridge. 'You may not know it, but the screws on this gunboat are in tunnels right inside the hull.'

Trewin nodded slowly. 'The chief did mention it.'

Mallory eyed him admiringly. 'You've been doing your homework! Anyway, what you may *not* know is that at half-speed or so you need very little helm. She's flat-bottomed and will sail on wet grass. Also, she'll swing round like a terrier if you put the wheel hard over.'

Trewin made a mental note of it. 'Thanks again. And I'm taking her out this morning. I might have muffed it.'

'Too right you would.' Mallory scowled and rubbed his eyes. 'He'd have *loved* that!' He sounded bitter.

'The captain?'

'Who else?' Mallory dropped his voice as a bridge messenger hurried past. 'He's off his nut; you realise that, I suppose?'

Trewin did not know what to say. Around and below him he could feel the ship coming alive, yet there was something strangely compelling in the Australian's tone which held him and made him listen.

Mallory shrugged. 'You're the first lieutenant now, so naturally you can't say anything.' He touched Trewin's arm. 'And I'm not giving you the cold shoulder either. No, you'll have to watch your step and see for yourself.' He grinned and breathed out noisily. 'Well, that's that. I guess from what I've heard you can take care of yourself.' He looked meaningly at the open hatch which led down to the captain's quarters. 'Apart from his lordship, you are the only joker aboard who has seen any action!'

Trewin replied slowly, 'I'd have thought you were the obvious choice for number one?'

'Me?' Mallory's grin broadened. 'I was mate of a bloody meat freighter. I used to make the run from Aussie to the U.K., and very nice too. But I *am* an Aussie, and, let's face it, there are too many stuck-up bastards in this Navy to allow a common bastard like me to get on. With no disrespect to you, of course.'

Trewin smiled. 'None taken.'

Mallory continued thoughtfully. 'The skipper thinks that all Aussies are a cross between bushrangers and the bloke who says *fair dinkum* and *good on yer* in every second breath. In fact, he likes everyone in a nice, neat category, so you'd better conform if you want to stay in one piece.'

A look-out muttered, 'The captain, sir.' He was addressing Mallory.

The Australian winked and looked down at his chart. 'Here we go then!'

Commander Corbett climbed briskly on to the freshly scrubbed gratings and stared fixedly at the forecastle.

Trewin saluted formally. 'Ship ready to proceed, sir.' He saw Mallory watching him and wondered how much of what he had said was true.

Corbett said, 'A fine morning, Trewin.' Then, 'Very well. Carry on.' He looked across and Mallory and added, 'Pilot here will have the necessary charts, I *hope*.'

Mallory spread his hands. 'Oh too right, sir.' He spoke in the most terribly assumed drawl, and Trewin stared at the captain expecting him to cut the Australian down to size, but he merely nodded and then lifted his glasses to study the other gunboat.

Trewin leaned across the chart table and hissed, 'What the hell are you trying to do?'

Mallory's big hands moved the parallel rulers with skilled ease, and he replied calmly, 'I always speak like that to him. It makes him feel secure.' He grinned hugely. 'Wogs and Aussies, the skipper likes to know who he's dealing with.'

A signalman shouted, 'Signal, sir! Proceed when ready!'

Corbett frowned. 'I'm ready now!'

Trewin tried to ignore him and walked to the side of the bridge. He saw Hammond wave back to his signal and heard the steady clank of the capstan. He said, 'Stand by.'

Below his feet he heard the clang of telegraphs and felt the responding tremble of engines through the soles of his shoes.

Clank, clank, clank. He watched the cable jerking through the hawsepipe where Chinese seamen were busy scrubbing each link with their brooms before it vanished below decks. Then Hammond yelled, 'Up and down, sir!'

It was now or never. Trewin held the picture of the current in his mind like a chart and snapped, 'Slow ahead together! Starboard fifteen!'

'Anchor's aweigh!'

Trewin watched narrowly as the blunt bows started to swing across the backdrop of green hills. He had done the first part. Not too quick, but not too late either. He crossed to the compass, and checked the slow swing around the anchorage.

'Midships. Steady. Steer one one zero!' Around him the business of paying salutes was well under way. Trilling pipes, and once when they surged past a massive cruiser, the lordly blare of a bugle.

Trewin suddenly found that he had almost forgotten about Corbett. He was actually enjoying conning the little gunboat down the Strait towards the open sea. As Mallory had predicted, the *Porcupine* answered well to minimum helm on her triple rudders, but he knew that but for the man's warning he would have made a mess of it. In the M.L. he had found it necessary to put the wheel hard over for anything but full speed.

30

Once when he glanced sideways at Corbett he saw him staring astern at the other gunboat which had weighed and picked up station automatically with the *Porcupine*. It was odd that Corbett had failed to mention about the ship's handling. It might have been an oversight, but Corbett did not seem the sort of officer who overlooked anything.

Minutes dragged into half an hour, and Mallory unclipped the chart and replaced it with another as the finger of Changi Point reached out to starboard and the channel began to widen and fall away on either beam. He said quietly, 'Sandbars now. Check your bearings.' He made sure that Corbett was facing the other way. 'He's waiting to dash in and rescue the ship from your clutches!'

Trewin frowned but checked the bearings from the compass. A nodding buoy dipped in the gunboat's wake and a motionless junk threw its shadow across the port rail as the bows lifted slightly to another increase of speed.

Corbett said suddenly, 'Fall out harbour stations. Red watch to cruising stations, if you please.' He settled himself in a tall wooden chair which was bolted to the port side of the bridge and tilted his cap over his eyes. Then he said, 'You're getting the idea, Trewin. But don't be too impulsive next time. A ship is a living thing. Not a lump of scrap.'

Hammond scrambled on to the bridge and saluted. 'Secured for sea, sir.'

Corbett did not turn. 'When you weigh anchor again I want the Jack and the Ensign hauled down *together*, not when the signalmen *feel* like doing it.'

'Aye, aye, sir.' Hammond looked at Mallory who merely shrugged.

'And get the cable repainted. It looks like salvage!'

Trewin walked to the other side of the bridge and stared forward. Already the hands were busy with brooms and scrubbers, and he could see the chief bosun's mate supervising a party of men who were armed with paint and brushes. He wondered how they could all be kept so busy. Like the offending anchor cable, the whole ship looked absolutely perfect.

31

The decks were so clean that he would have been happy to eat off them. Upperworks and rigging shone in the morning sunlight and would not have seemed out of place aboard the Royal Yacht.

Corbett said abruptly, 'Make a signal to *Squalus* in fifteen minutes, Trewin. Tell them to exercise secondary armament in accordance with the admiral's instructions. We will do likewise.'

'Ay, aye, sir.'

Trewin beckoned to a signalman but stopped as Corbett added, '*Without* ammunition, of course. There is absolutely no point in squandering war materials.'

Once again Trewin's mind returned to England. When he had left Liverpool the summer was already finished. Now it was November, but out here there was no reality or comparison. In London they would have the additional hazards of long nights in which to cower in shelters and beneath stairways as the bombs hammered down. Like the other November when he had returned from Harwich for an unexpected twenty-four hours' leave. He had telephoned Chris from a railway station where the train had stopped for some unaccountable delay. She had been laughing over the telephone. Laughing. Two hours later he had stood at the end of the street. Or where the street had once been. It still did not seem possible.

They had only been married for a year. Even that had seemed like an accident at the time. They had drifted into it, and had both been surprised by the intensity of the love which grew between them. Now she was dead. Wiped away as if she had never been.

Mallory picked up a pair of glasses and studied the low green coastline and the jutting fingers of pale sand. 'Do you think the war will come out this way, Number One?' He kept his voice down and he had to repeat his question before Trewin was dragged from his brooding thoughts.

He replied harshly, 'I should think so. The Japs are playing merry hell right through Indo-China, so what is to stop them having a crack at us?'

Mallory grimaced. 'They'll never attack Singapore, that's for sure. The Yanks will be the target this time.'

Corbett turned in his chair. 'I hope they do attack Singapore!' Beneath his cap his pale eyes flashed with sudden anger.

'My God, our country could do with a few victories! Just let them come, that's what I say!'

Mallory asked innocently, 'Singapore's that good, is it, sir?'

'Of course! If you spent a little more time studying our defence systems and a little less on the local fleshpots you might tend to understand it better.'

Mallory winked behind his back, but Trewin still felt strangely angry. They all looked on it as some sort of game. What the hell was the matter with them?'

He said coldly, 'They thought the Maginot Line was good, too!'

Corbett sighed. 'The danger out here is infiltration and sabotage. We must all be on our toes. We won't have *time* for making excuses, eh?'

A silence fell over the bridge, and apart from the occasional helm order Trewin was prepared to let it remain so.

On the battery deck the gun crews went through their drills like regimented dummies, with nothing more warlike to break the silence than the occasional click of metal or Tweedie's grating bark of command. It struck Trewin that the gunnery, like the ship's very presence off the coastline, was merely a pretence, an annoying necessity which had to be tolerated, but which must in no way interfere with the daily routine and the preservation of old standards.

He stared up at the bright sky and tried not to think of what would happen if it suddenly filled with attacking aircraft. They would all die bravely, no doubt. But that was not enough. It never had been enough. It was strange how in every recent war it seemed to take several years to weed out the empty minds of peacetime strategy. Men who had reached their powerful commands by seniority or influence, and were more amateur in their trade than those untrained beyond the requirements of battle. Except that in this war there was no longer any time left. England was walled up behind her defences, feeding from the lacerated Atlantic convoys which daily ran the gauntlet of bombers and U-boats. Only the Far East possessions were so far immune from the heat of battle. But for how much longer?

Corbett snapped, 'Signal the *Squalus*, Trewin! She's out of station!' He moved in his chair as if it was restricting him. 'You must try to watch these things!'

The flags soared up the *Porcupine*'s yards almost before Trewin could pass the order, and the other gunboat's acknowledgement was just as swift. Either they were all well trained or they were used to Corbett's sudden complaints.

Mallory tapped the chart and said, 'We shall be putting into the Talang River, Number One. It's about one hundred and fifty miles up the east coast and pretty treacherous. The Army are building a fuel dump there and we usually drop in to show the flag.'

Corbett had excellent hearing. 'I shall expect you to con her into the anchorage there, Trewin. Good practice for you, eh?' He was looking the other way but seemed to be expecting a reply.

Trewin said flatly, 'I think it's a mistake to do these patrols so regularly, sir. If there are any Japanese agents hereabouts they'll not hang around to wait for us!'

Mallory laughed but fell silent as Corbett said scathingly, 'The very fact that we are here is enough! Anyway, we are not at war with Japan. In the last war they were our allies. And damn good ones, too!'

Trewin walked to the rear of the bridge. To himself he muttered angrily. 'And so were the Italians!'

*   *   *

Four o'clock the following morning found the *Porcupine* steaming steadily northwards parallel with the Malayan coast. After the clammy stuffiness of his cabin Trewin found the upper bridge cool and refreshing, and he stood relaxed by the voice-pipes as Sub-Lieutenant Hammond finished writing his

34

comments in the log before handing over the watch. The sky was full of stars, but already there was a brightness above the horizon, and Trewin knew that it would soon be like an oven in the open bridge.

Hammond signed his name in a flourish and said with a yawn, 'She's all yours, Number One. Course three five nine.'

Trewin leaned over the chart table and nodded. 'Still knocking up a steady eight knots, I see.'

Hammond half listened to the gabble of voices in the pipes by his side. 'You've got a good quartermaster in Jardine. He never falls asleep at the wheel!' He turned towards the ladder. 'The captain's down for a shake in two hours, sir. He always likes to be on the bridge when we turn into the Talang River.'

Trewin glanced astern. Still on station, as if pinned to an invisible towline, he could clearly see the white crescent of the other gunboat's bow-wave and the gleaming eyes of her navigation lights.

Hammond followed his glance. '*Squalus* will push on another twenty-five miles to Kuantan. We rendezvous again in forty-eight hours.' He yawned even wider. 'God, you can set your watch by it. I wish that just once we would change places or something.'

Petty Officer Kane, the ship's G.I., loomed out of the darkness. 'Blue watch closed up at cruising stations, sir!'

Trewin nodded. 'Very good.'

Hammond threw one leg on to the ladder. 'I'm for bed.' His head vanished over the side of the bridge, and Trewin had the watch to himself. Methodically he filled and lit his pipe and hung his cap on one of the voice-pipes. Then he leaned on his arms on the screen and stared emptily over the pale wedge of the gunboat's forecastle.

He could feel the gentle tremble of the engines coursing up through his shoulders, and occasionally caught the acrid tang of funnel smoke as it fanned down over the bridge, caught by the offshore breeze.

It was strange that they were going into Talang, he thought. *Porcupine* was the senior ship, the *flagship* in fact, and from

35

what he could gather Talang was a pretty remote outpost compared with Kuantan to the north.

He frowned. It was useless to keep on thinking about Corbett's systems and motives for anything. He thought back over the previous day, when under a blazing sun the gunboat had moved inshore and then followed the coastline, sometimes with the nearest beach less than half a cable clear. The ship's shallow draught took a bit of getting used to. On several occasions the water had been so clear he had seen large, isolated rocks which looked as if they were lying merely inches below the surface. But the gunboat had pushed above them with complete indifference, her own stubby shadow moving along the sandy bottom to mock at his fears.

The scenery had been breathtaking. Rolling banks of green jungle, broken here and there by small clustered villages. There were craft in plenty, too. Fishing boats and sailing coasters which looked like something from another century.

It was not surprising that people failed to comprehend that other war, Trewin thought bitterly. Given time he might even begin to feel the same.

Corbett had spent most of that day on the bridge, saying very little, but apparently seeing everything that went on about him. When a watch was relieved he would make a point of glancing at the bridge clock. If there was too much noise on the maindeck he would crane forward and make some crisp comment about slackness in discipline. Trewin decided that if that was the worst Corbett could do he could learn to live with it.

Routine aboard the *Porcupine* was formal and regular. Trewin took every available minute to familiarise himself with the ship's company, and his good memory for faces and names was already proving useful. The petty officers seemed a very capable bunch. Most of them were a breed apart from the Navy Trewin had come to know. Old 'China hands', they showed none of the whimsical nostalgia for Chatham or Devonport, Portsmouth or Scapa, which he might have expected. Like the ship, the men who served her seemed to belong to a navy within a navy. Some of the other British ratings were already forming personality and meaning, too. They made up the bulk of the ship's key men, gunners, communications and the like. But the Chinese seamen, or *natives* as Corbett chose to describe them, were still a mystery. They looked alert and happy enough, but it was impossible to know what they were thinking.

The *Porcupine* had originally served on the Yangtze, so it was quite likely that some of her Chinese crew had once lived in that part of the world. The homes of some of them were probably suffering the agony of Japanese occupation or worse, yet there was nothing to show either worry or apprehension on their smooth faces.

Trewin wondered how his own parents were getting on in Dorset. His father kept a small boarding house near Lyme Regis, and Trewin had often spent his summer holidays helping to run their hire boat for the benefit of the carefree visitors. Now the boarding house was used for military billets, and the beach lay enmeshed in barbed wire. It was a different world again.

Petty Officer Kane stepped up on to the gratings and held out a large mug of tea. 'Char, sir.' His eyes glittered in the masthead light as he watched Trewin cradle the cup in his hands. 'I expect you're finding all this a bit strange, sir?'

Trewin smiled. 'A bit, but I hope it doesn't show too much.'

Kane relaxed slightly. He was testing the new officer. Feeling his way. 'The old *Porcupine* seems to have taken to you, sir.' He grinned. 'She can be a right little tartar when she has a mind.'

Trewin asked suddenly, 'My predecessor. Where did he go?'

Kane looked away. 'Lieutenant Foley. A nice gentleman he was.' He said awkwardly, 'There was a spot of trouble. He ran the ship on to a sandbar off Dungun. No damage, of course, but it didn't look too well.' He studied Trewin thoughtfully. 'The admiral was aboard at the time.'

Trewin pondered on these bare details. The admiral. He had a quick picture of the headquarters with its green lawn and deserted offices.

Kane added, 'The admiral is an old shipmate of the captain's. In the thirties that was, of course.' He shrugged with the indifference of one who is not involved. 'Still, you can't always choose your mates in this regiment.'

A look-out called, 'Light buoy on the port bow, sir!'

Trewin lifted his glasses and then checked the flashing light against the chart. 'Very well. Report when it comes abeam.' He turned back to the tall petty officer. 'Have you been aboard long?'

'Three years, sir.' He seemed to read Trewin's thoughts. 'The captain joined us early last year. We've been senior ship ever since.'

'I see.'

'Light abeam to port now, sir!' The look-out sounded bored.

'Very good. Starboard ten.' He listened to Jardine's voice from the wheelhouse and peered down at the shaded compass repeater. 'Steady. Steer zero one zero.'

Kane said, 'You sound as if you've been doing it all your life, sir, if you'll pardon the liberty.'

Trewin grimaced. 'That's how it feels, too!'

A telephone buzzed and he groped his way across the gratings. 'Bridge. Officer of the watch speaking.'

Corbett's voice scraped in his ear, distorted and edgy, as if the captain had just emerged from a deep sleep. 'You just altered course!' It sounded like an accusation. 'Is everything all right?'

'We've just passed Rompin Light Buoy, sir. We are on the new course now.' There was a long pause and he could hear Corbett's heavy breathing.

'I see, Trewin. Very well. But watch out for other shipping, fishing boats and so on.'

Trewin waited and Corbet added sharply. 'Did you hear what I said?'

'Aye, aye, sir.'

'Well answer, dammit! And if you're not sure of anything, anything at all, for God's sake call me, d'you understand?'

The phone went dead and Trewin stared at the handset for several seconds before dropping it on its hook.

Kane coughed. 'He's a light sleeper, sir.'

Trewin relit his pipe with quick, savage movements. 'In the English Channel you won't see any damn lights at all, and if you meet another ship the chances are it'll blow the bloody guts out of you!' He sucked hard on the pipe. 'Fishing boats indeed!'

Kane grinned. 'I'll be off on my rounds, sir. I'll call the captain myself when it's time.'

Trewin glared at the slow-moving bow-wave and felt angry with himself for his outburst. It wouldn't help anything if Kane told his cronies that the new number one was ruffled by what the captain had said. After all, the captain, *any* captain, could say what the hell he liked!

Another hour went by, and the ship regained her personality from the shadows as the masts and upperworks were bathed in pale sunlight. The hands were called, and soon the calm air was filled with the mingled aromas of eggs and bacon and the sweeter, more alien smells from the Chinese galley.

Corbett appeared on the bridge, freshly shaved and dressed in crisp new whites. He checked the log and peered for several minutes at the chart. He shaded his pale eyes to stare at the haze-shrouded shoreline.

'First of December today, Trewin. It'll be Christmas before we know it. My boy'll like that.' He looked hard at Trewin's unshaven face. 'He's six, you know. Got his name down for Dartmouth. A fine boy. You must meet him.' He nodded sharply. 'Yes, next time we're in harbour.'

Trewin eyed him carefully. Perhaps he had not seen Corbett through the right eyes before. He asked, 'Does you wife like it out here, sir?'

Corbett stared at him as if he had uttered some terrible obscenity. 'That's none of your damn business!' He swung on his heel and almost knocked Mallory off his feet as he entered the bridge from the chartroom.

Mallory watched him go and said thickly, 'I told you, didn't

I? Round the bloody twist!' He ignored Trewin's expression and began to unroll a fresh chart.

*   *   *

Right on time the *Porcupine* altered course yet again and headed towards the Talang River Inlet. From the seaward approach it was difficult to see any break at all in the long, undulating bank of green jungle which in some places appeared to come right down to the water's edge.

Trewin stood tight against the screen as the growing sunlight glinted on a bright arrowhead of water, which even as he watched seemed to open up across the ship's bows like a gateway. The river mouth was well hidden, and at its widest part was less than a quarter of a mile across. The northern side of the entrance was marked by a low, lopsided hill, which with the sun filtering across the water looked for all the world like a crouching beast.

Mallory was busy taking bearings, his tanned face creased with concentration as he passed one course after another, while the gunboat snaked amidst the scatted sandbars without reducing speed. It was a hazardous approach, Trewin agreed with Mallory's earlier description. At any second he expected to feel the ship shudder helplessly across the waiting humps of pale sand, as had once happened to the luckless Foley.

But as soon as the gunboat was past the entrance the river opened up on either beam, so that the ship was dwarfed by the high banks and the rolling, impenetrable jungle beyond. At reduced speed they pushed further and further upstream until the crouching hill and the open sea were lost around several wide curves.

Mallory pushed his cap to the back of his head and joined Trewin by the screen. 'It's easy from here on, Number One. There's a long pier around the next bend where we tie up. That's Talang settlement. We drop a few stores and drink tea with the gentry and then go back again.' He chuckled. 'A hard life.'

Trewin lifted his glasses as the *Porcupine* rounded the bend of the river and watched the rickety pier reaching out towards him like a gnarled finger. There was a good clearing in the jungle and several neat wooden buildings beside a rough dirt road which vanished inland into the trees. A line of brown-skinned Malays were already on the pier pointing and waving, and several more were paddling small boats out to meet the gunboat as she edged towards the rotten-looking piles.

Trewin saw Corbett gripping the edge of the screen and said sharply, 'Slow ahead together.' He watched Hammond in the bows and two seamen with heaving lines. The sun lanced up from the clear water and almost blinded him as he stooped to gauge the last approach.

Corbett shouted, 'Be careful, Trewin!'

'Stop together!' Trewin did not look at Corbett but watched the narrow sliver of water between the hull and the pier. 'Slow astern together!'

The bows squeaked against the bunches of old motor tyres which were strung alone the pier like blackened fruit, and first one then a second line snaked ashore to be seized by several chattering natives.

'Stop engines!' The telegraphs jangled and the ship shuddered comfortably as the mooring lines took the strain. Then Trewin said, 'Shall I ring off main engines, sir?'

Corbett stood up and adjusted his cap. He seemed agitated and did not reply for several seconds. 'Yes, yes, Trewin. Carry on.'

He walked to the rear of the bridge as the deck gave one more quiver and then fell motionless and still.

Trewin watched Corbett through narrowed eyes. If the captain was so worried about his handling of the ship on a difficult approach under entirely unfamiliar circumstances why did not he take over as most captains would have done? Trust in training was one thing but Corbett's attitude could have ended in real disaster.

Corbett stopped by the ladder. He appeared to have regained his composure. 'Not a bad effort, Trewin. Just be careful, that is all I ask.' He glanced at Mallory searchingly. 'I shall be going ashore in five minutes. Turn the hands to unloading the medical stores for the hospital.' He blinked rapidly. 'There'll be a drink at the club for anyone who needs it, I expect.' Then he was gone.

Mallory stuck his pencil in his shirt pocket and straightened his back. 'Club!' he said scornfully. 'Flaming hut on sticks!'

Tweedie clambered on the bridge and said harshly. 'Duty watch is swaying out stores, sir. Sub-Lieutenant Hammond is O.O.D.'

Trewin picked up his cap. 'Is he? I thought he was duty in Singapore, too?'

Mallory nudged him. 'He was a naughty boy. Let the awnings get slack. So Father got angry with him.' He grinned unfeelingly. 'Still, it'll do him good. He's only a kid!'

Trewin looked quickly at Tweedie. 'You can carry on here then, Guns. I'll go and stretch my legs for an hour. I'll stand you a drink when I get back.'

Tweedie's red face remained unsmiling. 'I never drink on passage, sir.' He saluted and clumped back to the maindeck.

Mallory sighed. 'Lying bastard!' He followed Trewin down the ladder. 'Has it in his bloody bunk just in case he has to buy someone else one!'

The two officers stepped on to the pier and pushed through the cheerful crowd of onlookers. Trewin remarked, 'Quite an event it seems.' Then he asked, 'Where did the captain say he was going?'

'The hospital.' Mallory gestured to the road. 'It's up there. Built for a big rubber plantation some years ago. But the place went bust and the jungle moved in again. The hospital has been kept on because of,' he tapped his nose, 'the *International Situation*!' He quickened his pace and pointed towards the tall, ramshackle house which was indeed built on stilts. 'The club!'

It was a dreary placed, filled with small cane tables and battered chairs to match. The walls were open to the river and covered with mosquito netting, and the fan which churned the humid air back and forth across the threadbare carpet was hand-worked by a wizened Malay who sat on an upended beer crate as if he had been there since the place was built.

Mallory banged the zinc-topped bar. 'Two beers!'

An unsmiling Malay brought the beer which looked better than it tasted.

Malory slumped in a chair and said, 'Dead as a doornail! It livens up a bit at nights though.'

'Who comes here, for God's sake?' Trewin sipped the beer and watched two flies crawling on his knee.

Mallory shrugged. 'Engineers mostly. They're adding to a big fuel dump about a mile up the road. The Army are a bit cut off up here and will need a lot of stores if the balloon does go up.' He groaned and banged down the glass. 'The Japs'd be nuts to come this way! The insects would eat 'em alive!' He saw Trewin was interested and added, 'Ten miles to the north of where we're sitting there's a whole brigade dug in.' He grinned. 'Aussies, of course! They always stick our chaps out in the bloody bush!'

Trewin considered the remark. Penned in by jungle away from the smell of the sea it was hard to picture the overall strategy which went to the defence of Malaya.

Mallory said soberly, 'It's a good spot, *militarily* speaking, of course. They've got the Pahang River to the north of them, which is better than any Maginot Line. And this little river down here to protect the flank. Next time we come this way I'll take you up there. They're a good lot of boys. One or two of 'em from Queensland, too.'

Two more beers were placed on the table and Mallory said gloomily, 'We had the admiral aboard on the last visit. Hell, he nearly blew his top. He wanted to do a sort of grand tour, and old Corbett insisted on visiting the flaming hospital just when he was about to go inland.' He shook his head. 'God, there's no love lost between those two jokers!'

Trewin recalled Kane's words. He said, 'The captain knew the admiral before, I gather?'

'S'right. I don't know what happened.' He shook his head.

'But whatever it was has made Corbett very edgy indeed. He's like a cat on hot bricks when the top man appears.'

'Oh there you are, sir!'

They both turned as Petty Officer Masters, the yeoman of signals, clattered across the rough flooring and handed Trewin a crumpled signal flimsy. Masters was very overweight and sweating badly. He added. 'For the captain, sir. Immediate.' He peered at the bar and sniffed.

Mallory said, 'Some sort of flap on?'

'Recall to Singapore, sir.' He sounded vague. 'We are to assume state *Medway*.' He shrugged. 'The captain'll know, sir.'

The portly yeoman walked away and Mallory said slowly, 'Hell, it looks like you may be right, Number One. State *Medway* is the bloody code for the squadron's emergency!' He grabbed his cap. 'I'd better go aboard and get things started. Will you tell the Old Man?'

Trewin was staring at the crumpled signal. 'Yes. I'll tell him.'

Leaving his second beer untouched Trewin walked out into the sun and along the dirt road. All at once the frustrations and disappointments of Singapore seemed unimportant and the green jungle walls were no longer inviting and tranquil. He quickened his pace, the sun fierce across his shoulders so that he almost walked right past a long, low-roofed bungalow building with a faded red cross painted on the roof.

Several Malay women were washing clothes in big enamel troughs on the hospital veranda, and there seemed to be about thirty children playing noisily in the dust below. An orderly in a white coat bobbed his head and smiled. 'You wish to see doctor?'

Trewin nodded, and as he followed the little Malay into the shade of the entrance hall he saw rows of neat iron beds, mostly filled with native women and more children. In another ward he saw some tough-looking Malays bandaged and splinted, and he guessed that they were injured workers from the new fuel dump.

The orderly stopped by a door. 'I go see if doctor is busy.'

At that moment there was a crash of crockery from the ward and a chorus of indignant yells. The orderly frowned. 'I go there first! Someone make trouble!' He hurried off clucking his tongue angrily.

Trewin thought of the brief signal and without waiting further thrust open the door. The room was in complete darkness with the shutters drawn tightly across the windows. Trewin blinked, half blinded from the blazing sunlight outside, and in the few seconds which followed he got a vague impression of Corbett's pale figure sitting in a chair, his head thrown right back and his eyes shining like blue stones in the beam of a small lamp which another man was holding barely inches from his face.

'What the devil!' Corbett thrust the other man away and lurched to his feet, sending the chair crashing to one side. He saw Trewin and strode to the windows, where he flung back the shutters with a further crash.

Trewin saw that the other man was a tall, distinguished-looking European with a neat dark beard. He had a calm, serious face, and as he turned his gaze from Corbett's anger to Trewin's uncertainty he said quietly, 'I'm Dr. Massey. Do you mind telling me what you mean by bursting in here?' His voice was mild, but there was no mistaking the annoyance in his eyes.

Corbett snapped, 'This is my first lieutenant!' He turned on Trewin. 'I might have expected something like this.'

Trewin said, 'I'm very sorry. I did not realise you were doing anything . . .'

Corbett interrupted angrily, 'You must forgive him, James. He imagines that he is the only one who has ever done anything worth while!'

The doctor relaxed. 'I was just examining your captain's eye. I think there is a bit of inflammation, or maybe it's dust there.' He looked at Corbett searchingly. 'As I was saying when we were interrupted.'

Trewin said, 'I have a signal, sir. It was urgent or I would not have come.'

Corbett appeared to have recovered himself. 'Well, now that you *are* here you'd better let me have it.' To Massey he added calmly, 'If it's not one thing it's another.'

Trewin held out the flimsy, but Corbett said, 'Read the thing out. That damn light has half blinded me!'

Trewin glanced uncertainly at Massey, and Corbett shouted, 'For God's sake, I've known the doctor for years! Are you afraid he'll tell everyone what it says?'

'We are to assume state *Medway*, sir.' The pencilled letters on the signal seemed to dance, and Trewin saw that his hand was shaking with suppressed anger. When he lifted his head he noticed that Corbett was quite controlled, as if nothing had happened.

'Very well, Trewin. That wasn't too bad, now, was it?' He turned to Massey 'All blow over, I expect. Still, it's just as well to be ready.'

Trewin walked from the room and waited in the passage outside the door. He heard Corbett and Massey speaking quietly together and felt the same dull sensation of resentment and anger creeping through him once more. It seemed to take so little to get him on edge now. In spite of every precaution he repeatedly had to find time to cool down, to reason with himself like a wary spectator. He plucked his shirt away from his shoulder and tried to see himself as he had once been before Crete.

At the very beginning of the war, for instance, when serving aboard an escort destroyer, he had had a captain who was generally considered mad by everyone who crossed his path. A character larger than life, he had goaded his officers almost beyond endurance, yet when the storm broke and the ship ran the gauntlet of the Atlantic for the first time Trewin had been the first to admit to his complete coolness under fire, his ready grasp of every phase of attack. While Trewin and his fellow officers seized the rare opportunities of sleep, a few hours at a time in damp blankets while the ship rolled drunkenly across the steep Atlantic troughs, the captain had stayed stolidly on his bridge. Whenever Trewin had fought off the clinging desire to sleep and had climbed once more to the nightmare of wind and sea, the captain had always been there, waiting and watching, like some superior being.

But once the ship had returned to harbour the same captain had returned to his old outward mould of insulting impatience.

Why then was it that Corbett was getting under his skin so much? He tried to tell himself it was because of his own bitterness at not getting another command. But deep inside his soul, gnawing like some half-healed disease, he thought he knew the real answer.

Unlike the men who had died beside him in the water at Crete, or those who had survived as broken shadows of their former selves, he had been spared for a later, more treacherous fate. His body was healing from the burns and the agony of his dying ship, but his mind was still undecided which path to follow.

He looked up as Corbett stepped into the passage, his face once more alert and controlled.

'Right, Trewin. Back to the ship. We'll return to Singapore immediately. The rest of the group will be on their way there, too.'

They fell in step together and walked quickly along the dirt road. Corbett said suddenly, 'I met Dr. Massey several years back, before the war. He has been a good friend in many ways. Had a great career ahead of him in England but threw it all up to come out here and work for these people. His wife died in a fire just after he came out here to start work.' Corbett shook his head. 'That didn't help much. But I think he's got over it now. And he had his daughter with him, of course.'

Trewin did not answer. Massey was probably just one more failure, he thought bitterly. Could not stand his own inability to find success in England so he had come out to Malaya in the role of benefactor.

Corbett glanced at him coldly. 'Without such men this country would be nothing.'

47

They reached the pier and Corbett said, 'Now just remember what I told you. Our flotilla of gunboats has been welded into something to be proud of. I won't stand for anything or anyone getting in the way of efficiency or one hundred per cent readiness to perform whatever duty is thrown our way, d'you understand?'

Trewin saw the side party waiting by the gangway. 'Yes, sir.'

Corbett saluted as the pipes trilled in the unmoving air. 'And don't grit your teeth, Trewin. I can't stand people who sulk!'

Mallory sauntered across the sidedeck and watched Corbett hurry towards the bridge. 'You told him then?'

'I did.' Trewin suddenly wanted to be left alone. To go to his cabin and take a drink. Or *sulk*, as Corbett had put it.

But in spite of his anger Mallory's unruffled question helped to ease away the tension which had gripped him all the way to the ship. He said wearily, 'I suppose I'll get used to this sort of life . . . eventually!'

Mallory grinned. 'The first ten years are the worst!'

They both looked up as Corbett called from the bridge ladder, 'When you are *ready*, gentlemen!'

Mallory said under his breath, 'Given some encouragement I could take quite a dislike to that one.'

Fifteen minutes later the *Porcupine* sidled clear of the pier and with her screws churning the water into white froth backed out into the centre of the river.

As before Trewin conned the ship downstream while Corbett remained silent and watchful in his tall chair. Only when the bows lifted slightly to the sea's greeting did he say anything.

Then to the bridge at large he remarked. 'That was a little better. But there's still room for improvement.' He sat back in his chair and tilted his cap across his eyes.

Trewin sighed and handed over the watch to Mallory. With men like Corbett you could never win, he thought.

3
In the Space of an Hour

The nightmare mounted to its usual terrible climax, and with a sudden cry Trewin rolled on to his side and switched on the bedside light. For a full minute he stared dazedly around the neat hotel room while his disordered thoughts moved back into some sort of pattern. He was sweating badly, and he could feel his heart pounding painfully against his ribs. How long would it be before he could shake off the repetitive dream? he wondered. It had no true order or realism, yet the distorted faces and leaping flames were always there.

Wearily he climbed from the damp sheets and stood beside the bed. With something like hatred he stared at the empty gin bottle on the table and at his clothes which lay where he had thrown them just a few hours earlier. His watch told him it was almost four in the morning, and he knew he would not be able to get back to sleep.

He had hoped that a change of surroundings, if only for one night, would make some sort of difference. Wandering from hotel to hotel, or allowing himself to be carried this way and that by the ceaseless, jostling throng of townspeople should have produced a sensation to replace the anticlimax which had greeted the *Porcupine*'s return to Singapore Island. What sense of emergency there might have been seemed to have given way to an atmosphere not unlike a strange carnival. As the gunboat had dropped anchor ahead of her consorts any idea of impending danger or urgency seemed to fade.

The crowded waterfront had abounded with optimism and relief, and even Trewin had to admit there was some foundation for the wild gaiety. In the centre of the crowded anchorage, dominating every other ship by their size and power, were two great capital ships and their newly arrived escorts. The battle ship *Prince of Wales* and the battle cruiser *Repulse* seemed to represent a visible sign that this time there was to be no nonsense. That sure shield which every Briton had come to take for granted had reached out protectively even to Singapore.

Of course there had been no shortage of rumours. The Japanese were moving ships and troop convoys westward from Indo-China. They would invade Siam, or they might even attack the American bases in the Pacific. But one thing was sure, they would not be so stupid as to try a seaborne attack on Malaya without ships to match the new power of the Royal Navy.

For five days the *Porcupine* had remained in a state of semi-readiness, and even that had been broken by ceremonial and drills as the newcomers to the fleet had been royally entertained both ashore and afloat. Then on the Sunday, immediately after Divisions on the *Porcupine*'s small quarterdeck, Corbett had granted local leave to all but the duty watch. Trewin had decided, almost without thinking, that he would spend his brief freedom in luxury. Now, after a night of colour and noise, of unfamiliar food and heavy drinking, he was able to appreciate his mistake.

With a sigh he held his head in the handbasin and let the lukewarm water run over his hair.

It was strange how the appearance of the big ships in the anchorage had affected Corbett, he thought. He had been almost gay compared with his usual cold watchfulness. As the *Porcupine* had cruised past the battleships and the towering upperworks and gun turrets had cast a black shadow across the gunboat's bridge Corbett had said, 'Well, this should make the moaning minnies change their tune, eh?' The pipes had trilled a salute, and from the deck of the *Prince of Wales* had come the acknowledgement of a bugle.

But after five repetitive days Trewin had had enough of it. No one knew for sure what was happening, and what was worse, nobody seemed to care.

As he had wandered aimlessly through the crowded streets of the city he had seen the shop windows bright with Christmas gifts, and after the hard sunshine of the day it made the place seem all the more unreal and alien.

He stared at himself in the mirror and decided he should have stayed aboard. Mallory was the duty officer, and although he had not asked directly, Trewin knew he was desperate to get ashore for his own kind of enjoyment. Tweedie and Hammond had left the ship and gone their own ways, and Corbett had gone home to his wife—the face in the photograph on his desk.

He walked to the open window and leaned his hands on the sill. He could feel the night air cooling the heat of his naked body, and he could see the endless lights and reflections of a city which never slept.

The full moon cast a silver reflection on the sea beyond Keppel's harbour framed between two tall hotel buildings, and he could see small dancing lights far out on the calm water where Chinese fishermen worked busily to supply the island's teeming population. There were aircraft flying somewhere to the north, their distant, regular throbbing somehow confident and reassuring.

In the next room he heard the dull murmur of a man's voice and a responsive female giggle before they both lapsed once more into silence. Trewin stared down at his disordered bed and tried not to listen to the furtive sounds in the adjoining room. They were too much a memory. Too much a part of something lost in the past.

He jumped as the bedside telephone jangled noisily. He sat on the bed and pressed the receiver to his ear. 'Yes?'

'Thank God!' It was Mallory. 'I've been trying to get through to your hotel but all the lines are humming like bloody hell!'

Trewin sat quite still, his eyes fixed on the opposite wall. 'Well?'

'There's a flap on!' In the background Trewin could hear the shrill of a bosun's pipe and the clang of metal. Mallory continued quickly, 'The R.A.F. have reported unidentified air-craft approaching the city! You'd better get your skates on and return to the ship at once!'

Trewin's mind became suddenly clear. 'Right. Have you sent out a recall?'

Mallory sounded strained. 'As best I can. I sent a messenger to fetch Corbett.'

Trewin reached for his underpants. 'Clear away the anti-aircraft guns and make sure that you've blacked out the whole ship.' He dropped the telephone and began to pull on his clothes. Through the window nothing had changed, and the sky was shining with a million coloured reflections. Perhaps it was yet another false alarm.

He swept his razor and scanty belongings into his pockets and hurried for the door. At the end of the corridor he almost ran into a pair of shadowed figures who were half lying against one of the windows. The girl was in a long evening dress, and even in the half-light Trewin could see that her breasts were bare and her eyes were closed as her eager companion sought to complete his conquest.

Trewin hurried by and heard the man shout, 'Bloody fool! Must be stoned!' The girl laughed, but the laugh was cut short as the floor seemed to buck beneath Trewin's feet and the whole corridor rang to the maniac sound of shattering glass. Then came the explosions, hard, nearby detonations which rocked the hotel like a ship in a sudden storm, and which filled the warm air with clouds of choking dust.

Trewin thought of the aircraft noises and reeled down the deserted stairway his ears deaf to the shouts and shrill screams from the rooms behind him. As he reached the ground floor he had to fight his way through stampeding figures, mostly in night attire, and a handful of hotel servants who seeemed too stricken to move.

Another pattern of loud explosions rocked the building, and glass spewed inwards across the reception desk and splintered against the floor.

A thickset man with a white moustache, dressed in a purple

bathrobe, pulled at Trewin's arm and shouted into his face, 'What the hell is going on?' When Trewin pushed him aside he yelled wildly, 'That's right, run, you bastard! That's about all you're fit for!'

In the crowded street it was even worse. Screaming crowds surged in every direction. Above the din of aircraft engines and the shrill whistle of bombs Trewin heard the telltale rumble of falling masonry, the exploring crackle of fire.

It was all the more frightful because the whole city still blazed with lights. As he ran along the road he saw the same cardboard Father Christmas standing in one big window, his painted grin all the more grotesque because of the broken glass and twisted steel in the shell beyond.

Police whistles called above the cries, and Trewin saw an ambulance trying to force its way through a throng of shouting Europeans in dinner jackets and gay evening dresses who had just emerged from one of the nearby clubs.

A man shouted, 'They've hit Raffles place! Guthrie's has been knocked for six!' He sounded both angry and incredulous.

There were searchlight now, pale and slender across the bright sky, and once when Trewin looked up he thought he could see the dancing silver shapes of slow-moving aircraft.

He heard a woman sobbing hysterically. 'What is it? What are they doing?'

A man's voice, harsh and desperate. 'It's all right, dear. It's only a practice of some kind.'

An Australian soldier, hatless and clasping a bottle in each hand, shouted, 'Some bleeding practice, mate!'

Trewin found a taxi parked in a sidestreet, a gravel-faced Indian driver sitting behind the wheel. He snapped. 'Take me to the base!'

The Indian eyed him thoughtfully. 'It's thirteen miles, boss.' He peered up at a tall column of smoke beyond the street. 'It could be dangerous!'

Trewin wrenched open the door. 'Move!' He stared at the man's turbaned head. 'Or I'll drive the bloody thing myself!'

The taxi jerked into motion and Trewin heard the tyres crunching over broken glass as it moved out into the stampeding people and din of traffic.

The drive seemed endless. Several times they had to wait while abandoned cars were dragged from the road by sweating angry soldiers. And on several occasions Trewin had to fight off vague, distorted faces which surged against the doors like part of his nightmares.

At the waterfront he found some sort of order at last. Apart from the occasional flash of gunfire from the anchored ships, the whole area was in darkness. Motor boats chugged back and forth, full to the gunwales with men of every age and rank who were trying to reach their ships. Some were yelling questions which nobody ever seemed to answer, others were still too dazed or drunk to care.

By the time Trewin climbed back aboard the *Porcupine* the sky was already brighter and the sound of aircraft was gone. Men were clustered at the guns and others stood uncertainly by the guardrails watching the glowing fires ashore and listening to the distant wail of sirens and the murmur of a million voices.

Mallory gripped Trewin's sleeve. 'You made it then.' He sounded relieved. 'It's been like a madhouse here!'

Trewin ran up the bridge ladder and entered Corbett's day cabin. Corbett was speaking into the shore telephone, but his pale eyes fastened on Trewin's face as he waved him to a chair.

He said, 'Very well, sir. I got that.' His fingers drummed on the desk in a sharp tattoo. 'I said I *got* that!' He slammed down the telephone angrily. 'Bloody civilians! They should have ratings on the switchboard.'

Corbett looked alert and neat, and Trewin found time to wonder how he had managed to arrive aboard before him, if at all.

'Prepare to get under way.' Corbett stood up and stared absently at a chart. 'This is the real thing, I'm afraid.' He looked hard at Trewin's face and added shortly, 'Our military defences at Kota Bahru to the north are under attack. Intelligence reports a strong Japanese assault over the border in Siam as well. He tapped the chart. 'Two landings there apparently. Patani and Singora. But the Malayan one is the more serious. Kota Bahru has our main northern airfield. They say the enemy are pouring in troops and aircraft by the hour, and the whole coast is under bombardment from warships.'

Trewin felt his stomach muscles tense. 'So the impossible has happened?'

Corbett's eyes gleamed in the desk light like stones. 'Don't be so damned melodramatic! The attacker always has the advantage. This had to be expected.' He picked up his cap. 'Anyway, in twenty-four hours the Japs'll have a bit more to deal with than a few dozy soldiers!'

Trewin asked, 'Why was the city left unguarded, sir?' He seemed to hear the cries and the sullen thunder of collapsing buildings. 'They went and dropped their bombs just where they pleased!'

Corbett picked an invisible thread from his shirt. 'The R.A.F. gave warning in plenty of time. Trewin. It appears that the city authorities neglected to keep the A.R.P. headquarters manned at night, and no one could be found to switch off the light power supply!' He eyed Trewin coldly. 'As I just said. Damned civilians! You just can't rely on 'em!'

There was a rush of feet along the sidedeck and the sound of a boat thudding against the hull. Corbett stared at his clock and said firmly. 'We sail in one hour. All libertymen should be aboard by then.' He frowned at Trewin. 'If not, I'll want to know why!'

Nimmo, the chief E.R.A., tapped at the door and peered at the captain. 'Engine room ready, sir.' He was unshaven and dishevelled, and his white overalls were open to his navel. He must have run naked from his bunk at the first alarm.

Corbett said, 'Thank you. You can stand by as from now.' As Nimmo turned to leave Corbett added, 'And, Chief! In future try to make yourself more presentable when you go to your station! Remember that most of your people are native

55

Chinese. From now on a good example will be all the more important.'

Nimmo's square face remained expressionless. 'Aye, aye, sir. I'll remember that.'

He walked away and Corbett said testily, 'A regular, too!'

Trewin said quietly, 'He realised it was an emergency, sir. That is surely a good thing.'

Corbett eyed him and then replied calmly, 'A high standard is not something you switch on for Sundays, Trewin. Aboard my ship at least it will remain standard and routine.'

Sub-Lieutenant Hammond looked round the door. 'Signal, sir. No enemy aircraft shot down.' He looked wide-eyed and very young, Trewin thought.

Corbett was unimpressed. 'We shall do better next time.' He stared at Trewin. 'Close up special sea dutymen. We'll weigh anchor in forty-five minutes.' To Hammond, he added sharply, 'Make a signal to Flag. Check the state of readiness of the whole group.'

Trewin followed Hammond into the passageway and said quietly, 'Well, this is it, Sub.' Through the chartroom scuttle he could see the red glow of fires beyond the crowded waterfront houses. They were well inland. Towards the airfields by the look of them. He finished grimly, 'At least we know where we stand!'

Hammond followed his glance, his eyes suddenly anxious. 'I hope we do better next time.' He licked his lips. 'Poor devils, they didn't stand a chance.'

He said it so fervently that Trewin asked, 'Is there someone special ashore for you, Sub?'

Hammond looked at him with immediate caution. 'Well, yes, as a matter of fact.' He seemed uncomfortable.

Trewin said, 'But it's none of my bloody business, is that it?'

'I'm sorry, Number One.' Hammond's cheeks coloured. 'I didn't mean that.' He faltered. 'She's a wonderful girl. But I'd rather you didn't say anything about her to anyone else.' He saw Trewin nod and continued more calmly, 'I was with her when the attack started. I didn't want to leave her.'

Trewin thought of the November drizzle across the bombed street, the silent A.R.P. workers and tired firemen. His feeling of loss and despair. He said shortly. 'You never do.'

He turned away from Hammond's curious stare as Leading Telegraphist Laird, the ship's senior operator, pushed his head from the radio-room door. He was a cheerful and irrepressible person on most occasions, but he was unsmiling as he said, 'Signal, sir! The Flag Officer, East Coast Patrols is coming aboard in fifteen minutes!' He grimaced and added, 'Shall I tell the captain, sir?' He waited the right number of seconds and then added with a sad smile, 'Or will you?'

Trewin said grimly, 'Leave it to me.' To Hammond he added, '*Porcupine* hardly seems big enough for an admiral!'

As he disappeared down the passageway Laird said under his breath, 'No ship'd be big enough for that bastard!'

And fifteen minutes later, as the sky brightened to display the blackened buildings and blasted rubble from the bombing, Rear-Admiral Mark Fairfax-Loring came aboard.

Shortly afterwards, with the frail sunlight filtering through the drifting banks of grey smoke, the six gunboats weighed and headed down the anchorage.

For them the waiting was over.

*   *   *

Trewin lifted his glasses and trained them on *Squalus,* the next gunboat in line astern. She was keeping perfect station about half a mile distant, and the other four ships of the group followed in a slightly curving formation as they rounded the jutting green headland of Gelang Point. It was halfway through the forenoon watch, and on the unsheltered bridge it felt like a steel oven. Nearly twenty miles astern lay Kuantan, which *Porcupine* and her consorts had left only a few hours earlier. It was two full days since they had left Singapore. Two days of rumour and uncertainty, of unfamiliar work and tempers stretched to breaking point. On the first day the group had embarked a battalion of Australian infantry, and two companies of Indian troops for good measure. Then with the deck space crammed with noisy, jocular soldiers they had steamed north to Kuantan to land their human cargo as reinforcements to protect the great coast road which ran straight down parallel with the sea from Kota Bahru to Kuantan itself.

Now they were on the move once more, still further north, with the green, unbroken coastline less than two miles abeam.

Trewin licked his lips and walked to the forepart of the bridge. He was feeling tired and strained, and now that the ship was kept at defence stations he was working four hours on and four off like every man aboard. Hammond was stooping over the compass as he took a fix on the headland as it dropped back astern, but apart from him and the look-outs, Trewin had the bridge to himself. That in its small way was something to be thankful for. With Corbett watching his every move it was bad enough. But now, with the admiral aboard, the ship seemed to have shrunk to half her size.

It was strange to see a senior officer moving about the decks. Fairfax-Loring's flag was hanging limp at the masthead, and not a breath of wind ruffled the blue sea to ease the tension of watchkeeping. At dawn the sky had been overcast with low cloud and the air still damp from the thunderstorms which had dogged them all the way from Singapore. Trewin had been grateful for the bad weather. It was something he understood. Heavy cloud meant that there would be no sudden air attacks, and with the apparent worsening of the military situation up north, even weather could be a valuable ally.

But now the sky, like the sea, was as clear and calm as it could possibly be, and with each thud of the screws Trewin could feel the apprehension mounting inside him as the little ships drove steadily northward. Whatever doubts and hopes he might have retained had been shattered at Kuantan. The estuary town was nearly two hundred miles south from where the fighting was said to be, yet already the place was in a state of panic. There was no other word to describe the scene as the six gunboats had sidled alongside the piers to discharge their troops. Trewin had gone ashore with some dispatches for the naval liaison officer, and had been shocked by the scenes of urgency and confusion which had greeted him on every side. Ox-carts and ancient cars thronged the streets, and the waterfront had been crammed with people of every colour and race, apparently looking for some ship or other transport to carry them south.

It had been a small but heartening sight to see the Australian soldiers marching away up the coast road, their rifles slung, their new orders sending them to the north-east coast where it was rumoured the Japs might attempt some small local landings behind the main fighting line.

Trewin wiped his forehead with his arm and trained his glasses on the rolling green bank of jungle which had been their constant companion. It was difficult to believe the Japanese would attempt to fight their way right down the Malay peninsula through that, he thought. His lips turned in a bitter smile as if to mock his own thoughts.

Today everything and anything was not only possible, it was more than likely. Who would have imagined the Japs would have attacked Malaya and America together? Yet only the previous day Corbett had announced that headquarters had released the news of a knockout attack on several American naval bases by carrier aircraft. Pearl Harbor had been laid in ruins in a matter of hours and the anchored fleet pulverised at its moorings. So nothing was impossible any more.

But like it or not, America was now in the war. Given time it would make all the difference. Trewin knew that time, on the other hand, was the one thing which never seemed to be available.

He turned warily as a shadow fell across the screen.

Rear-Admiral Mark Fairfax-Loring had a dark, aggressive face dominated by a pair of thick black eyebrows, and had once been a very handsome man, Trewin thought. Now beneath his impeccable white drill his waistline was just a bit too rounded, and the puffiness around his deepset eyes just that more noticeable than it ought to be in a man still in his forties. He had a heavily built, solid figure, yet gave an immediate impression of restlessness and impatience. It was hard to see him as Corbett's contemporary, and when they were together the comparison was almost grotesque. Corbett would sit impassively in his chair his pale eyes trained on some point on the horizon, while the admiral would move about the bridge as if its very restriction was affecting him like a caged tiger.

The admiral returned Trewin's salute with a casual flip of the fingers to his heavily oak-leaved cap and flashed him one of his fierce grins, which Trewin guessed was used more to charm than impress. He said briskly, 'Bloody hot day, Number One.' He glanced astern. 'Is the brood keeping station this morning?'

'Yes sir, The *Prawn* has been making a bit more smoke than usual, but she's holding her own now.'

The ship in question was a bit of a joke in the group. Apart from being the oldest on the Far East station, she was also plagued by being coal-fired. When the other gunboats were quietly resting at their anchors she could usually be seen half shrouded in a cloud of coal-dust, the air around her thick with curses and the clank of shovels and winches.

The admiral shrugged. 'Ah well, she'll just have to do what she can.' He seemed indifferent. 'Now where is that flag-lieutenant of mine?'

Hughes, his harrassed and overworked aide, was his only companion on these occasions, and from the moment the admiral had stepped aboard he had been either at his elbow scribbling signals or crouched beside the *Porcupine*'s telegraphists checking the steady inflow of operational despatches from the base.

The admiral asked suddenly, 'And the captain?'

'In his quarters, sir.' Trewin tried to see beyond the admiral's air of affable calm. It was still not possible to discover exactly the atmosphere between him and Corbett. Even when they were together on the bridge they seemed far apart. When one moved the other would watch. Like two cats enjoying a ritualistic manœuvre for mastery.

'Of course, I've known your captain for many years, Number One. He spoke off-handedly, yet Trewin felt that the admiral had his reasons for mentioning it. He seemed to be a man who always had a reason for everything he said or did, no matter how trivial. 'As a matter of fact he is married to my sister.'

Trewin's mind chewed on this information. If, as had been suggested, the two men disliked each other this marriage would certainly add to any awkward connections, he thought.

Lieutenant Hughes appeared on the bridge before the admiral could continue. 'Signal from base, sir.'

The admiral's brows knitted together. 'Well, Flags, what is it now?' He flashed his grin on Trewin. 'More bumph about the *situation*, what?'

Hughes said patiently, 'Kota Bahru airfield has fallen to the enemy, sir.'

The admiral scowled. 'I could have told *them* that!'

'Also, sir,' Hughes swallowed hard, 'The signal states as follows, "Fighter protection will not, repeat not, be possible".' He looked round the bridge. 'Nothing at all, sir!'

The admiral began to pace along the gratings, his face working angrily. 'That's ridiculous!' He gestured astern. 'Back there at Kuantan! What about *their* airfield, for God's sake?'

Hughes said carefully, 'It seems that there was some hasty order to evacuate the field, sir.' He shrugged. 'Of course, it might have been countermanded by now, but . . .'

His voice trailed into silence as Fairfax-Loring barked, 'Of all the cock-eyed reasoning!' He looked round as Corbett appeared at the top of the ladder. 'Did you hear that?'

Corbett nodded and readjusted the glasses around his neck. 'We must expect that sort of thing,' he replied calmly.

The admiral seized the screen in two big hands and breathed out noisily. 'Fortunately we are not quite alone on this patrol, gentlemen. Otherwise, army or no bloody army, I might consider pulling back to Kuantan!' He controlled his anger and said more calmly, 'Force "Z" is also at sea. It is sweeping almost parallel with us, so we should be all right no matter what happens.'

Trewin asked quietly, 'Force "Z", sir? What is that?'

Hughes eyed him sadly. 'The reinforcements. Admiral Tom Phillips sailed in *Prince of Wales* with *Repulse* in company and a full escort of destroyers on Monday afternoon.'

The admiral was watching Trewin's expression closely. Then he said, 'So not to worry, Number One! Whatever the other silly beggars do, the Navy at least is prepared!' He pounded the screen. 'We'll show the little yellow bastards when we get going!'

Corbett's quiet tone cut through the sudden silence like a knife. 'Are you not reassured, Trewin?' He was looking at the admiral as he spoke. 'What is bothering you now?'

Trewin said bluntly. 'I think it's madness, sir! Without air cover those big ships are worse off than we are!' He turned away, suddenly chilled in spite of the sun across his shoulders. 'They must be mad!'

Hughes exploded. 'Now look here!' But Fairfax-Loring held up his hand and said, 'Don't get excited, Flags. Young Trewin here is not quite used to things yet.'

Corbett said evenly, 'Lieutenant Trewin was awarded the D.S.C. for gallantry, sir, while serving aboard his own craft under fire.'

The admiral glared at him. 'What are you saying?' he seemed caught off balance by Corbett's pointed remark. 'I was not criticising his judgement, but obviously it takes more than bravery to gain a full measure of experience.'

Corbett did not pursue the point, but it was obvious to Trewin that he had meant to prick the admiral's confidence, and prick it hard.

Hughes moved quickly away towards the radio room, and Corbett took his place on his chair, his glasses lifted to study the coastline.

The admiral said stiffly, 'Make a general signal to the group. Extra anti-aircraft look-outs to be ordered immediately.'

Masters, the yeoman, said uncomfortably, 'Beg pardon, sir, but the captain 'as done that already.'

Trewin darted a quick glance at Corbett's profile. His face was shaded below his cap, but one corner of his mouth was raised in a small, tight smile.

The admiral forced a grin. 'Good show! Be prepared at all times!' He bustled towards the ladder. 'I'm going aft to my cabin for a bit.' He stared at Corbett's trim shoulders. 'Keep me informed.'

Corbett waited a few seconds then said flatly, 'If you must make those sweeping criticisms, Trewin, you must expect to get involved in argument.' Then in a milder tone he added, 'I do not happen to have much faith in reserve officers as a general rule.' He shrugged. 'However, you *are* one of my officers, and I will not have you insulted by anyone outside this ship!'

Trewin stared at him. 'Thank you, sir.'

Corbett turned his back impatiently. 'Just thank God I made that signal myself. You should have remembered to act yourself.'

In silence the watch continued.

Four hours later, as Trewin lay on his bunk, his chest bared to catch the churned air from the fan, he tried to understand what Corbett had really been trying to do. To use him to score points off the admiral? Or did he love his ship so much that even her officers and men were like personal possessions, part of a whole, which he would not stand to be criticised?

He frowned as Hammond slid back the cabin door and stared in at him. 'Hello, Sub.' He looked at his watch. 'Hell, it's too early for the Dogs.'

Hammond stepped over the coaming and sat down suddenly on the bunk as if his legs had been cut from under him. 'I thought you ought to know, Number One.' He sounded stunned. 'Force "Z" has been attacked by torpedo bombers.' He gestured vaguely. 'Hughes just handed the signal to the admiral.'

Trewin lay quite still, knowing there was worse to come.

Hammond continued in the same dull voice. '*Prince of Wales* and *Repulse* were sunk!' He ran his fingers through his fair hair. 'Both in the space of an hour!'

'I see.' Trewin rolled on to one elbow and stared emptily at the open scuttle and the straight horizon line which rose and fell with slow, timeless regularity. 'Thank you for telling me.' Then he stood up and walked to his mirror, and began to comb his hair. He could feel Hammond watching him, his eyes bright with shock and despair.

Hammond said suddenly, 'Look, Number One, you've been through this sort of thing.' He seemed to have difficulty forming his words. 'Dunkirk, Crete, and all that . . .'

He fell silent as Trewin wheeled round, his face hard and angry. 'That was different, quite different!' He pointed at the gleaming scuttle. 'This time there's nowhere to run! It's us or them!' Then he walked across the cabin and laid his hand on the boy's shoulder. 'We're on our own now. Face up to that and it won't feel quite so bad.'

Hammond was speaking almost to himself. 'I went aboard both of those ships just three days ago.' He shook himself. 'They seemed so confident, so *sure*.'

Trewin studied him and then replied gently, 'I expect the lads in the *Hood* felt like that, too.' He touched Hammond's arm. 'Come on, we'll go to the bridge. I expect the admiral will want to speak to all of us about it.'

Outside the cabin the deck seemed full of off-watch sailors. They stood either in small, silent groups or at the guardrails, staring towards the empty horizon as if they expected to see some sign or aftermath of the disaster.

Petty Officer Dancy, the chief bosun's mate, stepped forward and asked quietly, 'It's true then, sir?'

Trewin nodded. 'I'm afraid so, Buffer.'

Dancy looked towards the sea, his face suddenly grave. 'I never knew the battleship, she was new to me.' Unconsciously he took off his cap and held it to his side as if paying tribute in the only way he knew. 'But the *Repulse*, I knew her well enough. I was an A.B. in her.' He shook his head slowly.

'Twenty-five years old she was. Poor old girl, what a way to end up.'

But when Trewin reached the bridge the admiral was not to be seen. Mallory was on the gratings, his tanned face grim and thoughtful, and Tweedie stood beside the chart table, his hands clasped behind him as if on parade.

Corbett turned slightly in his chair, and Trewin saw that he looked very tired. 'I was just going to send for you, Trewin.' He studied his features for several seconds and added, 'I don't have to spell it out for your benefit.'

'No, sir.'

Corbett squared his shoulders and settled himself more comfortably in his chair. 'We're going on just the same.' It sounded final. 'Signal the group to close up the formation in fifteen minutes.' He sharpened his voice. 'At sunset we will go to action stations.'

As Trewin walked to the rear of the bridge he added quietly, We must hit back! There's been enough wasting time already!'

Trewin looked over the screen and along the sun-drenched battery deck. Against the blue water the *Porcupine* suddenly seemed very small and vulnerable.

4
No Use Being Bitter

Mallory's parallel rulers squeaked loudly as he pushed them across the chart. 'New course is three two zero.' From beneath the oilskin hood which covered the table his voice sounded muffled.

Trewin nodded and leaned slightly above the voice-pipe. 'Port ten!' The luminous dial of the compass repeater ticked slowly across the line. 'Steady! Steer three two zero!' He heard the coxswain's mumbled acknowledgement from the shuttered wheelhouse, but dismissed him from his thoughts as another great wedge of dark headland crept out towards the slow-moving bows. The ship's crawl up the coast was nerve-wracking enough, but to be so close inshore with the dark hills and occasional strips of beach reaching almost to the ship's side dragged at his concentration like a constant threat.

It had been going on for hours. At sunset the little group had been divided into two halves, and while Corbett led the *Prawn* and *Squalus* up the edge of the coast the other three gunboats were now wallowing a further five miles out to sea. So far they had sighted nothing, but from far inland their progress had been accompanied by a constant and distorted rumble of gunfire, like thunder, and every so often the jagged wall of jungle and low hills had been outlined with dull orange and red flashes, grim reminders of the war they had come to find.

Everybody aboard seemed to be holding his breath. Even the engines, throttled down to minimum speed, were lost in the steady swish of water against the hull, the creak of steel and wood as the ship rocked gently in the offshore current.

The heavy rain which had started just after sunset had

stopped with alarming suddenness, and after the steady drumming of the downpour against the decks and the bodies of the men at their stations the silence was all the more apparent and disturbing.

There was still plenty of low cloud, but every so often the moon managed to push through to throw strange patches of silver on the flat water or across the statue-like figures grouped around the *Porcupine*'s bridge. Apart from the howitzer, all the guns were manned and ready, and from either wing of the bridge came the quiet chink of ammunition belts as the two heavy machine-guns turned restlessly like black fingers against the dull and threatening sky.

Corbett snapped, 'Check the depth!'

A messenger by the voice-pipes said quickly, 'Six fathoms, sir!'

Corbett's pale shape shifted in his chair, apparently satisfied. Trewin had to admit that Corbett's knowledge of the coast was quite uncanny. To him the occasional soundings meant just as much as if they had been photographs. The weeks and months of pounding up and down this very coast had not, it seemed, been wasted.

On the starboard side of the bridge the admiral lifted his glasses and trained them towards the invisible horizon. He was still wearing a heavy oilskin, and against the pale steel he looked like some large piece of crude sculpture. He said harshly, 'Nothing! Not a bloody thing!'

Corbett remarked calmly, 'We're well past Trengganu now, sir. It'll be soon or never.'

Trewin wiped his face with his forearm. He knew it was no longer rain on his face and neck. Like the rest of his body, they were running with sweat. He blinked his eyes rapidly to clear them and looked around at the others. They were just shapes. What were they thinking? How would they behave if the shooting began?

Deep inside he knew he was only gauging his own strength. He had seen so many others crack. Outsiders described it jokingly as 'bomb-happy'. At the hospital the more well-

67

versed doctors merely labelled the victims as suffering from 'combat-fatigue'. Words, just bloody, meaningless words! Trewin bit his lip until the pain steadied his racing thoughts. He must get a grip of himself. It was sheer stupidity to go on like this.

Tweedie's rough voice, unreal through the microphone, floated from the rear of the bridge. 'Green six oh! Ship steaming left!' As the glasses swung across the screen he continued, 'Range oh nine two!' Above the bridge the rangefinder squeaked slightly as it turned to track the invisible ship.

Trewin gritted his teeth while his glasses moved vainly over patches of moonlit water and motionless black shadows. Tweedie's look-outs had done well. No doubt their powerful lenses had been helped by some freak sliver of light across the horizon. Out there, to seaward, any ship would stand out like a rock.

Corbett snapped, 'Inform the *Prawn*, Yeoman! Make sure the lamp is properly shaded!' He added slowly, 'We'll give it another two or three minutes. Then tell "A" gun to fire a star-shell.' He peered at Trewin's outline. 'Tell Hammond to make sure it *is* a star-shell.' He wriggled on his chair. 'I don't want to fire on some poor merchantman.'

The admiral remarked gruffly, 'Not likely to be!'

Corbett's voice was incisive. 'I am open to a suggestion to do otherwise, sir!'

The admiral moved his feet noisily. 'You carry on, Corbett.'

The shaded blue signal lamp flicked briefly astern, and Trewin wondered if the little ship was still on her station. At such slow speed there was no high bow-wave to betray her or the *Squalus*.

The long four-inch gun on the forecastle swung slowly across the side of the hull as Tweedie's rangefinder relayed bearings and distances over the intercom. Aft on the battery deck the other four-inch was also tracking the strange ship, something more powerful than star-shell already lying in the breech.

Trewin relayed Corbett's comment over the telephone to

68

Hammond, and faintly through the gloom he could see the young officer's white cap cover as he stood just behind the mounting. His gunners, their heads shrouded in anti-flash gear, were crouching around their breech like beings from another planet.

Hammond's voice was clipped, but he sounded calm enough. 'I've checked it myself, Number One. Actually there's not much chance of seeing anything anyway. It's over four miles away, whatever it is.' In the background someone laughed sharply, and Hammond added, 'Of course, as some idiot has just remarked, it may come after *us*.'

Trewin replaced the handset and walked back to the side. Hammond was doing his best to stay bright and relaxed in front of his men. It was part of the game. Trewin felt his stomach contract painfully and guessed what Hammond must really be enduring.

Tweedie's voice again. 'Captain, sir!' Target has stopped. Green four five. Range oh seven five.'

Corbett snapped his fingers. 'Stopped, has it?' He climbed to his feet and walked to Trewin's side. 'Just as I thought. There is quite a nice little bay around this headland. Ideal for a landing.'

A few agonising minutes dragged past while Corbett trained his glasses slowly in a full arc. Then he snapped, 'Fire star-shell!'

The gong rattled tinnily, and with an ear-shattering crash 'A' gun lurched back on its mounting, throwing a small, savage shockwave back over the bridge.

Trewin waited, counting seconds. He felt the pain sharp in his eyes as with sudden brightness the flare exploded far out on the starboard bow. The low underbellies of the clouds, the calm sea, all changed to an eerie moonscape in the flare's harsh, glacier light, and there, outlined like a black crag in the centre of the glare was the ship.

Nobody said a word on the gunboat's bridge. As each man studied the unlit and motionless ship Trewin could hear the distant bark of orders and the clang of a breech as 'A' gun reloaded. Then there was complete silence.

It fell to the yeoman to break the spell. He yelled, 'Signal from *Prawn*, sir! Two unidentified craft on our starboard quarter!'

A line of green lights lifted lazily from the strange ship's hull and rose in a graceful arc like a column of bright butterflies.

Trewin shouted, 'Tracer! She's opened fire!'

Corbett jabbed the button at his side, and as the gong rang again both guns fired almost together.

Trewin made himself stare at the green tracers, which were already being joined by two more bursts from further aft on the ship's black hull. How deceptively slow they were, then as they passed through the apex of their climb the tracer shells screamed down so fast that it was impossible to distinguish one from another.

Two tall water-spouts rose from the sea directly in line with the other ship. Tweedie's voice intoned, 'Short! Up two hundred!'

Corbett called, 'Signal *Prawn* and *Squalus* to engage the other craft!' To Trewin he snapped, 'Full ahead! Hard a-starboard!'

The star-shell was almost finished, but before the light could die two more flares burst directly above the other ship, which had already changed her outline as she increased speed and turned away.

The admiral said breathlessly, 'That'll be *Beaver* and the rest of the group.' He pounded his hands on the screen. 'Come on, hit the bastard!

As if in answer to his words there was a small orange glow from somewhere aft on the other ship. The light flickered, and then as it looked about to fade completely it soared skyward and clawed up and over the low superstructure in an outline of dancing flames.

Trewin heard some of the gunners cheering, and Hammond yelling above the din, 'Reload! Keep quiet there!'

The *Porcupine* was shivering like a mad thing as she worked up to her maximum speed, and the sea which had been so gentle along her flanks boiled away in two twin waves across the water like a giant white arrowhead.

From astern came the harsh rattle of Oerlikons and the sharper note of machine-guns. As another flare floated eerily overhead Trewin caught a vague glimpse of a flat, boxlike craft, with a high bow-wave breaking above her stem, steering directly across the *Porcupine*'s wake and making for the shore. He saw too the creeping tracers from the other gunboats flashing across the water and lashing the sea into high spectres of foam around the fast-moving craft and then ripping across it with the sound of a bandsaw.

Corbett snapped his fingers. 'Depth?'

A voice replied shakily, 'Nine fathoms, sir.'

Corbett grunted. 'Midships! Steady!'

The guns shifted smoothly as the ship settled on her new course, and maintained their steady fire in spite of the noise and flashing explosions around them.

The yeoman yelled, 'Signal from *Squalus*, sir! She's rammed a landing barge and sunk it!' He was almost choking with excitement. 'And *Prawn* is attacking another one of the bastards!'

Corbett said severely, 'Try not to get *too* excited, Yeoman.' Then in a sharper tone, 'Hard a-port!'

The deck canted as the helm went over and the *Porcupine* swung in a tight turn towards the other ship. The latter was well ablaze, and as the range dropped to less than two miles Trewin heard the crackle of exploding ammunition and the hungry roar of internal fires.

The admiral said sharply, 'Looks like a converted coaster. Just the job for towing these bloody barges!' He ducked as a line of whining tracer shells streaked overhead and vanished into the darkness.

'Midships!' Corbett sounded calm. 'Give me a course to pass the headland, Pilot.'

Mallory clung to the table as the deck heaved once more.

'Two eight oh, sir.' He slipped and almost fell. 'Bloody *hell*!'

Corbett said icily, 'Not like the meat business, eh?' He seemed to be enjoying himself. 'Steer two eight oh!'

There was a sudden explosion which threw a blinding red flash as far as the horizon. Trewin felt the shockwave like a hot wind in his face, and sensed the savage power which had torn the other ship apart. He could smell the stench of cordite and charred wood, of ignited fuel and the acrid stench of a hull being turned into an inferno. Before the light died and the sea closed over the shattered remains he saw the *Beaver* and her two consorts bright in the red glow, like ships from hell.

Corbett said, 'Half ahead together.' The vibration lessened slightly and he added, 'Report damage.'

Masters, the yeoman, sucked his pencil and said carefully, '*Squalus* reports that her bows are stove in, sir. Cannot make more'n two knots. Requests assistance.'

Trewin lifted his face from a voice-pipe and heard himself say flatly, 'No damage or casualties, sir.' He felt ice-cold, yet unable to sense any sort of reaction to what had happened. It was almost more unnerving than if his limbs had started to shake or his voice had refused to respond to his mind.

The admiral showed his teeth. 'Excellent work! Bloody marvellous!' He became suddenly businesslike. 'Signal *Beaver* to take *Squalus* in tow and return to base. *Prawn* can go as additional escort.' He laughed a little too readily. 'Provided she doesn't run out of coal, what?'

Corbett was watching him, his face white in a sudden patch of moonlight. 'Any further orders, sir?'

The admiral appeared to consider it. 'Er, yes. You can hang about here until daylight and make contact with the Army. Tell 'em we've done their work for them. *Shrike* and *Grayling* will stay with you, of course.' He watched the shaded signal lamp stabbing across the water and added casually, 'I'll shift my flag to *Beaver* and return to base with her. I must keep my finger on the pulse, y'know!'

'I see.' Corbett's tone was cool. 'As you say, sir.'

Mallory stepped to Trewin's side and whispered. 'He wants

to get back and grab all the glory for himself, the bastard!' He peered at Trewin's impassive face. 'You feeling all right?'

Trewin nodded. 'Yes.' He turned to watch the smoke drifting past the ship from the few remaining patches of wreckage.

A gesture, he thought. But it was something.

Corbett said, 'Signal for *Beaver*'s motor boat, Yeoman. And then tell the flag-lieutenant to collect the admiral's gear.' He added dryly. 'That is if he hasn't *swum* back to base already.'

Trewin heard the admiral retort sharply, 'That was not very funny!' He raised his voice slightly. 'You've done quite well tonight. Don't spoil it by bringing up old scores!' He seemed to sense that Trewin was behind him and added in a more normal tone, 'I'll send you fresh orders when I know what's happening at base.'

They heard the stutter of *Beaver*'s motor boat, and then Corbett asked mildly, 'Can I expect any air support at daylight, sir?'

The admiral threw his oilskin on the deck and flexed his muscles. 'You'll be all right here, Corbett. I'm the one who'll cop it if the Japs fly over!' He looked at Trewin and grinned. 'Towing a poor lame duck with a coal-fired relic as escort, what?'

They saw the admiral down to the motor boat and then returned to the bridge. Corbett watched the boat's wash fade against the dark water and murmured, 'We'll steam in a wide circle around the bay, Trewin. If it's clear of danger we'll anchor until first light.' He seemed to shrug. 'Then we'll just have to see.'

Trewin could feel the numbness in his body giving way to an uncontrollable shaking. Yet when he looked down at his hands they were quite still.

Corbett said, 'I wonder if there were any survivors from the landing barges?'

Trewin answered harshly, 'I hope not!' He saw Corbett's eyes watching him, but added, 'I hope the bastards found out what it was like before they went under!'

'I expect they did.' Corbett resumed his seat by the screen

and then said, 'I will take over the con. You go round the gun positions and tell them they did very well.' He waited a few moments before adding, 'So did you. But don't start getting bitter. It only blunts your judgement!' He removed his cap and laid it behind the screen. Then in a crisper voice he said, 'Now then, Pilot. Give me a new course. I don't want to run up on the damn beach, eh?'

Trewin climbed slowly down to the sidedeck and leaned against the cold steel ladder. He could hear the gunners chattering and calling to each other, their voices alive with both excitement and relief. He thought about Corbett's self control and wondered if he too knew that the quick success amounted to no more than luck. It had been a brave and necessary gesture. But tomorrow was a new day, and at daylight the enemy would come looking for them.

He saw Hammond talking with his gun crew and automatically straightened his back. Corbett was right about one thing. It was no use being bitter. It had got well beyond that stage, he thought grimly.

*　　　*　　　*

In the pale morning sunlight the bay looked peaceful and deserted. At its southern end the steep-sided headland cast a deep shadow on to the milky water, and from the thickly wooded shoreline which fringed the beach there rose a steady streamlike haze as the warmth penetrated the rain-swollen leaves and tangled creeper beneath.

The *Porcupine* tugged gently at her anchor, her shadow touching that of the headland, while at the other end of the bay the *Grayling* floated above her reflection like a scale model. The third gunboat, *Shrike*, had weighed before dawn, and under Corbett's instructions had rounded the northern arm of the bay to investigate the coast road beyond. From the bay itself the road was invisible, cut off from the sea by a razor-backed ridge of low hills and the thick, lush jungle.

Apart from the distant murmur of gunfire the scene was one

of absolute peace. During the night the coastal current had carried the few pieces of scarred flotsam, and what bodies there might have been from the landing barges, clear away from the shore, so there was nothing to show from the brief, savage action.

Corbett seemed unwilling to leave the bridge, or even to seek the comfort of his chair. As the sun cast more light and heat across the placid water so he became more restless and impatient.

Trewin felt the growing warmth across his neck and the smoky stiffness of his face and arms. He looked at the clear, inviting water alongside and the patches of pale green weed which swayed playfully on the sandy bottom, and imagined his body moving through it, soaking away the dirt and noise of the battle.

There was a mixed aroma of smells from both the galleys. Eggs and bacon and the spicy contrasts from the Chinese quarters. But the anti-aircraft guns were manned, and the slender muzzles moved occasionally from side to side, as if sniffing out possible enemies.

Corbett said abruptly. 'What the *hell* is the Army doing?'

Trewin looked at him. 'They must have heard the gunfire here last night. Perhaps they're too busy inland?'

Corbett stuck out his jaw. 'Rubbish! They must have been informed that we were making a sweep along the coast. The very least they can do is come and see us, dammit!' He lifted his glasses and peered at the empty beach. 'No wonder the bloody airfield got taken.'

Mallory appeared on the bridge holding a large sandwich in one hand. 'They'll be Aussie troops hereabouts. They'll have the job in hand all right.'

'I hope your optimism is well founded.' Corbett shot him an irritated glance. 'But it doesn't help *me*.'

Trewin found time to wonder how far the admiral had got with the other ships. They had heard aircraft during the night, but no sounds of gunfire from the sea. It was just as if each side was sitting back waiting to see what the other would do.

Corbett said suddenly, 'I want you to go ashore, Trewin. There's a village about a mile inland. The Army have a command post there. Go and ask the C.O. what he wants us to do, and be quick about it. I don't like sitting here waiting for the sky to fall.' He added, 'If they don't need us any more I'm heading back south, and fast!'

Trewin stared at the beach. 'Yes, sir.' He beckoned to a bosun's mate. 'Tell Petty Officer Kane to muster a landing party of six men with sidearms, and call away the motor boat.'

Corbett muttered, 'Take Hammond, too. You might need an interpreter.' He said with sudden anger. 'My God, if I've put this ship in danger for nothing I shall raise hell when we reach base!'

Ten minutes later Trewin and his small party waded through the cool water and on to the sand, while the boat turned and scuttled back to the *Porcupine*.

He glanced at his pocket compass and said, 'Let's get started, but have your weapons ready, just in case a few of those Japs managed to swim ashore last night.' He knew his voice was unusually harsh and that Hammond was watching him searchingly, but his mind was too busy with other things to care about that. He stepped through a fringe of salt-stained brush and started up the slope from the beach. It was hard going. It would be worse for fully laden soldiers, he thought.

Once into the jungle of small, gnarled trees they could have been one hundred miles from the sea. A few birds shrilled and squawked in the distance, but they did not see a single movement.

Petty Officer Kane kicked a scarlet fungus aside with a grunt of disgust. 'Bloody dump! Enought to give you the squitters.'

Hammond said quietly, 'What'll we do if we can't find anyone?' He looked up at the criss-cross of branches through which the sun was hardly able to penetrate. The air was humid and clammy, so that his shirt was already sticking to his body.

Trewin said shortly, 'They'll be here.' He hitched the unfamiliar pistol over to his hip and added, 'Where's that damned village?'

They plodded up the slope in silence, while the thorns and low branches plucked at their arms and legs like vicious, eager claws.

Towards the top of the ridge the trees thinned out and the sun swept down to add to their discomfort. Trewin said, 'Take a breather.' He pulled out his binoculars. 'I'll have a look around.' He looked at Kane, 'You come too, and bring your tommy-gun.'

Hammond sat down on a flat stone while the six sailors of the party threw themselves into a patch of shade, breathless and grateful for the rest from this unfamiliar exercise.

Trewin said, 'I won't be long Sub. I should be able to see the road from up there.' He turned on his heel without waiting for a reply and pushed through the bushes with Kane at his back.

Hammond tilted his cap over his eyes and stared at the tiny, busy insects which were already exploring his shoes. It was strange how easy it was to rely on everything Trewin said or did, he thought vaguely. He was quite unlike anyone he had ever met. He rarely seemed to smile or share his confidences, and he had an air of alert caution about him, like a wild animal surrounded by its natural enemies.

When he had first joined the gunboat as first lieutenant, and Hammond could recall the exact moment, he had seemed like a man who had seen and done too much in a short time. Hammond had imagined that he would resent serving under a temporary officer, but quite the reverse had happened. Trewin was unlike Mallory, for instance, who from the moment he had stepped aboard had kept up a steady flow of criticism and complaint about the Navy in general and the British in particular.

He tried to picture Trewin as he must have been before the war, but he could not visualise him as anything but what he was now. Even Corbett seemed content with him, and that was surprising. The captain had frequently and noisily disagreed with poor Foley, the previous first lieutenant. Foley had been an affable but not too intelligent officer, and it was quite impossible to see him playing Trewin's role during the past few days, Hammond decided.

Last night, for instance. He glanced quickly at the tired sailors. The rattle of tracers, and the terrifying scream of cannon shells whipping overhead, it had been far worse than he had believed it would be. But just before the guns had opened fire Trewin had spoken to him on the bridge telephone. His quiet, unemotional voice had acted as a buffer when the actual moment of danger had arrived. And afterwards in the noisy excitement and wild aftermath of battle Trewin had come to visit the gun position. He had been calm and cheerful, as if the whole thing had been part of a drill.

He recalled too the moment when he had almost confided in Trewin about the girl in Singapore. It seemed stupid now, but at the time, with the smoke from the air raid drifting over the island like a pall, he had wanted to tell Trewin about her.

A sailor rolled on his stomach and cocked his head nervously. He said, 'They're comin' back, sir.'

Hammond stood up thankfully and stretched his arms in the sunlight. His smile changed to shocked surprise as Trewin and the petty officer pushed through the bushes their faces streaming with sweat.

Between them, hanging like a limp puppet, was a young army lieutenant. His uniform was in tatters, and a revolver hung unheeded from a lanyard about his neck. His eyes and forehead were hidden under a filthy bandage, and his cheeks were covered in several days' growth of beard.

Trewin said sharply, 'Here, you men! Carry him to the beach, and be quick about it!'

The soldier groaned and rolled his head from side to side as the sailors lifted him from the ground.

Trewin gripped the signalman who had been sent ashore to keep contact with the ship. 'Bunts, run like hell for the beach and call up the *Porcupine*.' Hammond could see Trewin's chest heaving from exertion, the small lines of strain around his eyes. 'Tell the captain to up anchor at once. Tell him to recall *Shrike*, too.' He glanced back up the hill. 'Christ, what a mess!'

Hammond asked, 'Did you find the Army?' He waited, feeling his mouth go dry. 'What is it, Number One?'

Trewin pulled a map from his belt and stared at it. Then he said quietly, 'This section of the road is supposed to be controlled by the 50th Indian Brigade, or part of it.' He stuck the map carelessly inside his shirt. 'Yes, I found them all right.' He walked after the sailors and added shortly, 'The village has been burnt out. We found that poor devil crouching beside a useless radio set. I think he's been blinded.' He spat out the words, 'His men left him!'

Petty Officer Kane slung the tommy-gun across one shoulder. 'He's delirious, sir. But if 'alf of what 'e says is true, we're in a bad way.'

'I—I don't understand?' Hammond stared sideways at Trewin's unshaven face. 'Where did they all go?'

Trewin replied savagely, 'That poor, raving lieutenant was part of a battalion at Kota Bahru. They've been fighting and falling back, regrouping and falling back, since the whole thing started. Even now he doesn't believe his men have run away!'

Kane said angrily, ' 'E said there were tanks on the road. And 'is men 'ave never seen a bloody tank in their lives, can you imagine that?'

'Tanks, retreats, what the bloody difference does it make now?' Trewin quickened his pace. 'We've got the ship to worry about.' He steadied his voice with an effort and looked hard at Hammond. 'The Japs are further south already!' He watched his words strike home. 'They by-passed this sector *yesterday*!' He slammed his hands together. 'Anyone left back here will go in the bag when the Japs start mopping up the stragglers.' He wiped his face wearily. 'God knows how they missed the lieutenant when they came over the ridge, but he was lucky.'

Kane muttered, 'Not like them others, sir.' He shot Hammond a glance. 'We found about a dozen Aussie soldiers on the edge of the village.' His voice shook with anger and barely suppressed horror. 'Their hands were tied behind 'em! They were dead!'

Hammond asked quietly, 'Had they been shot?'

Trewin had hurried ahead, but over his shoulder he called harshly, 'Tell him, Kane! Tell him how the bastards had left them!'

Kane looked away. 'Their 'eads 'ad been cut off, sir! They was stuck on stakes by the side of the road . . .' He broke off, his normally impassive features sick with disgust.

Breathless and gasping they reached the beach where the motor-boat waited to receive them. The *Grayling* was already under way, and the *Porcupine*'s cable was bar-taut and ready to up anchor.

Hammond sat with the soldier's shoulders propped against his legs as the boat spurted towards the ship, his eyes fixed on the man's loose, sun-dried mouth. On the opposite side of the small cockpit Trewin stared fixedly at the shore, his eyes cold and hard beneath his cap.

The soldier's body twisted in a sudden convulsion and he shouted, 'Sergeant! Tell those men to march in step!' A thread of saliva ran down his chin as he continued in a flat, toneless voice, 'Remember that this is the *First* Battalion, not the bloody sappers!'

Trewin said, 'Keep that man *quiet*, Sub.'

One of the seamen muttered, 'My God! Poor bastard!'

As the boat reached the ship's side and men jumped down to help the delirious soldier aboard, Trewin said, 'Get the boat hoisted, Sub! I'm going to the bridge.'

Hammond waited by the guardrails until the motor boat was lashed, still dripping, against her davits, then with a quick glance towards the empty beach ran up the bridge ladder. The deck was trembling as the ship gathered way, and from forward he could hear Dancy yelling at the anchor party. Corbett was in his chair, as if he had never moved, and Trewin was standing beside him on the gratings, his face hidden in shadow.

Hammond heard Corbett say, 'We should have been *told*. We were sent too far north.'

Trewin replied, 'It's the most stupid piece of bungling I've ever seen!' He sounded calm, but his hands were bunched at his sides gripping his torn trousers as if for support. He continued, 'The whole front must have collapsed. They're falling back like a lot of bloody rabbits!'

Corbett turned and looked up at him, his face expressionless. 'Right now we have to get under way, Trewin. There'll be time enough later to hear your interpretations of all this.'

A look-out's voice echoed around the bridge. 'Aircraft, sir! Bearing green four five! Angle of sight two oh!'

Trewin did not look round. 'The admiral must have known, sir! He *must* have realised this could happen!'

Corbett snapped, 'Full ahead together!' Then he looked again at Trewin's tall figure and said flatly, 'We had our orders.'

'I see.' Trewin turned and stared straight at the sun. 'I'll go aft to the A.A. guns.' It was as if he were forcing his thoughts into words.

Hammond heard men running along the sidedecks, the rattle of voices across the bridge intercom, yet he felt unable to move.

Trewin crossed the bridge in three strides and then paused, seeing Hammond for the first time. His voice was cold, like a stranger's. 'Well, Sub, you once asked me about war, remember?' His eyes were blazing like a man with fever. 'So now you know!' He looked unwinkingly towards the distant growl of aircraft engines. 'This is what it is all about!' He turned away and ran quickly down the ladder.

Corbett's voice cut into Hammond's dazed thoughts like a knife. 'Forget what you just heard, and attend to your duties!'

Hammond climbed down to the deck and looked astern. The *Grayling* was gathering speed, her bows shrouded in spray as she cross the *Porcupine*'s wake. Of the *Shrike* there was still no sign.

He thought of Trewin's cold anger, of the poor, helpless soldier across his knees in the boat. Through it all he heard Trewin's words like an accusation . . . 'This is what it's all about!'

And at that moment the guns started to fire.

5
Direct Hit

The rating at Trewin's side said sharply, 'Four aircraft, sir! Port quarter, angle of sight three oh!'

Trewin did not raise his glasses. The aircraft were well out of range, and after turning in a wide circle were climbing rapidly towards the horizon and the sun. Four bright silver chips against the pale sky, the growl of their engines rising in time to their climb.

There were still a few minutes more to wait, Trewin decided. There was a small breeze whipping across the battery deck, but it did little to ease the heat thrown back from the armoured gun mounting, and the small protected position beside the ammunition hatch where Trewin was crouching. From here he could supervise either the four-inch gun or, if required, the Oerlikons which were mounted on either side of the upperdeck, just abaft the funnel.

He peered astern to watch the *Grayling* as she followed purposefully in the *Porcupine*'s white wake. They were less than a quarter of a mile apart and were steaming at full speed on the new southerly course. Further astern, her antiquated shape shrouded in haze, the little *Shrike* endeavoured to maintain her maximum speed, and smoke pouring from her thin funnel in a low, unbroken plume.

Trewin saw the *Grayling*'s guns following the distant aircraft, and guessed that the third gunboat would also be ready when the time came. Six four-inch guns between them, and with the additional power of the short-range weapons they might well give good account of themselves.

He rested his palms on the hot metal surrounding the gun position and watched the seamen training their sights towards the enemy. The men who were so engrossed in their preparations were no longer faces as they had appeared when he had first stepped aboard. Now they were names and personalities, and already the strengths and weaknesses were beginning to show, like small parts of a large canvas.

'X' gun grated slightly and the long grey muzzle tilted towards the dazzling sun. On either side of the gleaming breech the trainer and gunlayer eased their wheels very slowly and kept their eyes glued to their sights.

Able Seaman Walker, the breechworker, banged his gloved hands together and muttered, 'Come on, you bastards! Let's be 'avin' you then!' His black beard jutted through his anti-flash hood, and Trewin was reminded of a painting he had once seen of a jovial monk.

He said, 'They look like fighters. So watch your aim-off, and allow for a speed of three hundred knots.' He saw the layer and trainer glance at one another across the gun and added sharply, 'They'll come right out of the sun, so keep your heads and ignore everything else but the one in your sights.'

Trewin turned aside as the communications rating called, 'Barrage . . . *commence*!'

Trewin heard the bells ringing beside the gunshield and automatically held his breath. The gun lurched back on its mounting with an ear-splitting roar. From forward the other gun also opened fire, and as Trewin lifted his glasses to watch the dirty brown smudges drift across the sun they were joined by other shellbursts from the ships astern.

The port Oerlikon broke into a fierce rattle and then fell silent as Trewin yelled, 'Hold your fire, damn you!' He saw the gunner's face staring at him, angry and embarrassed. 'Don't open up until the range falls below a thousand yards!' He looked grimly at the other Oerlikon to make sure the man had understood him.

The rating beside him shouted, 'Aircraft, sir! Bearing red one one five! Angle of sight two oh!' He dashed the sweat from his eyes. 'Approach angle three oh left!'

Trewin clung to a stanchion as the deck canted in response

to the wheel. He could see the first plane clearly now. Coming down fast in a shallow dive and swinging astern towards *Grayling*. The wafer-thin wings rocked from side to side, bracketed with shellbursts, but with the sunlight gleaming on its blood-red insignia as it tore down on its quarry.

Then the Oerlikon opened fire, the green tracers lifting and joining to form a bright cone of fire across the aircraft's path. Trewin watched the fast-moving aircraft as it dived still closer to the water, so that it seemed to be pursued by its reflection into the converging maelstrom of cannon shells and machine-gun fire.

Trewin yelled, 'Here comes the next!' He pointed towards the sun as the second fighter streaked across the blue water, so low down that the surface rippled like corn in a strong wind. Vague and distorted above the crash of gunfire and exploding cannon shells he heard the hoarse rattle of machine-guns almost swallowed completely in the rising scream of the fighter's engine. He saw the water churned alive from the fighter's guns, and heard the clang of metal from somewhere on the side-deck.

The man at his side ducked as the plane's shadow blacked out the deck for a split second and the guns swung round in a full circle to follow it.

It was a small, snub-nosed aircraft, probably from a carrier, Trewin thought. He could see the sunlight on the perspex cockpit cover, the black outline of the pilot's head as he gunned the engine and threw the fighter almost on its side as it climbed steeply away from the ship.

The guns turned away, smoking and impotent, to search out the next attacker. They did not have to wait long. The final pair of fighters flew in wingtip to wingtip, their guns blazing even before they were in range. Again they went for the *Grayling*, and Trewin could see the gunboat's hull surrounded with leaping white feathers of spray as the bullets hammered across her in a torrent of steel.

One of the fighters swung drunkenly aside from its charge, and with black smoke pouring from its tail dropped dangerously

84

close to the sea. Trewin could see the flashing tracers reaching after it, plucking pieces from its wings, as the plane's engine coughed and reared in a final effort to escape.

The pilot might have succeeded but for the distant headland. Or maybe he was already dead at the controls. But as Trewin watched with cold fascination the aircraft dropped its nose and ploughed straight into the hillside above the coast road, vanishing instantly in a bright red explosion.

Some of the gunners were cheering, and Trewin yelled, 'Watch your *front*!' He swung his glasses to follow the remaining fighters. They were already swinging away in a tight arc, climbing for another attack.

He shifted his glasses slightly to look at the other ships. Both were on station, and every gun seemed to be trained and ready. The first kill would be a great encouragement. And the odds were getting better. It was strange that the Japs had sent only four fighters, he thought. They must have hundreds on the peninsula already, and more at sea on their carriers.

He swung round, caught off guard as a man shouted wildly, 'Aircraft! Bearing green nine oh!'

There were two of them, twin-engined and flying very low. The fighter which had fallen to the gunboats' combined attack had set the whole hillside ablaze so that the trees and dry gorse made one bank of leaping flames from the hilltop down to the water's edge. Over the lip of the hill, and seeming to fly through the flames themselves, the two new attackers swept down towards the ships before many of the gunners were aware what was happening.

'X' gun swung swiftly on its mounting, the breech opening and closing with a click across yet another shell, the sweating seamen kicking the used and smoking cartridge cases aside as they fought to follow the low, roaring shapes.

Trewin saw the bombs tumbling from the leading's plane's belly even as the first shellburst drifted some twenty feet above its tail. *Porcupine*'s guns fell silent, unable to bear on the fast-turning bombers as they passed astern of *Grayling* and climbed away in a tight turn.

85

There was one bright flash, and as Trewin craned over the tail he saw *Shrike* fall out of line, her forecastle and bridge hidden in a great pall of black smoke.

'Three fighters attacking, sir!' The communications rating was holding his earphones against his head, shutting out the echoing roar of the exploding bombs, the scream of attacking aircraft.

This time the fighters concentrated on the *Grayling*. In spite of the combined barrage of fire laid across their path they pressed home their attack, so that through his glasses Trewin could see the holes appearing in the gunboat's superstructure and funnel and pieces of deck planking lifting skywards as if thrown by some invisible maniac.

But another fighter got caught in the mesh of leaping tracers, and dived straight into the sea within feet of the *Grayling*'s stern. Spouting flames and smoke it bounced several times, throwing up spray like a maddened shark, then with one final bang it tore apart and sank out of sight.

Trewin looked again at the *Shrike*. Already she seemed to have grown smaller as she fell further and further astern. She was listing steeply, and the dense smoke hung above her shattered decks, rising and spreading until even the sun seemed to lose its power.

A Chinese messenger climbed gasping over the rim of the battery deck, his head encased in a steel helmet which only made him look more defenceless. 'Cap'n want you on bridge, sir!' His black eyes were fixed on the *Shrike* as he spoke, and Trewin could see the fear on his face like a mask.

'Very well.' He slapped the gun captain on the arm. 'Take over, Dunwoody!' He paused to scan the horizon with his glasses. The two fighters were already mere slivers of silver, half shrouded in sea haze. 'They'll not be back yet, and the bombers seem to have gone, too.'

The big leading seaman wiped his mouth and grimaced. 'They've done for *Shrike*, sir.' He sounded hoarse. 'Christ, I can see flames!'

Trewin pushed by him and ran towards the bridge. As he

passed the Oerlikons with their gunners leaning back in the harnesses he yelled, 'Check your magazines! They might be back!'

The seamen stared at him without recognition. They understood and would obey, but their minds were lost in the fury and sickness of battle.

As he climbed up the ladder Trewin felt his weight growing on his fingers, and when he glanced down he saw that the water was leaping beneath him in a surge of white froth as the *Porcupine*'s helm went hard over.

Corbett was standing by the screen, his glasses hanging on his chest as he watched the ship's wake curve away in a crisp arc. 'Ah, Trewin!' He looked away and said sharply, 'Midships! Tell the cox'n to steer straight for the *Shrike*!'

At the rear of the bridge Phelps, the red-haired signalman, was standing straddle-legged on the tilting deck, his Aldis cradled on his elbow as he flashed a signal towards the *Grayling*.

Corbett said, '*Grayling* is to cover us, Trewin. I am going to help *Shrike*. Take her in tow if I can.'

'*Grayling* 'as acknowledged, sir!' Phelps lowered his Aldis and wrinkled his freckled face against the glare. 'She reports that all guns are still operational, but that she's 'ad twelve men wounded, sir.'

Corbett did not seem to hear. 'Signal *Shrike* and ask her what has happened.' To Trewin he added quietly, 'That was a pretty sharp attack, eh?' He rubbed the teak rail behind the screen and said, 'She did very well.'

Trewin felt a hot breath across his neck, and when he turned he saw that the *Shrike*'s maindeck was enveloped in flames from end to end. Exploding ammunition crackled in an insane barrage, and he could see that the little ship's list had grown more acute in the last few minutes. He said flatly, 'She's going! It must have been a direct hit!'

Corbett stared at the other ship, his eyes glittering in the flames. 'She was hit twice, as a matter of fact.' His mouth hardened. 'We'll do what we can.'

Trewin made himself watch the *Shrike*'s last agony as more

87

internal explosions rocked her hull and sent her foremast crashing into the water alongside. He had seen many ships go like this, and he was disturbed to find that he was nevertheless moved by what he saw. Perhaps it was because of the unruffled surroundings. The clear sky and calm, placid water with the green line of hills abeam. And the ship herself made some difference, he thought dully. She was too old, too fragile for this sort of war. For any war.

'Slow ahead together!' Corbett lifted his glasses. 'Stand by with rafts and heaving lines!'

Men were already leaping from the *Shrike*'s sidedeck which was barely inches above the water. Small white figures which jumped from gun mountings and the scarred battery deck, to break the surface again black and obscene through the great slick of oil which surrounded the ship like blood.

'Stop together!' The *Porcupine* glided slowly through the oil and odd pieces of wreckage, while grim-faced seamen lined the rails and waited to haul the survivors aboard.

Rafts were lowered and tied alongside, and Trewin saw Baker, the ship's sick-bay attendant, already down in one of them, his red-cross bag slung on his shoulder as he gestured towards the nearest swimmers.

Corbett said, 'Tell them to get a move on! We're a sitting duck at the moment.' He shielded his face as another internal explosion shook the *Shrike* as if she were a toy.

She tilted slowly on her side, and Trewin heard the grate and crash of heavy machinery tearing loose and thundering through the hull. This time she did not resist, and with an increasing roar of inrushing water she rolled right over, her mainmast and shattered funnel cleaving through a few struggling survivors who were either too weak or too wounded to get clear.

Her flat, weed-coated bilges showed for a few more minutes, and as the first swimmers were hauled choking and retching on to the *Porcupine*'s deck the *Shrike* lifted her bows and vanished in a swelter of air bubbles and oily flotsam.

There were very few survivors. Trewin counted twenty all told. The two bombs had hit the bridge and penetrated the engine room. By rights there should have been nobody rescued at all.

While the *Porcupine* gathered way again and steamed in a circle around the few bobbing remains of her old consort, the look-outs reported two more aircraft approaching from the south. But as the gun crews swung their muzzles towards them Trewin heard the bridge tannoy intone, 'These are friendly aircraft!'

The men on deck watched in silence as the two elderly Buffaloes dipped their stubby wings and roared noisily overhead. From the bridge an Aldis flashed briefly, and together the two aircraft turned towards the shore.

Baker, the S.B.A., was trying to wipe oil fuel from the face of a wounded petty officer. With each attempt the man screamed, and his face seemed to come away like bloody waste in Baker's fingers. As the two shadows flashed overhead Baker looked up, his face pale and shocked. 'Where *were* you, you bastards?' His voice sounded about to crack. 'You rotten, cowardly bastards!'

Trewin dropped his hand on to the S.B.A.'s shoulder. 'Easy, Baker!' He saw the man's mouth quiver. 'You're more use to us right now than they would be!'

Baker nodded dumbly and then turned back to the moaning man at his knees. His face was still stricken, but Trewin saw that his hands were firm and gentle as he continued with his task.

Trewin returned to the bridge where Corbett remained by the screen, still staring towards the unmoving slick of oil. He said, 'Make to *Grayling* that we will head for Talang Inlet. We can send the survivors to the hospital there.' Almost to himself he continued, 'I knew her captain very well. He was a good officer.'

Trewin looked down at his hands. They were quite relaxed, and he was almost more shocked to discover that he could feel nothing but relief that he had survived yet once more.

Corbett was looking at him, his eyes empty and cold. 'I asked for air support, Trewin. It was denied.' He turned away as if angry with himself for displaying an unnecessary confidence. 'I expect they have their reasons.'

Trewin studied him calmly. 'Anyway, they'll have an *excuse*, sir, I have no doubt of that.'

Corbett replied as if he had not heard Trewin's bitterness. '*Grayling* are claiming both aircraft for themselves. You'll have to see that our gunners get the next bag.'

Mallory called, 'Steady on new course, sir! One five zero!' He cleared his throat noisily. 'That was a bit scary all round, I'd say.'

Corbett climbed on to his chair and leaned forward to watch 'A' gun swinging back into line. For once he seemed disinclined to contradict or rebuke the Australian.

Trewin brushed the dust and flaked paintwork from his shirt and said quietly, 'We're not out of the wood yet!'

From somewhere below a voice cried out in sudden agony. Trewin thought of the dazed and blinded soldier and the headless corpses beside the empty road. Of the *Shrike*'s tired acceptance of her fate and the cool arrogance of her destroyers. The doorway on to this particular war had been opened very slightly, but what he had seen had been more terrible than he had visualised, even in his worst nightmares.

He looked at Corbett's shoulders and wondered what he really thought about it all. If he had been equally shocked, he was certainly hiding the fact well enough.

All at once Trewin felt something like hatred for him. For him and his ship. This poor, creeping ship which had become Corbett's whole world. The stupid, meaningless remarks which acted like a shield for what they were all really thinking and enduring. Like a headmaster's report at the end of term.

The ship had done quite well. . . . Very well. . . . Or not well enough. . . .

He felt the sweat running down his spine and he wanted to run from the bridge with its air of silent purpose. He walked to the screen and took several long breaths. It was madness to let it get a hold like this. You had to fight it like a living enemy. Otherwise the despair closed around you, stifling, grinding you down until you were without meaning or reality. Like those poor, oil-sodden things who were gasping out their lives at the hands of a half-trained sick-berth attendant, or, the brave soldier who was even now issuing his empty orders to the men who had left him to die.

With a start he realised the signal man was staring up at him, his round, freckled face curious and questioning. Trewin asked sharply, 'What is it, Phelps?'

'Char, sir? Do you want a cup?'

Trewin felt the grin spreading across his face in spite of his screaming nerves. 'Thank you, Bunts. Yes, I would, very much.'

He watched the young signalman ladling the over-sweetened tea out of an enamel jug, his face entirely engrossed. His were the sort who never cracked, Trewin thought vaguely. They went on obeying orders until there were no more to give and none to give them.

He leaned against the warm, vibrating steel and looked into the cup. The tea was nearly cold and there were flecks of grit floating on the surface. But at that moment, as Trewin fought his lonely battle with himself, it tasted better than champagne.

*   *   *

Leading Steward Yates placed a glass of gin on the wardroom table by Trewin's elbow and ran a finger around the collar of his white jacket. ' 'Ot, annit, sir?' Yates stared round the untidy litter of rolled bandages, discarded stretchers and dirty crockery which stayed as reminders of the wounded sailors who had been taken ashore to the Talang hospital. It was late evening, and with the deadlights closed across the wardroom scuttles the air was sticky and oppressive, in spite of the revolving deckhead fans.

Trewin tasted the gin and grimaced. It was warm and made a sour passage to his empty stomach. He was dog-tired and his eyes felt as if they were lined with sand. He was still dressed in the same stained clothes, his face was stiff and stubbled, and yet he felt incapable of any more movement.

At first light the *Porcupine* and the *Grayling* had felt their way into the Talang Inlet, their crews weary at their stations, the guns still cocked skywards in readiness to repel another attack. And after leaving the place where *Shrike* had fought her last battle, the two ships had indeed been attacked. As before, the aircraft had dived out of the sun, searching and probing for an opening, their machine-guns churning the water into a wilderness of foam and flying steel.

Porcupine had remained luckier than her consort. *Grayling* had been raked on each attack, and seven men had died, including Quarrie, her captain.

Porcupine had not completely escaped. During the final attack, made by two large fighters, the port Oerlikon had jammed, and at that very moment one of the aircraft had been making its final approach some twenty feet above the water. Trewin had seen the gunner struggling in his harness and yelling to his loading number for a fresh magazine. He had watched the deck planking rip apart around the mounting, had seen the gunner torn from his feet and hurled screaming from his broken harness. From a man to a bloody pile of rags in the twinkling of an eye. Trewin had run from behind his shield and pushing the shocked seaman with the fresh magazine aside had swung the gun round and after the roaring fighter. He had hardly noticed the second plane, and had concentrated his whole being on the wafer shape which moved sideways through his gunsight. He had heard the bullets striking sparks from the superstructure around him and had shut out the shouts of warning from the other gunners. Only when the magazine had emptied and both aircraft were winging away towards the shore did he realise that there was blood running down his arm. Leading Sick Berth Attendant Baker had come running with a dressing but Trewin had snatched it away from him, his mind dulled with anger and sudden despair.

Now as he sat in the deserted wardroom he could feel the dressing tugging at his shoulder where a wood splinter had ripped up from the deck with the force of an arrow.

He followed Yates' disapproving stare around the wardroom, remembering all the pain and effort which had followed their arrival at the pier. There had been so much to do. The wounded to be taken by stretcher to the hosital, and the dead to be buried. For the latter there was no time for a sea burial, and within months their graves would be lost in the encrouching jungle.

For the whole day they had worked like dazed automatons to get the ship ready to fight again. In spite of the repairs and the replacement of ammunition, routine must be maintained. Meals had to be procured for sailors too tired to notice what they were eating, and the men had to be coaxed or driven to the countless tasks which needed doing, when all they wanted to do was sleep. Sleep like the dead.

And through it all Corbett had remained an ever-moving force. He showed no sign of fatigue or despair, and seemed to make no allowances for anything his men might be feeling. As he had said to Trewin that afternoon, 'I want this ship on top line. You don't win battles with slackness, eh?'

To Trewin's knowledge Corbett's untiring energy had taken him ashore and back to the ship more than a dozen times. He had organised a telephone link with the base, and had even bullied the local military to supply some anti-aircraft guns for the inlet to cover the two ships at their moorings.

Trewin had stepped ashore only twice. At the hospital and in the village he had been stunned by the change which had shown itself since his other visit. There were Malay refugees everywhere. Whole families were camping in the open or sitting amidst scanty possessions along the roadside. All had fled from the north, and not one of them seemed to know where to go or with what purpose.

It was comforting to see more soldiers about. Mostly Australians, they moved in and around the village, sorting out lost families and supplying endless quantities of food and fresh water. They appeared cheerful enough, and treated the news from the north with the usual serviceman's indifference. As one sergeant had said to Trewin, 'What can you expect from flamin' Indians? They're lost without their friggin' elephants!' He had gone off laughing to himself a Malay baby in one arm and his rifle in the other.

At the hospital things had been chaotic but under control. Every bed space, and each passageway as well, was filled to capacity with sick and injured refugees. The wounded sailors had been laid in Dr. Massey's own quarters to wait for army transport to take them south. The Chinese and Malay nurses moved quietly amongst them like pale nuns, showing no emotion or strain, and not sparing themselves for an instant, in spite of the fact they had not slept for two days.

Yates said suddenly, 'Will you be needin' me, sir?'

Trewin shook his head absently. 'No. But leave the bottle. You can get the messmen to clear up all this stuff tomorrow.'

Yates shrugged. 'We'll be wantin' it agin soon, I wouldn't wonder.'

He padded out of the wardroom and Trewin poured out another full measure of gin. As he leaned back in the chair he winced as a stab of pain lanced through his shoulder. The splinter was still there. He would have to do something about it. The gin dulled his aching mind, and it was hard to drive his thoughts into order.

How quiet the ship felt. Just the whir of fans and the muted hum of a dynamo from aft. Occasionally he could hear the uneasy pacing of the quartermaster at the gangway and the squeak of fenders against the pier. But the ship was resting. Gathering her spent strength.

Normally at this time the messdecks would be alive with noise and music. But when Trewin had done his rounds half an hour earlier he had found the men asleep. Some had not even reached their hammocks and lay like corpses at the mess tables, heads on forearms, their faces strained even in sleep as their minds relived the noise and fear of battle.

He had looked into the petty officer's mess. It had been the same there. The ship's professionals had been in their bunks. Nothing had stirred.

He had seen Chief Petty Officer Unwin, the coxswain lying flat on his back, his mouth open, a filled but unlit pipe still

94

grasped in one hand. On his chest, sleeping like a small extension of himself, had been Toby, the ship's black-and-white cat, his body rising and falling in time with Unwin's uneven breathing. The coxswain had taken out his teeth before climbing into his bunk, and in the shaded police light his face looked old and sunken. Yet this was the man who had stayed at the wheel during each attack, his ears deaf to all but the ever-demanding voice-pipe from the bridge.

And Kane, the G.I., with one arm across his face, his clothes neatly folded beside his bunk. A true gunnery man, Trewin thought. He recalled Kane's lean features beside the road as together they had stared at the line of sun-blackened heads with their obscene expressions of horror and grisly malevolence. Kane had been trained to control his emotions, yet even he had muttered, 'Now I *know* there's no God!'

Trewin stood up violently and pushed the bottle aside. He would go to the sick bay and remove the splinter himself. He cursed as he remembered that Baker was ashore at the hospital and the sick bay was locked. It always was in harbour, by Corbett's direction. Apparently it had once been raided by a cat-footed Chinese searching for drugs, and the captain had never forgotten the incident.

Trewin seized his cap and walked out on to the deck. There was a small breeze, and after the wardroom it felt almost cold.

Petty Officer Dancy shielded a cigarette in his palm and said, 'All quiet, sir.'

'I'm going to the hospital, Buffer. This splinter is bothering me.'

'If you come to the mess I'll have a go if you like, sir?'

Trewin turned away. 'No! I can manage!' He saw Dancy's eyes glinting in the darkness and added, 'I'm sorry. I didn't mean to bite your head off.'

He walked past the quartermaster and down the gangway. He saw Dancy pause to speak with the quartermaster and wondered if they were discussing him. He strode quickly and angrily up the dirt road, ignoring the little groups of villagers and refugees, his mind returning again to the signal which

Corbett had received that afternoon.

Corbett had seemed to be quite content with it. 'It makes up just a little bit for what has happened, Trewin.' Corbett had been busy shaving when Trewin had entered his cabin. 'The R.A.F. could not send fighter protection in time because all their planes were busy elsewhere.' He had turned to study Trewin's grave features. 'It doesn't help the *Shrike*, but it shows that they tried, eh?'

Trewin had waited, wondering why Corbett had bothered to call him from the work on deck.

Corbett had wiped his blade carefully. 'I've fixed up a telephone line with the troops ashore. Go and get through to base and tell them to pass a signal to the R.A.F. for me.' He sounded vague. 'You know the sort of thing. Thanks for trying! and so forth.'

Trewin had gone to find the army signal section, his mind buzzing with Corbett's words. 'Thanks for trying!' That was a big comfort to the *Shrike*!

The line had been bad and noisy with interference, but Trewin had discovered that there was more to the signal than he had imagined. A harassed staff officer at the other end of the line had snapped, 'The R.A.F. wanted to help you, old boy. But Rear-Admiral Fairfax-Loring refused to allow it. Said he wanted every available plane to cover *his* withdrawal.'

Even now he could hardly believe it. The admiral's small group had been nearer to ready help, yet he had stopped the air cover for the *Porcupine* which was in greater danger. What the hell was going on? Was it spite or stupidity? Either way it was beyond any sort of sane reasoning.

Trewin recalled with sudden clarity the admiral's words to Corbett on the darkened bridge. 'Don't spoil it by bringing up old scores!' It was unlikely that anyone would settle any scores, no matter how personal, in this way, but of one thing he was sure—somehow or other he would have it out with Corbett. Or, he quickened his stride in time with his thoughts, apply for a transfer back to England. Anywhere but in this ship and this place!

He reached the hospital compound and groped his way up the wooden steps. All shutters were drawn, but chinks of light made a mockery of the black-out. Not that it mattered, he decided. The hospital was surrounded on all sides by jungle and steep hills. It would take a very eager pilot to find it as a potential target.

Dr. James Massey was standing outside his room, arms folded, a long cheroot in his teeth. He looked tired and worn, and his white smock was daubed with dried blood. He nodded briefly, 'Can I help you?' His tone was automatic, as if he had been asking that question since time began.

Trewin said, 'Just a wood splinter. I'd do it myself, but . . .'

Massey said briskly, 'Don't *do* anything. Not out here.' He saw Trewin shift his shoulder awkwardly. 'You're more likely to die of blood-poisoning than anything in this place.' He gestured with his cheroot. 'Get in there. Take your shirt off and wait until I send someone.' He turned away as a nurse called to him from one of the wards. Over his shoulder he remarked, 'It seems as if the military have made a pretty mess of things.'

Trewin walked into the room, suddenly wishing he had let Dancy have a go at the splinter as he had suggested. He did not trust first judgements, but something about Massey made him feel resentful. His offhand summing up of the fighting in the north, for instance. If there had been a mess made of it, it had been decided long ago, and certainly not by a handful of over-optimistic soldiers!

'Ah, here you are.'

Trewin swung round and stared at the girl who stood framed in the open door. She was wearing a khaki shirt and slacks and her long black hair was tied back to the nape of her neck with a piece of bandage. She looked in her early twenties and was extremely attractive. Even the crumpled shirt could not disguise the firm curve of her body, and in the lamplight her tanned skin looked cool and smooth.

She studied him gravely, watching the uncertainty on his face. 'Well? You are the one with the splinter?' Her dark brown eyes flashed with sudden impatience. 'Look, Lieutenant, I've got plenty to do here without waiting for *you*!'

Trewin managed to reply, 'It's not important. It's just that I couldn't reach it myself . . .'

She interrupted shortly, 'Some of the sailors in the other ward are really ill! But they make less fuss than you are doing now!'

Trewin caught sight of himself in a wall mirror and saw the lines of anger on his face. He looked and felt dirty and crushed, yet the words he wanted for this cool, arrogant girl would not come. With something like defeat he tore off his smoke-stained shirt and threw it on the floor.

She was still watching him, her small hands firmly placed on her hips. Then her head moved towards the table. 'Lie on that. I'll get that old dressing off first.'

Trewin rolled face down on the table, his face buried in his forearm. By pressing his eyes into the skin of his arm he could blot out the glare from the hissing pressure lamp, shut out everything but his feeling of desperate urgency. To get out of here. To return to the ship and get that bottle.

He could hear the girl moving back from the wall cabinet. Then there was a sudden silence, and he could sense her standing beside him, very close and unmoving. As if from far away he heard himself say. 'Well, don't just stare at it! For God's sake get it over with!' His body went rigid as she laid one hand on his back. It felt very soft and cool.

She said quietly, 'Forgive me. I did not know.'

Trewin could not stop himself. The words seemed to force themselves between his clenched teeth, breaking down his control, pouring out in a flood. 'Would you like to get someone else? Or would you rather leave me the bloody tools and let *me* do it?'

He stiffened, holding his breath as the hand moved slowly up his back. It did not falter or flinch but moved on until it lay motionless again on his disfigured shoulder with its great patch of mutilated skin.

She said, 'It's all right now. Just rest quietly.'

Trewin lay silent as the hands removed the dressing. It was so easy, so gentle that he hardly noticed it. Then she moved around the top of the table, and he could feel the pressure of her waist against his arm.

She paused. 'Just another second.' There was a sharp stab of pain, followed by the enclosing warmth of a dressing. Then she added in the same level voice, 'Let me help you up.'

Trewin threw his legs over the side of the table and stood up, his fingers reaching for his tattered shirt. As he pulled it across his shoulders he looked at the girl, his mind suddenly empty. She was watching him, her eyes no longer impatient. She was still holding the scissors in one hand, and Trewin could see her breasts moving with emotion.

She said quietly, 'You don't have to be ashamed. I'm the one who should feel that!'

There was a step outside the door and she added quickly, 'You must be Lieutenant Trewin.' She held out her hand. The action was impetuous yet very genuine. 'I'm Clare Massey.'

Trewin took it and stared down at it, fighting to control his confused thoughts.

She said, 'You've had a bad time.' She squeezed his fingers very slightly. 'But things will get better, you'll see.'

Trewin looked into her eyes and then nodded. 'Thank you.' He tried to smile but it would not come. 'I should like to talk to you again. Later.'

She nodded slowly. 'Very well.' She released his hand and stood to one side to let him pass.

He stared down at her, feeling her hand still on his back. At the moment of breaking he had wanted to shock her, drive her away with shame and disgust. But her simple gesture had held all those things back. Had driven them away with that one action. Later he might see it as pity or embarrassment. But now he would let nothing spoil it.

As he walked away from the crowded hospital his step was almost brisk, and his mind was calmer than he could remember for a long while.

6
Then There Were Four

Trewin wedged himself firmly in a corner of the darkened taxi and watched the last dwellings of the city's outskirts giving way to open country and small scattered clumps of trees. The Indian driver seemed glad to get away from the densely crowded streets and gunned his engine despite the deep, savage ruts in the road which had been left by a recent thunderstorm and its attendant downpour.

Now the sky over Singapore was bright with stars, and the air tasted fresh and clean. Trewin had intended to walk to Corbett's house, but the city's atmosphere of desperate gaiety had left him dazed and slightly unnerved, so that he had seized the solitary taxi as something like a refuge.

It was New Year's Eve, and the *Porcupine* had moored to a buoy in Keppel Harbour just twenty-four hours earlier with her sister ship *Beaver* lashed snugly alongside. It was just over two weeks since Trewin had watched the *Shrike*'s death agony and her pitiful survivors hauled aboard the *Porcupine*'s deck. Two weeks in which the world and the war seemed to have contracted and shrunk to the smallest confines of the hull, a green blur of coastline and the merciless sky above.

The gunboats had continued their duties without a break. They had carried troops, stopped and searched native craft for enemy guerillas, humped stores to the more isolated garrisons, and had hit back at the ever-prowling aircraft. There was never a let up, and nobody aboard even bothered to ask about air cover any more.

Grayling had returned to base for some quick repairs, but had reappeared on her patrol area in much the same condition, her hull scarred and pitted from the first fighter attack. With her she brought news of heavy and constant air raids on Singapore's dockyard and base, and a reminder of the personal side to war.

The *Squalus*, her bows smashed after ramming the Japanese landing craft in that first gesture of jubilant victory, had been sunk at her moorings while awaiting the attentions of the dockyard. Fortunately the loss of life was small, her company having been ashore enjoying the attractions of Singapore. Her captain, Lieutenant-Commander Nye, a man once known for his ready humour, had taken command of the *Grayling* to replace Quarrie who had died on his bridge under the air attacks, and he too seemed to bring the realisation of despair and danger even closer by his presence. He was a good captain, but *Grayling* was only a substitute for his own ship, his *Squalus*. His humour too seemed to have gone with her.

But at last they were given a small reprieve, and for most of them it was not a moment too soon. With ammunition down to a last few rounds, and fuel tanks below minimum requirements for safety, the little ships had sailed back to Singapore. The northern side of the island was deserted of ships, but for wrecks and tiny patrol boats, and rather than run the gauntlet of more air raids over the dockyard the gunboats had been ordered to the southern side, to Keppel Harbour and the approaches, which were anything but abandoned. Busy freighters and supply ships queued to unload their munitions and supplies, and from graceful troopers there came a steady stream of khaki reinforcements for the fighting up north.

But once ashore Trewin had sensed the immediate end to reality. In spite of the casual attempt at a black-out the city was quite obviously in the throes of festivity and wild celebration. Restaurants and clubs were jammed to capacity, and even during the occasional air-raid alerts the queues waited with persistent optimism outside every cinema and theatre. It was as if the people were refusing to accept danger. Were drowning it with noise and high living. Shutting off the embattled peninsula like a tap.

Yet the fighting drew remorselessly nearer, none the less. In the three weeks and two days since the first landings, the Japs had fought their way some two hundred miles down either coast. Over half of Malaya was in their hands, and never a day passed without some vague rumour of defending troops being cut off and decimated. All the impossible things were happening. The Japs were using tanks in plenty to smash down troops who had been assured that such weapons would find no way through the jungles of Malaya. Their aircraft controlled the skies, their ground forces moved with a speed and a mobility which was more than a match for mere bravery.

Trewin stared moodily from the taxi window to watch a small trudging group of Australian soldiers making their way towards the city. That was another thing. Perhaps the worst of all. When the time came, as come it must for Singapore, every soldier would be worth his weight in gold and more. Yet Trewin had been stunned, and then outraged to see that such soldiers were being treated with something like contempt by many of Singapore's citizens. There appeared to be a rigid system of segregation. Officers were accepted in the homes of leading businessmen and the like, N.C.O.s and other ranks had to manage as best they could. On this very night, as Trewin had pushed his way through the jostling crowds he had seen some wounded British soldiers being given a firm dressing-down by a man in a dinner-jacket outside one of the hotels. 'This is out of bounds to you!' He had stared at each soldier in turn. 'God, there are *plenty* of places for your sort!' Trewin had turned away, sickened, as the three soldiers had turned obediently back into the crowd. The man in the dinner-jacket had called after Trewin, 'Must keep up standards!' Trewin had not trusted himself to reply.

The taxi slewed to a stop and the Indian said with a yawn, 'Here t'is.'

Trewin paid him and stood staring at the neat white house with its low wall and overhanging trees. This was the next phase in unreality, he thought.

Ever since the *Porcupine* had picked up her moorings Corbett had been restless and on edge. Trewin knew that the captain had been hoping to return to Singapore in time for Christmas. As that had been impossible it now seemed a New Year's party was to be the next best thing.

Trewin had toyed with the idea of getting out of attending the party by standing in as O.O.D. Corbett had apparently foreseen this. '*Beaver* will be alongside while we're here. I've arranged for her O.O.D. to cover both ships, Trewin.' He had rubbed his hand with a rare show of excitement. 'I want *all* my officers to be there when the gin pennant is hoisted, eh?'

Pushing his gloomy thoughts aside, Trewin stepped through a porch and handed his cap to a Malay houseboy. He was shown into a wide, low-ceilinged room which was filled from wall to wall with people. Music was being provided by a large radiogram, but it was all lost in the din of conversation and laughter. They were mostly naval officers and their ladies, the latter making bright splashes of colour against the white drill tunics and the occasional khaki of the military.

A glass was thrust into his hand, and when he sipped it gratefully he decided it was almost neat gin. He would have to be careful.

He recognised a few of the faces around him. Some of the *Beaver*'s officers, dominated by Lieut.-Commander Keates, her captain. He was a giant of a man with a shaggy, prematurely grey beard. As he stood surrounded by an intent audience of women he looked for all the world like an Old English sheepdog, Trewin thought.

A houseboy took the glass from his hand and gave him a full one in exchange. Trewin loosened his collar and began to work his way through the press of figures towards the far corner. He would make his number with Corbett and then leave, he decided.

His heart sank as he caught sight of Fairfax-Loring's massive shape beside a well-laden table of drinks and caskets of fresh ice. He tried to ease back into the crowd but the admiral boomed, 'Ah, your number one, Corbett! Better late than never, what?' He looked flushed, and his fierce grin was fixed and unwavering.

Corbett stepped forward and looked at Trewin's glass. 'Glad you got here.' He shot the admiral a quick glance. 'Keep it to yourself, Trewin, but Kuantan has just fallen to the enemy.'

The admiral stared at him. 'It's no secret now, Corbett.' He smiled knowingly. 'This time I think we've done the right thing. We've got a firm line from east to west, and Kuantan or no Kuantan, our lads'll hold 'em on the Pahang River.' He jabbed Corbett with his finger. 'So don't be so bloody pessimistic! This is what we should have done from the start!' He looked at Trewin, 'Don't you agree?'

Trewin pictured the admiral's casual information as it would appear on a chart. He recalled the first visit to the Talang Inlet with the troops invisible but reassuringly close by in the jungle. He remembered Mallory waving his arm towards the north and telling him about the line of defence along the river and the carefully planned chain of stores and fuel dumps. That was only three weeks ago, but it felt like a lifetime. He thought too of Kuantan itself, with its milling columns of refugees and the newly landed infantry singing as they marched away northward along that coast road. He shuddered inwardly. Now the Japs were there, less than twenty-five miles from the Talang Inlet.

He replied quietly, 'They should never have been allowed to reach so far south, sir.'

Fairfax-Loring signalled to a houseboy. 'Well, of course you can't be expected to see the wider plan of things, Trewin. I have been at a conference most of the day. Believe me, things are starting to hum around here!' He became suddenly grave. 'But we must all pull together as a team. No more going off at half-cock!' He stared into his glass. '*Shrike* and *Squalus* are gone now. It makes for harder effort all round!'

Trewin watched Corbett's impassive face and wondered if he was remembering the sinking gunboat and the signal from base about lack of air cover.

The gin was burning his stomach and he toyed with the idea of finding something to eat. But he kept thinking of the small line of gunboats and the nursery rhyme which seemed to fit so cruelly and so aptly: '... Then there were four!'

He saw Corbett turn his head as a slim, bright-eyed woman with pale, sun-bleached hair and bare, tanned shoulders entered the room from a curtained door and moved towards them. Unlike the photograph on Corbett's desk, she was smiling and she held her head and body as if she was used to being admired.

The admiral beamed. 'Hello, Mildred!' He gestured at Trewin. 'This is your husband's first lieutenant.'

Her handclasp was warm and surprisingly strong. She had a direct way of looking straight into a man's eyes which Trewin felt like an embrace. She said, 'I've heard all about you. It's very nice to meet a fresh man around here.' It sounded like an accusation.

Trewin replied, 'You seem to have a lot of friends, Mrs. Corbett.' He wished that she would release his hand and that Corbett would stop staring at him.

She shrugged, tossing the pale hair from one shoulder. 'You meet all sorts out here.'

A red-faced artillery major pushed through the crowd and asked plaintively, 'You promised me a dance, Mildred!' He stepped closer to focus his eyes properly. 'Mil-*dred*! You *promised*!'

She smiled at Trewin. It was a lazy smile, like a challenge, he thought. 'Very well, Benjy. As you've been a good boy.' She added calmly, 'See you later, Lieutenant.' She was still looking at Trewin as the major guided her tipsily towards the radiogram.

Corbett said tightly, 'I don't know where she gets the energy!'

The admiral grinned. 'Well, you *should* know!'

Trewin felt like an uneasy onlooker. It was not just the drink. Every word, each gesture seemed loaded with private meanings. It was hard to imagine Corbett living easily with a woman like that. He said, 'I suppose that most of the wives will be evacuated to England or Australia soon?'

The admiral stared at him in surprise. 'What an odd chap you are! There's no danger here. And as soon as we get more aircraft on the island it will be an even better fortress than before.' He shook his head. 'There'll be no running out this time, no more humiliating retreats!'

Hughes, his flag-lieutenant, appeared at his elbow as harassed as ever. 'The brigadier has arrived, sir. You wanted to meet him.'

The admiral placed the glass carefully on the table. 'Very well, Flags. I'll come and see him right away.' He shot them a sad smile. 'No rest for me, none at all.'

Trewin breathed out thankfully. To Corbett he said, 'He sounds confident enough.'

Corbett did not reply directly. He was still staring towards his wife. She was dancing with her arms wrapped around the soldier's neck while a circle of onlookers clapped in time with the music.

He said suddenly, 'Come with me.' He turned on his heel toward the curtained door without waiting for Trewin to reply.

Trewin shrugged and followed him. He caught sight of Tweedie's scarlet face beside the improvised bar, his eyes glazed, his chest heaving from drink and exertion as he tried to pour himself a further measure of gin under the anxious eye of a Malay steward. Mallory was sitting relaxed and unsmiling in a chair by the wall, smoking a cigarette, his eyes fixed on the clapping circle around the dancers. He looked very sober and alert and strangely watchful, as if he was waiting for something to happen.

Corbett opened a door and led the way into a small bedroom. A dark-haired Chinese *amah* sat motionless by the window, her hands resting in her lap, and the room was in darkness but for a small shaded lamp beside the bed.

Corbett said quietly, 'This is my boy, Trewin.' He stood aside watching Trewin's face, his pale eyes shining in the lamplight. He repeated, 'My boy, Martin.'

Trewin looked down at the child and wondered how many other sides he would see to Corbett tonight. Corbett's son was small and rather delicate-looking, his face relaxed in sleep. There was a photograph of his father beside the bed, and standing on a chest of drawers a small model of the *Porcupine*.

Corbett saw his glance and said, 'Petty Officer Dancy made it for him last year.' Then in something like his usual tone he asked crisply, 'Well, what do you think of him, eh?'

Trewin replied, 'A fine boy. You must be very proud of him.' He did not know how to react to this Corbett.

'Means everything to me, Trewin.' Corbett sounded distant. 'Him and the ship. Everything.' He patted the sheet into place and touched the ragged teddy bear on the pillow. 'A man needs an anchor. Must have one, you know!' He seemed to pull himself together with an effort. 'Well, must get back to my guests.' He closed the door quietly behind them. 'I've got his name down for Dartmouth, did I tell you?'

'Yes, sir.' Trewin felt uneasy. 'That'll be a few years yet.'

Corbett rubbed his hands. 'Ah well, we *must* plan. Can't just let life run all over you.' He added vaguely, 'After the war I suppose you'll settle down and be a journalist again, eh?' He smiled briefly. 'Write a great novel perhaps?' It seemed to amuse him. 'Well, God knows there's enough material in this island to fill a damn library!'

The big room was as noisy as before and the air was heavy with smoke and perfume. Tweedie was sitting on a chair, his head lolling in sleep, some paper streamers wrapped around his neck. There was no sign of Mallory.

A hand caught Trewin's sleeve and he turned guardedly, half expecting it might be Corbett's wife. But it was Hammond. He looked very bright-eyed, and there was little trace of the fatigue and strain of the past few weeks. He said quickly, 'I've been looking all over the place for you, Number One.'

Then Trewin saw the girl whose hand he was holding. She was tall and statuesque, and several years older than Hammond, he thought. She was a very striking girl, handsome rather than pretty, and her dark colouring and wide slanting eyes betrayed the mixture of blood and race which made her stand out from the women around her.

Hammond said, 'This is Jacqui, Number One.' He looked from one to the other, both pleased and nervous. 'Jacqui Laniel'

They shook hands and the girl said quietly. 'It is very noisy, yes?'

Hammond said, 'Jacqui is an interpreter at Government House. We met when I was doing my course.' He grinned awkwardly. 'We've become very good friends!' He looked at the girl and they shared the same smile.

At that moment someone started to ring a bell, and everyone crowded together singing and cheering. Hammond seized the girl's shoulders and kissed her, forgetting Trewin and everyone else in the room.

'Happy New Year, darling!'

Trewin turned away, suddenly feeling very alone. All around him people were embracing each other, laughing and shouting, or staring at familiar faces as if for the first time.

Corbett's voice cut through the din, and he turned to see him standing beside the table. He was holding a glass in one hand and offering him another. Corbett said, 'Happy New Year, Trewin.' He was watching him strangely.

It was then that Trewin realised something else about Corbett. He was drinking. It was almost a shock to realise that he had never seen him take a drink before.

There were beads of sweat on his brow, and in the bright lights his hair looked very grey. He said, 'Didn't want you as my first lieutenant, y'know! Thought it was a damned dirty trick when they posted you to me. Never had much time for amateurs. All right in the Army, of course, but the Service is different. Quite different!'

Trewin did not know whether to show resentment or amusement. He replied evenly, 'We do our best, sir.'

Corbett did not seem to hear. 'No, I'm very pleased with you.' He nodded. 'Very pleased, Trewin!' He lifted his glass and said suddenly, 'And I hope you have better luck all round.' He looked across at Hammond and all the others. He might have been looking for his wife. 'But you've got the ship, Trewin. It's not every man who can say that!'

Trewin felt the drink burning away his reason. The overwhelming press of noise and heat seemed to force the words from his mouth. 'I meant to ask you, sir. What is it between you and the admiral?'

For an instant he thought he had gone too far. But he no longer cared. In the middle of all this frenzy and excitement, seeing Hammond's obvious happiness and Corbett's faith in his son, he could no longer care about anything.

Corbett eyed him emptily. 'He was my first lieutenant, too, Trewin. Away back when I commanded the destroyer *Ariel*. We were on manoeuvres in the Med and I rammed the Captain (D)'s ship. It was actually his fault, and everyone knew it at the time.' He shrugged wearily. 'But in the cold light of a court of inquiry things appeared differently.'

Trewin frowned. He must have missed something. He tried again, raising his voice above the noise. 'But I still don't see . . .'

Corbett said sharply, 'Fairfax-Loring gave evidence against me, Trewin. That tipped the scales and I took the blame!'

Trewin felt the anger rising like a tide. 'That was a bloody terrible thing to do!'

'You think so?' Corbett's tone was calm. 'Well, I went on the beach after that. And Fairfax-Loring is a rear-admiral.' He stared at his empty glass with distaste. 'So it wasn't too terrible for *him*, was it?' He placed the glass on the table and then said, 'I do not wish to discuss it further.'

Trewin saw him stagger slightly and was strangely moved.

Corbett walked towards the door adding curtly, 'And don't put it in that damned book when you write it either!'

Trewin watched the curtains sway back across the door and then heard the admiral's booming laugh from across the room. With sudden determination he walked to the entrance and picked up his cap from the great pile beside the low porch. Outside it was very dark and cool without a trace of wind. Yet Trewin could smell the salt from the sea, and imagined the gunboat sleeping at her moorings, like the little model beside the boy's bed. Well, it was a new year, he thought vaguely.

And one thing was sure. It could not be worse than the last one.

Swinging his cap in one hand, Trewin started to walk back towards the town, and the sea.

*   *   *

Apart from three days in harbour the New Year brought little change or respite to the *Porcupine*. The coastal patrols continued, but whereas the proximity of danger left no time for relaxation, there were no direct attacks on the ship, and the news from the inland war remained vague and uncertain, so that officers and men came to accept their isolated role with patient forbearance. Then after a week at sea, broken only by a hasty dash to replenish the fuel tanks, *Porcupine* was ordered to take on a full cargo of ammunition and deliver it to the Army via the Talang Inlet.

At Mersing they had laid in the sandy shallows beneath a blazing sun, immobile and vulnerable to any hostile aircraft, while long lines of sweating soldiers had trundled crates of grenades and ammunition down the beach where they stood in great, inviting piles of destruction, while the hard-worked sailors heaved them aboard and stowed them on and around every available piece of deck space.

Now in pitch darkness, rolling uneasily in a choppy off-shore swell, the *Porcupine* pushed her way northwards once more, her bows throwing back arrows of spray as she maintained an unwilling ten knots. It was just past midnight, and some fast-moving clouds obscured the stars and left the sea's face like black glass, unbroken but for the ship's slow passage.

Trewin worked his teeth around the stem of his unlit pipe and tried to focus his glasses on the distant shoreline. Only an occasional garland of surf betrayed the line of crumbled cliffs, and in his mind's eye he tried to remember that first visit to Talang. Then there had been no actual war. Just uncertainty and apprehension. He recalled the half-hidden entrance to the Inlet and the hump-sided hill which guarded the northern side of it. Now in the darkness there was very little to go on, and the gunboat's top-heavy pitch and roll was made more obvious by the great weight of ammunition, and even Unwin, the coxswain, was having difficulty keeping her on course.

Within hours of backing away from the beach at Mersing they had received a signal. It had been brief but definite. 'Do not, repeat not, approach Talang Inlet during daylight. Approaches are under fire from artillery.'

Corbett had listened to the signal in silence. Then he had jumped from his chair and paced the bridge in quick, angry strides, as if to work off his irritation. 'Damn them! Why the hell can't they knock out a few guns?' He had glared at Trewin. 'We're holding them on the Pahang River, so that means these guns must be firing about ten miles or so.' As Trewin had kept silent he had snapped, 'So they must be big enough to *see*, eh?'

Trewin glanced sideways at Corbett's hunched figure on the forepart of the bridge. His body was swaying in the chair in time with the unsteady motion, but he could have been asleep.

It was hard, no impossible, to picture Corbett as he had been for just a few moments at the New Year's party. Once back aboard he had resumed his old isolated position of command. He showed no sign of having remembered any display of confidence with Trewin, nor did he ever mention his family.

Mallory stepped across the gratings and said quietly, 'We alter course in ten minutes. Course to steer is two eight zero.' He rubbed his eyes. 'God, it's as black as a boot!'

Trewin turned quickly, just in time to see a far-off flare drifting down across the mainland. For a brief instant he saw a ridge of hilltop and heard the vague crump, crump of gunfire. Just a murmur. A mere hint of what lay beneath. Probably even now men were stalking each other through the dense jungle. Straining their ears, deafened by their own frantic heartbeats, fingers on triggers or groping for grenades.

Corbett's voice broke the train of thought. 'This will have to be a slow approach, Trewin. Remember the sandbars. If we run aground it will be daylight before the tide lifts us off. By then it might be too late.'

Trewin nodded. The *Porcupine* was already a floating bomb. Beached on a mudbank, it would not be a difficult target to find.

The seconds ticked by. Then Mallory said flatly, 'Ready, sir!'

Corbett snapped, 'Port fifteen!' He waited, his hands outspread across the screen as if to feel the ship's sluggish response. 'Midships. Steady.' He half turned, his face pale against the backcloth of land. 'Well, Pilot?'

Mallory repeated. 'Course two eight zero, sir!'

Trewin passed the course to the wheelhouse, and as he straightened his back he heard Corbett say sharply, 'Well, tell *me* in future, Pilot! I'm not a damn mind-reader!'

Trewin said quietly, 'That was my fault, sir. He did tell me the change of course when . . .'

Corbett interrupted angrily, 'Oh, for *God*'s sake!' He swung back to peer at the darkening line of land. 'You can save your defences of the navigating officer's slackness for later!'

It was unfair, and Trewin was tempted to say so. He looked at Mallory's outline across the chart table and saw him shrug.

It was very odd. Corbett was acting as if he had never made this approach before. As if he was troubled by the mass of explosives around him. Yet how could this be? Trewin tried to see his face in the gloom, but could only make out the outline of his chin and the insistent tapping fingers of one hand on the screen.

While they had loaded the ammunition, each man expecting an air attack in every dragging minute, Corbett had stayed on the bridge, apparently indifferent, and more concerned it seemed with the damage done to decks and paintwork by clumsily handled crates.

Corbett rapped, 'Slow ahead together!'

The engines sighed and the motion increased as the ship wallowed heavily in her own bow-wave.

Trewin heard the scrape of steel from aft and pictured the gunners crouching by their breeches, ears and nerves strained to breaking point as they waited for a sudden attack. Not that it was likely, Trewin thought. The Japs were apparently prepared to depend on daylight, and with good reason. Air superiority was the main weapon for attacks on surface craft.

Corbett snapped his fingers. 'Depth?'

'Four fathoms, sir.' The seaman's voice was hushed.

Corbett nodded. 'Port ten. Midships.' He was moving his head from side to side, like a terrier sniffing out its adversary.

Mallory said suddenly, 'We'll run too close to the sandbars, sir! I suggest you stay on this course until . . .'

'When I require your opinion I'll ask for it!' Corbett slid from his chair and stooped over the compass repeater. He held his face so close that Trewin could see the luminous dial reflected in his eyes. He said, 'Steer two seven eight!'

Mallory sucked in his lip. 'Christ!' he said under his breath.

Trewin thrust his head under the oilskin hood and peered at the chart. It was a very bad entrance. In some places the sandbars were above water at high tide.

A voice said, 'Three fathoms, sir!'

Trewin studied the neat pencilled lines and the countless alterations which Mallory had entered on the chart. There had once been light buoys and a beacon on the headland. Now there was nothing.

He stood up and walked to the front of the bridge.

Corbett shot him a glance. 'Won't be long now.'

A darker blotch of land moved leisurely across the starboard beam. It was the crouching hill. Trewin breathed out slowly. He could feel the deck jerking steeply in response to the fierce current from the Inlet and heard the wheel creaking below his feet as Unwin fought his personal battle with sea and rudder. He tried not to stare at the hardening line of land across the bows. It made his head ache, like that of a blind man walking towards a solid barrier in his path. Seeing nothing, yet knowing that it was there.

'Two fathoms, sir!'

Corbett swung round. 'What? Repeat that!'

The seaman replied uneasily, '*Two* fathoms, sir!'

'It can't be!' Corbett looked back at Mallory. 'What the hell is he talking about?'

Trewin stepped up beside him. 'The sandbars may have shifted, sir. All that rain, and the tide-race through the Inlet.'

He broke off as a look-out yelled, 'Breakers ahead! Fine on the port bow!'

Corbett sprang across the gratings. 'Starboard fifteen!' He locked his fingers round the voice-pipe. 'Increase to twenty!' He was shouting.

Trewin saw a flurry of white spray, suddenly very close and stark against the darkness.

'Midships! Steady!'

Mallory said tightly, 'Too fine, we'll never make it for Chrissake!'

The *Porcupine* swung awkwardly across the current, her bows chopping noisily on the swell.

Corbett called, 'Steer two eight five!'

Trewin heard Unwin repeat the order and lifted his glasses to search for the other side of the Inlet. Then, just as the lenses settled on the hill's blunt outline, the gunboat struck the sandbar. It was nothing more than a slight quiver at first, but as Trewin clutched at the screen and the deck tilted beneath his feet he heard Corbett shout, 'Full astern together!'

The telegraphs jangled, and from aft came a sudden surge of wash as both screws screamed urgently in response. The bows lifted, trembled, and then struck hard down, so that the ship shook from bridge to keel as if in a giant vice. As the vibration increased Trewin felt the deck canting heavily to starboard and heard sudden cries of warning and alarm from every side.

Corbett said, 'Stop engines!' He ran across the bridge, his glasses banging unheeded against the screen as he peered down at the swirling water alongside.

There was a sudden silence, broken only by the steady sluice of the current against the hull and the occasional groan of steel.

Corbett sounded as if he was short of breath, but his voice was controlled as he ordered, 'Slow astern together!'

The painful jerking started again, then as the engines stopped the silence was shattered by the buzz of a telephone. Trewin heard Corbett say, 'if you think that, Chief, I'll abide by your advice.' He replaced the handset and said, 'Nimmo reports that the screws are drawing up silt into their tunnels. We shall shake the shafts out of the ship if we try again.' He took off his cap and ran his fingers through his hair. It was an unusual gesture for Corbett, and Trewin sensed his sudden anguish. 'We will have to wait for that tide, after all, it seems.'

Mallory's voice was without expression. 'That is at 0530, sir.'

Trewin looked away. It would be daylight by then. Daylight and the *Porcupine* would be squatting like a lame duck for all to see.

'We could signal for a tow, sir?' Trewin was surprised how calm he sounded.

Corbett shook his head. '*Beaver* is the nearest ship with shallow draught and the power to pull us off. She couldn't be here much before first light, if then.'

Trewin watched him in silence. There was no point in questioning Corbett's reasons for taking the southern side of the Inlet. It was known to be a difficult entrance by any method, especially by night. But his refusal to accept Mallory's suggested course was strange. He had a sudden picture of Corbett beside his son's bed, and in his mind he seemed to hear his words: '. . . means everything to me. Him and the ship.'

He heard himself say, 'I expect we'll slide off all right, sir. We might even try and kedge her into deep water.'

Corbett sounded distant, as if his mind was elsewhere. 'We must get the ammunition to the Army, Trewin. They were the orders. The hazards of the trade don't come into it.'

Trewin thought of the far-off Japanese guns. Even they might be preferable to what the admiral would do when he found out what Corbett had done.

115

The *Porcupine* settled more firmly in her new berth, her stem still pointing towards the shore. Like the men who controlled her, she had nothing more to do but wait.

*　　*　　*

The *Porcupine*'s small dinghy slewed violently in a sudden eddy and then wobbled back on course as Trewin, who was squatting uncomfortably on the transom, pushed the tiller hard over to the full extent of his arm. The two Chinese seamen at the oars were pulling with all their strength, and Trewin heard their combined breaths bursting with sharp gasps with each savage effort. In the bows, a boathook poised like a whaler's harpoon, Ordinary Signalman Phelps peered ahead ready to thrust away any threatening sandbank or some of the many waterlogged branches swept down from the Talang River.

He said sharply, 'Pull harder! Not much further.' He could sympathise with the oarsmen, but any failure of effort now and the little boat would be carried past the crouching hill on the far side of the Inlet to the open sea beyond.

Still, it was better than just standing about and waiting, he thought. Corbett's restlessness was almost more unnerving than his normal attitude of impassive calm. Quite suddenly he had said, 'I think you'd better go ashore. Before the dawn comes up.' He had stared at Trewin's face through the gloom. 'There is an army signals post on the headland. Get through to Talang and rouse the army commander if you can.' He had sounded tired. 'Tell him what has happened and why we didn't get up there on time. He may think we didn't start out at all.'

Trewin had asked, 'Is that all, sir?'

'If he has some river craft at his disposal he can get them sent down to meet us. If the worst comes to the worst the troops may be able to unload some of the ammunition in midstream.' He had added bitterly, 'If there's any time for it!'

Trewin stared up at the sky. The clouds had all but gone and the stars seemed much paler and more indistinct. Dawn was very close, and when it came it would be immediate, as it always was here.

Phelps called, 'Here we are, sir!' He lashed out at a small rock, and with a final thrust of the oars the dinghy grated on to a tiny sliver of beach below the headland.

Hammond, who had been sitting in silence at Trewin's side, stood up and jumped over the gunwale. He said, 'Better pull the boat into those bushes, Number One. This might take a little time!'

Trewin waded ashore, straining his eyes to separate the various dark clumps of hillside and tangled brush. When he looked back across the swirling water he was shocked to see that he could already determine the gunboat's outline, even the darker line of weed and slime along her exposed bilge. He glanced at Hammond, 'As soon as we've contacted the Army you had better make your way up the Inlet. They'll need someone who understands the problem of unloading.'

Hammond said quickly, 'I'd rather go back with you!'

Trewin smiled. 'What about the girl in Singapore? She wouldn't thank me for letting you get killed.'

Hammond replied, 'I hope you don't think I'd stay ashore because of my personal feelings?' He sounded strained. 'If I thought that . . .'

He broke off as Trewin said, 'Forget it, Sub, I was just pulling your leg. But all the same, you *are* going to stay ashore. That is an order!'

He turned as Phelps said cheerfully, 'Dinghy's safe an' snug, sir!'

Hammond stared at the small boat and said quietly, 'To think that I was sailing her in the regatta only a month ago. It feels like a lifetime!'

Trewin peered up at the hillside. 'We always seem to be searching for the Army!' He tightened his webbing belt and added, 'Well, let's get on with it.' He started up the slope knowing that the others would follow. He could almost feel Hammond's mind working. But whatever he suggested, Trewin had already decided to hold to his original order. If the enemy opened fire in sufficient force the *Porcupine* would be hard put to reach the high-sided safety of the Talang River. And just a near miss would be enough to blast her to fragments. Hammond would be well out of it. And it was right that someone should be spared to talk about the futility of it all.

He controlled his fresh wave of bitterness with a physical effort and increased his stride as if to drive the thoughts from his mind. You could not expect to live for ever. Today was as good a time as any other, he thought savagely.

The higher they climbed the lighter it seemed to become. Already they could see the hazy outline of the horizon and the individual eddies and swirling currents which marked the hazardous approaches between the littered sandbanks outside the Inlet.

Then Trewin saw the hut. It was very small and camouflaged from the air by netting and freshly cut branches. Faintly on the fresh dawn air he could hear the beat of dance music, and his mind rebelled at this impossible situation which could only be found in war. The soldiers were no doubt drowsing over their radio, while just a few hundred yards away the gunboat lay helpless, awaiting death from an invisible enemy.

He quickened his pace again. Over his shoulder he said, 'Go and wake those bastards, Phelps!' As the signalman ran across the flattened ground he added to Hammond, 'Were you surprised when the captain decided to make his approach the way he did?'

Hammond shrugged. 'We always used to take that channel, Number One. When I first joined the ship I've seen him con her right into the Inlet within yards of the south bank.' He sounded troubled. 'But I can't understand why he did it this time, *and* in the darkness.'

Trewin nodded. 'Thank you, Sub. I have a feeling there will be questions asked about it.' He thought of the stranded gunboat and thought, What the hell does it matter now?

He saw Phelps' pale shape outlined against the hut. He seemed to be bending over as if studying the ground. Then Trewin heard the young signalman retching uncontrollably.

Suddenly all the dangers and frustrations seemed to give way to an icy calm. Trewin pushed Hammond aside and called

'Stand still, Phelps!' To Hammond he snapped, 'Stay here!'

Ignoring him and the two Chinese seamen he strode across the small clearing and seized the signalman's arm. As he stood by the half-open door the dance music seemed deafening and obscene. 'Easy, boy!' He shook his arm. 'Easy now!' He reached out and very slowly pushed the door back on its hinges.

There was a single lantern flickering from the top of a steel locker, but the light was sufficient. It was more than sufficient.

Two soldiers lay spreadeagled on the dirt floor amidst the remains of the radio transmitter. Trewin felt the bile rising in his throat as he stepped inside the hut, his mind and being rebelling against the horror around him. Each soldier had been impaled on the floor with his own bayonet. One of them, a corporal, had his fingers wrapped round the bloodied hilt, his mouth and eyes wide with agony and terror. He must have died trying to tear the bayonet from his own stomach while his murderers stood and watched him.

They had taken their time with the other soldier. He had been hacked in so many places that it was hard to recognise the corpse of a man. The hut's walls were splashed with blood, and in the flickering lamplight it looked like the mural of some bestial maniac.

He heard a cry of horror and turned to see Hammond's face by the open door. Trewin said harshly, 'Get outside! There's nothing you can do here!'

Hammond gasped, 'My God! How could they do that?' His body began to shake uncontrollably. 'To see them lying there!' He clapped his hands over his ears. 'And that damned, bloody music all the time!'

Trewin saw the two Chinese staring at him, their eyes like black stones. Phelps was squatting on his knees, his face in his hands as if in prayer.

Trewin shook Hammond's arm. 'Get a grip, Sub! For God's sake, control yourself!' He shook him harder. 'Whoever did that cannot be far away!' He let the words sink in. 'So we've got to see that it doesn't happen to *us*!'

Phelps looked up, his eyes wet in the growing light. 'Shall I turn that radio off?'

Trewin looked down at him. 'Leave it, Bunts. Those murdering bastards will feel safer if they can hear the music.' He swallowed twice to control the nausea which threatened to engulf him with every word. Then he gripped Hammond's arm again. 'Get their rifles, Sub. They're by the table.' He thought he saw rising panic in Hammond's eyes and added coldly, 'Force yourself! If you give way now you're no use for the future!' He shook his unprotesting arm and added, 'You can take my word for it!'

He walked across the clearing, unable to watch the young officer dragging himself back through the door. He shut his ears to Hammond's vomiting and to Phelps' quiet sobbing. He had to think. *Had to think!*

It was four miles upriver to the settlement. They could never get there in time to rouse the Army and collect boats to unload the *Porcupine*'s lethal cargo.

He rubbed his palms across his face. The skin felt like ice.

The dead soldiers had been tortured and killed quite recently. The blood was still wet. Probably a small raiding party behind the lines, or a dedicated group of guerillas with some particular object in view.

Hammond walked from the hut and laid the rifles on the ground. There was blood on his hands and shirt. He said in a flat voice, 'Anything else?'

Trewin stared at him fixedly. He wanted to explain, to sympathise, but the words held back. 'We'll get some real daylight in a moment, Sub. Then we can signal the ship from up here, right?' He raised his voice, 'Do you read me?'

Hammond nodded dully.

'Good. Now post the men around the clearing. We don't want to get jumped ourselves.'

He pulled the revolver from his holster and turned it over in his hands. The touch of the warm metal was not reassuring. It just seemed to bring the nightmare a little closer.

7
Face to Face

The first indication of the dawn showed itself in a soft purple glow which threw the hillside into deep shadows while the sea below the headland seemed to come alive in the growing light. Across the centre of the Inlet, moving like swamp gas above the swift current, a low haze drifted seaward, momentarily blotting out the shape of the *Porcupine*'s hull but leaving her funnel and masts disembodied against the far shore.

Trewin lifted himself to his feet and peered at his watch. He had intended to tell Phelps to use his semaphore flags to call up the gunboat, but the haze made that temporarily impossible. Above and around him he could hear the growing twitter of birds and the drowsy murmur of countless insects. Otherwise it was very still, and he felt his eyes drawn back to the hut as its shape re-formed in the hardening light. The radio had mercifully fallen silent, and he tried not to think of the two mutilated corpses behind the closed door.

He looked across the small clearing where Hammond sat unmoving on an upended crate, his revolver cradled on his lap. He was hollow-eyed and pale, and the least sound from the dense scrub made him jerk as if he had been touched. Phelps was further down the slope facing the sea, his bright ginger hair making a patch of colour above the swirling water at the foot of the hill. On either side of the hut the Chinese seamen lay with their rifles pointing towards the trees, their faces grim but intent, their dark eyes showing nothing of their thoughts.

Phelps called quietly, 'The *Porcupine*'s shiftin', sir!' As Trewin tugged his glasses from their case he added glumly, 'She's settled again!'

Trewin peered at the distant ship and tried to see some

change in the angle of the masts. It would be soon now. He could see a steady wisp of smoke from the funnel, the mast-head pendant whipping occasionally in some freak breeze. He thought of Corbett pacing his bridge and watching the river entrance. He would be expecting some sign of Trewin's mission. Maybe even some boats from the settlement to lift off part of his cargo.

Phelps suddenly jumped to his feet, his hands around his ears. 'Sir! There's a ship comin'!' He turned slightly to the right, his body craned forward as if willing the sounds to reach him.

Then Trewin heard it too. A steady swish, swish, swish, echoed and distorted by the tall sides of the Inlet.

Hammond clambered over the bushes and stood at his side. He listened for several seconds and then said in a strained voice, 'I know that noise. It's the old *Nonouti*.' He shaded his eyes and added, 'She's a clapped-out paddle steamer which does the coasting run from Talang to Singapore about once a week.' He screwed up his eyes as if to clear his thoughts. 'She shouldn't be here now!'

At that moment the ship in question appeared around the sharp bend below the headland. She was a very old ship indeed. On either beam she was powered by a huge paddle wheel and her low hull was bare of superstructure but for a tiny, box-like bridge and a long, spindley funnel from which poured an unbroken trail of black smoke.

Trewin watched her churning past, shocked by the packed humanity which filled the deck from rail to rail. There must have been hundreds of them. Men, women and children jammed together shoulder to shoulder in a tight, unmoving mass. He could see crates of chickens, even livestock lashed around the bridge, and the ship was so obviously overloaded that it was only her wide beam which prevented her from capsizing in the offshore current.

Hammond said dully, 'She's the deepest draught vessel which can get into the Inlet.' He lifted his revolver and pointed towards the horizon. 'She has to use the main channel. It runs almost north-east for about two miles before she can make her turn.' He shuddered. 'It's also the worst channel. She'll have to pick her way like a blind man with all that weight aboard!'

As he spoke the *Nonouti* swung around a darker path of water on to her next course, and Trewin saw the packed masses of figures sway sideways in unison, like an uncontrolled crowd on a cup final terrace.

Through the haze across the Inlet Trewin saw the intermittent blink of light and guessed that Corbett was trying to warn the other ship of the possible danger. Either her captain did not see the signal, or he had got beyond the stage of reason and order, but the paddle steamer maintained her zigzagging course with no reduction of speed.

He recalled the crowd of refugees at the settlement. The air of hopelessness and despair. They must have looked upon the *Nonouti* as a last chance to escape from the war. He could see the ship's port side swaying to within inches of the frothing water, and imagined even more wretched refugees crammed below her decks in total darkness.

Trewin heard Hammond gasp, and as he swung his glasses he saw a tall water spout rise like a spectre, far out, but in line with the *Nonouti*'s present course. Almost simultaneously he heard a sharp, abbreviated whistle, but nothing more. The gun, whatever it was, was firing at very high trajectory. The shell had fallen almost straight down, like a bomb.

He watched coldly as a second shell fell within a minute of the first. It must have struck a sandbank just below the surface, for it exploded in a bright flash, throwing up a great wall of water and mud which seemed to take an age to fall back to the sea. When it did, the explosion left a wide yellow stain and a growing circle of dead fish.

Hammond said hoarsely, 'That was closer, and still in line!'

Trewin turned towards him, their eyes locking with sudden understanding. He said quietly, 'That means they must have a spotter! No battery could track a ship otherwise!'

Together they looked up past the hut towards the deep green of the hillcrest.

Behind them another shell exploded with a dull roar, and they heard the distant scrape of steel splinters against the *Nonouti*'s hull.

Hammond swallowed hard and said bitterly, 'At least our ship will stand a better chance now. She can slip into the Inlet while those poor devils are being massacred!'

Trewin did not reply. He was thinking of the two murdered soldiers. Not as people any more, but as parts of a puzzle. The Inlet had been under fire for some time, yet the enemy had not bothered to interfere with this solitary signal post before. He glanced at Hammond meaningly. 'These shells, Sub? What do you make of them?'

Hammond lifted his glasses and watched as another tall water-spout rose about fifty yards from the *Nonouti*'s starboard quarter. 'Not all that big.' He looked at Trewin. 'Five-inch maybe. The Japs do have a five-point-nine field piece, I believe.'

Trewin nodded. 'Exactly. Well, it isn't firing ten bloody miles, is it?' He waved his arm towards the hill. 'They must have infiltrated a battery behind the lines for some special purpose. And near enough for their spotters to keep contact.' He winced as another shell exploded in shallow water, and he tried not to think of those packed refugees.

Then without a word he walked into the darkened hut, and pausing only long enough to throw a ground sheet over the body by the door he began to pull the litter of wreckage from the radio set. He shut his ears to the distant shell-bursts and the sounds of buzzing flies from the other corpse. It was all beginning to fit. Some of the batteries were missing. The Japs must have come in the night to take some replacements from this hut.

As he walked out into the clearing he heard Phelps call, 'The *Porcupine*'s floating off, sir!' His voice was trembling with relief. To him the ship meant order and safety, and her survival represented something more precious even than the lives of the refugees.

Hammond said slowly, 'The *Nonouti*'s getting to the narrowest bit of the channel. It's like a funnel there. If the Japs can hit her there she'll block it completely. Then only the gun-boats'll be able to get upstream!'

But Trewin ignored him. He was staring at the *Porcupine*'s masts above the surface haze. He had seen them go astern. The ship was off the sandbar at last. Then, just as he had been about to take the others back to the dinghy and return to the gunboat, he had noticed with something like shock that the masts were slowly turning into line. As he blinked to clear his vision he saw the *Porcupine*'s blunt bows nose from the mist, her fore-castle shining faintly in the first hint of sunlight.

Hammond said in a strangled tone, 'She's going about! Cor-bett's heading for the *Nonouti*!'

As one they turned their glasses back to the paddle steamer. The paddles were still churning bravely, and there was a drift-ing cloud of cordite smoke almost alongside. But there was no bow-wave under her battered stem, and the water around her was yellow with silt and mud.

'She's gone aground!' Hammond spoke between his teeth. 'She's stuck!'

Trewin turned back to the gunboat. He could see tiny white figures on her quarterdeck, the gleam of sunlight shining briefly on the big towing swivel.

No more shells fell, and Trewin could imagine the sudden consternation caused by the *Porcupine*'s appearance. The in-visible spotters would just have to wait until the gunboat was harnessed to the other ship and then . . . Half to himself he mut-tered, 'You poor, brave bloody fool!' Then in a calmer voice he said, 'Take Phelps down to the foreshore, Sub. Tell him to call up the ship on the double!'

He saw the uncertainty in Hammond's eyes and added sharply, 'There is a Very pistol in the hut. If I can mark the spotters' position with a few flares, maybe Tweedie's howitzer can hit the bloody thing!'

He turned to go but Hammond clutched at his arm. 'You'll get killed! It's impossible!'

'We don't know till we try, do we?' Somehow he forced a

125

grin. 'You get that signal off, Sub! The ship'll find her way through the channel before you can say whistle!' He turned and ran into the hut, hating the smell of the place, hating himself for pretending to Hammond that there was room for hope.

He wedged the fat cartridge into his shirt and rammed one into the pistol. As he left the hut he felt a fresh pang of alarm. The others had already gone and he was momentarily tempted to follow them. Then with a quick glance at the ship he started to push his way through the clinging brush towards the top of the hill.

The sun was hardly clear of the sea yet already his chest and legs were streaming with sweat and his breath was hot across his parched lips. At the foot of a rotting tree he found a shaded tunnel of black mud left from some recent downpour. Gratefully he sank on his knees and dipped his handkerchief in it. The sodden rag felt cool across his face, and as an afterthought he tore off his shirt and kneaded it in the mud before dragging it back across his shoulders. It stank, but Trewin knew it would be harder to see than a white shirt. As he replaced the heavy cartridges against his skin he thought suddenly of the girl, Clare Massey. What was she doing at this moment? Would she ever hear what he had done, and if so, would she care?

He lurched to his feet and hurried on up the slope, ignoring the stinging thorns and the cruel whips of low branches across his shoulder. Not far now, he thought dazedly. They had to be near. To be in a safe place from which they could see seaward and back inland at the same time.

He tried not to think about the dead soldiers and how they had died. He looked at the revolver in his hand. They would not take him alive, he was quite sure of that.

A lance of weak sunlight glittered momentarily through the trees, and instinct made him drop to his stomach in one quick movement. Then, holding his breath, he began to drag himself forward through an unbroken carpet of gorse. It tore his hands and knees, but each second took him closer to the place where he had seen the light. The light made by the sun shining on glass.

Flies buzzed around his streaming face and other insects explored his thighs and chest, but he dared not move. Suddenly, muffled by the trees, he heard the dull bang of a shellburst. They had started again. Within minutes they would have the exact range and the *Porcupine* would be detonated like a giant bomb.

He thought of Corbett's sudden impulse and wanted to bury his face on his arms as he had that day in Talang Hospital. Shut it all out. Forget Corbett and his hopeless determination to prove himself and his ship.

He was shaking badly, and he knew that he was only waiting to hear one final explosion.

Then he looked up. They were so close that for an insane instant he imagined that they had seen him and were already closing in on his hiding place. As the mist cleared from his eyes he saw the whole position like a small picture. There was a camouflaged hide made of reed thatch in which they had laced loose branches to disguise it from any aerial survey. In front of it was a long telescope mounted on a brass tripod, and almost hidden beyond the thatch roof was a signal lamp pointing towards the next ridge of hills. And grouped around the telescope, intent and motionless, were the Japanese spotters.

They were dressed in filthy, camouflaged uniforms and tight-fitting jungle caps. One, who appeared to be in charge, wore glasses and was calmly smoking a cigarette. Across his knees was a long, curved sword, and Trewin had a sudden stark picture of this calm, composed officer slashing at the pinioned soldier in the hut.

The man at the telescope moved his sighting bar and spoke quickly from the corner of his mouth. Another soldier's head and shoulders appeared behind the hide, and Trewin saw him crouch behind the signal lamp. It was a very small light, but no doubt it was being watched by a powerful telescope from the distant hills. Trewin heard the brief whistle of a shell passing overhead and the distant roar of an explosion.

The officer stood up and snapped something to the man at

the telescope. The latter nodded violently and pressed his eye to the sight once more.

Trewin gently eased back the hammer of the pistol. It took two attempts as the metal was slippery with his sweat. It was useless to attempt to shoot any of the soldiers. There were probably more of them down the far side of the hill guarding the inland approaches until the spotters had done their work.

His eye fixed on the thatch roof, and with sudden calm he lifted the muzzle and aimed directly for it. The sharp thud of the pistol was lost instantly in a great roar of flames and diamond-bright sparks as the whole roof erupted with the exploding flare. The soldier by the telescope made as if to run away, but the officer screamed at him, his pointed features distorted with fury. Then as the flames and black smoke began to spread across the surrounding bushes he drew his sword and yelled an order to some more men who had come running through the trees behind him.

Resting his revolver on a fallen branch Trewin squeezed the trigger, and saw one of the men spin round like a top before pitching back down the slope. He fired again and again, but as he peered through the smoke he saw that the soldiers had vanished. But for the telescope and the blazing hut it was as if he had imagined them.

Then somewhere to his right a rifle cracked out and he felt some clipped leaves falling across his neck as the bullet whined overhead. Someone was calling orders, and he heard the crash of running feet around the back of the blazing pyre.

With his heart pounding against his ribs he started to wriggle back down the hill. A shadow moved against the smoke and he fired again, feeling the revolver buck in his fist like a wild thing. He could not remember how many he had fired, and with something like panic he rolled over and started to run down the slope, expecting to feel a bullet slam into his back at each step.

He saw the trees ahead of him shiver as if in a strong squall, and some last ounce of warning made him throw himself flat as the first shell arrived from the *Porcupine*'s howitzer. Like the gun, the shells were old and outdated, but the effect of the first one was staggering.

Timed to explode on impact, Trewin had heard Tweedie describe them lovingly as daisy-cutters, they sprayed out a lethal hail of shrapnel and splinters in every direction, and at ground level.

He dug his fingers into the ground as the air came alive with shrieking sounds and the crackle and splinter of torn trees. The pyre from the burning flare would make a perfect target, but it was no time to wait and watch. He had expected to die, but now that this incredible reprieve had been allowed him he could feel nothing but fear.

He ran forward, stopping yet again as another shell screamed down on the hillside and rent the air with splinters and sharpnel. Before he ran on Trewin peered back at the smoke and flames from the blazing hill-top. Surely nothing could live there now? That stone-faced officer would have died with the others. Trewin found himself praying that he had died slowly. Slow enough to realise what had done this to him.

Trewin ran faster, his vision swimming with effort as trees and bushes leapt to impede his path and tried to trip his desperate feet. Then he was in the small clearing with the sea opening up below him like blue silk. He could see the *Porcupine* turning towards the Inlet again, her wake creaming out astern in a wide crescent. And the old paddle steamer under way once more through the narrow channel and heading to the south, with her plume of black funnel-smoke streaming in a jubilant banner to mark her escape.

The sea was pockmarked with wide patches of discoloured water and the distant battery was still firing. But it was blind and without the guidance necessary for a kill.

Trewin turned dazedly and then stopped dead in his tracks. Facing him on the opposite side of the clearing was the Japanese officer. His uniform was torn and scorched, and there was a cut above his eyes, but his face was quite composed, and in his hands the naked sword was steady and unwavering as he stepped slowly on to the cleared ground with the sea at his back.

Trewin lifted the revolver and then saw the Japanese officer's face change its expression from concentration to something like pleasure as the hammer clicked on an empty chamber.

The sword moved slightly above the man's right shoulder as he moved easily across the clearing. He was holding it with both hands, and Trewin could see the early sunlight shining like blood on the razor edge of the blade. Trewin stood quite still. It was over. He could not turn his back, nor could he get to grips with the slowly advancing soldier.

There was a sudden sharp crack from beyond the bushes, and Trewin dodged sideways as the Japanese was hurled forward by the force of the heavy bullet which had struck him squarely in the spine. As if in a dream he saw the man writhe from side to side, his teeth bared like a savaged animal, his hands still clutching at the sword as his blood soaked into the dry ground around him. Then he rolled on to his back, kicked once, and lay still.

When Trewin lifted his head he saw Hammond framed against the sea, his revolver hanging on his hand shrouded in pale smoke.

Hammond did not lift his eyes from the dead soldier. 'Had to come back! Couldn't leave you to die without trying to help . . .'

His voice trailed away as Phelps burst across the clearing and after the smallest hesitation snatched the sword from the corpse and held it up to the sunlight.

Trewin rested his arm on Hammond's shoulder and stared at the dead man at his feet. His teeth were still bared, but his face seemed to have fallen away like a shrunken mask. He said thickly, 'So this is the enemy. Well, now we know.' He swayed and added tightly, 'Thanks, Colin. I shan't forget what you did!'

Hammond holstered his revolver and shivered. Then he laughed, the sound brittle on the warm air. 'You can say that after what you just did!'

Phelps called, 'The sword, sir? Can I have it?'

Trewin stared at him for several seconds. 'Sure you can, Bunts. You're more than welcome!'

He felt the creeping fingers of nausea exploring his limbs like fever. 'We'd better make our way upriver.'

Discordant but triumphant they heard the *Porcupine*'s siren as she pushed on up the river towards the settlement.

Hammond said at length, 'She sounds pleased with herself.'

Trewin looked quickly at his companion and nodded. 'So she should.' He felt the grin spreading over his face in spite of his nausea. 'The crazy bitch!'

*　　*　　*

The Massey residence was built on the rear of the hospital, and from outside resembled little more than a lean-to. It was as if it had been constructed only from material left over after the needs of the hospital had been satisfied. But once inside, the effect was entirely different.

Trewin lay back in a deep cane chair a tall glass of brandy and ginger ale at his elbow, his eyelids drooping in spite of his resolve to remain alert and attentive to what Dr. Massey was saying. Behind the lowered blinds and in the glare of several pressure lamps the long room looked comfortable and pleased with itself. One wall was lined with books, and there were several pieces of solid furniture which Massey had managed to bring from England. Trewin guessed that but for the strength and durability of such furniture it would never have withstood the hardship and strain of this strange outpost.

Massey sat with his legs crossed smoking one of his black cheroots and watching a moth attacking the glass of a pressure lamp. In spite of a long day's work he looked relaxed, and his large scrubbed hands rested on his lap, as if they too were enjoying a brief moment of respite.

Massey was saying, 'When I came out here first the people were dying like flies. One damn epidemic after another, with no doctor within fifty miles.' He grinned at some old memory.

'And fifty miles out here is the longest distance in the world.'

Trewin thought of the long trudge upriver from the headland, the endlesss jungle landscape and overlapping ridges of low hills. When he had finally reached the settlement the *Porcupine* had been tied to the pier with lines of soldiers busily unloading the crates of ammunition and carrying them inland along the dirt road.

Corbett had met him on the sidedeck and had said, 'That was a fine piece of work, Trewin!' He had stood back, studying his face as if looking for some clue to his actions. 'I shall see that it is brought to the proper notice in Singapore.' He had rubbed his hands and watched the sweating soldiers on the pier. 'Most satisfactory, eh?'

Even Tweedie had appeared to be more cheerful than usual. Trewin had said, 'Your howitzer did the job right enough, Guns. Bang on the target!'

Tweedie had tried to look unimpressed and pouted his lower lip as if contemplating some disagreement. Then he had replied gruffly, 'Always said it was a good weapon. Nobody listened, but I was right.'

Trewin found time to wonder if Tweedie had thought of him as he had personally supervised the firing of his little howitzer, and whether it had bothered him to realise that each shell might be the one to kill the gunboat's first lieutenant as well as the enemy. If he had considered it, he gave no sign.

Hammond had gone to his cabin, and when after a hasty shower and change of clothes Trewin had gone to see him, he found him lying on his bunk still dressed in the same torn shirt and slacks as before.

Hammond had said without looking up, 'Today I killed a man! I shot him down with no more thought than for squashing a beetle!' He had shuddered violently. 'I never thought it would be like that. Before it was always faceless and without real meaning. A gunsight, or a position on a range map.' He had examined his hands, turning them over as if searching for some sign of what he had done. 'But I shot that Jap. I *killed* him!'

Trewin had answered quietly, 'I'm damn glad you did, too. But I know what you are feeling. It always comes later. Sometimes it never leaves you.'

Hammond's head had dropped and the next instant he had fallen into a deep sleep. Shock and exhaustion had drained away his last resistance, and Trewin had stood for several minutes looking down at him. Then he had covered Hammond with a blanket and had left the cabin.

Given a chance, Hammond would get over it all right, he thought. He was young, and had someone to live for.

Massey said, 'And now I've got two more doctors to help me. Both Chinese, and excellent chaps.' He grinned. 'I was afraid the Army might foist some of their doctors on to me and turn this place into a military hospital.'

Trewin brought his tired mind back into focus. 'Would that be so bad? There *is* a war going on.'

Massey became serious. 'This hospital belongs to the local people. It was theirs by right, and will remain so after all this wretched fighting is over.'

'I see.' Trewin thought of the stench of death in the hut above the headland, the merciless whine of shells through the trees. 'It isn't always possible to stay out of a fight, Doctor.'

Massey lumbered to his feet and replenished Trewin's glass. He said calmly, 'I was in the last war, as a matter of fact. Not as a doctor either.' He straightened his back and stared at the moth by the lamp. It was dead and shrivelled, its beauty gone. 'I was in the infantry. Flanders.' He shrugged vaguely. 'That changed me. For the better, I hope. I couldn't find what I wanted in England, so I specialised in tropical medicine and came out here. This is my home now.' It sounded final.

'And your daughter?' Trewin watched him over the glass, but there was neither resentment nor caution on Massey's bearded face.

'Clare wanted to come. She's happy most of the time.'

Trewin waited, feeling the tiredness dragging at his senses like claws. He had not intended to come to the hospital at all. After going to the army command post and passing over the information about the concealed battery, he had returned to the ship with little in his aching mind but sleep. But Corbett had said almost jovially, 'We'll go and eat, Trewin. We have an invitation to dinner with the Masseys.'

Together they had walked along the road, greeted by cheerful waves from the soldiers who were loading the last of the ammunition into their vehicles above the pier.

When Trewin had asked Mallory if he had been invited to the dinner he had exploded, 'Not bloody likely! And I wouldn't have accepted anyway!' He had watched Trewin angrily, his dark face creased into a frown. 'I knew the skipper was off his rocker, but this last day has done it.' He had drawn one hand across his forehead. 'I've just about had it, up to here!'

In quick, staccato sentences Mallory had described the events which had followed Trewin's departure in the dinghy. 'Corbett was like a bear with a sore arse. He never stopped snapping at me.' Mallory had banged his fists together. 'And when the shooting started he was passing more bloody orders than an admiral's wife.' He had dropped his voice suddenly. 'I know you did well, Number One, and I'll be the first to admit that I couldn't have done it myself. But Corbett's part in all this was quite different. As soon as that clapped out scow came under fire he deliberately steered towards her! He knew that the admiral would have his guts for garters for running the *Porcupine* on the putty, so he did the only thing he knew. He didn't give a tuppenny damn for the lives of his men, he only cared for how it would look when the top brass heard how brave he had been.'

Trewin had interrupted firmly, 'I think you'd better calm down. This is no help to anybody, is it?'

Mallory had sighed. 'Sure, sure! You are the first lieutenant. Loyalty to the ship and all that.' He had added lazily, 'I was in a proper old rust-bucket once as third mate. We had a skipper who was so drunk most of the time he didn't know his arse from his elbow. His first mate carried him along, but one day the Old Man went too far. The ship had been badly stowed, and when we were two days out the bloody cargo started to shift. God, I can see it now. A crew of half-baked Lascars, and the skipper so tanked up he could hardly see the funnel.'

Trewin had asked, 'I don't see what that has to do with this situation?'

Mallory had continued calmly, 'Well, our skipper had already been warned for slackness. That rusty old freighter was the bottom of the ladder for him, the last chance, so to speak. He knew bloody well that when the owners heard what had happened he would be given the bum's rush.' Mallory had spread his hands. 'Then we got an S.O.S. from some Greek tanker which had lost her rudder. There were plenty of ships nearby, but our skipper had to get there, too. He damn near wrecked the ship and lost a man overboard to do it, but he got there in the end. When we reached port the papers were full of it. Our skipper was the hero of the day. Even though the tanker broke up in the storm before we could get a line across, the skipper was spoken of as a man who had risked his life and his ship for the brotherhood of the sea!' He had shaken his head. 'Fortunately the bastard died of alcoholic poisoning the next year before he could kill anybody else!'

'And you think the captain only acted out of self-interest?' Trewin had felt his sympathy for Mallory giving way to anger.

'Could well be! He made me con the ship upriver. Treated me like a kid and watched me every foot of the way. But if I'm asked, I shall tell what I think about it. He ran aground because he's past it! And he's too damn pig-headed to admit that anyone else could handle the ship as well as he can!'

Trewin felt his eyelids drooping and said quickly, 'I think I'll be getting back, Doctor. It's late.'

'I suppose you think it thoughtless of me to keep you talking?' Massey regarded him gravely. 'But I believe you needed to talk. To get away from what you had to do this morning.' He shook his head. 'When I was told what you did I guessed what you must be feeling.' He studied Trewin with his deepset eyes. 'You've had a tough time. I've heard about some of it from your captain. Some I worked out for myself.' He smiled.

'And you can wipe that guarded look from your face, my lad. I'm a doctor, remember?'

At that moment the door opened and Corbett came into the room with the girl at his side. He said, 'I've just been looking at Clare's garden, James. It's very good. Just like a little piece of England.'

Clare Massey looked across at Trewin. 'Feeling better now?'

Trewin replied, 'Much.' It was strange how tongue-tied she made him. From the moment he had returned to Talang he had known that he wanted to see her again. Perhaps it was fear of a rebuff, or some mistake in his memory of that other meeting which made him tell himself not to leave the ship. To invent tasks when his whole being was crying out for rest and reprieve from those hours on the hillside. All through dinner he had watched her across the table. She looked so young, so sure of herself, and when she spoke with her father it seemed more as a companion than as a daughter.

She said, 'The rains have battered the flowers down a bit, but they're very hardy.' She shivered. 'It's getting dark outside now. I don't know if I shall be able to sleep tonight knowing the Japs were so close last night.' She checked herself and added to Trewin, 'I'm sorry. You've been fighting them, and I'm moaning about myself.'

Trewin watched her hair shining in the lamplight. He could see the fine line of her neck and throat, the firmness of her body beneath the khaki shirt. He said, 'It seems quiet enough now.'

Corbett was watching them with his cool, unblinking eyes. 'We must be going, Trewin. We sail tomorrow for Singapore and the next job to be thrown our way.'

Trewin wished that he could make some excuse to be alone with the girl. He did not know what he wanted to tell her, or how he would begin. But it was suddenly very important to him.

Massey stood up and yawned hugely. 'I'm sending Clare down to Singapore in a day or so, Greville. Do her good to get away from this place for a bit.'

Corbett nodded, his eyes still on Trewin. 'I agree, James. She can stay with Mildred again, eh?'

Trewin thought he saw a quick exchange of glances between the girl and her father, but she replied quietly, 'I should like that.'

Trewin heard himself say, 'Maybe you could have dinner with *me* if I'm in harbour?'

Corbett picked up his cap 'I expect we shall be very busy, Trewin.' It sounded like a warning.

But the girl replied, 'I should like that, too.' She smiled, showing her even teeth. 'So mind you look after yourself this time.'

As they walked back to the ship Trewin noticed Corbett's sudden change of mood. He seemed deep in thought, his foot-steps quick and impatient. He snapped, 'She is a fine young girl. Known her since she was a child.'

Trewin tried to see his face in the darkness. 'I know, sir.'

Corbett added stiffly, 'I wouldn't like to see her upset in any way, do you understand?'

Trewin felt so weary and drained that he did not know whether to laugh or be angered by Corbett's remarks. He sounded possessive and guarded, as he did when speaking of his ship. Perhaps there was some grain of truth in Mallory's explanation after all. He said carefully, 'There might be an enquiry at Singapore, I suppose, sir.'

Corbett sniffed. 'I shouldn't wonder. Still, we can report that we've done very well. Very well indeed!'

But if Trewin thought he had successfully changed the sub-ject he was wrong. As they reached the darkened gangway Corbett said, 'She'll meet someone one day, and be happily married.' He paused with one foot on the sidedeck. 'So just keep that in mind, eh?'

Trewin walked into his cabin and slammed the door. For a moment he stared at his reflection in the mirror and then nodded. 'I will bear it in mind,' he said. 'Indeed I will!'

8
Stabilise the Line!

Trewin soon found that Corbett had been right about one thing. Within three days of their return to Singapore Island they were ordered to sea yet again, but not the familiar eastern coastline which had become part of everyday life. Under cover of darkness, while the city waited for yet another air attack, the four gunboats steamed west and then north into the Malacca Strait. So restricted had life become for the crews of the gunboats that even the other part of the war away from the east coast had seemed remote, a matter for someone else to worry about.

There had been talk of fierce fighting from the moment the invasion had started, of the same pattern of retreats and desperate counter-attacks. Penang had fallen, and Kuala Lumpur had followed quickly in the list of defeats.

But British resistance was hardening, and as the enemy pushed down on each side of the Malay Peninsula more troops and artillery were rushed northwards to fill the gaps and stem the fast-moving tide of destruction and death.

On the third day at anchor Corbett had received a summons to Fairfax-Loring's H.Q. The once neat buildings were now little more than blackened skeletons, victims of the many air raids over the dockyard and anchorage, but in the sandbagged cellars beneath the admiral had set up his operations room, and if anything seemed to thrive on the inconvenience.

All the gunboat captains and their first lieutenants had been there, and the admiral had wasted no time in getting to the point.

'The enemy has made another breakthrough *here*!' His flag-lieutenant had moved a long pointer across the map until it reached the town of Malacca. 'It's the same sort of pattern as we had on the east coast, but here the country is more difficult for supply and communications. The Army is pulling out of the town and falling back *here*,' he had paused for the pointer to move slightly, 'so they will need support from the sea.'

He had looked around their intent faces. 'The C.-in-C. is pleased with our efforts over the past weeks, and I suggested that we should lend our strength to the west coast for a change.' He had chuckled. 'At least on the eastern side things have hardened a bit, what?'

It was true that the Pahang River line was still intact. There had been much patrol activity on both sides and a good deal of artillery fighting. But the line was holding, and every day meant more reinforcements and a better chance of hitting back. The war was like a pendulum. If the Japs were held on one coast, the momentum of their pressure swung to the opposite side. So far both fronts had stayed about level, but now with this latest breakthrough the enemy were smashing south again, nearer and nearer to the final goal. Malacca was only one hundred miles from Singapore. On the map it had not looked half that much.

Fairfax-Loring had continued in the same brisk tone. 'We know more about the enemy now. We've got the feel of him.' His smile had shown nothing but confidence. 'This time we'll give him a bit of a shock!'

Keates of the *Beaver* had plucked at his grey beard. 'What support are we getting, sir?'

The admiral had wagged one finger. 'Everything I can throw your way! You'll have an anti-aircraft cruiser and her destroyer escort tracking you along the coast, and just to make everyone happy I've laid on some good air cover.' He had saved this part for the last. 'Hurricanes! Fresh out from England and raring to hit the Japs where it hurts!'

He had looked around their faces, suddenly solemn. 'I only wish I could come with you, gentlemen. But unfortunately I have to stay and control the operation from here. And the way things are going it does look as if I shall be given the responsibility for both coastal sections until further notice.' He had shrugged, and brought out his old smile. 'But now is not the time to think of oneself, what?'

As they had finished writing their notes the admiral had added casually, 'I have not had the opportunity to speak to all of you about the *Porcupine*'s little adventure at Talang.' His eyes had rested momentarily on Corbett. 'It looked very nasty for a bit, but things came out quite well in the end.'

That was all. No censure, not even an inquiry about the grounding report which Corbett had already delivered. The business of getting the ship ready for sea again had pushed this realisation to the back of Trewin's mind. Even the shock with its aftermath of nightmares had lessened in the general air of purposeful preparation.

But now, as the *Porcupine* steamed slowly along the south-west coast, Trewin found time to ponder over Fairfax-Loring's apparent indifference.

One thing was sure, it seemingly had a strange effect on Corbett. From the moment the gunboats had left Singapore he had been unable to restrain his irritation and impatience. It was as if he felt out of place on this new coastline, for as Hammond had remarked, Corbett had never been away from the east coast since he had taken command.

For another three days the gunboats had steamed slowly back and forth along a set patrol area, the first tension of expectancy giving way to the usual air of anticlimax and un-certainty. It was true that the admiral's prophecy about support was correct. They had seen the cruiser *Canopus* and her destroyers far out on the horizon, and regularly twice a day they had been alarmed and then cheered by the sight of low-flying Hurricanes as they flashed overhead following the coast-line like birds of prey.

Then on the third day as Trewin had climbed to the bridge to take over the First Watch the news had broken. He had been standing by the starboard screen, his glasses trained on a group of motionless fishing boats, when Corbett had hurried up from the radio room, his face stiff and apprehensive.

Just had a signal, Trewin. The Japs have bypassed the Army to the south of Malacca and have made a seaborne landing behind them!' He had pushed Mallory away from the chart table. 'They've cut the coast road and are already in command of the hills there.' He had smacked his hand on the chart. 'Damn them!'

Trewin had asked. 'And our orders, sir? Do we try a bombardment on the enemy positions?'

Corbett had stared at him as if he were talking gibberish. 'My orders are to enter the pocket between the two enemy-held areas. There is a fishing port of some sort and a whole brigade pinned down inside it.' He had controlled his voice with an effort. 'We will evacuate the troops at first light and take them further down the coast to stabilise the line.' He had glared at Mallory's grim features. 'So get cracking, Pilot! I don't want any mistakes this time!'

The group had turned away from the coast, and when darkness fell *Porcupine* had led the little line of gunboats back towards the shore. Navigation for once was made easy in the early stages. The fishing village, such as it was, was lit repeatedly by shellbursts, and far away to port, lighting the night sky like an early dawn, was an unmoving pink glow.

Mallory had said quietly, 'That must be Malacca. It'll be burning like hell to give a glow like that.'

Now the glow was fainter, and Trewin was reminded of the hillside above the Talang Inlet as he and Hammond had waited for the dawn.

Corbett sat restlessly on his chair, his glasses trained over the screen towards the flickering arrowhead of water which marked the entrance to the village. The approach was littered with sunken or drifting fishing boats, and more than once Trewin saw a corpse floating face down on the surface, seeming to come to life when caught by the gunboat's wash.

Corbett said, 'Slow ahead!' He seemed unable to sit still. 'Have you checked the bearing, Pilot?'

Mallory's face lit up momentarily in the glare of a bursting

141

flare. He said curtly, 'Oh four five, sir! But once past the breakwater it'll be all guesswork.'

Corbett snapped. 'Don't be impertinent, Pilot! Don't you overstep the mark again!' He swung round as Trewin made to leave the bridge. 'And where do you imagine you're going?'

Trewin flinched as the air shivered to a sudden barrage of gunfire. He replied, 'Aft sir. My action station is with . . .'

Corbett banged his fist on the screen. 'You stay here, Trewin. We'll not be engaging any ships this time!' He peered towards the village. 'Just get those soldiers aboard and then get out, that's what I say!'

Trewin lapsed into silence and turned to stare at the dancing patterns which lit up parts of the village and surrounding hills in bright, stark pictures, only to leave him blinded again as the fires died only to break out again elsewhere. He saw a line of small houses by the waterfront blazing from end to end, and thought he saw running figures flitting across the flames, like victims in hell.

The low breakwater crept out to meet them, a black line across the flat, glittering sea. Then Corbett said sharply, 'We'll check this side of the breakwater first. Just to make sure there's no obstructions for when we come out!'

Trewin trained his glasses along the breakwater. It was surprisingly undamaged, and nothing moved along its length. It was a waste of time to carry out an inspection, he thought. It would hold up the other gunboats, too.

Corbett said calmly, 'Starboard fifteen.' He craned his head to watch the bows swinging round. 'Midships! Steady!' Over his shoulder he added, 'Signal *Beaver* to lead the way to the picking-up point, Trewin. No use in wasting time, eh?'

The signal lamp stuttered briefly, and as *Porcupine* glided clear of the entance *Beaver*'s pale shape crossed her wash and pushed on towards the village. Even as she passed the breakwater she was enveloped in drifting smoke, and Trewin could see the burning houses reflected in her bridge screen like individual pictures of despair and misery.

Corbett was studying the breakwater with obvious interest.

As the other two gunboats followed the *Beaver* through the entrance he said, 'Very well, Trewin. Follow them in. It all seems clear enough on this side.' He slid from his chair and walked to the chart table. 'Can you hold her yourself, Trewin?' He picked up the parallel rulers and dividers and made to lift the hood from the table. 'Just long enough for me to do some checking.'

Trewin stepped on to the centre grating. 'I can, sir.' Corbett's question had got under his skin. 'Starboard twenty!' He watched the compass repeater glowing just below his chest. What the hell was the matter with Corbett? He seemed more concerned about handing the con to him than he was about the actual operation of evacuating the trapped soldiers.

He snapped 'Midships! Steady!' He heard Unwin's reply from the voice-pipe and concentrated his whole mind on the smoke-shrouded shape of the ship ahead. It was the *Prawn*, her boxlike superstructure ploughing through the smoke, her own funnel adding to the dense fog which covered the narrow inlet from end to end.

Mallory stepped up beside him. Between his teeth he said harshly, 'So we're the last to go in. That means we'll be the first out!' He looked down at Corbett's shape above the chart table. 'There was no need to hang back, Number One. You know it and *I* know it!'

A drifting flare showed briefly through the smoke, and Trewin saw the pale upturned face of a swimmer almost along-side. It might have been a boy or a young girl. He turned away, sickened as the swimmer kicked vainly away from the churning froth of the *Porcupine*'s propellers.

He looked at Mallory and replied, 'For God's sake shut your mouth! I'm sick of your bellyaching, *sick* of it!'

He ignored Mallory's anger and leaned forward to watch the *Prawn*'s shape lengthen as she swung around a half-sub-merged cabin cruiser. 'Port ten!' He wiped the stinging tears from his eyes. 'Meet her!' Damn Mallory! His words still moved in his mind like barbs. It was as if he had read his own thoughts. Had said what he dared only to think.

'Midships!' He lowered his head over the voice-pipe. 'Head straight for the jetty, Swain! Can you see it?' He pictured Unwin at the wheel, leaning over the spokes to stare through the narrow slits in the armoured shutters.

Unwin replied in his usual expressionless tone, 'Aye, aye, sir! I can see it fine!'

Masters, the yeoman called, 'Sky's brightenin', sir! The dawn'll be up shortly.'

Trewin glanced quickly across the opposite screen. It was true that the fires seemed paler and the smoke more plain to see against the hills beyond the village.

The jetty was little more than a mud wall supported at intervals by thick wooden piles, and as Trewin brought the gunboat swinging round in a tight arc he heard Dancy yelling to his men on the forecastle and saw two seamen leaping over the rail to receive the mooring lines.

The hull shuddered against the piles, and Trewin put the starboard engine astern to bring the stern closer to the jetty. 'Stop engines!' He had to shout above the crackling fires, the confused stammer of machine-guns and the heavier bark of mortars. It was hard to believe that anyone could live in this inferno, let alone fight in it. What had happened to the Malay fishermen and their families? he wondered. Maybe like that solitary swimmer they had been driven into the sea like rats before a forest fire.

Corbett was suddenly beside him. 'Good.' He looked over the screen towards the *Prawn* which had somehow managed to tie itself to a waterlogged lighter while the other two ships were moored together just ahead of her. He said, 'Now let's get on with it!' He stood looking up at Trewin's smoke-smeared face. 'We've got about three hours. No more!'

Trewin felt unable to move. Suppose it was all true what Mallory had said? That Corbett's attempt to help the stranded refugee ship had been a gesture, just for the record? That he was even now thinking more of his own safety than that of the men who were depending on him? He felt the thoughts turning in his mind like panic. Men like Hammond and Dancy. Like himself.

He said flatly, 'I—I'll make contact with the Army right away, sir.'

As he turned to go Corbett caught his arm and in a quiet voice said, 'Now hold on, Trewin. Just keep calm. Try and think of it as an exercise, eh?'

His eyes seemed to glow in the reflected fires, and across his shoulder Trewin could see Mallory watching both of them, his face tense and angry.

He ran down the bridge ladder, not trusting himself to say another word. Corbett must be mad. Had to be.

Petty Officer Dancy called, 'Sir! What'll I do about those poor devils?' He pointed down at the jetty where a small group of Malays had appeared, as if conjured out of the fires at their backs. There were only about six of them and three small children. They neither waved nor called out, but stood in the drifting smoke like statues, staring up at the *Porcupine*'s bridge.

Trewin shook his head. 'Don't do anything, Buffer. We must wait for the soldiers first.' He saw the agony on Dancy's face, remembering suddenly that Corbett had told him it was this man who had made the model ship for his son. Curiously the memory seemed to steady him. He said, 'Later perhaps. We'll have to see.'

Then he was running across the jetty between the flickering lines of burning huts which had once offered life and hope for people like those on the jetty. He almost collided with a helmeted army lieutenant who was squatting on a shooting stick, a pipe in his mouth, as he watched the distant shellbursts above the village.

He took the pipe from his mouth and nodded, 'Ah, the Navy, I presume?' He waved the pipe towards a crumbling wall at his side. 'Don't go past there, old son. You're liable to get your head shot off.'

In the grey dawn light his face took on shape and personality, and Trewin saw that he had a small jaunty moustache and about three days' growth of stubble.

Above the crackle of gunfire the soldier said, 'You wouldn't have any tobacco, I suppose? Left my pouch in Malacca.' He laughed, and Trewin saw the strain breaking through his mask of casual indifference like a raw wound.

He handed him his own tobacco and asked, 'I have to find your brigadier. We've only got three hours.'

The lieutenant's fingers paused above the pouch. Then he said quietly, 'I'm in charge now, old boy. Me and Sergeant Hall, if he's still alive.' He continued to press the tobacco into his pipe, but most of it fell on the ground between his legs. He handed his pipe to Trewin and asked shakily, 'Would you do the honours, old son? I seem to have lost the knack.' He stood up and folded the shooting stick carefully. 'Fact is, the brigadier, his staff and practically the whole bloody outfit is now in the bag!' He spoke slowly, as if to make sure he was putting his words in the right place. 'Yesterday it was, I *think*.' He rubbed his face. 'My lot got separated. We decided to make a fight of it.' He took the pipe and lit it slowly, the flame quivering as if in a wind. 'Actually, I think I'm getting too old for this sort of thing.'

He looked about the same age as Hammond. Trewin asked gently, 'Can you bring them back? I'll go and warn the ships you're coming.'

At that moment a tall, gangling sergeant ran round the wall and skidded to a halt beside them. His battledress was in tatters, but he looked very calm and competent.

The lieutenant said briskly, 'Ah, Sarnt Hall! The Navy has brought some ships for us!'

The sergeant jammed a fresh clip into his rifle and said, 'One ship would do for our lot, sir.' He showed his teeth. 'I'll start the ball rollin' right away.' He blew two blasts on a whistle and added, 'I've got the perimeter mined for the bastards. The rearguard know what to do.' To Trewin he said calmly, 'You'll have to leave them behind, sir. You'd never get out of the harbour otherwise.'

As he strode away into the smoke the lieutenant called, 'Goodbye, Sarnt. And thank you!'

The sergeant paused and then saluted very formally.

The lieutenant said in a small voice, 'We drew lots for the rearguard, Sergeant Hall is one of them.' Then he started to cry, the pipe still clamped in his teeth.

Trewin turned and walked slowly back towards the waiting ships.

* * *

Before the sun had fully cleared the range of hills behind the burning village the evacuation was completed. Then led by the *Porcupine* the gunboats picked their way seaward amongst the bobbing flotsam and past the deserted breakwater. A few stray shells whined overhead, but the dense pall of smoke from the gutted buildings made an effective screen for the final withdrawal, and as *Porcupine*'s telegraph rang down for full speed those on the upper bridge heard the ragged salvo of explosions and knew that the mines around the village had been detonated.

The *Beaver* was the last to pass the breakwater, and as she turned in a flurry of white foam to follow her consorts her upperdeck was wreathed in her own gunsmoke as she opened fire blindly and savagely towards the hidden enemy.

Some thirty wounded soldiers were aboard the little *Prawn*, and the remainder, numbering less than seventy all told, were spread between *Porcupine* and *Grayling*. As they headed southeast, hugging the coastline in the strengthening sunlight, flights of Hurricanes roared overhead, and from far out on the horizon the A.A. cruiser *Canopus* could be seen steaming at full speed, her signal lamp flashing like a bright diamond across the lingering sea mist. But aboard the *Porcupine* there was neither interest nor satisfaction. Over the whole ship there was an air of stunned despair, as if each man shared some private grief with the silent, exhausted soldiers who lay about the decks like dead men.

By midday they had rounded the great elbow of jutting headland called Tohor Point, and right on time the four gunboats dropped their anchors in the clear water of a protected sandy bay. As the engines sighed into silence so the noises of the war intruded and stayed to remind them of what lay only ten miles behind them. The continuous murmur of artillery and the harsher explosions of bombs. High above in the washed-out blue sky they occasionally saw the entwined vapour trails of grappling fighters, the sounds of their death struggles lost in the general mixture of distant battle. Twice they saw anonymous aircraft fall like flies far out over the sea, and a single parachute drifting aimlessly towards the horizon. Trewin had watched it through his glasses for several minutes. It was like a child's balloon. Lost, and already forgotten.

Corbett had left him in charge of the bridge while he went to the radio room. The anti-aircraft guns were manned and ready, but on the gunboat's decks there was some attempt to gain order and purpose, if only to break the tension of waiting for fresh instructions.

He saw the cook and his assistants stepping over and around the listless soldiers, their arms laden with freshly cut sandwiches and great fannies of tea. The soldiers took what they were given, but their actions were automatic and without expression. Trewin turned away, unable to watch their faces. They still could not grasp the fact that they had survived.

Petty Officer Masters said, '*Prawn* has just weighed, sir!' He closed his long telescope and exchanged it for a mug of tea. 'She is takin' the wounded out to the cruiser. They'll get better looked after aboard 'er.' He pouted his piggy face and added, 'Not that it matters much now. The show's over as far as we're concerned.'

Phelps, the signalman, asked, 'Won't we be doin' any more 'ere, Yeo?'

Masters eyed him coldly. 'Use yer loaf, Ginger! We was supposed to bring out a brigade an' put 'em ashore further south to,' he frowned as if memorising the original signal, 'to stabilise the line. You can't *stabilise* nothin' with seventy 'alf dead squaddies, now can you?'

Trewin sipped his mug of tea and watched the *Prawn* butting fiercely through a shallow offshore swell. Masters was right. This part of the operation was over. They might as well go back to Singapore.

He thought suddenly of Clare and her father's description of the hospital at Talang. Was it really possible that he still believed it could survive? Maybe he was only pretending for Clare's benefit, and he was sending her to Singapore to avoid the terror of the inevitable breakthrough.

He turned as Corbett climbed through the hatch, and noticed with surprise that the captain had managed to find the time to shave and change into a clean shirt.

Corbett said, 'The show's still on, Trewin. We sail in three hours.' He pushed the cover from the chart table and continued calmly. 'The enemy are well placed on those hills at Muar. When they bring up their main artillery support they'll be able to command the whole road system and stop our people bringing reinforcements.'

Trewin was still on the gratings, the cup gripped in one hand as he stared at Corbett, unable to conceal the dismay and horror which his words had aroused. 'But, sir, that's ridiculous! We were supposed to have a whole brigade, or at least a thousand men to support this operation!' He waved the mug violently across the screen. 'My God, we can't expect to do anything with these poor bastards!'

Corbett was still examining the chart. 'The cruiser is sending additional support, Trewin. Fifty marines, to be exact.'

Trewin closed his eyes against the sun, 'Now I've heard everything! My christ, that's *perfect*!' He felt Corbett watching him coldly but he could no longer control the flood of bitter anger. 'One hundred and twenty men to be thrown away because some bloody fool behind a desk can't see further than the Aldershot Tattoo!'

Corbett snapped, 'You don't know what you're saying!'

'Oh yes I do, sir!' Trewin swayed, feeling the sun across his neck like hot metal. 'I've seen it before, remember? Dunkirk and Crete were enough for *me*!'

Masters said in a hushed tone, 'Signal from *Canopus*, sir.

149

Marines are bein' embarked now.' He stepped back, pushing the open-mouthed Phelps out of earshot.

Corbett said irritably, 'Well those are the orders. It's settled!'

Trewin stepped down beside him and said quietly, 'Look sir, if you made a signal, if you explained that it was hopeless . . .' His voice trailed away as he saw Corbett's eyes settle again on the chart.

'It's not my decision, Trewin. We have to land these men as close to the hills as possible. There's no time for a big regrouping of forces. This may be decisive, even critical.' He looked up sharply, examining Trewin's features. 'What I may think personally about all this is quite irrelevant.' He folded his arms and stared up at the masthead pendant. 'And whatever you consider is more practical is equally unhelpful.' He walked back towards the hatch adding curtly, 'Orders are not made to be discussed! They are to be obeyed!'

Trewin walked out on to the bridge wing and looked towards the lush green coastline, hating it, and dreading what had to be done. Then, as he glanced down he saw the young infantry lieutenant crossing the forecastle, his helmet swinging in his hand, his pipe still jutting from his mouth. There was little trace of the beaten, dazed soldier Trewin had seen climb aboard with the last of his troops. He had shaved, and his step was almost springy as he walked amongst his men, his voice low but confident as he spoke to each soldier in turn. He must know exactly what lay ahead, just as every one of his men did. Neither he nor they gave any sign of despair or anger. It was as if they all knew that their reprieve from death had been merely temporary.

Once the lieutenant looked up at the bridge, perhaps feeling Trewin's eyes following his improvised inspection, and threw him a mock salute. Across the heads of the *Porcupine*'s gunners and the resting soldiers they shared a small moment of understanding. Then, as the young lieutenant turned back towards his men, the moment was past.

They started the attack at the end of the afternoon. For half an hour the cruiser and her two destroyers maintained a steady bombardment from the sea, the air torn apart by their shells as they ripped overhead with the sounds of tearing silk. It was easy to see them exploding along the ridge of hills as the earth and trees erupted in bright flashes and the pale sky became smeared with brown cordite and woodsmoke.

An elderly flying boat droned lazily back and forth across the water, reporting the fall of shot and dodging the occasional retaliatory bursts of enemy gunfire. But otherwise the ships had the scene to themselves. In line abreast the four gunboats headed for the great spread of sandy beach with its ever-present backcloth of jungle, their forward guns high angled as they joined in the raking barrage as fast as their sweating crews could reload the demanding breeches.

The *Porcupine* steamed on the left of the line, while the others were spaced out at regular intervals with less than a cable's length between them. Next abeam was the *Grayling*, and Trewin could see some of the cruiser's marines crowded aft on her quarterdeck, the sunlight glinting on their fixed bayonets. He knew without looking that it was the same picture on his own ship, the weight of men very necessary to hold the bows as high as possible in readiness for grounding. For here the beach shelves steeply and suddenly, and with luck the gunboats would be able to unload their human cargoes on to the land with hardly more than their feet wet.

Mallory stood beside the compass, his glasses levelled straight ahead. He said to the bridge at large, 'The coast road is down behind that first section of jungle. Our lads have got to cross the beach and get through that before they can join up with the rest of the troops.' He licked his lips as a tall water-spout rose steeply abeam and threw a pattern of spray over the gunboat's hull. 'Close!'

Corbett said coolly, 'A dud! Probably a six-inch from the cruiser.'

Mallory looked at the back of Corbett's head and muttered beneath his breath. Then after a quick fix from the compass he said loudly, 'We are running in now, sir! About half a cable to go!'

Corbett nodded. 'Slow ahead together!' He turned sharply as a shell clipped through the trees on the left of the beach and exploded deep inside the shadows with a sharp crack. 'Pass the word to the soldiers.'

Masters remarked hoarsely, 'Well, at least the Jap artillery has been took care of. The bastards are only gettin' off one shot to our ten.' His assessment did not mean much, but it helped to ease the tension.

Corbett swung his glasses towards the other ships. All were moving very slowly as if tensing for the impact. He said, 'Tell the chief to prepare to go astern immediately we unload.' He might have been discussing an unwanted deck cargo.

Trewin saw the patches of weed swimming up to meet the gunboat's stem and heard Corbett snap, 'Stop engines!'

The cease fire gong rang beside the forward gun, and Trewin saw the seamen holding on to the shield as the *Porcupine* glided soundlessly above her shadow towards the empty beach. He held on to the screen, but when the impact came it was hardly more than a dignified shudder. A whistle shrilled, and the decks came alive with thudding boots as the soldiers tore along either side and hurled themselves over the bows. The water was deeper than it appeared, and more than one man fell cursing and kicking before he could scramble up on to the firm sand.

When Trewin tore his eyes from the running soldiers he saw that the men from the other gunboats were already scrambling ashore, urged on by hoarse cries from N.C.O.s and a tall major of marines.

From individual faces and torn, battle-stained uniforms the *Porcupine*'s soldiers were transformed into a trotting khaki line. Then as the other men from the gunboats fanned out to meet them the whole line began to move steadily towards the green wall of jungle.

Then as Trewin lowered his glasses the beach seemed to burst skyward with short, ear-splitting explosions. There was no whine of shellfire, and for one terrible moment Trewin imagined that the soldiers had run into a minefield. The line of men faltered, and others lay bleeding beside their rifles and the blackened patches of sand.

He heard Tweedie's voice, magnified over the bridge tannoy. 'Mortars! They're using mortars!'

Mallory shouted. 'The Japs must be in the jungle too, for God's sake!' He sounded frantic. 'They'll never make it!'

But the line began to move forward again. The marine major was waving his revolver, and in the lenses of Trewin's glasses his face looked defiant and angry.

The mortar shells continued to fall, throwing up small fountains of sand and cutting down the running men in a tide of splinters. Far out on the left flank a heavy machine-gun added to the horror, and Trewin saw soldiers and marines crouching and firing their rifles as they ran, ignoring the clutching hands of their fallen companions, their ears and minds deaf to all but revenge.

He saw too the young army lieutenant, his helmet gone, using one hand to drag a wounded man behind him towards the trees. But the man fell, and as the lieutenant turned to look at him Trewin saw his body jerk violently like a rag doll as the machine-gun whipped the beach into yellow feathers around him. When the murderous bullets passed on the lieutenant lay face down in the sand, his shooting stick standing upright beside him like a memorial.

Trewin looked at Corbett. He was standing quite motionless by the voice-pipes, his face set like a mask.

He shouted, 'Call them back, sir! For God's sake get them *back*!'

Corbett gripped the voice-pipes as if the ship was moving. Then he said quietly, 'Slow astern together.' He did not even flinch as a mortar shell exploded near water's edge and splinters clanged against the hull and ricocheted screaming over the sea.

The screws began to beat the water into froth beneath the counter, and one by one the gunboats started to move astern. When Trewin looked again at the beach the running figures had vanished into the trees. He could hear the rattle of small-arms and the dull thuds of grenades, but the jungle hid the final scene and betrayed nothing of the fighting and the dying. On the beach the corpses lay like discarded bundles, while here and there a wounded man crawled aimlessly or lay crying for help which would never come.

Corbett's voice scraped his mind like a saw. 'Hard a-star-board. Full ahead together!' To Masters he rapped, 'Signal the group to take up station astern!'

Then as the four gunboats curved away on a bright arc of white wash he looked at Trewin and said simply, 'They had their orders, too.'

Masters said thickly, 'Signal from *Canopus*, sir. Operation completed. Return to patrol area forthwith.'

On one corner of the bridge Phelps was standing with both hands digging into his signal flags, his face pale, his eyes blinded with emotion.

Trewin saw the gunners leaning around their shield as they stared astern at the rising pall of smoke and the deep foot-prints in the sand which were already fading in the rising tide.

When he looked again at Corbett he saw that he was back in the chair his head sunk in his shoulders as he stared fixedly at the horizon.

Trewin remembered the signal 'Operation completed.' It sounded like an epitaph.

9
Massey's Secret

The *Porcupine*'s presence on the south-west coast was mercifully short. Within two days of the Japanese breakout from the Malacca pocket there was virtually no part of the Strait safe enough to patrol. Day by day and hour by hour the enemy intensified his air attacks, and as the gunboats zigzagged in and out of the shallows, their guns hardly having time to cool, it became obvious that the Army's retreat was turning into a rout. On the fifth day the signal came to release the little ships from their torment, and with ammunition lockers almost empty their hulls grimed with smoke and scarred with splinters, they headed south-east for Singapore.

Apart from a few minor injuries they had escaped the fate of many others. They had seen a destroyer blasted into two halves by a stick of bombs, the swimming survivors machine-gunned from the air with methodical savagery. An ammunition lighter had gone up like a bomb within yards of the shore, and so swift and terrible had been her end that no one knew the cause of the disaster. The blast from the explosion had fired and flattened the trees for miles inland, and had whipped the topmast from the *Beaver* like a straw in a strong wind.

But the gunboats had survived, and had even managed to hit back. They had shot down one fighter, and the *Porcupine*'s own gunners had sent a solitary Zero limping back over the land, a trail of smoke pouring behind it and growing with each second to show the sure certainty of a kill.

Once in harbour they had gone on immediately with the tasks of refuelling and taking on more shells and supplies. Everybody was either too tired or too shocked to care about the nearby city or the air raids which came and went with the regularity of time itself.

Just one day at anchor, and then in the middle of a sudden rainstorm the four ships had weighed and headed through the Singapore Strait and up towards the old familiar area. Only then did Corbett seem to regain some of his original self-control. Maybe he was reassured by the unchanging coastline, by the very feel of the sea and wind about him.

But his calm was only skin deep, and at dusk on the first day out of harbour, when the *Prawn* signalled plaintively that she had an engine failure, he seemed beside himself with anger. The lights blinked back and forth, and even Masters, the imperturbable yeoman, felt the edge of the captain's abrasive tongue when he was slow to comprehend one of *Prawn*'s signals. But no ship as old as *Prawn* could take such usage without something giving way, and in spite of all Corbett's persuasions and threats he had to give her permission to withdraw back to harbour. *Beaver* took her in tow, and as the rain lashed the *Porcupine*'s upper bridge like steel needles the two gunboats moved guiltily into the darkness and vanished from sight.

Trewin pushed himself tighter into one corner of the bridge and readjusted the soggy towel around his neck. He could feel the rain battering his oilskin and splashing up from the gratings to soak his legs and feet. There was a lot of cloud, and he knew that the rain was here for some time.

He heard Corbett tearing at the chart table hood and the scrape of instruments as he leaned down to study the ship's course and estimated position. He could not imagine what was holding Corbett together. He never slept, and rarely left the bridge for more than minutes at a time. On occasions he was like a stranger, brooding and pacing, or slumped in his chair his eyes staring straight ahead as if for some new encounter.

Trewin managed to avoid any open conflict. He forced his mind to stay in the tight confines of duty, shutting out the agony and despair of the massacred soldiers, the pathetic attempt at normality by his own men.

Corbett stood up, his face gleaming momentarily in the

shaded chart light. For an instant as he gathered his thoughts he showed some of the strange inner force which was tearing him apart. He looked much older, and Trewin noticed that he had developed a small, persistent tick in one eye.

Corbett saw him looking down from the gratings and snapped, 'Keep an eye on your quartermaster! He's wandering about the sea like a drunken duck!' He seemed to be trying to think of another reproach when the handset buzzed at the rear of the bridge. Before Trewin could move he ripped it from its rack and barked. 'Bridge!' Then in his old tone he added coldly 'This *is* the captain, you fool!'

Trewin thought of the luckless telegraphist on the other end of the line and sighed.

Corbett dropped the handset and said, 'I'm going down. There's a long signal. I can't trust them to deal with it.' He peered at Trewin's dark outline. 'Just remember what I said, that's all. Don't let them slack!'

Trewin asked quietly, 'Who, sir?'

Corbett clung to the rails of the ladder, his head craned, like a ferret ready to strike. 'Don't you get clever with me, Trewin! I've just about taken all I can from your sort!'

When Trewin remained silent he turned violently and ran down the steps.

Trewin found that his anger was quite gone. It was now merely a sensation, like all the others. Fear, shock and complete tiredness left little room for more outward emotion. Perhaps later, he thought dully. Later, there might be time.

When Corbett returned to the bridge he was quite calm again. He stepped up beside Trewin and lifted his glasses to search for the *Grayling*. She was still astern, her shape little more than a smudge above her bow-wave. He said slowly, 'We are going to Talang.' He sounded as if he was wrestling with his inner self again. 'The enemy has landed a striking force further down the coast, about fifty miles below the Pahang River.'

Trewin looked away. It was all happening in an exact pattern of what they had shared on the opposite coast. If the line held then the enemy drove a pincer behind it from the sea. He said bitterly, 'What the hell is the matter with our people? Why can't they stop them landing like this?'

Corbett opened the voice-pipe by his side and shouted above the drumming rain. 'Full ahead together!' To the crouching signalman he added, 'Make to *Grayling* "Keep close station astern".'

Then he seemed to consider Trewin's outburst. He replied, suddenly, 'It's not as easy as that. There are offshore islands, countless creeks and inlets. The enemy can afford to bide his time.'

'And without air cover we just have to take it!'

Corbett said coldly, 'Air cover is not everything, Trewin.' He shrugged his shoulders beneath his oilskin. 'Anyway, this is the plan. We enter Talang and take off all unwanted personnel immediately.'

Trewin had a sudden picture of the settlement lying inside the arms of the two enemy pincers. He spoke his thoughts aloud. 'At least Clare Massey's out of it. I only hope that your friend the doctor will agree to leave.'

Corbett stared at him. 'That's just it. She's still there. I checked with my wife while we were in harbour.' He shook his head. 'I wish she *were* out of it, believe me.' He watched the rising bow-wave sluice back through the hawsepipes and around the forward gun mounting. Then he said firmly, 'We will have the destroyer *Waltham* to cover us from seaward. But it will have to be quick this time.'

It always is, Trewin thought bitterly. He said, 'Have you told base about *Prawn* and *Beaver*, sir? We're at half strength now.'

Corbett shrugged. 'No to your first question. Radio silence is the thing at this stage. As to your other piece of pessimism, we can manage better without the others. We don't want to attract attention.' In a rising tone he added, 'Surely even you can see that?'

Mallory clumped up the ladder from the chartroom before Trewin could retort, and Corbett swung round to face him.

'You took your time, Pilot!' He glared at Mallory's shape by the chart table. 'Well, have you calculated what I asked?'

Mallory said evenly, 'Our E.T.A. at the Inlet will be 0430, sir.' He added, 'Low water at that time.'

'I *know* that.' Corbett joined him beside the table and rolled back the hood a few inches. 'Signal *Grayling* to take the lead. She draws a foot less than we do. We will follow up when the tide gives us a better channel.'

Trewin turned back towards the sea. He was thinking of that last time when the *Porcupine* had gone aground outside the Inlet. The captain was obviously taking no chances.

He swung his glasses slowly over the port beam and tried to see the darkened shoreline through the steady rain. But they were standing too far out. Maybe that was just as well, he thought grimly. The Japs might have no intention of using their new landing to waste time striking north. The troops caught between their two armies would have to fight their way out anyway, so the Japs could well use their fifty-mile advantage to increase their march on Singapore.

But surely to God they would be able to stop the Japs soon. In the narrowing strip of the Malay Peninsula the line would be shorter, easier to hold.

He sensed that Corbett was again standing beside him and he asked quietly, 'Where will we make a stand, sir?'

Corbett took several seconds to reply. When he did his voice was calm, almost gentle. 'We're not, Trewin. That signal was from the admiral. It seems that we are going to abandon the peninsula altogether. Singapore is the fortress, and was after all the main purpose of our defence commitment.'

Trewin felt his mouth go dry. 'Just like that?'

Corbett nodded firmly. 'Just like that.'

Trewin tried not to think of the hundreds of miles of hard-fought jungle, the ships sent to the bottom in the face of persistent and carefully planned attacks. Of the pain and the hopeless bravery. He said, 'So it was all for nothing!'

Corbett lifted his glasses to watch the *Grayling*'s pale shape surging past to take the lead, her blunt bows throwing up the

159

spray in a white curtain. He replied, 'No sacrifice is in vain. No matter how great or how small.'

Trewin clenched his hands and then let them drop at his sides. What was the point of trying to argue with Corbett? He was unreachable within himself.

Corbett slid on to the chair, heedless of the rain which bounced from his cap and oilskin. If there were any doubts in his mind, the *Porcupine*'s captain concealed them very well.

*　　　*　　　*

With her engines at dead slow the *Porcupine* pushed stubbornly against the fierce offshore current, the swirling water on either side of the hull giving a false impression of urgency and speed.

For the tenth time Corbett snapped his fingers and asked, 'Time?'

Mallory replied, '0445, sir.'

Corbett muttered, 'Where the hell *is* she? She should have been in and out by now!'

Trewin moved his glasses very slowly from bow to bow. It was still very dark, although the rain had given way to a steady, soaking drizzle. But for it and the persistent cloud he might have been able to see something, but although the dawn was very close the actual line of the shore remained hidden and remote. The waiting was getting on his nerves. Corbett's anxiety about the *Grayling* was more than justified, he thought. She had gone on ahead hours earlier with Corbett's orders to carry out the first and main part of the evacuation of nonessential personnel.

He blinked as another pattern of dull red flashes outlined the hills inland. All the way up the coast it had been hard not to watch the ominous reflections of duelling artillery and the glow of burning trees.

They had arrived off the Inlet ahead of time, and while the ship stayed in deep water, steaming in a wide circle, every look-out had strained his eyes for the *Grayling*'s returning shadow, so that Corbett could go in to complete the task. He could not enter the Talang River without waiting for *Grayling*'s return, as it was quite impossible for two craft to pass in its treacherous bends and deceptive shallows.

Trewin wondered why Corbett had not taken the plunge from the first and accompanied *Grayling,* instead of waiting for the dawn light and an extra foot of water.

Was it his imagination or was it already lighter? He peered over the screen and saw the restless gunners behind the four-inch and the pale blob of Hammond's cap. He listened to the sporadic rattle of machine-guns and watched a flare drifting palely above the headland. No doubt the enemy were probing with their patrols again and the defenders of the river line were searching for them in the treacherous tangle of jungle below the hills.

Corbett snapped, 'Give me a course for the centre channel, Pilot. I can't wait any longer.' He sounded hoarse.

Mallory said at length, 'Two five two, sir.'

Corbett grunted. 'Very good. Bring her round and increase to half-speed.' To Trewin he said, 'We've still got a mile before we are committed to the last approach. *Grayling* should be showing herself by then, eh?' Half to himself he added harshly, 'That ass Nye! If he gets stuck halfway downstream I'll have something to say about it!'

The gunboat gathered way, her powerful screws sending a steady tremble up through the bridge and the limbs of the men at their action stations.

The starboard bridge look-out suddenly jerked upright behind his glasses. 'Sir! A light in the water!' He fumbled for words. 'It's gone now, but I think it was a red light!'

Corbett leaned forward on his chair. 'I don't see anything!' Then, 'Slow ahead together!'

Trewin stood beside the look-out and peered over the wet steel. 'Are you sure? What sort of light?'

The look-out sounded confused. 'It was red, sir. Yes, I'm sure it was there. Very low down. Very small.'

His voice faltered as Corbett said impatiently, 'Well it's not there now!'

Mallory called, 'There are no buoys hereabouts either.'

The look-out said stubbornly, 'It was too small for a buoy.'

Corbett twisted in his chair as if it was restricting him. 'Oh, for God's sake! We'll be here all morning at this rate!' To Trewin he added, 'Go forrard and see if you can see anything from the stem. The drizzle might not mist your glasses from there.' He called after him, 'And get a damn move on!'

Trewin climbed down the ladder and hurried along the spray-dashed forecastle where he found Petty Officer Dancy already leaning over the guardrail, his figure crouched like a runner waiting for the gun.

'Anything Buffer?' Trewin dropped on one knee and pulled his glasses from inside his oilskin.

'Nah. I came when I heard the look-out, but it looks just as bloody horrible as it always does.'

Corbett's voice, metallic through a megaphone, made them both look back at the bridge. 'Well, is there anything, Number One? I'm still waiting!'

Trewin almost fell as Dancy seized his arm and pointed excitedly. 'I saw it, for God's sake! Look, sir, fine on the port bow!'

It was little more than a pale red glow, and appeared to be half submerged in the water

Dancy added in a grim tone, 'I think it's a lifejacket lamp, sir. There must be some poor bugger in the drink.'

'Maybe.' Trewin strained his eyes through the drizzle and wondered why they had not seen the light from the moment the look-out had reported it. It must have been hidden, but by what?

With sudden apprehension he clambered to his feet and ran back towards the bridge. As he reached the gun mounting he cupped his hands and yelled towards Corbett's hunched silhouette. 'Sir! Use the searchlight!'

Corbett shouted, 'Are you mad? We'll be visible for miles!' But something in Trewin's voice made him reconsider, and as

Trewin ran back to the bows the bridge searchlight cut the darkness apart in a blinding, glacier beam which threw Dancy's shadow ahead of the ship like a grotesque figurehead.

The light was only switched on for a few seconds, and as Trewin clung to the guardrail he imagined for one terrible moment that the ship was taking the wrong course and heading straight for a weed-covered sandbar.

Far away he heard Corbett yelling, 'Full astern together! *Emergency full speed!*' But his eyes remained riveted on the long, slime-covered thing which lay across the *Porcupine's* path, and as the deck jerked violently to the reversed thrust of the screws he knew it was the upturned keel of the *Grayling*.

The bobbing red light came from her stern, where a sodden corpse in a lifejacket twisted and turned with the current, caught firmly in one of the triple rudders.

Dancy yelled, 'Get back, sir! We're going to ram her!'

Without the searchlight Trewin's eyes were momentarily useless, and he had vague impressions of men throwing themselves to the deck and the whole ship shuddering like a mad thing in her efforts to pull clear.

When she struck he felt the pain of the collision lance up through his chest as if he too had been injured, and he lay quite still for several seconds listening to the scream and scrape of torn metal, the grinding embrace which seemed endless, until with a final convulsion the *Porcupine* jerked clear and backed away from her stricken consort.

Trewin lurched to his feet and watched the other hull rolling and yawning in a great pattern of exploding air bubbles. He could smell the stench of oil fuel, the harsher odours of fire and charred paintwork.

He tore his eyes away and ran after Dancy. Through screen doors and down half-lit ladders, his mind only barely recording his urgent journey. He saw the deserted messdeck and garish pin-ups on the lockers. Freshly laundered clothing hanging across deckhead pipes, and a half-eaten sandwich forgotten behind the mess radio.

Right forward, beyond the collision bulkhead, he stopped,

and with Dancy listened to the surging roar of inrushing water. He stared at the small, spurting jets around the edges of the massive watertight door and stood back as Dancy began to hammer the clips hard home.

Torches were flashing through the half-light, and he heard Hammond call, 'The lower store is flooding, Number One! I've got the men sealing it off right now.'

Trewin turned wearily. 'The cable locker is flooded, too. She feels heavier in the bows already.' He swore savagely. 'The *Grayling* never got to the Inlet. She could not have turned over in the shallows beyond the channel.'

He was half shocked and ashamed by the sense of relief which had replaced his first horror. For one terrible moment he had pictured the *Grayling*'s hull packed with helpless refugees as she turned over. Deep down he knew that he did not even care about them. Just one. And she was still in Talang.

His voice sounded calm as he said, 'Carry on here, Sub. I'll send you some men from the engine room to help with shoring up.'

Hammond said hoarsely, 'She was capsized! I couldn't believe it!'

A seaman skidded to a halt and said, 'Beg pardon, sir, but the cap'n wants you on the bridge at once.'

Trewin nodded and then said to Hammond, 'It might have been us if we had gone in first.' He rested his hand on his shoulder. 'It doesn't help those poor devils, but it's still a thought to carry around.'

The seaman was still there. 'The cap'n sounded as if he wanted you urgently, sir!'

Surprisingly, Corbett seemed almost cool as Trewin made his report. In the growing light his eyes were watching the bows and the sluggish lap of water around the dripping anchors. He said, '*Grayling* must have hit a mine. As she drifted clear I saw a great gash on her port bow. She always was top-heavy.' He sighed. 'But she was a good ship.' Then he continued more briskly, 'We seem to have escaped with little more than a buckled frame and one hole just abaft the stem. The storeroom below the forrard messdeck is flooded, but we can pump it out as soon as Nimmo has finished checking for other damage. The pumps should be able to control it. But the cable locker is another matter. That'll have to be dealt with at base.' He looked hard at Trewin. '*Porcupine* is a lucky ship, Trewin. But we can't rely on damn miracles every day.'

Trewin looked across at the waiting headland, grey tipped in the reluctant dawn. 'Do we go in, sir?'

'Immediately.' Corbett turned slightly as Mallory called, 'Chief reports no damage aft. He is ready to proceed.'

Corbett grunted. 'Good. Tell him to start the pumps and try and lift the bows by draining off his forrard fuel tanks. We shall still have enough for our present task.'

He waited until Mallory had passed his message and then snapped, 'Slow ahead together.'

As the *Porcupine* pushed slowly and painfully between the treacherous sandbars towards the Inlet the sky suddenly blossomed into a fiery red glow. Then, while the men on the bridge shaded their eyes, the explosions split the air apart, cowing them, beating them down with the power of its detonation. It went on and on, echoing round the hills and dulling every other shot and sound, as if they too were crushed into submission by its passing.

Trewin shouted, 'The fuel dump and magazine! The Army must have blown them up!' He watched the rising bank of black smoke and saw the underbellies of the low clouds flickering with red and orange reflections.

Corbett said, 'They must be falling back.' He sounded distant. 'We will have to get a move on. You and Mallory will take twenty men as soon as we reach the settlement and get ashore as quickly as you can. I want the whole settlement cleared in thirty minutes. Nurses, engineers, *everybody*, do you understand?'

Their eyes met. 'And if anyone refuses, sir?'

Corbett turned away. 'Bring them anyway. By force if necessary.'

The trees above the headland were tinged with reddish gold,

165

and Trewin imagined that somehow the explosions had even reached this far. But he heard Masters mutter, ' 'Ere comes the sun. I was beginnin' to wonder if I'd see another one!'

'It'll be the last one for you if you don't keep your mind on your work!' Corbett glared at him. 'Now get aft and hoist another ensign, the biggest you've got!'

The yeoman stared. 'Sir?'

Corbett looked at Trewin. 'When we steam upriver it may be the last visit for a very long time. I want this ship to look as if she means business, see.'

The shadow of the headland crept out to greet them, and Corbett said suddenly, 'I'm going round the ship myself to check the damage, Trewin. Take her upriver and keep away from the south bank.' His eyes glinted as a second ensign broke out from aft. 'That's more like it, eh? Give 'em something to remember at Talang.'

Mallory watched him go and asked, 'Do you think we'll *ever* come back here?'

Trewin watched the Inlet opening up across the sagging bows. He had not heard Mallory's question. He was still thinking of the slime-covered keel and the mocking red light from the entangled corpse.

He said quietly, 'Three down and three to go!'

*   *   *

As the watery sunlight finally broke through the drifting smoke and thinning patches of cloud the *Porcupine* rounded the last bend into the widest part of the river below the settlement. At first glance it was hard to recognise it as the same place. Only half the pier remained intact, the outward end having been reduced to a tangle of broken beams which jutted from the fast-moving stream like decayed teeth. The air was thick with smoke and noise and a drifting curtain of ashes and black smuts from the burning dumps further inland. At regular intervals the ground shook to the onslaught of bursting shells, most of which were hitting the ridge of hills beyond the settlement. But some cleared the high ground completely, and as the gunboat nudged cautiously into the remains of the pier the shells screamed overhead to plough deep amongst the jungle on the south bank before exploding and adding to the fires which were already there.

Quickly and nervously the landing party clambered across the pier and waited for Trewin and Mallory to join them. As the shells whimpered through the smoke and the air vibrated to their explosions the men crowded together as if for mutual support, their eyes on the shattered houses and the great craters along the dirt road.

Trewin said harshly, 'You know what to do! Two parties up the road on the double and get every available person here right away!' He pushed his holster across one hip and added to Mallory, 'They've had a few air raids too by the look of it.'

Mallory pointed at the remains of the stilted clubhouse. It was little more than a ruin, but miraculously the zinc bar still hung in position, a broken bottle at one end. 'Never did like the bloody place!' He grinned, but his eyes were dark with strain.

Trewin watched Petty Officer Kane trotting up the road with his men at his back. The sailors looked clean and alien against the chaos and charred houses, and he saw several of them glancing back at the ship as if to reassure themselves of safety.

As he followed them towards the road Trewin also looked back. The *Porcupine* was swinging gently at her mooring lines, and he could see the livid gash on her waterline by the stem, a smear like blood where *Grayling*'s red lead had broken the final embrace.

Then as the two officers quickened their pace they saw the soldiers. They were coming down the road towards the river. They came in groups or singly, running, or just dragging themselves along at the last stages of exhaustion. Hardly any of them were carrying arms, and some of them had thrown away everything but their boots and shorts in their eagerness to get away.

An officer was standing in the centre of the road, a revolver in his hand as he shouted hoarsely, 'Get back there! I'll shoot the first man to pass this point!'

But the soldiers hurried by not even sparing the officer a glance, some even brushing against his revolver, their eyes glazed and empty as they pushed on down the road.

The officer, he was a young major, lowered his revolver, and as individual soldiers thrust their way past he called out, 'You, Jackson! Tell them to stop and dig in! We can still hold the line!' To another, 'Here, Bill! Let's show 'em what we can do!'

Mallory said thickly, 'Christ, they're Aussies!'

The major saw them and called in a pleading voice, 'For God's sake, what can I do? They won't listen!'

Mallory asked, 'Are there any more behind you?' He seized the major's arm. 'Well, *are* there?'

The major stared at him vacantly. 'No ammunition left. No food. No goddam anything!' He shook his revolver at the jungle. 'Jesus bloody Christ, what did they expect us to do?'

Mallory said, 'Easy, mate! There's nothing you *can* do now!'

The soldiers had reached the river and were throwing themselves into the current and striking out for the opposite bank. Even those who could obviously not swim were following the blind stampede, heedless of everything but the need to escape the holocaust behind them. Not a single man made for the moored gunboat. It was as if she represented authority more than safety. Something to be avoided to the last.

Trewin saw several bobbing heads being swept downstream and heard the feeble cries above the din around him. He said grimly, 'We must get on with the job, Pilot. There's less time than ever now.'

Mallory was still staring at the last of the soldiers, his face creased with despair. 'I never thought I'd live to be ashamed of being an Aussie!' He turned to watch the major who was already striding back up the road towards the jungle. He was shouting out orders to the few remaining stragglers, his voice cracked and inhuman. Mallory added, 'What about him, for God's sake?'

Trewin said, 'He'd not thank you for helping him now.'

At that moment Kane appeared around the bend of the road, his eyes searching for his officers. He yelled, 'We're bringin' out the nurses now, sir!' He ducked as a shell ripped overhead and exploded against a tall tree in a blast of splinters. 'The 'ospital's been 'it, sir. A raid last night, they tell me.'

Trewin broke into a run. He ignored the little groups of figures, the sailors carrying improvised stretchers and a civilian engineer who was holding a caged bird and a bottle of gin. His eyes were fixed on a separate pall of smoke, and his mind was ringing with Kane's words. The hospital had been hit. Massey's red cross, his efforts to stay apart from the war, had been in vain.

In the clearing by the hospital he saw the lines of covered corpses, splattered with drying mud from the night's rain, the broken furniture and great fragments of charred timber from what must have been a direct hit.

He shouted wildly, 'Get those people out of it, Kane!' He saw the nurses, smoke-stained and dazed as they stood amongst the wreckage. They did not resist as the sailors pushed them towards the road. They were like children. Mindless children, Trewin thought.

He put his shoulder against a door at the side of the building and ducked as a sheet of corrugated iron scythed down from the remains of the roof. But for the splintered bookcase he would not have recognised it as the same room.

Massey lay on a sofa, his eyes open and staring at the sky overhead, his teeth bared in agony as he clutched a bloody bandage against his stomach. The girl was on her knees beside him, her black hair speckled with ashes. There was blood on her hands and her shirt was almost torn from her shoulders.

Trewin dropped beside her. 'We got here, Clare! For God's sake what happened?'

She did not look at him. 'It hit the centre ward. There were fifty people there. It was ablaze from end to end before we could get to them!' Her shoulders began to shake, but as

Trewin put his arm around her she said fiercely, 'Please help him! I—I can't do anything for him!'

Massey seemed to see Trewin for the first time. His lips opened and closed, and even that effort appeared to be tearing him apart. He gasped, 'Get her away, Lieutenant!' His eyes blinked. 'Oh, it's you!' He tried to smile. 'So Greville got here after all!' He clamped his teeth together, and Trewin saw the sweat breaking across his forehead and running down his beard. 'Just *get her out!*'

Mallory stepped through the door, his feet crunching on broken glass and splinters. He said harshly, 'I've sent most of them down.' He saw Massey and added, 'How is he?'

The girl turned and stared up at him. 'He can't be moved! I'm not leaving without him!' Her voice quivered and there were tears cutting through the grime on her face.

Trewin lifted his head. The gunfire had stopped, and he was conscious of the small sounds outside the shattered room. The hiss of charred wood, the distant cry of a wounded animal, or man.

He said, 'You must go now, Clare.'

She stared at him, her eyes wild, '*No!* I won't go!' To her father she said brokenly, 'Please! *Tell him!*'

Petty Officer Kane shouted from the clearing, 'Come on, sir! I can hear the bastards on the hill!' As if to back the urgency of his words Trewin heard the *Porcupine*'s siren. It was eerie and somehow frightening.

'You will go with Lieutenant Mallory.' He could not look at her. 'I will stay with your father.'

She screamed, 'No!' But as Mallory seized her arm she shouted, 'I hate you! I'll never forgive you!' Her other words were lost in an outburst of sobbing as Mallory picked her bodily from the floor and carried her into the sunlight.

Massey seemed to relax. 'Thank you.' He coughed, and two small threads of scarlet ran down his beard. 'I know what that cost you. What she means to you.'

Trewin looked at the sodden bandage. The sudden silence outside the ruins was worse than gunfire, and his whole being called out to him to run. To keep running, like those soldiers. But he could not move.

Massey muttered, 'Can't help me. Finished. Matter of minutes.' He rolled his eyes. 'All my work gone, Trewin. All finished.' He tried to lift himself on his elbows. 'You'll see her safe, won't you?' His eyes were desperate. 'She's had nothing out of life!'

Trewin nodded, not knowing what to say. 'Try to rest, Doctor.'

'I'll rest. Later.' He lay back, his eyes again on the sky. 'Tell Greville to look after himself.' One hand gripped Trewin's wrist with surprising force. 'He must be careful!'

Trewin looked away. Massey was obviously going fast. He was delirious.

But Massey continued in the same urgent tone, 'You must help him, Trewin! I know he trusts you.'

Somewhere a rifle cracked and the agonising screams were cut short before the echo had faded. Trewin tried to smile. 'He doesn't need my help, Doctor.'

His voice seemed to bring Massey a last reserve of life. He struggled up on one arm, his eyes blazing. 'He does, Trewin! He *does*!' His teeth were bared in what might have been a smile. 'He's a stubborn fool. But he's going blind!' His head lolled against Trewin's shoulder. 'Been treating him, but he can't be helped now. Nearly blind!'

He coughed, and this time the blood did not stop.

Trewin felt his pulse and then stood up. Hardly daring to allow his mind to function he stepped out into the sunlight and then, with Massey's last words ringing in his ears, began to run down the road towards the river.

The last mooring rope was flung clear as he was hauled up and over the bows, and he saw the guns swinging round to cover the bend in the road as the ship thrashed astern and started to edge her way towards the opposite bank.

The rescued wounded and the handful of refugees had been taken below, and of the girl there was no sign. Trewin had been dreading the reproach and hatred in her eyes. Now he would not have to tell her about her father's last minutes. Not now, not ever.

He climbed to the bridge and watched dully as Corbett leaned across the port screen to peer at the river bank as it swung to meet the gunboat in her tight turn. But I'll have to live with Massey's last words. He heard a shell whine overhead and felt the increased vibrations from the *Porcupine*'s screws. Another failure. Another bloody retreat.

He stared at Corbett's shoulders, seeing all the past moments, the occasions of uncertainty with sudden clarity and understanding. The time he had found Corbett in the darkened room with Massey. His unwillingness to attempt to enter the Inlet at night. It all made stark and terrible sense now.

Corbett turned and saw him leaning against the chart table. He said sharply, 'Take over the con, Trewin. I want to keep an eye on the shore, just in case they try and block our escape.' He waited and then asked, 'Are you all right?'

Trewin heard his mind screaming back at Corbett. Throwing the stupid excuses straight at those pale, opaque eyes which could see nothing but the need of this ship. He lurched past him and took his place behind the screen. In a voice he no longer recognised he replied, 'I've got her!' The cry in his mind continued. Tell him you know! *Tell him!*

Instead he said emptily, 'Massey's dead.'

When he looked again Corbett was resting his hands on the teak rail by the ladder, his face suddenly lined and old. 'He was a good doctor, Trewin.' He turned away, his hands groping for the ladder. 'More than that, he was a good man.'

He vanished down the ladder and Trewin heard the chart-room door slam. He looked at Mallory and the others. They were all watching him, as if they already shared his secret.

He rasped, 'Half ahead together!'

The settlement disappeared around the curve of the river, but Trewin knew that now he would never be free of it, or its secret.

The Impregnable Fortress

Leading Steward Yates leaned his buttocks comfortably against the wardroom sideboard and watched as Ching, the Chinese messman, refilled the officers' coffee-cups. He had just pulled the screens across the shuttles for the night, and had adjusted the fans to give maximum relief from the heavy, humid air which stayed as a reminder of the relentless heat.

He asked, 'Anythin' more, sir?'

Trewin sat at the head of the table, deep in thought, his eyes resting on the flat surface of his coffee. 'No, you can clear up, Yates.' He glanced across at Tweedie and Hammond, but they too seemed immersed in their own particular problems.

It was strange to feel the ship moving gently beneath him again. Ever since they had limped back to harbour from the fire and terror of Talang they had been committed to the indignity and danger of a crude stone slipway, while Chinese dockyard workers had done their best with limited facilities to repair the damage to the bows and restore the ship to fighting trim. There had been time to think and brood during the hot nights while the bombers droned above Singapore city and the sky flickered to bursting shells and the glow from burning buildings below.

For as the *Porcupine* completed her hasty repairs, so the Japanese reached the southern coastline of Malaya. There had been a fierce rearguard action to allow every possible group of soldiers to retreat to the island, and then, as the last organised resistance of Australians and troops of the Argyll and Sutherland Highlanders had been withdrawn, the Causeway had been destroyed and the final link with the mainland cut. It was like hoisting the drawbridge of a great fortification, and with it

Singapore settled down to withstand attack and siege for as long as was required.

The Japanese forces entered Johore Bahru at the close of January to find it deserted. Like a ghost town, with only the buildings and abandoned animals to watch their jubilant capture. Within two days the enemy's guns were firing across the water, and at night, even aboard the *Porcupine*, they could hear the mutter of the bombardment like an ever-present threat.

The final loss of Malaya had had a mixed effect on the island. There was new determination amongst the fighting men, brought about mainly by a simplification of objectives and purpose. Their strength was more condensed, and even the attacking aircraft no longer had it all their own way. Singapore's own fighters flew to meet them without a break, and the island was littered with wrecked aircraft, friend and foe alike.

But there was plenty of apathy and stupidity, too. Trewin had spoken to an officer whose duty it was to dig fresh defences for the infantry. He had told him how the secretary of a golf club had refused point-blank to allow slit trenches to be dug on his greens without proper authority. And even the rumble of the distant artillery would not budge him.

The harbour was busy with two-way traffic. As the days dragged past Trewin had watched the troopships bring more reinforcements to the island and leave almost immediately, their decks crammed with women and children, dependants of those left to defend and fight.

The evacuation had had a marked effect on the *Porcupine*. Many of her company were married and had settled down years earlier to Far East service. There was an air of gloom over the whole ship, something quite different and apart from past events and common suffering.

Perhaps now that the *Porcupine* was afloat again things might improve, if only out of the harsh necessities of survival.

Trewin stirred his coffee and wondered how Corbett was getting on. Within a few days of the ship being hoisted on to the slipway Corbett had been ordered to take the remainder of the group back to sea. He had sailed in *Beaver* to take overall charge of the motley collection of craft which the admiral had formed into one force to help forestall any attempt by the enemy to land isolated groups of shock troops. Apart from the two gunboats, Corbett had taken three trawlers, an M.L. and one converted yacht. It was not much of a force, but as the admiral had said before they had sailed, 'We must put all our shoulders to the wheel now! Not a man or a ship can be wasted!'

It was difficult to see through the confident daily orders and bulletins, and quite impossible to know exactly how safe the defences really were.

The reinforcements were heartening, and only a few days earlier the fleet had been joined by the veteran cruiser *Exeter*, heroine of the River Plate battle. Her name seemed to represent another war to Trewin. She came from a time when the lines between friends and enemies were clear-cut, when people still believed that to win a war you merely had to be in the right.

The quartermaster's voice echoed harshly through the tannoy. 'Hands darken ship! Duty part of the watch fall in!'

Trewin smiled to himself in spite of his thoughts. Routine went on, no matter what was happening elsewhere.

He tried not to let his thoughts stray back to Corbett. By throwing himself into the work of getting the ship ready for service, with all the additional burdens of temporary command, he had managed to shy away from what he knew must be done. On the slow trip down from Talang he had found himself watching Corbett's every move, had even gone out of his way to test him with a cunning he never knew he possessed. He had wanted to prove Massey's dying words to be imaginary, part of a mistake, and up to the last moments he had still hoped that Corbett would surprise him. He had offered the captain hastily scribbled signals, and felt his heart sink as Corbett had made casual excuses for leaving them until later to read, or had asked Trewin to summarise them for him.

'Be good training for you, Trewin,' he had remarked on more than one occasion.

His mind had gone over all the little remarks Corbett had made in the past. His testy complaints on smartness or the cleanliness of paintwork. He knew now that they had been part of a carefully planned façade, and he could almost feel pity for Corbett and the misery he must be enduring.

Trewin had even considered going to see the admiral about it, but had dismissed the idea instantly. He knew about Corbett, and as first lieutenant he had to do something about it.

But as a man he knew he would have to tell Corbett himself.

Tweedie, who had been reading one of his accumulated letters from home with laborious concentration, sat up with a jerk and threw it on the table. 'God Almighty! They've been an' put some snotty-nosed evacuee kids in me new bungalow!' He glared at the others as if he could not believe it. 'Bloody Battersea kids at that!'

Hammond asked politely, 'Does Mrs. Tweedie object, Guns?'

Tweedie scowled. 'Object? No, she bloody well seems to enjoy it!' He stood up violently. 'All me flower beds. All that work! I'll bet the little sods'll trample over everything.' He snatched up a torch and peered at his watch. 'I'll go an' do me rounds. I need to think about this.'

He stamped outside and Hammond said, 'I'm sorry for any of the lads with a scruffy messdeck tonight.'

Trewin watched him thoughtfully. He knew that Hammond had been ashore trying to persuade his Jacqui to take a place in one of the evacuation ships. He knew from Hammond's worried face that he had failed. He asked, 'What will your girl friend do, Sub?'

Hammond shrugged. 'I keep telling her she must go. It's not safe here, no matter how good the defences are.' He stood up and walked restlessly to the sideboard. 'I—I want to marry her and send her home to England.'

Trewin thought of the girl's calm, sad eyes as she had watched Hammond at the New Year party. Quite apart from being a bit older than Hammond, it was unlikely that his family would welcome a half-caste girl into the fold without some protest. His father was an admiral. One of several in a long line of naval ancestors.

Trewin said quietly, 'Did she say why she would not go?'

Hammond stared at him and then grinned awkwardly. 'You know damn well why it is!' He became serious again, 'I had a letter from my father yesterday. Just between ourselves, he said he's arranging a transfer for me. To a destroyer this time. So you see, if I can't get Jacqui fixed up before that we may never get together.' His mouth hardened. 'And I happen to love her. I really do.'

Trewin put his coffee down. It was stone cold. Hammond's casual remark about his father opened up yet another door in his understanding. His was a different world, where things were 'arranged'. To Trewin they just happened. He could easily picture Hammond in a few years' time. Cool and confident, with all his youthful uncertainties left behind in the *Porcupine*. Maybe his father had found out about the girl and was using this transfer for more than a mere advancement.

Hammond looked up at the ship's crest and said with sudden desperation, 'I don't want to leave the *Porcupine*. Not yet.' He swung round and faced Trewin across the table. 'What do you think I should do?' He spread his hands awkwardly. 'You've been around more than I have. You must have some ideas.'

Trewin looked away. 'It's for you to decide.' He knew his voice was cold but he could not control it. Hammond's faith, his simple way of looking at things, had touched his reserve like a raw nerve.

Even as Hammond had been discussing Jacqui, Trewin's mind had strayed again to Clare Massey. She was always close by, haunting him with her bitter words, the desperate sadness of her eyes. Yet he had hardly seen her since Mallory had carried her from the bombed hospital. When the ship had reached harbour to unload the dazed and injured passengers he had seen her briefly from the upper bridge. A slim, upright figure as she had climbed down into a launch, one of Corbett's jackets slung across her torn shirt like a cape. She had not looked back, although he had sensed that she knew he was there, watching her.

He had been to tell the captain's wife that Corbett was sailing in the *Beaver*. He could have sent a messenger, but he wanted to see the girl, although he knew he was unwanted. He had caught sight of her sitting with Corbett's son at the back of the house and had gone to speak to her. He had tried to tell her of her father's last moments alive, that there was nothing anyone could have done for him.

She had looked up at Trewin's worried face, her eyes shadowed by her dark hair. 'Then there's nothing more to be said, is there, Lieutenant?' She had turned her face away. 'You should have let me stay, too. Now please leave me alone.'

Corbett's wife had been waiting beside the windows. She had been wearing a silk robe, her tanned face fresh from a shower. She had said, 'You'd better leave her. She's still shocked.' She had tossed her damp hair as if it were of no importance. 'What about a drink, Ralph? You can probably do with it.' It was not just the casual use of his name which flashed a warning. There was something very inviting in Mildred Corbett. She had an almost animal warmth about her, as if it was all she could do to control her inner emotions.

As he had made his excuse to leave she had brushed against him, letting her breast move over his arm, while she had kept her eyes on his with that bright, direct stare he had seen at the party.

'Well, anytime you're passing, Ralph. Anytime.'

As he had walked down the drive he had heard her humming to herself. Perhaps she was just another reason for his inability to think clearly about Corbett. Angrily he told himself that it was not his concern. Corbett's wife and career were nothing to do with it. Corbett's stubborn conceit was the only thing to consider. He must realise what he was doing, the risks he was taking with lives other than his own.

He looked back at Hammond and said evenly, 'I'm sorry, Sub. I didn't mean to jump down your throat.' He saw Hammond relax slightly. 'But I still think it has to be your decision. She may feel worried about going to England. This is her home.' He bit his lip. He was really speaking about Clare. He tried again. 'Things have moved so fast, it is hard to plan anything too far ahead.'

Hammond slumped in an armchair. 'Two months since the Japs landed in Malaya. Just two months. And now, here we are back in Singapore.' He sighed. 'It doesn't make sense.'

Trewin watched Ching moving around the wardroom gathering up fallen newspapers and replacing them in their rack. He looked shrunken and vaguely sad. We've all got our worries, he thought. Hammond and his girl, Tweedie and his bungalow in Hampshire. And no doubt Ching was feeling a personal disgrace for himself and the whole ship. In the past few days eight of the Chinese sailors had deserted, vanished without a clue. They had probably heard the rumours that the Japs were making savage examples of the Chinese they had captured in Malaya. After years of fighting them in Manchuria and Indo-China they were apparently doing their utmost to butcher any found in their advance, partly to impress and cow the Malays, but mainly it seemed for their own amusement. *Porcupine*'s Chinese sailors were probably trying to get back to their families, and who could blame them? But Ching felt it deeply. It was a matter of honour. Of loyal service. In some ways he was rather like Corbett, Trewin decided.

Maybe Corbett would explode when he heard about the desertions and blame him for them. Trewin found himself hoping he would. By losing his temper and his control he might be able to have it out with Corbett, once and for all.

He thought of Mallory, ashore drinking with some woman or other. *He* would not hesitate, nor would he worry about personal involvements. Only that evening, just before he had stepped into the shore-boat, he had said calmly, 'It's better already with you in command. You ought to keep it!' He had looked towards the distant hills, his eyes dark and expressionless. 'A word in the right place would do it fair enough. Nobody amongst the brass likes Corbett. He's a has-been.' He had cocked one eyebrow. 'So why not give it a try?'

Now, looking back, there seemed more to Mallory's advice than he had first seen.

He stood up, defeated and angry. 'I'm going to turn in, Sub. I want a couple of hours before the night's "hate" gets going.'

Hammond stood alone in the wardroom and then ran his fingers over the ship's crest. 'Touch me not.' He spoke half to himself, and was really thinking of the girl. 'It could have been written for you, Jacqui!'

* * *

Trewin awoke with a start to find the cabin flooded with light and Tweedie's hand dragging roughly at his shoulder. He struggled into a sitting position and stared at the clock. He had been asleep less than half an hour. He said, 'What is it, Guns? Another raid?'

Tweedie shook his head. 'The admiral wants you ashore double quick.' He jerked his thumb at the door. 'There's a launch alongside waiting right now.'

Trewin shook the dullness of sleep from his mind and began to fumble for his shoes. He asked, 'Do you know why?'

Tweedie looked away. 'The Japs 'ave landed on the island. I got it from the cox'n of the launch. The bastards are crossing the Johore Strait in a full-scale attack!' He sounded as if he was still unwilling to believe it.

Trewin snatched his cap, his mind now working at full speed. 'Are all the libertymen off yet?'

'All but three petty officers, *and* the pilot.'

'Right. Tell the chief to flash up and get ready to get under way. Call all hands and prepare for sea, and make sure that nobody tries to desert.'

Tweedie eyed him bleakly. 'The Chinks, d'you mean?'

'I mean anybody!' There was a rasp in his reply. 'Some of our people have got native women ashore who weren't evacuated. They'll want to see them, to make sure they're safe at a time like this.' He jammed on his cap and added flatly, 'So see that they stay aboard!'

He ran on deck where Hammond was waiting by the rail above the swaying grey shape of a powerful launch. It was very dark, but the sky was paler towards the north-west, and he could hear the steady rumble of gunfire.

As the launch shoved off from the side he called to Hammond, 'Get hold of Mallory, and send someone for the P.O.s. They'll be in the harbour canteen.' Hammond's reply was lost in the throaty growl from the launch's screws as it curved towards the inner harbour.

Trewin hardly noticed the looming shapes of moored ship or the busy bow-waves from other launches. He was thinking about Clare, of the sudden closeness of new danger.

At the steps he found an open car waiting for him, a marine at the wheel. At his side was another with a sub-machine gun across his knees. They both looked grim and tense.

But as the car roared through the outskirts of the city Trewin found time to wonder if the threat was as serious as Tweedie had made out. There were plenty of people in the streets, and at least one cinema had a 'house full' sign at its doors.

He craned forward, suddenly realising that the car was not taking the usual route. But in answer to his question the driver yelled, 'The admiral 'as changed 'is H.Q., sir! 'E's on the other side of the town, by Kallang Airfield.' He swore savagely as a crowd of shouting figures jumped across the shaded headlights and swayed drunkenly at the side of the road. 'You'd think they *wanted* to be killed!'

They paused momentarily at a barbed-wire barrier, and after exchanging shouts with armed sentries, roared forward again towards a low-roofed, concrete bunker, where a messenger greeted Trewin with something like relief. 'The admiral's waiting, sir. This way.'

Trewin found Fairfax-Loring beside a map table surrounded by busy staff officers and jangling telephones. The air was thick with tobacco smoke and the urgent voices of officers who received a constant barrage of demands and questions from the ever-ringing telephones.

The admiral looked up as Trewin entered. His face was grim, and his normally immaculate drill uniform was darkly patched with sweat. 'Good. You got here then.' He gestured at the map. 'They've landed in force to the north-west. About four places, as far as I can make out. Corbett's group ran right into some of them at the entrance to the Johore Strait.' He scowled. 'The M.L. and one of the trawlers have been sunk, and *Prawn* has been damaged, how badly I don't know.' He swung round and barked, 'Flags, have you got any more news?'

Lieutenant Hughes looked remarkably calm. 'Nothing, sir. I'm still trying to get some confirmation.'

The admiral stamped his foot. 'Well, get a bloody move on!' Then to Trewin he said heavily, 'I want you to put to sea immediately. Can you do it?'

Trewin replied. 'We are very low on fuel, sir. We've only just come off the slipway. But I have already ordered the chief to get steam up.'

The admiral nodded. 'That will have to suffice. Sail as soon as you can and head for the Strait. Nothing larger than a gunboat can get close enough to get a crack at the bastards. They've got their artillery pounding across from the mainland, and some heavy naval units coming down the Malacca Strait to support them.' He was breathing heavily. 'I have been assured that if we can control the rate of landings the Army can contain the situation.' He glared at Trewin's doubtful face. 'God, it's not the end of the world! We were *expecting* them to try and land sooner or later!' He calmed himself. 'General Percival the G.O.C., is pushing up his reserves, and in twenty-four hours we should have either killed or surrounded the Japs who have managed to land.'

Hughes called, 'The twenty-second Australian Brigade have reported that more of the enemy have crossed the Strait, sir. They're using rafts and rubber boats.'

An army liaison officer said quietly, 'So blowing the Causeway didn't make all that difference?'

The admiral turned and stared at him. 'I could have told *you* that! You've only got to look at the chart to realise that

Causeway or not the water's only four feet deep there at low tide!' He banged the table loudly so that some of his staff turned to watch him. 'Bloody fools, they couldn't organise a bottle party in a brewery without some idiot forgetting to bring a corkscrew!' He wiped his forehead and looked at Trewin again. 'So get going. Join up with the group and do what you can. I wouldn't drop this in your lap, but I'm hard-pressed for officers right now.'

Trewin smiled faintly. 'I'll manage, sir.'

The admiral studied him thoughtfully. 'I hope so.' Then he conjured up a shadow of his old grin. 'Yes, I'm sure you can!' He turned away as another officer began to shout into a telephone. 'One thing is certain. We're not giving up the island!'

Trewin hurried out into the darkness and found the car waiting for him, the engine still ticking over. An air raid was in progress, but it was far away on the other side of the city, the bursting flak making small necklaces of red and gold beyond the darkened buildings.

He said, 'Put your foot down.' As the car bounced forward he added, 'Go round the other way, driver. I want to stop for a minute at Commander Corbett's house.' He regretted the impulse immediately, but forced himself to remain silent as the car swung around the blacked-out streets, its tyres screaming in protest.

Fairfax-Loring might be right about the ability of the defenders. But if not . . . He felt the sweat cold on his face as the car roared along the deserted road and skidded to a halt outside the low white building.

The driver said tightly, 'You won't be long, sir?' He was looking towards the glow in the sky.

'Two minutes.' Trewin ran through the gates and groped his way across the deep porch, recalling with sudden clarity the brightness and gaiety of the New Year's party. He thought too of Corbett, fighting with his motley collection of craft against the enemy. Thank God for Keates of the *Beaver*, he thought. He at least would be able to cope, if anyone could.

A sleepy Malay servant answered his knock, buttoning his

white jacket as he ushered Trewin inside the door before switching on the lights.

Trewin said, 'Where is your mistress?'

The man shrugged. 'She out.' He rubbed his eyes dazedly. 'She bin out all evening, sir.'

Trewin ground his teeth. 'Well, when she returns tell her to pack some things.' He felt like hitting the man's blank features. 'Just in case she has to leave, see?'

'Who is that?' There was a step in the passageway. 'Is that a visitor, Mali?'

Trewin stood quite still as Clare Massey stepped into the light, her slim figure shrouded in a dressing gown. She saw him and stopped, one hand at her throat, the other pushing the hair away from her face.

Trewin walked towards her, feeling her eyes fixed on his face. He said quietly, 'I came to tell you. To warn you.' He heard the marine driver revving his engine meaningly. 'The Japs have landed on the island. I think you should get ready to leave. Just in case things get out of hand.' He faltered, not knowing what to add.

She said, 'Thank you, Mali. You go back to bed.' As the servant hurried away she added. 'Would you come into the other room? The boy is asleep there.'

He followed her along the narrow passage and into the room he remembered so well. Corbett's son was asleep in his bed, his face away from a small light, one arm around his teddy bear.

Then the girl said quietly, 'I will tell Mrs. Corbett what you said.'

In the silence of the small room Trewin could hear her breathing, could smell the faint perfume of her dark hair. He said, 'I really came to see you. Commander Corbett is still at sea, and I have to take *Porcupine* to join him.' She did not turn, but he could see her fingers gripping the sleeves of her gown. 'Things may get worse. I think they'll probably get very bad. I expect you will be evacuated, and I may not see you again. I just wanted to tell you . . .'

She said suddenly, 'What did my father say?' Her voice was very quiet but controlled. 'What did he tell you before he died?'

Trewin replied slowly, 'He told me what you meant to him. He died with the wish that you should be safe.'

'Is that all?'

Trewin pictured the charred hospital, the sudden loneliness and terror. 'There was not much time. But I waited until the end. That I promise you.'

She turned and looked up at him, her face in shadow from the lamp. 'Thank you.' Her hands moved vaguely against the gown. 'I don't know what to say. Once before you made me feel ashamed. Now I do not know what I can add to repair the wrong I did you.'

Trewin said, 'I understood exactly what you were feeling.' He heard the horn gain. 'I will have to leave now.'

The urgency in his tone seemed to bring her to life. She said, 'When my mother died in a fire Greville Corbett saved my life. After that I had only my father, and his work out here.' Her shoulders moved in what might have been a shrug. 'Now he is dead, and Greville is away fighting.'

Trewin said gently, 'Your father told me about Corbett's eyes. He's been going blind for some time. He's kept it to himself, but there's too much at stake now to keep it secret.' He added quietly, 'So I expect he will be sent to a shore job. Then you will be able to keep in touch.' He felt helpless. 'It's not much, Clare, but it's something to hold on to.'

She was looking fixedly into his face, her eyes shining through the shadow. 'I never knew about his eyes!' She stepped forward and gripped Trewin's hand. 'Poor Greville, but you must try and help him. Make him see it's for his own good as well as yours.'

He replied, 'I'm not thinking of myself, Clare.'

She nodded. 'I know.' She kept hold of his hand as he stepped back into the passage. 'But I am.'

They walked to the door and stood with the cool air on their faces. Then she asked quietly, 'Why did you come here? What was the real reason?' She pulled her hand away and added firmly, 'I *must* know.'

Trewin found that it was quite easy to answer. 'Because I love you, Clare. I've wanted you since we first met. Your father seemed to understand that, too.'

She said, 'And now *I* know.' She looked towards the gates. 'Come back soon. I won't go until you tell me again. Properly.' Then she stepped close to him and kissed him briefly.

He tasted the tears on her cheek and felt the determination of her body not to break down. He said, 'I'll get back. Somehow.' Then he turned and ran back along the drive and threw himself into the car.

When he looked back the house was already lost in the dust from the racing wheels, but in his mind he could still see her face, just as he could feel the touch of her mouth against his own.

He pressed his head in his hands, feeling suddenly lost and defeated. What was the use? It was hopeless before he had started. And if Corbett was taken from the *Porcupine* there was less chance than ever of getting back to see her. She would disappear, and his memory would soon fade from her mind, left behind with the rest of the pain which this place had come to mean to her.

He barely noticed the transfer from car to launch, and when he climbed aboard the gunboat he had to force his mind to grapple with the protests and problems which waited for his attention.

Chief Petty Officer Nimmo, stubbornly anxious to point out the dangers of too little fuel. Mallory, bleary-eyed in the wardroom with a pot of black coffee. And Tweedie making it all too obvious that whereas he was prepared to serve under Trewin at anchor it was another matter entirely to have him in command at sea.

Trewin pushed his way to the upper bridge, suddenly anxious to get away, if only to speed the possibility of return. 'Stand by to slip from the buoy in five minutes!' He knew his voice was hard, but he no longer cared. 'Hands will go to action stations as soon as we leave the harbour limits.'

Only when his eye fell on Corbett's empty chair did he realise exactly what lay ahead. He had often disagreed with Corbett's decisions, but decisions they had been. Now his was the strength or weakness which could commit the ship and her company to the fates of *Shrike* or *Grayling*, and all the others.

Hammond said quietly, 'Engine room standing by, sir.'

Trewin rested his hands on the screen, feeling the waiting power pulsating gently through his palms. His hands felt clammy and he was sweating badly.

'Very well. Slow ahead together.' He heard the telegraphs clang beneath him. 'Slip!'

The single wire snaked back through the fairleads and he felt the ship edging forward, nudging the buoy aside with calm indifference.

'Starboard fifteen. Half ahead together!'

He watched the mounting froth creaming back from the bows. The *Porcupine* too seemed glad to be leaving the land behind.

II
Just a Matter of Time

Mallory straightened his back above the chart table and said sharply, 'Alter course now. Steer two five eight!'

Trewin nodded but remained motionless behind the screen as Mallory relayed the order to the wheelhouse. His whole body felt tensed as if to receive a blow, and he was conscious of the steady engine beats as the *Porcupine* steamed through the next leg of the narrow Sinki Strait. It was nerve-racking and frightening, and he had the feeling that the ship would strike full tilt into a jutting headland or charge across a lurking sandbar. The ship was steering into complete blackness, broken only by the outflung arrowhead of her white bow-wave. What he had first thought to be a bank of unbroken cloud was in fact a drifting pall of smoke, and only occasionally could he see the stars beyond, aloof and indifferent to the world of men.

Mallory said, 'I think we should reduce speed.' He waited for Trewin to reply and added harshly, 'You'll rip her guts out if you strike now!'

Trewin ignored him and concentrated his full attention on a darker path beyond the starboard bow. He knew Mallory had been against his choice of route, and now that the ship was committed to this treacherous, unlighted channel he had to force himself to ignore the warning which moved through his mind with each swing of the screws. By taking this channel between the offshore island around the south-west coast he could save an hour. *Or lose the ship*, the warning voice persisted.

He saw the wash break into dancing spectres against the foot of a tall-sided cliff less than fifty yards abeam, and held his breath until the jutting spur of land had dropped astern into the darkness.

The gun below the bridge squeaked on its mounting as it was trained towards the next piece of channel, and he could imagine the men at the controls straining their eyes into the drifting smoke and waiting for the first tell-tale sign of an enemy.

The gunfire was still constant, but more muffled by the cliffs and hills, and every so often the upper bridge was lit by brief, savage explosions from inland, which made the tense look-outs and gunners stand out like crude waxworks before they vanished once more into one solid outline.

A feeble green light moved to greet them, and as the *Porcupine* dashed past without faltering Trewin saw that it was a warning lantern hanging dismally from a listing freighter which had run aground five days earlier after being bombed and set ablaze.

Mallory said, 'That bloody wreck gives me a good fix. We seem to be more or less where I estimated.' He sounded doubtful.

'Well, you're the navigator!' Trewin found himself grinning, but his face felt like a mask. 'Just another few miles and we'll be clear.'

A telephone buzzed and Petty Officer Dancy said, 'Masthead reports a fire ahead, sir. A ship by the look of it.'

Trewin licked his lips. They were parched and dry. The look-out could probably see over the next clump of islets to where the channel widened out to meet and mingle with the entrance to the Johore Strait.

Mallory said, 'Alter course again. Steer three two zero!'

Trewin watched the thin line of breakers moving past the hull and then said, 'All guns prepare to open fire. And tell the chief to stand by for emergency full speed!' He wiped the mist from his glasses and trained them over the screen as the dark edge of the nearest islet hardened in a new flickering glare, low down, somewhere close inshore.

As the *Porcupine* nosed out into open water a star-shell burst with blinding brilliance less than a mile ahead. For a moment it was impossible to see anything but the searing glare pinioned between the unruffled water and the drifting smoke above.

Then a look-out yelled, 'There's the *Beaver*, sir! Fine on the port bow!'

Trewin shifted his glasses and watched as the distant gun-boat was suddenly bracketed by two tall water-spouts. There were so many flashes from both the mainland and the island that it was not possible to gauge the bearing and distance of the hidden battery. He saw the *Beaver* swinging in a fierce turn, her bow-wave silver in the drifting flare, her guns firing back over her port quarter, their muzzles high-angled for maximum range. Following in her wake were the two remaining armed trawlers, their guns joining in the barrage as they zigzagged between another set of water-spouts, their hulls shining like glass from the spray thrown up by the Japanese shells.

Then as the last piece of islet moved away to starboard Trewin saw the *Prawn*. She was nudging into a smooth-backed sandbar, if not actually aground, and smoke was billowing out of her aft superstructure, where tiny figures flitted across the eager flames, their efforts to control the blaze made puny by distance.

Mallory said between his teeth, '*Prawn*'s had a direct hit by the look of it. Her after gun has gone, and so has her mainmast.'

They ducked as a shell shrieked overhead and exploded with a vivid flash on a small islet far abeam.

Trewin shouted, 'Full ahead together!' Then to Mallory, 'Get a fix on that gun if it fires again!' Another shell whipped above the bridge and he added, 'There! Did you get it?'

Mallory yelled, 'About green four five! The Japs must be firing from Singapore Island itself!'

Trewin watched the flare drifting slowly towards the sea and said. 'That would make them about five miles inland already!'

Masters touched his arm. '*Beaver*'s signalling, sir!' His face looked blue in the eerie light. 'Signal reads, "The group will retire forthwith and return to base."'

The *Beaver* was still swinging in a wide arc, her masts and upperworks dipping to the power of her screws. Trewin saw her signal lamp stabbing urgently from the bridge and imagined Corbett watching the *Porcupine* and waiting for her to respond.

The *Beaver's* outline shone briefly in a bright scarlet glare, and beyond her one of the trawlers reeled out of line and began to capsize in a welter of flames and escaping steam.

'Direct hit, sir!' Masters turned back to Trewin. 'Shall I acknowledge?'

Dancy was still staring at the *Prawn*. He said suddenly, 'They're jettisoning coal by the looks of it. By God, they've got that fire nearly out!' He waved his cap in the air. 'That's right, lads! We'll show the buggers!'

Trewin watched the *Beaver* as she surged towards him, the last trawler close on her tail like a shadow. There was no sign of the armed yacht, so she was probably sunk also. Two trawlers, an M.L. and a small pitiful yacht, all sunk within hours. With sudden desperation he stared towards the *Prawn*. Now that the flare had almost died he could see that the fires were nearly out, while from alongside her listing hull he could see the white splashes of coal cascading into the shallow water as Adair, her captain, fought to save his ancient command.

Trewin made up his mind, 'Signal *Prawn*. Ask what assistance she requires.' He waited until Phelps had started to use his lamp and added. 'We'll not leave her now!'

'From *Prawn*, sir. "One direct hit from heavy shell. Engine room flooded but ship still afloat. Would appreciate your shoulder to cry on!"'

Trewin smiled tightly. 'Acknowledge. We will go alongside and take her in tow.'

Phelps came back in less than a minute. 'She says, "God bless you!", sir.'

'Tell her that porcupines are very partial to prawns, Bunts!'

Trewin felt Mallory gripping his sleeve. 'What is it, Pilot?'

'You're not going to do it, surely?' His face was inches from Trewin's. 'The enemy has the range! They'll be on to us as soon as another flare goes up!' When Trewin did not answer he shouted, 'Corbett left that trawler, so why do we have to go after *Prawn*? Are you trying to prove something?'

Masters called, 'Signal from *Beaver*. "Obey my last order instantly!"'

Trewin felt a strange anger moving through him. Corbett was watching him, just as if he were here on this bridge. He was afraid of losing his precious *Porcupine*, just as he mistrusted his first lieutenant's competence to deal with the task of saving *Prawn*.

Savagely he said, 'Well, if he won't do it, *I* will!' He pushed Mallory away, adding, 'Now get aft and turn to all available hands to rig towing gear, and be sharp about it!'

He watched Mallory groping for the ladder and looked towards the *Beaver*. She was sweeping past about half a cable clear. He could see the pale blobs of faces on her bridge, the distant gunfire reflected in the raised binoculars along her screen. He turned away. 'Starboard fifteen. Slow ahead together.' *Porcupine*'s stern would be a better reply to Corbett than any signal, he thought bleakly.

He winced as another flare exploded almost directly overhead. He heard some of the men whispering with alarm and said, 'Now we can see what we're about!' He made himself watch the narrowing strip of water between the two gunboats, but half of his mind still rebelled and waited for the first, obliterating salvo.

'Midships. Port ten.' In the harsh light he could see every detail of the *Prawn*'s shattered deck, even the glittering mounds of discarded coal on the sandbar below her hull. The coal had definitely saved her. The shell's lethal power had dissipated itself inside one of the bunkers instead of breaking the old gunboat's back or ploughing into one of the magazines.

'Stop engines!' He saw someone waving his cap at him from the *Prawn*'s bridge, but turned as Dancy called, 'All ready aft, sir!'

It was all taking too long, although he knew from the position of the drifting flare that it had only been a matter of minutes and seconds.

There was an explosion like a thunderclap from the opposite side, and as he turned he saw a giant column of water shoot skywards while the deck heaved beneath his feet as if on a tidal wave. A shell had exploded in the shallow water merely yards away. As the white column fell in a blinding torrent across the bridge the men staggered back coughing and gasping, their eyes and mouths filled with salt and the stench of cordite.

Dancy was calling, 'Wheelhouse reports that the wheel don't answer, sir!'

Trewin stared at him for several seconds, waiting for his voice and wits to return. He spat the filthy water from his mouth. 'Get aft and find out the damage.' In a calmer tone he continued, 'All departments report damage immediately.'

When he looked again he saw that the *Prawn* was almost touching and already they were joined by dripping heaving lines. On one was attached a strange hawser, and as he watched he saw the thick towing line moving slowly across the narrow strip of trapped water between the two ships.

Aloud he muttered, 'We'll use *Prawn* like a drogue and rely on the engines for steering.'

A messenger thrust a telephone into his hand. 'Engine room, sir.'

Trewin hid the sudden anxiety from the watching men and said, 'Yes, Chief, what is it?'

'Just been having a look at the steering gear, sir. Two of the rudders are buckled right over. You'll not be able to use 'em until the dockyard has fixed 'em.'

Trewin waited, hardly daring to hope. Then he asked, 'No other hull damage?'

He heard Nimmo laugh. He sounded a long way away. 'Not a bloody thing. She's a tough old bird, this one.'

As Trewin replaced the handset Nimmo was still laughing. 'Tow secured, sir!'

'Very well.' He glanced shorewards but there was no tell-tale flash from the searching battery. Maybe it had been engaged by the island's defenders, he thought vaguely. 'Slow ahead port!'

Like a crab the gunboat veered away from the other ship and then took the strain on the unreeling tow rope. Twice it jerked bar taut from below the surface, and Trewin caught his breath, waiting for it to part. Then *Prawn* without power and *Porcupine* with no rudder would be drifting targets awaiting the dawn and any enemy gunner who chose to take advantage of them.

Mallory scrambled on to the bridge soaked in water and filthy. He gasped, 'She's taking the strain!' Then he shook his head. 'You mad bastard! You're as bad as bloody Corbett!' But he was grinning.

'Just to please you I'll take the main Strait this time.' Trewin could feel his hands shaking violently. 'We shall have to go very slowly.' Over his shoulder he snapped, 'Slow ahead starboard!'

Mercifully the flare dipped and died with startling suddenness, and above the mutter of duelling artillery and the thud of engines he heard *Prawn*'s men cheering.

He said, 'We'll try and keep going due south for an hour or so. Then I'll signal for a tug.' Now that the actual moment of decision was past he found he could not stop speaking his mind aloud.

Mallory replied quietly, 'Corbett will not be pleased, whatever you do or say now.'

Trewin thought of what he must say to Corbett when he reached harbour, and wondered what Mallory would think if he told him.

He said steadily, 'Just watch the tow, Pilot. Leave the diplomacy to me, all right?'

Mallory shrugged and then walked to the rear of the bridge. Under his breath he commented, 'Rather you than me, my friend!'

By the screen Trewin stood alone with his thoughts. It would be a very slow crawl back to harbour, Corbett would have plenty of time to work up a rage and prepare to act against him for disobeying his orders. Deep down Trewin wondered if he had deliberately given Corbett a weapon to use against him, if only to ease the pain of what he had still to do.

He heard the telegraphs ring violently as Mallory wrestled with the engines and tried to keep the tow in line astern, and smiled in spite of his uncertainty.

With or without Corbett, the *Porcupine* seemed to have a life and mind all of her own, he thought.

*   *   *

No tug was sent in response to Trewin's signal, merely a brief but definite order to maintain radio silence and return to harbour using whatever resources available. It was a slow and painful journey, with much of the time spent hiding amongst the offshore islets while processions of bombers and solitary reconnaissance aircraft droned overhead, obviously intent on searching for such targets as the crippled gunboats now presented.

They finally crossed the harbour limits on the morning of the following day, the success of their arrival immediately overshadowed by the unmoving pall of smoke above the city and the fresh wrecks which littered the harbour like so much scrap.

It was difficult to believe that the harbour and anchorage could have changed so much in less than thirty-six hours. Transports and supply ships were gone, and the largest warship in sight was a destroyer busily engaged in taking on fuel from a lighter, even as her seamen prepared the lines for getting under way without a second's delay.

A harbour launch assisted the *Porcupine* to tie up to a buoy, and then towed the listing *Prawn* towards the slipway where a crowd of reluctant dockyard workers awaited her arrival under the eyes of an armed platoon of soldiers. Trewin imagined that but for the latter the workers would have left the *Prawn* to fend for herself. Of the *Beaver* there was no sign, but as Trewin leafed hastily through a bunch of despatches hurled aboard by the guardboat he read that she had been ordered to embark some two hundred civilian refugees and wounded troops and sail with a convoy bound for Java. From the look of the deserted harbour it seemed as if it was to be the last convoy to go. The island was digging in to make a final fight of it. Even the wardroom radio sounded determined, and the voice of the newsreader trembled with emotion and resolution as he ended with the words: 'We will not surrender! Singapore lives, and will never give in to the invaders!'

Trewin switched off the set and looked at the *Porcupine*'s officers. They were lolling around the table, too tired even to eat the hastily prepared breakfast. He said, 'I shall go ashore and report to headquarters. The captain will most likely be there and will have our orders.' He glanced at Mallory's unshaven face. 'Make a signal requesting fuel. We should be able to get that lighter alongside as soon as the destroyer puts to sea. It may be our last chance, and the chief tells me we are down to the rivets in all the tanks!'

Nobody answered. Each man seemed totally immersed in his own thoughts. He continued, 'I think that all officers and P.O.s had better wear sidearms as of now. And any shore parties must also be armed.' He saw Tweedie glance at the pistol rack. 'When I get back we might know a bit more, but from what I've already seen, I'm not too hopeful.'

As he walked towards the door the others stood up, as if to some secret signal, and followed him into the bright sunlight. They seemed unwilling for him to leave. That by staying together they might forestall any additional disaster.

Hammond asked, 'What about the steering? Can we get on the slipway after *Prawn*?'

Trewin shrugged. 'I will find out.' He forced a grin. 'I'm as eager as you to get mobile again.'

As he sat in the motor boat he stared back at the ship with a sense of shock. Her hull was streaked with dirt and rust, and it was impossible to visualise her as she had been when he had first seen her. Then she had looked like a yacht. Now she was showing the signs of wear and survival, like the men who served her.

At the landing stage he found freshly erected sandbag barriers and helmeted soldiers with machine-guns. The whole area seemed swamped with military police and armed troops.

An army lietuenant met him at the barrier and glanced briefly at his papers. He said, 'Can't be too careful. The place is crawling with saboteurs and spies.' He glanced across at the *Porcupine.* 'I hope you're staying well at anchor. We've already had several riots with our brave citizens fighting or bribing their way aboard anything still afloat.' He smiled bitterly. 'A few days ago any soldier was treated like dirt around here. Now he could become a millionaire in exchange for a pass aboard some ship, *any* bloody ship.' He signalled to a camouflaged car. 'He'll take you to the airfield, or what there is left of it!'

Trewin did not trust himself to reply. As the car nudged out into the street he was immediately aware of the changes all around him. The crowds of silent Malays and Chinese. Of abandoned vehicles and bomb-blasted buildings. Several times he saw corpses piled at the side of the road, only barely covered by sacking and crawling with flies. The driver did not even glance at them, and Trewin saw that he had a revolver resting across his legs as he steered through the streets at breakneck speed.

Trewin asked, 'Much trouble here?'

The soldier grimaced. 'It's not safe to go out alone at nights. Some of our lads have been done up by the locals recently.'

Trewin remembered the friendly faces he had seen before, the air of gentle tolerance and patience.

The soldier added, 'They think we've let 'em down. That we should be protecting 'em from the Japs.' He laughed angrily. 'Protect *them*!'

'It's as bad as that, is it?' Trewin saw the man's eyes harden.

'Yeh, it's a bloody sight worse by now, I expect. The Japs are supposed to have taken Timah Hill, the highest point on the whole ruddy island.' He cocked his head sideways. 'That's only about five miles from the city's perimeter, for God's sake!'

He swung the wheel and skidded the car through the barbed

wire gate and braked outside the familiar concrete bunker. Then he leaned on the wheel and added softly, 'Protect those bastards? We can't even protect our bleeding selves!'

Trewin climbed down and stared at him. The soldier had a plain, ordinary face. He seemed to personify every soldier he had ever seen. He said, 'Maybe they'll be able to hold them yet.'

The man pulled a cigarette from beneath his helmet and squinted against the harsh sunlight. 'Save it, sir. I've been a squaddie too long to believe that sort of thing. They drop you into one mess after another. I was in Greece before this.'

Trewin looked away. 'So was I.'

The man lit his cigarette and leaned back comfortably. 'Well, you know then, don't you?' He smiled. 'Fair makes you want to throw up, don't it?'

Trewin walked into the cool confines of the bunker and was almost knocked over by some marine orderlies who were man-handling a large steel filing cabinet out of the entrance. Inside the operations room the telephones were silent and unmanned, and only the map table remained as before, a colourful mockery in the middle of chaos.

The admiral was sitting in a canvas chair dictating a signal to his flag-lieutenant. At the far end of the room staff officers were bundling files into cases or throwing papers into a large incinerator beside which stood a can of petrol.

Fairfax-Loring looked up and nodded calmly. 'You always seem to be dropping in for a visit, Trewin.' He looked at Hughes. 'Pass that to all sections and then carry on with my order.' He pulled out his gold case and lit a cigarette. 'Fact is, Trewin, things are getting a bit dicey here.'

A telephone buzzed impatiently, but a staff officer lifted the receiver and then laid it on the table and continued with his work. Trewin stared at the telephone. At the other end there was probably some wretched junior officer like himself. Perhaps out of fuel or ammunition, and wanting help and instructions.

He said coldly, '*Prawn* is on the slip, sir. I think we should get *Porcupine*'s rudder seen to immediately.'

The admiral watched him through the smoke. 'Quite so. Actually I have already got it in hand. *Prawn*'s damage is not too bad. When she's pumped out and so forth she should be able to get steam up again. Pity about your steering though, I could have used the *Porcupine* right now.'

'I understand that *Beaver* has already gone, sir? Is Commander Corbett still here?'

'Of course he is, Trewin!' The admiral frowned. 'He is the senior officer of the group. What did you expect?' Then he yawned. 'I'm about bushed, but there's a lot to do yet.' He eyed Trewin thoughtfully. 'You'll hear soon enough, so it might as well be from me. The Army is in a bad way. They are mounting a counter-attack as of now, but if that fails I'm afraid we can't hope for much. The Japs are almost at the reservoirs, and some of the other water supply has already been poisoned,' he shrugged, 'so it's just a matter of time.'

Trewin felt the room closing in on him. He said, 'But the troops, sir? Surely they're not going to leave the whole lot to be killed or captured?'

The admiral leaned over the map, then took a paper knife and scored a deep line right across it. 'They've got half the island, Trewin! In less than forty-eight hours they cut the bloody place in two!' He threw the knife aside. 'There's nothing we can do about it. Nothing anyone can do at the moment!'

Trewin thought of the soldier in the car outside and replied bitterly, 'The stupid, incompetent bastards!'

The admiral smiled dryly. 'There's more to fighting a war than just one campaign, my lad. You'll learn that if you live long enough.'

Hughes reappeared at the door. 'Car's ready, sir.' He glanced at Trewin and gave a small shrug.

Fairfax-Loring stood up and picked his briefcase from the table. 'I am sending *Prawn* after the *Beaver* as soon as I can, Trewin. She'll probably be the last ship to go of any size, and I want every available person crammed aboard. Hughes has a list, and I've got my people rounding them up right now.' He became vague. 'Some nurses, a few wives, and so forth. All those who did not take advantage of the more comfortable transport last week.'

Trewin could not withhold his anger. 'Perhaps they were stupid enough to believe the bulletins, sir! Maybe they really trusted the people in authority who promised their safety and final victory!'

Fairfax-Loring watched him unmoved. 'Corbett will be sending his wife and child with the *Prawn*. You had better see that Massey's daughter goes, too.' He looked around the bunker. 'Ah well, one command post is much like another!'

As he crossed to the entrance the admiral added calmly, 'You can send your people ashore if you like. Those you can trust. It'll be your responsibility of course. Some of them may want to make sure their homes are in order and so on. But get them back aboard as soon as you can, so that the ship can be repaired while there's still time.' He showed his teeth. 'You don't want to be stuck here all alone, do you?'

Trewin wanted to hit him. You smug, hypocritical bastard! You don't really give a damn about anyone, do you?

He said quietly, 'How long have we got, sir?'

'Two or three days.' The admiral studied him, as if surprised by the question. 'Not much more.' He added suddenly, 'But if you need any help I shall be ready to do what I can.'

Trewin replaced his cap and then replied bitterly, 'No, sir. I don't want anything, thank you.'

He walked back to the car and leaned for several seconds against the warm metal. He could hear the rumble of guns and the unending murmur of voices in the street beyond the gates. It was like a new nightmare.

The admiral had said nothing about his disobeying Corbett's signal. It was surprising how little it mattered any more. One thing stood out foremost in his mind. Clare must be got out as soon as possible. He would check with *Prawn*'s captain and then fetch her himself. When the final battle started it would be something to know that she was safe.

The soldier looked down at him and grinned. 'All done, sir?'

Trewin climbed into his seat and stared straight ahead. 'Yes. All done.' He saw a polished staff car with a rear-admiral's flag on its bonnet nosing through the compound towards the bunker.

The soldier let in the clutch and said, 'Well, at least we've got the harbour intact. The Navy'll lift us out, like they always do, eh?' He was looking at the road and did not see the despair on Trewin's face.

*　　　*　　　*

As the motor boat darted alongside the landing stage Trewin sensed that Corbett had returned to the *Porcupine* before him. Both the coxswain and the bowman were in spotless whites and in spite of the wired-off jetty being deserted but for two sentries they went through the full drill of getting the boat neatly laid by the stone steps, as if they were under the eye of the commander-in-chief.

Trewin saw Hammond waiting at the gangway, and as he climbed from the boat he asked, 'Well, Sub, why the anxious look?' Even his attempt at humour sounded hollow. His mind was still buzzing with thoughts and impressions he had gained on his short visit ashore. The admiral's casual acceptance of defeat, the grim-faced soldiers and the thought of Clare Massey waiting for someone to help her.

Hammond said, 'Thank God, I was beginning to think you were making a day of it, Number One' He dropped his voice. 'The captain came aboard just after you'd gone. He's been yelling for you every other minute. He tried to get through to H.Q., but some joker said that the lines are all disconnected.'

Trewin frowned and glanced at the bridge. 'That was no joke, Sub.' He looked along the deck where men were busy with hoses and scrubbers and Dancy was instructing some Chinese seamen in the art of repairing a torn awning. 'What the hell is happening?'

'Captain's orders. He went right over the ship as soon as he returned. Every deck and flat, even the boiler room. He's had the people hard at it all forenoon so far.'

Trewin thought of the tired, unshaven faces in the dawn light. The empty expressions of men too weary even to feel relief at their return or to find pride in seeing the *Prawn* towed to safety. Now Corbett had them all at work, as if the ship was about to receive a full inspection.

He said flatly, 'I'll go and see him.' He ran up the bridge ladder and stared with disbelief at the deserted wheelhouse. The brass telegraphs gleamed like gold, the helmsman's grating was still damp from scrubbing, and there was even a smell of new varnish in the air.

He walked down the connecting passageway and rapped on Corbett's door. Corbett was sitting behind his desk writing slowly in his order book. Trewin said, 'I've just come aboard, sir.'

Corbett did not look up. 'Yes. I heard you talking with Hammond. I wondered when you might get to me.'

Trewin gripped his trousers by the seams and tried to control the remains of his patience. 'As temporary officer in charge I went to see the rear-admiral, sir. I wanted fresh orders.'

Corbett replaced the pen on a silver stand and raised his eyes. They looked cold and dangerous. 'Never mind that, Trewin! When I came aboard I expected to find you here. With an explanation in writing. I'd have thought that as an ex-journalist you'd not have found that too difficult?' He did not wait for a comment. 'In all my experience I have never seen a ship, *any* ship in such a pot-mess! Had I behaved as you did, I would certainly have tried to present some front of efficiency, if only for decency's sake!

Trewin eyed him warily. 'Have you finished, sir?'

Corbett stood up. 'No, I have not finished, and be good enough to pay attention!' He was breathing quickly and the nervous tick had appeared below one eye. 'The night before last you disobeyed my signal. The result of which is obvious, even to you. This ship is disabled, and the fault is entirely yours! Ever since you came aboard I have tried to tolerate your lack of experience, and to guide you towards a chance of making yourself useful in the future. And this is how I am repaid!'

Trewin said quietly, 'The *Prawn* had to be saved, sir. The enemy were already close to that part of the coast. They would have taken her as soon as it was daylight.'

Corbett stared at him as if he had uttered some obscenity. 'Do you think I don't know all that? My responsibility is to the group, Trewin. God knows, I don't want to lose men, some of whom are dear friends of mine. But I'm not permitted to think of that sort of thing, and neither are you. The group must stay intact. *Porcupine* and *Beaver* are the two biggest ships in the group. And now, thanks to you, there is only the *Beaver*. When she returns we may still be stuck here waiting for the dockyard idlers to carry out our repairs. *Prawn* will never be any use as a first-line ship. She has always been the lame dog, and now it looks as if she will be the only one here in commission until *Beaver* comes back!'

Trewin replied, 'She's not coming back, sir.'

'Don't change the subject!' Corbett was shouting. 'I want to know why you disobeyed my signal!' He swung round. '*What* did you say?'

Trewin repeated, '*Beaver*'s not returning, sir. Not soon. Not ever!'

'I don't believe it!' Corbett sat down at his desk and stared at the neat piles of signals. 'Even the admiral would not jeopardise efficiency like that!'

'It was the admiral who told me, sir.' Trewin waited a few more seconds. 'And the *Prawn* is to leave Singapore as soon as she's able with the last available evacuees. There should be a signal about it already. He said that you should get your wife and son to the slipway as soon as you can, sir.'

Corbett was still staring at his desk. 'I don't believe it,' he said again.

Trewin leaned over the desk and turned over the top clip of signals. 'It should be here if . . .'

Corbett knocked his hand away. 'I can look, Trewin! I'm

not a damn cripple!' In his sudden anger his sleeve caught his open book and knocked it aside. Before he could replace it Trewin saw a large magnifying glass lying underneath. It was so powerful that the wording on a sheet of typed paper looked about an inch high.

Trewin looked away, holding down the embarrassment and pity, and forced himself to say, 'The admiral told me that it's nearly over. We're finished. The powers that be are going to surrender and drop the whole army in the bag!' He could no longer conceal his anger. 'So it doesn't really matter what we do now, does it?'

Corbett did not speak for several seconds, and from the ship and beyond Trewin could hear the familiar sounds as if from another world. The sluice of water alongside, the patter of feet on the battery deck, and over all the steady murmur of guns.

Then Corbett said, 'I've been over the whole ship myself. There's a lot to do to get her back to shape.' He seemed to be talking to himself. 'But she's a sturdy ship. She can take this sort of trouble, and a lot more beside.'

'I know that, sir.'

Corbett lifted his gaze, his eyes empty of expression. 'You only think you know. You just look on a ship as a piece of equipment, a means to an end. But you're wrong, believe me!' He slewed round in his chair and looked across the cabin. 'The size and power of a ship does not matter. It's the *heart* of a ship that counts. If the ship is treated badly so will she react.' He shook his head. 'Because you've seen war it does not make you some sort of super being, Trewin!' He glanced up at him briefly. 'You had better go ashore and fetch my wife and son. Dr. Massey's daughter will accompany them in *Prawn*.'

He fixed Trewin with a cold stare. 'I would go myself, but I have work to do. This ship will return to normal duty as soon as possible. You don't get that sort of standard by allowing our people to lounge about like a lot of damn vagrants, or by letting the ship get in a state of filth.'

Trewin said, 'Very well, sir. I'll go now.'

'And when you return I will want a full written report about your disobeyance of orders. When I write mine I shall not be slow to point out to the admiral your better achievements also. They will be taken into full consideration at the enquiry. To you, the Navy's ways are still strange, perhaps. But they are fair and just, notwithstanding what you may or may not believe.' He picked up his pen. 'Now go and see Adair and arrange for my wife to go aboard when *Prawn* is ready.' He dropped his eyes. 'She seems to like you well enough, so you should be able to manage that all right!'

Trewin left the cabin, knowing that it was useless to start into a head-on row at this moment. It would be just like Corbett to relieve him of his duties entirely. And there was still Clare's safety to consider.

He walked to the gangway and beckoned to the motor boat. To Hammond he said quietly. 'There's to be local leave for those with responsibilities ashore, Sub. Tell Guns to take O.O.D. and get ashore yourself.' He shot him a meaning glance. 'Just between us, the *Prawn* is pulling out with the last organised evacuees.' He saw Hammond's eyes cloud over. 'I suggest you put your Jacqui aboard, by force if necessary!' Then to the coxswain he shouted, 'The slipway, as quick as you can!'

Lieutenant Adair, the *Prawn*'s commanding officer, was an extremely tall man, all arms and legs, and with a cluster of large, protruding teeth which seemed to give him a permanent grin. Trewin found him on the slipway squinting up at his ship's wood-encrusted hull, his cap on the back of his head and his shirt as filthy as any of his men's.

He said enthusiastically, 'Pretty good show! Just a few dents, but otherwise as sound as a bell. And a few more dents won't be noticed.' He patted the scored and pitted plates with affection. 'Lost a lot of coal, but the bomb would have blown *your* ship to blazes, literally that is!' He rubbed his hands on his shorts. 'You know about the old Noah's Ark stunt then?'

Trewin nodded. There was something very likeable and reassuring about Adair. 'Yes. I'm to fetch Mrs. Corbett and bring her aboard immediately you're ready.'

Adair shrugged. 'I'm ready now. We'll unslip her as soon as I can kick the arses of the dockyard maties, and then my chief'll try and get steam up again.' He eyed Trewin with sudden seriousness. 'I hope you get away, too. I don't like to think of running out like this.'

Trewin glanced up at the ship's smashed and sagging battery deck, the dried bloodstains around the severed gun mounting. 'I think you've done your share.'

Adair grinned, himself again. 'Poor old cow!' He signalled to another filthy figure. 'Number One! Tell the top man to prepare the slipway. He can drop her in the drink as soon as he's ready. You can take over for a bit.' He looked at Trewin. 'I'm going to drive this gentleman on an errand of mercy.'

Trewin followed him up the greasy slipway. Then Adair added, 'I've got a shooting brake laid on. I'll drive you myself. It'll help to blow the jitters away.'

Trewin beckoned to Petty Officer Dancy who had accompanied him in the boat, and Adair said cheerfully, 'Good! An extra pair of hands will be useful at a time like this.'

The drove in silence through the shadowed and sunlit streets, the battered shooting brake the only civilian vehicle in sight. There were plenty of soldiers on the march, their feet churning up the dust, their eyes unseeing beneath their helmets as they headed towards the northern side of the city. More troops stood in listless columns, leaning on their rifles, staring into space. They did not look defeated, merely baffled, as they stood and waited for something to happen to them.

As they passed a narrow sidestreet Trewin saw some people smashing into a native store while the owner and his family screamed and pleaded in the faces of the determined looters. Some Indian policemen stood at the corner, their backs turned to the scene, and Adair said shortly, 'This is the worst part. When order gives way to empty vandalism. They are merely hurting each other, maybe because they are afraid, like the rest of us!'

They swung aside as a line of ambulances bounced down the road towards the hospital, and Trewin caught sight of limp khaki figures with brightly bandaged limbs and pale dazed faces.

Adair drove on again, his eyes on the shuttered houses and the aimless groups of townspeople at every intersection. He said, 'I had to come with you on this trip. I wanted to see it all for myself. So that I shall remember. Always!'

Dancy said sharply, 'Heads up! There's an aircraft!'

Adair gunned the engine as a black shadow flashed overhead and craned his neck to watch as the plane lifted above the line of houses as if following the road.

Trewin felt the sudden down-draught of air and heard the sigh of wind against the plane's wings, and saw that its prop was stiff and motionless and a long streamer of smoke was already pouring out from beneath the fuselage, above which he could see the pilot's helmeted head and the red sun insignia of Japan.

Adair said tightly, 'The bastard's going to crash! He must have been trying to get back to his own side.'

The brake swung round the bend in the road and Trewin seized Adair's arm with sudden anxiety. 'He's coming down now! For God's sake, he'll land right on Corbett's house!'

Adair said, 'Christ Almighty!' Then he pressed his foot hard down and simultaneously blared a shrill alarm on the horn. For a moment it seemed as if the pilot was going to clear the house completely. Then as the black shadow crossed the gates the nose dipped, and with a shattering roar the plane ploughed into the roof and exploded, so that the car was showered with falling stonework and pieces of torn metal from the aircraft itself.

As the car's engine stopped Trewin heard the crackle of flames and saw the rising plume of black smoke lifting and spreading until it reached out to engulf the whole building. He was running, heedless of the others behind him or the menacing sound of flames and the attendant stench of petrol.

He reached the porch and saw with despair the gleam of sunlight where the roof should have been. At the end of the long room he could see the smashed nose and engine of the enemy fighter with the cockpit still intact. Its perspex was soaked in blood, and he saw the pilot moving from side to side like a trapped animal as the creeping flames licked up and around his prison, but Trewin hardly spared him a glance.

He shouted her name, his voice all but lost in the sound of flames and falling woodwork, and he was pulling aside the splintered timbers with his hands, fighting to break through the barrier, his mind empty of everything but finding Clare Massey.

The passageway was already alight, and he felt the old terror welling up inside him, and he was held momentarily motionless by the flames' cruel glitter. They seemed to be burning again at his shoulder, and in his reeling mind he seemed to hear his men crying out as they perished one by one in the creeping fire across the water.

Then he found he was through, and he heard her calling his name.

12
Even the Innocent

For a moment Trewin could see nothing. The passageway was thick with smoke being sucked greedily downwards from the shattered roof, and his eyes were streaming, leaving him half blind. Then he saw her. She was crouching beside a fallen beam, her face pale against the black rectangle of a door. He reached her in two strides and pulled her against his chest. He did not know what he was saying, but was only conscious of holding her, of feeling her face and arms as he tried to soothe her and protect her from the growing heat around them.

She cried, 'I can't get the door open! Oh, Ralph, the boy's in there!'

Dancy appeared in the passage, his shirt blackened and torn as he pushed through the debris, his arms groping as he yelled, 'Lieutenant Adair's getting help, sir!' He retched then added, 'The whole place'll go up any second!'

Trewin released the girl's hands from his shoulders and said harshly, 'Get her out the back!' Then he stood back against the wall and threw his full weight against the door.

With a crack it flew open, and Trewin felt the flames searing his face like hot knives. There was no roof, and he could see the thick smoke pouring towards the sky, the eager fire leaping from one piece of furniture to the next, as if guided by an invisible hand.

The Chinese *amah* was lying face down on the floor pinioned by a smouldering beam, her clothes and body already alight like a human torch. The child sat against the opposite wall, his eyes fixed on the dead woman, and for a brief instant Trewin imagined that he was too terrified to move.

There was a dull explosion beyond the wall and a great

tongue of orange flame burst upwards through the floor as the plane's fuel tank exploded.

Trewin could hear the girl sobbing and screaming his name, and Dancy shouting through the rising roar of flames, but he could not bring himself to move. His shirt was flaking in the heat, and when he tried to draw breath his lungs felt raw and seared, yet still he could not move.

Dimly he heard the clang of a bell and more voices far off and confused. As another piece of flooring gave way in a burst of sparks he held his breath and threw himself across the room, his mind empty of all but the child. As he scooped his body into his arms he realised that the flames had joined behind him and the whole place was full of fire and noise. He knew he was shouting, yet could hear and see nothing but the flames.

Then Dancy was at his side, and he found himself being pulled bodily from the room, his feet like lead as he stumbled blindly through a door and out into the air and hazy sunlight. Vaguely he saw Adair gesturing to a group of helmeted firemen and some soldiers running with a stretcher. Then he sank to his knees and lowered the boy on to the grass.

He looked up, trying to control the rising nausea in his throat. He said, 'He's dead!'

The girl dropped beside him, her eyes suddenly bright in the flames. She whispered, 'His eyes are open!' It sounded as if she was pleading with him to be wrong.

Trewin looked at the boy's face. It was just as it had been when he had sat watching his dead *amah*. He closed the child's eyes. His face was still warm from the burning room, as if he was indeed alive.

'He must have died instantly. Probably from a shock-wave from the plane's bomb.' He looked across at the girl. 'Is Mrs. Corbett there, too?'

She did not take her eyes from the dead child. 'No. She went to visit someone in town.' Her lips was trembling but her voice was strangely controlled. 'I told her we should leave here. I told her. But she insisted on making her last visit.'

Then she looked up, her eyes filling her face as she stared at

Trewin. 'That was a wonderful thing you did just then. I saw your face as you looked at the fires. I never understood what war could do before. Not until today, when I saw it in your eyes.'

Trewin stood up slowly and swayed. He heard Adair say, 'There's nothing more we can do here.'

Dancy was looking down at the boy's relaxed body. Then he brushed his blackened hand across his eyes and said, 'Damn them! Damn them all to hell!'

Trewin felt the girl's arm around his waist and heard her ask, 'Are you all right, Ralph? Please tell me you're all right!'

He looked down at her and tried to smile. 'I'm over it now.' Then very gently he ran his hand over her hair, feeling it, gaining strength from the small contact.

'Thank God you were safe, Clare!'

She replied quietly, 'The admiral telephoned and told us to go to the harbour. He even sent a car for our luggage.' She shuddered violently as she relived each moment. 'Then Mildred Corbett left us here.' She looked up at him, her eyes filled with anxiety. 'We must tell her, Ralph!'

Adair said thickly, 'I'll go and tell Commander Corbett myself. I've known him for some time. It might come better from me.' He looked down at the child. 'What shall we do with him?'

Dancy knelt on the grass and gently covered the body with his shirt. Harshly he said, 'I'll take him, sir.'

Adair watched the petty officer carry the small bundle towards the car. Then he said, 'I forgot. Dancy was his friend.'

Trewin turned away. 'You'd better go with them, Clare.' He felt her tense beneath his arm. 'I shall not be long. Just tell me where Mrs. Corbett was going. I'll fetch her myself.'

She stared at him, her face grave. 'Are you sure you want to?'

He nodded. 'I must.' He walked with her to the car, past the onlookers and the busy firemen. Then he said, 'I'll see you before you leave.'

She reached through the car window and gripped his arm.

'I shall never forget what you did today. What it must have cost you.' She was smiling at him but her eyes were running with tears.

Then the car jerked away and Trewin watched it until it had turned the bend in the road.

He did not want to be the one to face Mrs. Corbett, and deep in his heart he knew that he was only giving himself the task to avoid seeing Corbett when he was told of his son's death.

He made himself look at the gutted building and tried to remember it as it had once been. All Corbett treasured in life was his son and his ship. And now there was only the ship.

As he walked slowly towards the road he knew that whatever else happened he would not be the one to take that away away from Corbett. There was nothing else left.

*   *   *

When Trewin finally found his way back to the landing stage it was already getting dark. It had taken him longer than he had expected to find the address Clare had given him, and then on his way back to the harbour he had been forced to take cover during a sudden air raid.

As he had sat in the sweltering heat of the crowded shelter he had found himself going over what had happened again and again. Maybe it had been because it was so unexpected that the final scene was still riveted in his mind.

The place where Mrs. Corbett was making her visit was an expensive apartment in a small block of flats. Several people had paused to watch him pass, but he no longer cared what they thought of his stained and dishevelled appearance. He had found the flat on the first floor, and after pressing the bell had waited, almost holding his breath, his eyes fixed on the closed door.

It had seemed like an age before the door had finally been opened. There had been the sound of dance music from a radio and the smell of gin. But all these brief impressions had faded instantly as he had come face to face with Mallory.

The Australian had been wearing a dressing gown and carrying a glass in one hand. For a moment he had stared at Trewin with something like stunned disbelief, then he had shrugged.

'So I just came ashore, Number One! I wasn't expecting a visit from you or anyone else!' He had made to close the door and it had been then that Trewin had seen Corbett's wife in the next room reflected in the dressing-table mirror. She had been sitting relaxed and naked on the bed, her head moving slightly in time with the music while she poured herself a drink.

Trewin had heard himself say tonelessly, 'I suggest you take Mrs. Corbett to the harbour right now!' He had watched the hostility on Mallory's dark features. Then he had continued, 'Her son has just been killed. Tell her if you like, she may be interested!' Then he had swung on his heel and not looked back. If he had waited any longer he knew he would have hit Mallory.

In the air-raid shelter, as the walls and roof vibrated to the explosions overhead, he had found time to think clearly and restore his self-control.

By the time he reached the landing stage he was outwardly calm, but within he had an empty, dangerous feeling which made him watch his every move, like an onlooker, someone on the outside of himself.

It was only when the motor boat coxswain told him that he noticed the *Prawn* was afloat and the *Porcupine* had been moved further along the anchorage to another buoy.

The seaman said, 'The Japs flew across and dropped some bombs on the harbour, sir. They hit the slipway, but the old *Prawn* was just too quick for 'em. She'd been in the water some three hours earlier.'

Trewin did not answer. He did not want his mind to accept the true meaning of the man's words. If the slipway was wrecked, there was no chance of repairing the *Porcupine*'s rudders. It was the end.

He climbed the gunboat's side where Hammond stood by the rail with Tweedie. Hammond said softly, 'We've been waiting to tell you what a fine thing you did.'

Trewin studied him emptily. 'The boy was dead.'

'Yes. But you saved one life. It could have been worse.'

Trewin looked at the bridge. 'Is he aboard?'

'In his cabin. He's been ashore for a while with Adair.' Hammond licked his lips. 'Dancy went with him.'

'I see.' Trewin felt his shoulder throbbing in time with his heart. 'How is he?'

Hammond shrugged. 'Hard to say. He looks like a man in a trance.'

Trewin nodded. 'I'll go up.'

Tweedie said harshly, 'Tell 'im about the admiral!'

'What about the admiral?' Trewin knew his voice was hard. 'Tell me!'

'He's going with *Prawn*.' Hammond spread his hands. 'He's leaving us.'

Trewin looked at the red glow above the city. 'Well, that just about makes everything perfect, doesn't it?'

He climbed the ladder slowly, conscious of the seamen standing by the guardrails. Nobody spoke. No one turned to watch him.

He tapped on the cabin door. It swung inwards and he saw Corbett sitting behind his desk. As if he had not moved from the last time. Trewin said, 'I'm back sir. I tried to carry out your orders. I'm sorry, sir. I think you know that.'

Corbett was staring at the desk. 'Thank you.'

Trewin tried to shut out the pictures of the child staring at the dead nurse and Corbett's wife naked in the mirror. He said, 'I've just heard about the admiral, sir. It seems he's running with the rest.'

Corbett sounded distant. '*I'm* in charge of the group, Trewin.' He stood up and walked slowly to his bookcase. 'I've decided to drop the matter of the enquiry. I don't imagine you'll act so foolishly again.'

Trewin watched Corbett's hands moving aimlessly along the

leather-bound books. He was not deceived by his remarks. He could see the stiffness in his back, the fixed intensity of those pale, useless eyes. You poor, helpless bastard! Don't keep fighting it! Just let go, just once!

Corbett said, '*Prawn* will be sailing after midnight. I want you to take the motor boat and guide her clear of the harbour. I don't want her to hit any of the wrecks, she's enough ahead of her as it is.'

'Yes, sir.'

Corbett lifted his gaze and stared at Trewin for the first time. 'You look a mess. You'd better go and freshen up. God knows when you'll get another chance.' As Trewin moved towards the door Corbett said, 'Thank you for what you tried to do.'

Trewin paused. 'Is there anything I can do now, sir?'

Corbett's hands bunched into tight fists. 'Just go.' He turned away. 'Just leave me *alone*!'

In his cabin Trewin leaned against the bulkhead and closed his eyes. Ching opened the door and peered at him. 'You like a shower, Number One, sir?'

Trewin said tightly, 'Yes, I would.'

The old Chinese hovered by the door. 'Drink, maybe?'

Trewin pushed himself away from the cool steel. 'No drink. Later perhaps I'll need it very badly, but not yet.'

He did not resist as Ching helped him off with his clothes, but as the man moved away to arrange the shower he sank on the edge of the bunk and rested his head on his hands. Around him the ship was so quiet that she seemed to be listening.

*   *   *

Trewin pushed his way along the *Prawn*'s unfamiliar deck and began to climb the bridge ladder. He could feel the metal vibrating in his hands as the little gunboat's engines settled down to an impatient rumble, and as he reached the bridge wing he could see the smoke pouring steadily from her thin funnel. It should have been pitch dark, but there had been another air raid, and the glow of burning buildings painted the ship's upperworks like burnished copper.

When he looked down he saw the deck crammed with people. Here and there amongst the black, anonymous mass he saw the pale shape of a sailor as he patiently guided or placated one of the frightened passengers who were being led below without a pause. Most of them were women and children, but there were also some wounded soldiers and a few civilian males, whom Trewin guessed had been attached to some military establishment or other.

He found Adair leaning against the screen, a cigarette glowing at the side of his mouth.

'I've got our motor boat alongside ready to guide you clear.' Trewin heard a child whimpering and the deeper voice of a sailor. 'Are there many more to come?'

Adair sighed. 'A few.' He gestured to the sagging pier alongside, where the distant fires reflected on the fixed bayonets of the sentries. 'About two hundred aboard all told, I believe.'

Trewin shuddered. Two hundred in a ship this size. They would be jammed below like sardines in a tin.

Adair remarked, 'I've sent all my Chinese lads ashore. It's only fair to them. They can ditch their uniforms and try to get to their homes.' He threw his cigarette into the water. 'I've made up my crew with some spare hands from the base. It wasn't too difficult, as you can imagine!'

A telegraph rang noisily and someone spoke over a voice-pipe. Adair peered at his watch. 'About fifteen minutes and I'm away.'

Trewin asked, 'Is the admiral aboard?'

'Too right he is.' Adair sounded indifferent. 'Snug in my cabin, not that I'll have much use for it this trip.'

'You should be safe enough. *Beaver* will be waiting for you.'

Adair coughed. 'You've not seen the signal then? *Beaver* was sunk by Jap bombers in the Durian Strait. She only got about fifty miles from here!'

Trewin said, 'My God!'

'Keep it to yourself, old boy. We don't want a panic.'

Trewin saw Hammond on the pier at the top of the brow, his arms around a girl as they spoke to each other, oblivious of the desperate, struggling figures about them. So he got her to leave, he thought dully. That was something.

Adair said, 'Fairfax-Loring is not the only one to go. The Rear-Admiral, Malaya and his staff are going, too. About the last mobile M.L. is taking them. That'll be no picnic either!' He grinned. 'The *Prawn* is old, but at least she's iron and steel, not bloody wood!'

Trewin held out his hand. 'I'll be going. This is to wish you luck.'

Adair's grip was firm. 'Thanks. The one you're going to say goodbye to is in the wardroom. I thought it might be quieter there for you.' He chuckled. 'I'll look after her.'

As Trewin stepped on to the ladder Adair added quietly, 'You *could* stay aboard too. There's not much you can do here. I'd be glad to take you with me.'

Trewin replied, 'I can't. I'm not being heroic or anything, and I won't say I'm not tempted.' He shrugged wearily. 'But it's no go.'

Adair grinned. 'I knew you'd say that, I suppose.' He flipped his cap in a casual salute. 'Then I'll be seeing you somewhere.' A phone rang at his side and he answered it curtly. He was the captain again.

Trewin found the girl in the wardroom. She was watching the door, her hands resting in her lap. As he wrapped his arms around her she pillowed her head against his chest and said, 'I thought we would sail and I wouldn't see you.'

He tilted her chin and studied her face, as if to memorise every single feature. 'I have to go now. You'll be safe with Adair. He's a good skipper.' He thought suddenly of Fairfax-Loring and added tightly, 'You should be *very* safe with the admiral aboard too.' He saw the anxiety in her eyes and said, 'You'll soon catch up with some bigger ships. Then I expect you'll be taken to Australia.' He smiled. 'You see, it'll be all right.'

A pipe shrilled and he heard the cry, 'Hands to stations for leaving harbour!'

He said, 'Take this letter, Clare. I've written down my parents' address. You must go and stay with them when you get to England. You'll like Dorset.' The words were choking him.

'I'm not worried about myself, Ralph.' She reached up to touch his face. 'When will you follow? How long will you be?'

He swallowed. 'Soon. I'm not sure yet.'

She held herself away at arm's length and said, 'I shall be waiting for you. No matter how long it takes.' Then she kissed him hard with a desperate urgency.

He stepped back. 'I shall be guiding you out of the harbour. You won't see me, but I shall be there.'

She reached out for him again but he said, 'I *must* go.' He felt the resistance draining from his body. 'Take good care of yourself.'

Then he was outside in the smoke-tinged air and hurrying for the pier.

He paused beside Hammond and said, 'Get her aboard now. *Prawn*'s shoving off!' He saw the girl prise Hammond's hands from her shoulders. She was the strong one, he thought dully. Aloud he added, 'Go to the wardroom. Adair will fix you up later.' He looked from one to the other. 'I'm glad you decided to make a match of it.'

He was suddenly aware of a crowd of watching figures behind the wire barrier. They were all men, silently watching the ship which would soon separate them from their wives and families. One of the figures suddenly leapt over the barrier and ran towards the brow, just as Hammond was guiding the girl into the hands of two sailors. 'I want to go, too!' He was dressed in a white dinner-jacket, and in the reflected glow from the fires his heavy face was wet with sweat.

A petty officer said, 'No more, sir.' He signalled to the men at the barrier. 'We're full to the scuppers now!'

The man yelled, 'What about *her*?' He pointed wildly at the girl. 'You're letting her go!'

Trewin said harshly, 'Stand aside, for God's sake!'

The man peered at Trewin's shoulder-straps and shouted, 'She's a bloody wog! You'll not take her instead of me, you bastard!'

Trewin hit him hard in the face and said, 'I'm not leaving either, you gutless pig!' He pulled Hammond's arm. 'Come to the boat with me.'

They found it below the piles with Dancy at the tiller. A blue guiding light threw a strange glow on the frothing water below the stern, and Trewin imagined Adair watching from his tiny bridge.

'Shove off and wait in the channel, Buffer.' He heard the *Prawn*'s telegraphs and the squeak of fenders as she idled clear of the pier. From the figures still behind the barrier he caught a snatch of voices blended together in a hymn.

He said harshly, 'Take it slowly, Buffer. Nice and easy!'

Following the bobbing blue light, like a shark after a pilot fish, the gunboat slipped away from the land, her small wash rippling back over the silent wrecks and deserted buoys as she turned and headed for the open sea.

As the channel widened out across her blunt bows the *Prawn* gathered speed, her upperworks shrouded in smoke as the stokers threw more coal into her demanding boilers. The motor boat swung aside to let her pass, and Trewin stood swaying in the cockpit, his eyes fixed on the gunboat's outline, hardly blinking in case he should miss some small part of her departure.

Hammond was waving his cap, his face pale in the dull glare. Perhaps she was watching too, somewhere on that small, smoke-blackened ship which represented the last chance of safety and life. Trewin lifted his cap and held it above his head, ignoring the pitching boat beneath him as *Prawn*'s wash rolled out **of** the darkness and faded to blend with the night.

Then the motor boat had the sea to herself.

He said, 'Back to the ship, Buffer.'

Dancy swung the tiller hard over. 'Aye, aye, sir.' He sounded tired.

Hammond crouched in the cockpit, his cap still in his hands. He said, 'She has promised to marry me if I get back.'

Trewin did not look at him. *If* I get back. He replied, 'I'm pleased for you. I really am.'

He thought of Mallory and said, 'Did the captain go and see his wife before she sailed?'

Hammond shook his head. 'She wouldn't see him. I expect she was too upset.'

Mallory's face in the doorway, the dance music and the gin moved through Trewin's thoughts once more. He said coldly, 'I expect she was!'

Out of the darkness he heard the challenge. 'Boat ahoy?'

Dancy cupped his hands. 'Aye, aye!'

As they bumped alongside Trewin saw that the seamen were still at the rails watching the town and the angry glow of fires. He made himself run up the ladder where Tweedie stood like a pale rock beside the gangway, a telescope beneath his arm.

He said quickly, 'The captain wants you on the bridge. Number One.' He jerked his hand towards the ladder. ' 'E's bin waitin' for you.'

Corbett was standing on the upper bridge leaning against his chair, his face turned towards the shore. Without turning he said quietly, 'She got safe away then?'

'Yes, sir.' Trewin stepped forward and saw that Corbett was holding a glass in his hand and there was a bottle standing on the chart table.

'I have had some new orders, Trewin. The admiral was gracious enough to send them across before he left.' His tone was flat, with neither bitterness nor anger. He continued, 'The G.O.C. has started to negotiate a surrender with the enemy. His emissaries have already been in contact with them.'

Trewin remembered the girl's face against his own and the soft warmth of her mouth. He said thickly, 'When is it to be, sir?'

'About forty-eight hours. At the most.' Corbett gestured

with his glass. 'Help yourself. I brought a glass for you.'

Trewin made himself pour a full measure and downed it in one swallow. The neat spirit helped to steady his reeling thoughts, but his mind did not register what he was drinking.

Corbett said, 'All resistance will cease and the armed forces will stand down and await detention.' He ran one hand across his face. 'Any ships unable to leave will be sunk forthwith and their crews sent ashore to await capture.' He sounded as if the words were choking him.

Trewin asked, 'The *Porcupine*, sir?' He knew it was coming, but the shock felt all the greater.

Corbett said in the same tight voice, 'Mr. Tweedie will place charges for demolition at daybreak. You can carry on now. You'll need some sleep after today.'

'You can't do it, sir!' Trewin watched Corbett's upright figure, waiting for some sign of emotion. 'Not *this* ship!'

'I have my orders, Trewin. I have always tried to obey them in the past, and I expect you to understand that!'

'Have you told the ship's company, sir?'

'Yes. I have sent the Chinese crew members ashore already.' His shoulders sagged. 'They didn't want to go. I hope they understood.'

Trewin said quietly, 'Is that all, sir?'

'Yes.' It sounded final. 'I didn't think you'd come back, Trewin. I wouldn't have blamed you this time.'

Trewin moved towards the ladder. 'I would have blamed myself.'

As he climbed down towards the deck he saw Corbett grip the screen with both hands. As if he was holding on to his ship for the last time.

Somewhere on the far side of the town the sky lit up to one more violent explosion. It looked like an ammunition dump. Now that a decision had been made it seemed as if the abyss was already opening.

He walked to his cabin and threw himself across his bunk. But when he tried to think of tomorrow he could find nothing. Nothing at all.

13
Corbett's Decision

When the sun lifted itself above the placid sea it was greeted by so much smoke from the burning city that it was more like dusk than dawn.

Trewin stepped on deck and leaned heavily on the guard-rail. For some seconds he watched the drifting curtain of ashes while he waited for his mind to clear. Sleep had been impossible, and it was almost a relief to be on his feet again. He realised that the continuous mutter of artillery was lulled and the listless morning air was only occasionally troubled by infrequent and vague explosions which hung on the ear like echoes. In a way it was worse than the original sounds of conflict. It seemed to herald the final shots which would mean the end of Singapore and its exhausted defenders. Even now, senior British officers might be sitting across a table from Yamashita, the Japanese general, listening to his demands and enduring the first shock of humiliation and defeat.

Trewin looked up at the bridge but it seemed to be deserted. No doubt Corbett was sitting at his desk and waiting for the moment to destroy his ship and the remnants of his own life.

From the corner of his eye he saw some figures moving on the quarterdeck, and as he walked aft he realised that there were about half a dozen men gathered by the ensign staff, their heads together in discussion. Then he realised that all the chief and petty officers were present, neatly dressed and freshly shaved, as if this meeting was by arrangement.

They looked round as he approached, their expressions both guarded and determined.

Trewin asked, 'What's this then? Are you having a conference?'

Unwin, the coxswain, licked his lips and glanced at the others. 'Well, I'm the senior, so I'd better speak for the rest, sir.' He looked awkward, even unhappy about his task as spokesman. 'We know it's not our job to question orders, sir, but we think we ought to make a go at getting out of here.'

Trewin tried to keep his face impassive. These men were the backbone of the ship. Of any ship. They were the professionals who were all too often taken for granted. A man like Unwin who had given all his life to the Service would not find it easy to speak up in defiance of tradition and hard discipline.

'I'm listening, Swain.'

Unwin said quickly, 'We sat up most of the night discussing it, sir. I think we might have a shot at fixing the rudders.'

Nimmo interrupted, 'He's speaking for us all, sir.' The engineer gestured over the rail. 'I went in the drink meself at first light. If we could have got on the slipway I reckon I could have done the repairs in my workshop, and never mind the bloody dockyard workers!'

Trewin was conscious of the tension amongst the watching men. At first he had imagined that they wanted permission to leave the ship and try to escape individually in one of the abandoned harbour boats. Any such craft would have been useless, but he knew that to a sailor even a raft represented something better and more reliable than the land.

Nimmo continued in his gruff, matter-of-fact voice, 'It would be a temporary job of course, but at least we would have tried.' He fell silent and watched Trewin's face expectantly.

Unwin nodded. 'That's about it, sir.'

The other petty officers murmured in agreement. Then Dancy added, 'We can't use the slipway any more.' He pointed outboard. 'But we *could* take the anchor away in the motor boat and kedge the old girl yonder. There's a good sandbar not fifty yards away. If she dried out on that the chief and the rest of us could get down on the mud and have a crack at repairing the steering.'

Trewin replied, 'I take it you've been swimming, too!' They laughed, but he was aware of something very tense and brittle in the sound. He could feel it in his own body, too. It was stupid to encourage this sort of pitiful hope, and yet . . . 'Do you *really* believe we could fix it?'

Nimmo licked his lips. 'Well, sir, it's hard to say.' He looked at the others. Then he nodded sharply. 'Yes I do.'

Trewin breathed out slowly. 'I'll talk with the captain. Right now.'

As he turned he almost collided with Tweedie who was carrying a canvas bag and a roll of fuse. Trewin said quietly, 'Hold up the demolition, Guns. Nimmo seems to think we can fix the rudder.' He waited, watching the dull expression in Tweedie's red-rimmed eyes. 'What do you think?'

Tweedie did not answer immediately. He stood looking around the ship, as if realising for the first time what the demolition would mean. Then he said thickly, 'I'd try anythin'.' He placed the bag on the deck. 'I don't want to die 'ere!'

'Right then. I'll tell the captain.'

But when he knocked on Corbett's door it was some time before he heard any movement. Then with a start he realised that Corbett was having to unlock the door, and he received a further shock when he saw the captain's face around the edge. He was unshaven and his shirt was crumpled and stained with sweat.

'What do you want?' Corbett stayed behind the door, his eyes shadowed with strain, his fingers gripping the varnished wood like a claw.

'The hands will be falling in directly, sir.' Through the narrow gap Trewin could see the empty bottle on the desk, the papers scattered across chairs and desk alike. 'Can I speak to you a minute?'

Corbett stepped back and allowed him to enter. Then he walked to the scuttle and threw it open. The lights were all burning, and apart from the one scuttle the whole cabin was sealed as for the night.

Trewin began carefully. 'I have been talking with the chief and other P.O.s. We might try and do the rudder repairs ourselves, sir.' He waited for some change of expression but Corbett remained staring at the scuttle. He continued quietly, 'We can kedge her on a sandpit. The rest will depend on what we can do there.'

Corbett said emptily, 'You're a fool, Trewin.'

Stubbornly Trewin said, 'Nimmo thinks he could do it.'

'Then he's a fool, too!' Corbett swung round. 'You know my orders. There's no point in adding to the men's agony because of some crackpot scheme which would never work, even if we had the time for it!'

Trewin noticed that both photographs had vanished from the desk, and then his eye fell on a sealed envelope which was propped against the silver inkstand. He felt suddenly cold, as if he was standing in a chill breeze.

He said, 'You told me once about responsibility, sir. To the ship and all that she represents.'

Corbett slammed his hand on the back of a chair. 'My God, Trewin! Don't you think I've thought of all this?'

Trewin continued, 'Well, what about responsibility to your people, sir?' He saw Corbett's lip tremble and persisted, 'Young Hammond, for instance. His father could have got him away long ago. But he stayed with the ship, because he thought it was his duty.' He took another step towards the desk. 'And Tweedie, what has he done to be left to rot in some prison camp? He's given his whole life to the Navy!' He was speaking quickly now, if only to prevent a rebuttal. 'They're all good men! They *deserve* a chance!'

Corbett replied slowly, 'I'll not prevent their leaving. I wish to God I had told them to go with *Prawn*.'

Trewin leaned on the desk, his eyes fixed on the captain's drawn face. 'They don't *want* that, can't you see? They're not running away like the others! They want to go as a company, as *your* ship's company! God in heaven, don't take away their pride now!'

He dropped his eyes briefly and saw that the envelope was addressed in Corbett's scrawling hand to his wife.

Corbett stared at the carpet. In a small voice, he said, 'You mean well, but you don't understand what you're suggesting.'

'Yes, I do. I've been thinking. At first I thought as you do. But if it is only a chance, we will have tried, and that's what matters now.' He shot Corbett a quick glance. 'We could make for Batavia in Java, sir. We're bound to find some of the fleet there.'

Corbett shook his head. 'It's impossible. Even if the first part of your plan proved likely, I don't think you understand what you're asking. Five hundred and fifty miles through waters patrolled and dominated by the enemy. Our supporting ships have pulled back by now. We'd be quite alone. A crippled ship, too.' His voice shook with emotion. 'Gunboats are designed for rivers and inshore waters. Even *Prawn* will have great difficulty in getting away, in spite of leaving earlier.' He controlled himself with obvious effort. 'No, Trewin, it would be madness to give our people false hope and endanger their lives to no purpose.'

Trewin stepped around the desk and swept some papers on to the deck. Shining coldly on the blotting pad was a cocked and loaded revolver. He said harshly, 'Isn't this madness, too?' He saw Corbett's jaw drop open as he added, 'What good do you think it will do the ship and the rest of us by killing yourself?'

He expected anger or another controlled attack, but Corbett seemed to collapse into the chair, as if the muscles and sinews of his body had at last given out.

Trewin said gently, 'I'm sorry, sir. But I couldn't just stand here and let you . . .'

Corbett's head was hanging over his hands. 'It's no *use*, Trewin. I can't go on. You don't understand. I tried to do my duty as I saw it. I thought I was getting a second chance.' His shoulders shook. 'My wife was right after all. She always told me that I was a failure, but I didn't care then. I had the ship and Martin.' His voice trailed away, then he said, 'And there's something else I *didn't* tell you.'

Trewin replied quietly, 'Your eyes?' He could hardly bear to watch the astonishment on Corbett's face as he stared up at him. 'Yes, I knew all about them, sir. Dr. Massey told me.'

Corbett spoke with real difficulty. 'And you stayed quiet about it?'

'I had a lot of time to think. Time to remember. Like the time you ran the ship aground when we were entering the Talang Inlet. You knew there was a danger of grounding in the dark, but you were too stubborn and too . . .' Trewin sought for the right word, 'too *honest* to allow me to take the ship in. You knew that if anything went wrong I would be blamed. And your sense of justice would not allow that, even at the expense of this ship!'

Corbett stood up and walked back across the cabin, so that his head and shoulders were framed in the scuttle in silhouette. 'I'm going blind, Trewin!' The words seemed to break from his lips. 'It's been coming for months. There's nothing I can do.' He spread his arms. 'I'm finished! But I will write you some fresh orders. *You* take the ship. I'll not try and stop you this time!'

There was a tap at the door, and Trewin thrust the pistol into a drawer before calling, 'Enter!'

It was Tweedie, his face set and apprehensive. 'Any orders, sir?'

Trewin stepped in front of Corbett and replied, 'Prepare to lay out an anchor for kedging ship, Guns. The tide's on the turn, so we've not much time.'

Tweedie swallowed hard and peered towards the captain. 'Really?'

Trewin repeated, 'Lay out an anchor.' He stood quite still until Tweedie had left. Then he turned and said, 'We may make a hash of it, sir, but at least we'll have a bloody good try!'

Corbett was looking at him, his face in deep shadow. 'The amateurs have become the real professionals.' His voice was shaking badly. 'If you are sure, then I . . .' He broke off as a wave of cheering echoed along the *Porcupine's* upperdeck.

Trewin tried to grin. '*They* think you can do it, sir. I think that is your answer.'

227

Corbett sat down again, his head on one side as the cheering continued. 'They don't know what they're asking!'

Trewin moved towards the door. 'I think they do.' He turned away, feeling guilty at sharing Corbett's private grief. 'You tell us what to do, and we'll get the old *Porcupine* to Java, or bloody Australia if necessary!'

He stepped out on to the bridge wing and into the smoky sunlight, and looked down at the busy figures on the gunboat's deck. Then with a deep breath he climbed down the ladder where Unwin and the others were waiting for him.

The coxswain said gruffly, 'Well done, sir. You must have put a good case to the captain.'

Trewin felt the infectious excitement all around him. 'Well, let's hope the idea works!' He thought of Corbett's pistol and the sudden enormity of the responsibility which lay ahead. Then he said harshly, 'We sail tonight. Or not at all. So let's get to it!'

*　　*　　*

It took the best part of an hour to move the gunboat into what was considered to be the best position. Using one anchor and the power on the capstan, she was jockeyed this way and that while Trewin hovered near by in the motor boat, one eye on the work and the other on the tide, as on either side of the ship the long sandbar lifted above the water like some surfacing sea monster.

At last the *Porcupine* was settled firmly astride the bar, and even before the last of the falling tide had swirled clear of her plates Nimmo and his assistants were floundering in the thick yellow mud, their naked bodies soon caked from head to foot.

Trewin climbed back on board and walked aft to watch the frantic preparations. Everybody but the anti-aircraft gunners was employed doing something, and even the cook and his mate were slithering in the mud and ooze beneath the stern, helping to carry away the thick sand from the rough trench which was being dug around the rudders.

So intent were they on their desperate preparations that each man appeared oblivious to the distant shellbursts beyond the town and the curtain of smoke overhead.

Nimmo stood knee deep in the mud and shaded his eyes to look up at Trewin. 'The port outer is okay, sir. The starboard outer has gone completely, sheared off at the rods.' He wiped a smear of slime from his forehead. 'The centre one is badly buckled.'

Everyone had stopped work to listen, like patients around a doctor at some mass diagnosis.

Trewin rubbed his chin. 'What d'you think, Chief?'

Nimmo shrugged. 'I can remove the centre one. If I could use it to replace the starboard outer rudder you would have a fair purchase on your steering. Of course, it wouldn't be as good as having three, but it would see you all right.' He knelt down again. 'Trouble is, the rods are badly sheared. Even if I could straighten the rudder, I'd need a welding kit. And that we don't have, sir.'

There was something like a sigh from the watching men. Then Nimmo added, 'Still, we'll get on with the job. No point in looking at it.'

Trewin replied tightly, 'High water is at fourteen hundred, Chief. If we can't do it by then we won't do it at all.' He looked at the distant pier. 'There may be Jap soldiers standing there this time tomorrow!'

He turned away and saw Mallory staring at him. Mallory asked calmly, 'Anything I can do?'

'If we can get clear of here we shall need all the charts for sailing south via the Berhala Strait and on to Banka Island.' He kept his tone formal. 'Just check your stores and see if you've got them.'

Mallory stepped closer and dropped his voice. 'Look, Number One, I'm damn sorry about the kid, but how was I to know?'

Trewin eyed him coolly. 'If the captain's wife had done as she was told the boy would be alive today.'

'Hell, you're laying it on a bit thick! You know what she's

like. If it hadn't been me it would have been some other joker!'
He shrugged vaguely. 'She was a tart. She was fine in bed, but
I don't see her as the faithful wife.'

Trewin made sure no one was close by. 'Listen to me, and
listen good! You've never got on with the captain because
you've never even tried. Ever since I came aboard I've heard
nothing but moans and complaints from you about him and
the whole Navy in general.'

Mallory said angrily, 'I didn't exactly see you hitting it off
eye to eye with him.'

Trewin ignored him. 'I still don't. But just answer me this.
Would you have made a point of going for his wife if she had
not been married to Corbett?' He saw the uncertainty on
Mallory's dark features and added remorselessly, 'Don't bother
to answer now. It's written all over you.'

'So what do you want me to do? Go and apologise to him?'

Trewin looked away. 'If he ever found out about you, Mallory, because of something you say or do, I won't have to kill
you. *He* will!'

Mallory bit his lip. 'For Christ's sake!'

'We're not playing by the rules any more, Pilot, and one life
more or less doesn't count for much around here.'

At that moment the quartermaster called, 'There's a dinghy
comin', sir!'

Trewin walked to the rail and stared at the small boat with
its five bronzed occupants. From their forage caps and khaki
shorts he saw that they were soldiers. They were floating aimlessly with the sluggish current and watching the sailors working the rudders, like casual holidaymakers on the Thames.

Trewin cupped his hands. 'Boat ahoy! What do you want?'

The boat nudged into the sandbar, and one of the men
climbed out to stare up at the gunboat's deck. He was tall and
tough-looking, and his thick arms were covered with tattooes.
Surprisingly he pulled his heels together and threw a smart
salute.

'Sarnt Pitt, sir!' He nodded towards the other soldiers.

'Them's four of my sappers.' He lifted his chin with a touch of defiance. 'Royal Engineers, sir!'

Trewin had a sudden picture of the tall, gaunt sergeant marching back into the smoke with his small rearguard to lay the charges in the face of the Japanese advance. Of the officer dying on the beach beside his ridiculous shooting stick. Of a hundred other nameless faces.

He asked, 'What are you doing out here, Sergeant?'

The man moved a bit nearer. 'Nothing else to do at present. My last remaining officer is busy preparing to surrender himself so I thought I'd bring my lads out here.' He could not hide the bitterness in his tone. 'They are all I've got left now.'

Nimmo appeared from under the stern, his eyes peering through a mask of mud. 'Engineers, did you say?' He spat on the sand. 'Have you got any welding gear, you know, a portable unit of some sort?'

The sergeant smiled calmly. 'I have. Matter of fact, I saw what you were doing through my glasses. I wondered if you might want a bit of professional help.'

There was a dull clang and Donovan, the stoker petty officer, shouted, 'We've got the bloody thing off!'

Nimmo looked hard at Trewin. 'This is the answer, sir. If the sergeant could bring the gear out here we might still get the job done in time.'

Trewin felt the nerves jumping in his body like live things. 'Could you, Sergeant?'

The soldier squatted comfortably beside the watching sailors. 'We've been building pontoon bridges for the most part.' He nodded. 'Sure, it would be a piece of cake!'

Nimmo slapped his shoulder. 'Thanks a lot, mate!'

The sergeant stood up and added, 'I said that I *could*.'

Nimmo exploded, 'Now, just a minute!'

But Trewin held up his hand. 'Spit it out, Sergeant. What do you want?'

The soldier looked him squarely in the eyes. 'I want passage for me and my sappers, sir.' He glanced at the smoking town.

'I'm not staying here to die. Not now. Not for those bastards!'
He lifted his head again. 'They're my terms, sir.'

One of the other soldiers called, 'We can bring some Brens, too. We'll work our passage, don't you fear.'

Nimmo chuckled. 'You're a cool 'un chum.' To Trewin he added, 'I've lost all my Chink stokers, sir. Any help will be more than welcome.'

Trewin smiled. 'Take the motor boat and fetch the gear.' He returned the sergeant's salute and continued, 'I'd have taken you anyway, with or without your permission.'

The sergeant watched the motor boat muttering into life. 'This is a press gang I'll not argue with, sir!'

Hammond joined Trewin by the rail. 'What d'you think? Can we complete the change-over in time?'

Trewin rubbed his chin. 'Touch and go, Sub.'

'Er, how is the captain?' Hammond was still watching the hurrying motor boat. 'Will he be all right?'

Trewin thought of the slumped, beaten figure alone in the cabin. The letter propped on the desk, the cocked revolver. He answered, 'I think so.'

'Now then, what are we all waiting for?' They turned as one, momentarily caught off guard by Corbett's sharp voice.

The captain was standing on the battery deck beside the aft gun staring down at the lolling, mud-daubed figures by the stern. He was dressed in a crisp white shirt, and his face seemed to glow, as if from a recent shave and cold shower.

Trewin stared at him with amazement. Then he answered, 'I've sent some men for welding gear, sir.'

Corbett nodded. 'I heard that part, Number One. But what the blazes are you doing at this particular moment?'

'Well, sir.' Trewin could not take his eyes from Corbett's neat figure. 'As a matter of fact . . .'

Corbett nodded 'As I thought. Nothing.' He rubbed his hands. 'I suggest you send away the other boat and see if there are some stokers still in the harbour. You know, the ones who worked the harbour launches.' His brow was creased in thought 'And get a few extra life-rafts, they'll help to protect us from flying splinters if we are attacked, eh? And when you've attended to that, I think you ought to get that horrible object, whom I now recognise as the cook, to prepare a good solid meal for all hands.' He gave Trewin a flat stare. 'Right?'

Trewin saluted. '*Right*, sir.' For a split second he saw a slight softening of Corbett's stare. As if he was trying to say something, to thank him. Trewin added, 'I think we'll make it, sir.'

Corbett looked around at the filthy, breathless seamen. 'Make it? I should damn well hope so!'

He walked away, and Trewin stared at the empty guardrail, half expecting to awake from a dream. Then he looked at Nimmo. 'Well, you heard him, Chief.'

Nimmo bared his teeth in a grin. 'Loud and clear, sir!'

* * *

Trewin switched off his torch and stepped quickly into the shuttered wheelhouse. After the darkness and drifting smoke the light seemed too bright, and he had to wait a few seconds to restore his bearings. It still did not seem possible that they had succeeded in getting the ship ready for sea. Right up to the final minutes, as the rising water had lapped eagerly around the listing hull and slopped into Nimmo's sand trench, the men had worked with a kind of fanatical desperation, each one conscious only of the passing seconds which measured his last chance of survival.

Then, as Nimmo had dragged himself aboard, the gunboat had tilted upright with satisfied dignity and had allowed herself to be moved back to her buoy. For the remainder of the day the work of preparation had continued, although to all outward appearances the ship was as before, her A.A. guns manned, her awnings spread and the boats tied alongside.

Trewin was surprised to find that he was not totally exhausted. Perhaps deep down he had felt like the others. He had never really expected any real success from their efforts, and now that the ship was afloat again his whole being throbbed with nervous excitement in time with the pulsating engines.

Once darkness had fallen the ship had slipped her buoy and drifted with the current until well clear of the nearest pier. Then she had dropped anchor to await the final moment of departure.

Trewin looked around the wheelhouse and tried to make sure he had forgotten nothing. He had been right round the ship. There was little time left for second chances.

Unwin was standing loosely behind the wheel, idly watching his telegraphsmen. Feet moved restlessly on the upper bridge where signalmen and look-outs waited for the ship to move, and from right forward Trewin heard the sharp click of metal as someone made an adjustment to the capstan.

He sighed and walked along the passageway to the tiny chartroom. Mallory was leaning across the table, his face screwed with concentration as he ran his parallel rulers across a chart, while Corbett stood against the opposite bulkhead, toying with the strap of his binoculars.

Trewin said, 'Ship is ready to proceed, sir. All awnings stowed and boats hoisted inboard.' In the sealed stillness of the chartroom he thought he could hear his heart beating.

Corbett's eyes flashed palely in the chart light. 'Very good.' He sounded very calm. 'I want you to go forrard and make sure the cable comes aboard as quietly possible. Put as much grease as you can find on it. We don't want some spy to report our sailing. There'll be trouble enough later on without advertising our departure.'

Trewin looked at the clock. 'Five minutes, sir.'

'Yes.' Corbett dropped his gaze on Mallory's shoulders. 'I shall go up top in a minute.'

Trewin remembered *Prawn*'s passage through the littered channel and wondered if Corbett was gauging their own chances. Moving to this anchorage had cut some of the dangers but it would be far from easy.

As if reading his thoughts Corbett said, 'Put two good look-outs right forrard. They'll be able to see anything before we can on the bridge.' He looked hard at Trewin. 'But I shall take no chances.'

Trewin nodded. Was Corbett trying to reassure him? In this sort of darkness it hardly mattered how good a man's sight was. He said awkwardly, 'I'll go then.'

He walked out into the night air again, past the waiting seamen, his feet guiding him across hidden objects and fittings with a practice which had become part of his life. It was hard to remember any other purpose to living. More difficult still to see beyond these requirements of duty and routine.

He found Hammond in the eyes of the ship, his arms outspread on the guardrail as he stared towards the embattled city. Out here at the furthest extent of the anchorage they had a wider view of the port. The waterfront buildings looked black and stark against the unbroken crimson glow which covered the whole town. Carried on the warm breeze they could hear the actual sounds of fire and of shots, and every so often small cries, like voices in hell.

It was impersonal and remote, part of an insane holocaust, yet Trewin knew that just there across the glittering sheet of water men were fighting and dying, seeking shelter and cursing those who had betrayed them.

A seaman called in a hushed voice, 'Right, sir!'

There was a quick hiss of steam from the capstan, and then with a determined grunt the cable began to move slowly through the hawsepipe. Clank, clank, clank, each link jarring a fresh memory alive in Trewin's thoughts as he stood in silence watching the shore.

He knew he was seeing the falling of a fortress, perhaps the end of a whole era, but his mind refused to stay aloof from the separate, more personal pictures which flitted across it in time with the dripping links of anchor cable.

In the late afternoon he had been ashore for the last time. With Dancy and some armed ratings he had gone to collect a few more men to replace the Chinese sailors. That part had been easier than he had expected. He had found some stokers from the port launches altogether in a deserted canteen amidst a litter of beer bottles. They had been preparing to await the final collapse in their own way, and had stared at Trewin and the others like men watching a small miracle.

Above the crackle of flames he had suddenly heard the plaintive wail of bagpipes, and with his men had stood aside as a platoon of Scottish soldiers had marched through the smoke behind their piper, their arms swinging, their step as firm as if they had been on parade. Now, looking back, it seemed as if every soldier had had the same face.

He had found four marine bandsmen wandering aimlessly through a street carrying their instruments even in the face of disaster, and when he had ordered them to the motor boat one of them had burst into tears.

As they had made their way to the pier Trewin had glanced into an open-fronted restaurant. The place had been deserted but for a middle-aged couple. They had been sitting at a table holding hands and staring at each other across a last meal. They did not even look at Trewin as he passed. There had been candles burning on the table and wine in an ice bucket.

Hammond leaned right over the rail and called softly, 'Up and down, Number One!'

Trewin flashed his torch twice towards the bridge and heard the clang of telegraphs.

There had been other sights too. Of men driven beyond reason, robbing shops and stores with pointless fury and desperation. He had seen women amongst them, wild-eyed and screaming as they were caught in the hysteria of terror and defeat.

As they climbed on to the pier they had seen some native policemen wearing small Japanese flags on their tunics, and Dancy had pulled his revolver angrily from his holster, muttering, 'The bastards! They won't live to welcome the Japs!'

But Trewin had pushed his arm down. 'Leave them, Buffer! Let them find their escape their own way. It'll be hard to stay alive anyway, let alone for those who served the British.'

'Anchor's aweigh!'

Trewin watched the cable go bar taut and swing like a pendulum, then flashed his torch once more. The deck gave a nervous quiver, and he saw the water begin to froth away from the stem in a small but increasing wave. They were moving.

He said, 'Secure for sea, Sub.' Then he turned and made his way back to the bridge.

He passed Dancy by the four-inch gun and heard him say quietly, 'It's like watching the end of everything.'

Trewin sighed. 'Better to have your dreams shattered now than have nightmares for the rest of your life, Buffer.' He touched his arm and began to climb up the ladder. Looking down he saw Dancy still watching the fierce glow above Singapore, his body swaying stiffly with the ship's gentle movement. Like the day the *Prince of Wales* and *Repulse* had been sunk, Trewin thought grimly.

On the upper bridge it was very quiet, with the silent figures standing out in various hues from the reflected fires. Corbett was by the screen, head jutting forward towards the bows.

'Slow ahead port, half astern starboard.' His voice was clipped but quite calm.

Trewin watched the great panorama swinging slowly across the ship's bows, remembering Adair's words with sudden clarity. '. . . so that I shall remember. Always!'

'Stop starboard.' Corbett half turned, his face pale in the glow. 'Half ahead both engines. One one zero revolutions.'

The *Porcupine* shivered and then began to push steadily down channel, her wash rolling away and breaking against the forlorn and deserted buoys.

Corbett added sharply, 'Tell the coxswain to watch his steering! We can't be too sure of the rudder yet.'

A man said quietly, 'Listen to 'im! 'Is son's dead, all 'ell is burnin' over there, and 'e just sits there givin' orders like nothin' 'as 'appened!'

Trewin turned swiftly, his rebuke caught in mid-air as he heard Masters, the yeoman growl, 'An' just you pray 'e keeps on sittin' there, you stupid bugger!'

Trewin climbed on to the gratings and said, 'Ship secured for sea, sir.'

'Very good.' Corbett rapped, 'Port ten! Midships!' He leaned out across the screen to watch a sodden black shape slide abeam. It might have been a capsized boat or part of a bomb-blasted building. He said, 'We must get well clear of the island by dawn. It will be alive with enemy aircraft soon.'

'Yes, sir.' Trewin watched the drifting clouds of sparks from a tall, gutted warehouse. It was impossible, but he imagined he could feel the savage heat on his face even across the long stretch of water.

He heard Corbett say distantly, 'There's no defence against one's imagination. I suppose that's where our real weakness lies.' He turned and stared at his profile, but Corbett was again looking at the bows.

Trewin said, 'Shall I take the con, sir?'

Corbett shook his head. 'Not yet, Trewin.' He ran his hands along the screen. 'She'll be all right.'

Trewin stepped down and waited beside the voice-pipe. To Corbett their stealthy departure must mean so much more. Over there, amidst the flames and the despair, he was leaving part of himself. His hopes, his beliefs and what happiness he had ever known.

Trewin shook his head. No, this was not a moment Corbett would want to share with anyone.

14

The Hunt Is On

Once clear of the port waters the *Porcupine* made a wide turn and headed west for the Durian Strait. The slow journey was an agony of strain and concentration as the little ship picked her way between the sprawling mass of islands and reefs, narrow channels and tiny islets which guarded the southern approaches to Singapore and through which lay the only safe path to the Strait.

Hardly a full five minutes would pass without alterations of course and speed, and twice on the first leg of the journey the ship ran aground. With white breakers leaping from nearby rocks the engines were coaxed astern until finally the gunboat backed clear and picked up her course once more into the darkness.

Still under cover of night they turned south into the Durian Strait and increased speed, caution giving way to urgency as the first pale gleam of dawn showed itself above the nearby islands.

With every man holding his breath the *Porcupine* swung inshore towards the southernmost island in the group and dropped her anchor within yards of a smooth, deserted beach. The sunlight was already touching the topmasts as seamen swarmed ashore to gather palm fronds while others rigged nets and shredded awnings across the bridge and superstructure. When at last a look-out reported an approaching aircraft the ship was completely camouflaged in a mass of freshly cut palms and bushes, so that from the air she would appear as just one more extension to the land.

Food was served on deck as the ship's company seemed unwilling to go below except for matters of duty. As the day wore on they squatted or lay about the decks, staring up through their flimsy protection at the regular comings and goings of enemy aircraft. Mostly they flew low overhead, confident and indifferent, each pilot aware that there was no longer fear of attack or of a sudden barrage. But no aircraft altered course to inspect the little bay, nor did anyone apparently notice the thin wisp of funnel smoke which drifted skyward as evidence of the ship's readiness for instant departure.

Nimmo and the resourceful Sergeant Pitt took turns in diving in the clear water to inspect the rudders, but as far as they could judge the repairs had withstood the rough passage well.

Trewin made himself go to his cabin to shave and change his shirt. It was more as something to keep him occupied than for any hope of wiping away the strain of the first part of the journey. Looking at the chart did not help either. It had taken the whole night to cover a total distance of forty miles, and there were still over five hundred to go before any sort of help could be expected. The ship was very quiet. Just the whirr of fans and the gentle murmur of a generator, nothing else moved. It was strange that he had not considered this part of the plan. He was not even sure that he had thought of anything but the actual moment of escape.

During the nerve-dragging hours of darkness, while every man on the bridge had strained his eyes into the black curtain beyond the bows, Corbett had said suddenly, 'We'll stand no chance at all if we just try and run for it. That was why *Beaver* was caught.'

Nobody had turned to look at him, yet Trewin knew that every man within earshot was hanging on Corbett's words. Even now, in the privacy of his cabin, he could hear the steady swish of water against the hull, the monotonous bleep of the echo sounder, the rasp of his own breath as he had waited with the others.

Corbett had continued, 'We shall steam by night and take cover during the daylight hours. We will keep well clear of Sumatra and instead hug the islands as far south as we can.' He had turned to look at Mallory. 'We should pass through the Berhala Strait tomorrow night and make for the Seven Islands Group.' He had paused to allow his words to sink in. 'That'll mean crossing open water, sixty miles or so. After that we just have to wait our chance to cross the next big stretch of open sea to pass round the Banka Island.' He had become suddenly grave. 'Once through the Banka Strait we will be on the last lap.'

Corbett was there now on the upper bridge, sitting in his chair, absorbed in his thoughts and sharing them with no one. It was impossible to reach Corbett. What little understanding there may have been seemed to have been severed and left behind in Singapore. It was just as if Corbett needed every ounce of power and strength concentrated in his mind and that his body and personal thoughts had become merely incidental.

There was a tap at the door, and Trewin turned to stare at Ching's gaunt, bearded face, as if he was looking at a ghost. 'I thought you had left the ship with the others, Ching.' Even as he spoke Trewin's tired mind registered the fact that his bunk was neatly made and his shirt had been freshly laundered.

Ching's hooded eyes glittered. 'This ship my home also, sir. I not leave now. Not when I am needed.'

Trewin felt strangely moved. 'Did you want something?'

'Captain send for you, sir. On bridge.'

Trewin reached for his cap. 'Trouble?'

The old Chinese shrugged. 'All kinds of trouble, sir. Some worse than others, but all bad.'

Trewin smiled. 'Well, it's good to see your face again. I thought I'd made a complete check before we sailed.'

Ching showed his yellow teeth. 'I hide in paint store, sir.'

Trewin shook his head. 'When did you get out?'

'This morning, sir. Mr. Tweedie found me an' say he going to kick my bloody arse for me!' The old man's grin widened. 'But I think it worth it all same.'

Trewin climbed up to the bridge and found Hammond standing grim faced beside Corbett's chair. The captain had a steel mirror propped against the screen and was shaving with an open razor. He gestured with the blade. 'Tell the first lieutenant.' Then he carried on shaving.

Hammond looked hollow eyed, and Trewin saw that his shoes and legs were caked with slime and wet sand. He said, 'I have been ashore on a reccee, Number One. This island is supposed to be uninhabited, but I went to make sure.'

Trewin nodded. That again was typical of Corbett to remember the small but essential matters of detail. Like paragraphs in a long-discarded training manual, he seemed to produce each item with neither effort nor conscious thought.

'I took Petty Officer Kane.' Hammond looked at his shoes. 'On the far side of the place there's another little bay, just like this one.' He was speaking more quickly now, describing each moment just as he had seen it. 'Kane said that there was driftwood in the water, and I thought it might be some wreckage from the *Beaver*.' He looked directly at Trewin. 'They were dead bodies. A whole line of them, just rolling about in the surf, forgotten, left like slaughtered pigs!'

Trewin asked flatly, 'Some of our men?'

Hammond gripped the chart table. 'They were all women. Nurses!'

Corbett was wiping the razor on his towel. He said, 'They had apparently been marched into the sea and machine-gunned from the beach.'

Hammond said in a choked voice, 'They didn't *have* to do that, did they? For Christ's sake, *nurses*!'

Corbett turned and looked at him impassively. 'The point is that the enemy have been here recently. We will have to be more careful than ever.'

Hammond looked at Trewin, his eyes pleading. 'Couldn't we go back and bury them? It wouldn't take long, and I know that our people would want it that way.'

Corbett said, 'I'm afraid that is impossible. It would simply be asking for trouble if the graves were seen by a patrol.'

Trewin took Hammond's arm and guided him to the rear of the bridge. 'He's right, Sub. I'd have said the same.'

Hammond bit his lip. 'I kept thinking of Jacqui. I walked

through the surf looking at their faces. Some of them were just girls!'

Trewin said, 'I know. Thank God Adair commands the *Prawn*. He knows these waters well. His passengers will stand a better chance.' He thought of Clare's dark, pleading eyes. 'The best chance in the world.'

A seaplane droned slowly overhead, and together they stared up at it between the criss-cross of netting and palm fronds. It was strange how safe the camouflage made them feel, how remote from that symbol of ruthless power. The plane dipped over the island and the sound of the engine was lost in the murmur of surf.

Trewin said, 'Go round the ship. Try and keep the men cheerful. I still don't believe they realise what is expected of them.'

He watched Hammond climb down to the deck. There was little left of the young, impressionable officer Trewin had met when he had saluted the gunboat's quarterdeck for the first time.

When he turned again he saw that Corbett was asleep, his head resting on one outflung arm across the closed voice-pipes. In sleep his severe features looked relaxed and almost youthful, and Trewin felt vaguely like an intruder.

Apart from the look-outs, most of the ship's company had followed the captain's example, and Trewin wished that he too could find a temporary escape in empty dreams.

During the dog watches the camouflage was removed, and with little fuss the ship weighed and headed away from the quiet bay. Darkness was still a few hours ahead, and by the time the first purple shadows had reached the islands the *Porcupine* was heading south at full speed towards the Berhala Strait and the first challenge of open sea.

*   *   *

The first part of the journey went better than anyone really expected. Once clear of the shallows, but keeping within a few miles of the larger islands, the *Porcupine* lost no time in working up to her maximum speed of fourteen knots. Not since her keel had cut through the cold Scottish waters on her first trials had she made such supreme effort to show what she could attain. Every plate and rivet shook and vibrated to the tune of her engines, and the steep waves pushed aside from the bows rolled away into the darkness on either beam in solid white furrows.

And the *Porcupine*'s speed was now doubly important. Shortly after midnight the radio room had intercepted a brief but important signal. All resistance in Singapore had ceased. The entire British garrison was at the mercy of the conquerors.

Corbett had listened to the telegraphist's message and had replied slowly, 'Now they will know we've sailed. The hunt is on.'

'Trewin stood on the starboard wing of the bridge moving his glasses slowly back and forth in an effort to distinguish sea from sky. The hunt would indeed be on. The Japs would search every inlet and island amongst their newly acquierd territories. No ship would be allowed to escape. No efforts would be spared.

A look-out's voice, sharp and urgent, broke into his thoughts. 'Light, sir! Bearing green one one zero!'

Corbett's body moved swiftly across the bridge like a pale ghost. 'Stop engines!'

As the power was cut from her whirling screws the gunboat seemed to sag heavily into her own wash, as if she had smashed her blunt bows into some solid object. Men cursed and staggered while they sought to train their glasses, and Trewin felt the steel sides of the bridge biting into his shoulder as the ship slewed awkwardly against the demands of her rudders.

He saw the light almost immediately. A few bright flashes, far out on the starboard quarter, followed at once by answering pinpricks even further away, maybe on the horizon itself.

Corbett said abruptly, 'Slow ahead together. Port fifteen.' To Trewin he called, 'Two ships. Probably patrols. We will have to move closer inshore.'

Minutes dragged by, and then the waiting look-outs saw another stammer of signal lamps. This time they were closer together, and Trewin heard Mallory breathing heavily as he made a few quick calculations. Then he called, 'They were on converging courses, sir. To cover that distance in six minutes they must be knocking up about twenty knots at least.' He sounded wary.

Corbett reseated himself before replying, 'Hmm, destroyers, if I'm not mistaken.'

Trewin did not have to consult the chart to picture the two powerful warships sweeping up and down the wide curve of the Berhala Strait. Here it was no wider than the English Channel. But as one seaman had remarked earlier, there was no green and friendly Kent to offer hope and safety like there had been at Dunkirk.

Corbett said sharply, 'Give me a course for the southernmost point of Singkep Island, Pilot.'

Trewin was still staring through his glasses, but the sea was black and empty once more. He listened to Mallory's pencil on the chart, half wondering if the Australian ever thought about Corbett's wife and what might lie ahead for both of them.

'One two zero, sir.'

'Very good. Bring her round now.' Corbett twisted in his chair and beckoned to Trewin. Then he said, 'Singkep Island is the last one in the group. I had hoped to head straight out into the open sea for the Seven Islands and be there before dawn. But these enemy patrols make it too risky. Any fool could see our wash miles away. We must reduce speed for the rest of the night and lie inshore off Singkep until tomorrow.'

'That will mean losing a day, sir.'

'I know.' He removed his cap and ran his hand over his hair. 'There's a lighthouse around the point. It's not in use, of course, but I do know that there is a reliable keeper in charge of it. I met him once. We might be able to find out from him what the Japs are doing.'

'Is it safe, sir?'

'No, of course it isn't!' Corbett sounded tense. 'We don't have any damn choice!'

Singkep Island was small, barely twenty miles across, but it was more than formidable. The coast was high and rocky, and in many places the cliffs fell away on to steep barriers of reefs. The chart showed the whole area to be littered with wrecks, mostly unfortunate traders caught in past storms which swept down from the South China sea with neither warning nor mercy.

Trewin stood beside Corbett, listening to the echo-sounder and watching the writhing barrier of tossing breakers which girdled the point with everlasting spray. At one moment the ship seemed to be entirely surrounded by white-dashed rocks, and he tried to stop himself from holding his breath and waiting for that final impact.

But the *Porcupine*'s small draught saved her, when any other ship would have long since foundered. Corbett could see no more than any look-out, probably much less, yet he seemed to be feeling his way towards the wedge-shaped bay beyond the point, building up a picture in his mind from Mallory's stream of information and the imperturbable echo-sounder.

At three in the morning they dropped anchor, with the spray from the nearest reef drifting across the upper bridge like tropical rain.

Corbett wasted no time. 'Lower the dory and send Hammond ashore to the lighthouse. It's at the top of that ridge. The only building there, so he should be able to find it.'

Men scampered to the davits, and within minutes the small boat was bobbing uneasily in the surging tide-race alongside.

Corbett said to Hammond, 'Make it quick. The man you want is Javanese, but he speaks good English. Find out all you can. Ask him about enemy ships.' He seemed restless. 'Anything which you think can help.'

They watched the boat as it curtsied over the creaming back-wash from the foot of the cliffs, and then Corbett said, 'I'm not happy about all this.'

Trewin waited, but Corbett again lapsed into silence. He said

'I didn't know you had been down here before, sir. That was a fine piece of navigation.' He could not disguise his admiration.

Corbett shrugged. 'The last time I was here was ten years ago.' He ignored Trewin's quick intake of breath. 'We were doing a survey at the time. I was navigating officer.'

Trewin stared at him. 'And you mean you remember from that far back?'

Corbett sounded indifferent. 'I have not been wasting all my time out here, you know!' He added, 'You have to learn to use all your faculties, even when some of them fail you.'

Trewin walked across to the opposite side to watch for the dory. He saw Mallory leaning against the chart table and wondered what he would say if he knew Corbett had conned the ship through the reefs and breakers with little more than his memory to help him.

An hour passed, and then they saw the dory pulling back towards the ship, the oars dipping and slicing as the small hull bounced across each succeeding line of retreating waves.

Hammond panted on to the bridge even as the falls were hooked on and the boat returned to its davits. He said breathlessly, 'I found him, sir. He says that there was a Jap destroyer and some small patrol boats here yesterday afternoon.' He gulped painfully. 'And he thinks that there are some troops on the other side of the island.'

'He only *thinks*?' Corbett's voice was toneless.

'Well, sir, they were there in the morning. Searching for anyone who might have escaped from Singapore.' He continued more calmly, 'They did capture some soldiers who had got away in a yacht.'

'I see.' Corbett slipped from his chair and walked absently across the gratings. 'Anything else?'

Hammond said tightly. 'They shot them, sir.' He paused, as if expecting Corbett to speak. Then he said, 'There is a small fishing village here too, sir. The soldiers were hiding there after their boat capsized on the rocks.'

Corbett stopped his pacing. 'And the fishermen betrayed them, I suppose?'

247

'Yes, sir.'

Corbett nodded slowly. 'The natives will be more afraid of the Japs than of us.' He squared his shoulders. 'We shall have to leave immediately. Stand by to break out the anchor.'

Hammond walked towards the ladder, his limbs moving like a man under drugs.

Trewin asked quietly, 'The Seven Islands, sir?'

'What else can we do?' Corbett was watching the men on the forecastle, their bodies dark against the distant surf. 'If we are caught here we can neither run nor fight. We would be in the jaws of a trap.' He became suddenly brisk. 'Ring standby on the engines.' To Mallory he snapped, 'As soon as we clear the reefs I want a course direct to the Seven Islands.' He did not wait for a reply but picked up the engine room handset.

'Chief? Captain speaking.' He paused as from forward came the steady clink of cable. 'I shall ring for full speed in about fifteen minutes. But I want more than that.'

Trewin could not hear Nimmo's face, but Corbett's reply was flat and final. He said, 'We have sixty miles ahead of us. It will be daylight in two hours. Do I have to say more?' He slammed down the phone and added, 'Now we shall just have to see, eh?'

*   *   *

Daylight found the *Porcupine* pounding steadily south-east, her wake creaming astern in a ruler-straight line. When the sun finally rose above the hazy horizon the men on watch saw that they had the sea to themselves. Instead of dark shadows and pale stars the air was crisp and very clear, and the sea a flat, glittering expanse of deep blue, the surface throwing back a million reflections and tiny mirrors from horizon to horizon. It was then that many of the ship's company came to realise for the first time the smallness and frailty of their ship and the vast, latent power of the sea around them.

Trewin felt the heat beating back from the steel plates at his side and pitied the gunners who waited beside their weapons

248

unprotected from the sun and salt-dried air. He saw that the soldiers had been true to their word and had mounted their Bren guns below the bridge under the watchful eye of Sergeant Pitt. The marine bandsmen were not being wasted either. Pitt had detailed one for each bren as loader, and Trewin wondered if they had brought their instruments aboard, too.

He glanced up at the quivering funnel and watched the smoke pumping astern in a steady stream. The bridge was shaking and groaning, and his own body felt as if it was in the grip of some mechanical fever. The gunboat was bursting her heart, and Trewin imagined that even the meticulous Nimmo had long given up watching the red gauges of warning.

He walked to the uncovered table and glanced at the chart. Mallory did not look up but laid the points of his dividers on the diagonal pencilled line. The Seven Islands were only miles away. It was incredible. At any minute the masthead look-out would actually see them, and every man would draw a small comfort from the sight of land. Not that these islands represented much in the way of salvation. The whole group was only ten miles wide, and some of the islets were little more than humps which had somehow managed to avoid sinking below the surface. Some fluke of nature had thrown them there. The last cluster of visible land at the southernmost extremity of the South China Sea. Beyond them there was another stretch of open, hostile sea and then the Banka Strait.

Once through that and they would be in the Java Sea. Trewin licked his dry lips. With luck they would find the remnants of the Far East Fleet there. Big ships, order and stability. They would be alone no longer.

Almost as the thought crossed his mind a voice yelled, 'Aircraft, sir! Red four five! Angle of sight two oh!'

Corbett seized his glasses. One second he had been sitting as if in a doze. Now he was craning forward, his whole body tensed and rigid.

Trewin fought back the sudden feeling of despair and trained his own glasses over the screen. Around and below him he heard the bark of orders and the crisp snap of metal as the bridge tannoy intoned, 'Repel aircraft! Repel aircraft!'

He blinked rapidly to clear his vision. For a moment he thought the haze and distance were playing games with him. The small hovering shape seemed to be stationary, like a flaw on the backcloth of empty sky.

Tweedie's voice came up from the bridge speaker. 'Flying boat, sir. Turnin' towards us now.'

Corbett nodded. 'Very good.'

The solitary aircraft was moving very slowly indeed, its high-mounted engines giving it an awkward top-heavy appearance which reminded Trewin of a toy glider.

Tweedie spoke again. 'Permission to open fire, sir?'

Corbett snapped, 'Hold it!' He gestured to Trewin. 'This pilot is behaving very strangely. He must have seen us.'

Trewin viewed the approaching plane from a different light. It was true. The seaplane should be hauling off now to wireless the *Porcupine*'s course and position to the searching ships and bombers. It was holding the same height and bearing, and unless something happened very quickly, would fly directly over the gunboat's port bow.

Corbett said, 'Stand fast "A" and "X" guns! I want all short-range weapons to fire when I give the order.' There was no emotion in his voice. He might just as easily have been discussing a point of discipline.

Several times he lowered his glasses to wipe his eyes, and Trewin saw something like anger on his face as he rubbed vigorously with his knuckles. He saw too that the glasses were set at full power.

Corbett said slowly, 'He's probably never seen a gunboat before. My guess is that he doesn't even know about us yet.' He curled his lip. 'Well, he is about to find out!'

Trewin gripped the vibrating screen and watched the flying boat through narrowed eyes. He did not need glasses any more, and the air throbbed with the plane's high-pitched engines as it flew doggedly towards the ship.

Corbett reached out and rested his hand on the red button.

He was staring straight at the aircraft, his eyes running and blinded as he refused to turn away from the sunlight beyond the glittering fusilage.

At the last second the pilot seemed to realise what was happening. Maybe a long flight had tired him, or perhaps he was expecting to rendezvous with a ship similar in his own mind to the British gunboat. But as the bell screamed above the roar of engines and the air was filled with the jubilant bang and rattle of Oerlikons and machine-guns, the flying boat swung dizzily into a steep climb, its great shadow blotting out the sun as it lifted drunkenly up and over the bows.

Trewin saw the bright orange flashes ripple along its fat underbelly and the quick bursts of smoke from one of the engines. The plane carried two bombs, one on either wing, probably for use against submarines, but as the smoke thickened to envelop the tail and floats he knew it would never get the chance to use them.

Men were cheering and shouting like children. Even the gunners, strapped and jerking with their weapons, were mouthing unheard words with the rest.

Bullets and cannon shells were following and ripping pieces from the flying boat, and even more ammunition was streaking uselessly towards the sun. Nobody cared about wastage any more. They were hitting back. For once they were winning.

Then, surprisingly, the flying boat levelled off, one of its engines well alight and its perspex cockpit cover shining from fires within.

Masters shouted, ' 'E's goin' to ditch! Look at 'im go!'

They could hear the plane's motors coughing and roaring like the sounds of a dying beast, but somehow it stayed airborne, and as the guns fell silent Trewin felt Corbett's fingers on his arm like a steel vice.

'Hard aport! Put the helm *over*!'

Trewin dragged his eyes from the burning plane and threw himself at the voice-pipes.

He heard Unwin's crisp reply, 'Hard aport, sir! Thirty-five of port wheel on, sir!'

The whole ship swayed as if about to capsize as the rudders clashed with the racing screws and threw the gunboat into a savage turn. The startled shouts and curses gave way to other cries when some saw what had made the captain act so desperately.

The flying boat was turning, the pilot using all his skill and strength to hold it above the water as it belched flames and black smoke and glided nearer and nearer to its own reflection.

A man shouted, 'It's coming straight for us!'

Corbett's voice was like a knife. 'Midships! Steady!'

The ships sudden turn took her slightly away from the aircraft's desperate attack, and as the bell rang again every gun which could bear opened up to challenge the pilot's suicide attempt to drop his aircraft directly on the *Porcupine*'s hull like one giant bomb.

A wing crumpled like paper, and with a great bellow of noise the aircraft lifted its nose, staggered and fell into the sea within fifty feet of the quarterdeck.

But it was not quite finished. While blazing fuel spread around the sinking fuselage and two figures tried vainly to free themselves from their private furnace, one of the bombs exploded.

The explosion was below the surface, but Trewin felt the ship lurch as if hit by a shell. Splinters whined above the side-deck and whimpered away over the sea, and one of the marine bandsmen who had run from his gun position to watch the plane fall was picked from his feet and hurled back against the unyielding steel like a piece of rubbish in a strong wind. Trewin tore his eyes away as the man's blood ran across the canting deck and splashed unheeded down the side of a ventilator.

Corbett was shouting, 'Slow ahead together! Report damage!'

Trewin knew what he was thinking but made himself stay silent as he stood watching the engine telephone.

Corbett snatched it from its hook before it had finished ringing. 'Yes?' His pale eyes were fixed on Trewin's face. 'I see. Right!' He strode back to his chair. 'Rudders are intact and functioning perfectly.' His chest was heaving beneath his smoke-stained shirt. 'Bring her round on course. We must get a move on.'

Masters said humbly, 'Masthead reports sighting the islands sir. Fine on the starboard bow.'

Corbett did not reply. He looked hard at Trewin and then said, 'Number three fuel tank has been punctured. There's no risk to the hull as yet, and I've you to thank for taking on a full fuel load before we sailed.'

He walked to the bridge wing and stared fixedly astern. Trewin followed him and saw some of the seamen at the rails, they too were peering back along the sharpening wake. There was no sign of the flying boat, and for a moment longer he wondered what they were looking at.

Then he saw it. A long, unbroken silver line, spreading and mingling with the wake, but staying to mark their passing long after the latter had faded.

Corbett said distantly, 'There are twenty tons of fuel in that bunker, Trewin. That's a lot of oil.' He turned and walked back to his chair.

Trewin stayed by the rail, his eyes watching the spreading trail of fuel which followed the ship like blood from a hunted animal.

Far astern there was a small haze of smoke to mark the flying-boat's grave. Trewin stared at it until his eyes smarted with pain. Why didn't you kill us properly? Did you have to prolong the suffering this way?

He turned and saw Phelps, the signalman, watching him. He tried to smile at him but his mouth refused to move. He walked to the opposite side and groped for his pipe. But when he took it from his pocket he remembered the soldier in the burning village. A man with a shooting stick and a pipe he was unable to fill because his hands refused to obey him. He felt the nerves screaming at the back of his mind, like voices from a cave. There was a sudden snap, and when he looked down he saw that the pipe had broken between his fingers.

Phelps said, 'I can fix that for you, sir.'

Trewin replied harshly, 'Mind your own bloody business!'

Corbett half turned in his chair and looked across at him. The expression was cold, and felt to Trewin like a douche of ice water. It was as if Corbett understood and was telling him to go on playing the game to its end.

He thrust the broken pipe into his pocket and stepped up to the screen. By holding his body tight against the steel plates he could exclude everybody from his sight and his mind. Ahead there was only the sea, and the horizon which never got any nearer.

15
Unexpected Rendezvous

Trewin rested his hands on the vibrating voice-pipes and looked up at Corbett's silhouette as he craned forward across the screen. 'Both engines slow ahead, sir. Seven oh revolutions.'

Corbett muttered, 'Very good.' Over his shoulder he said, 'We will head for the centre island. We should be more concealed there.'

It was very quiet on the upper bridge, and every eye was fixed upon the widening spread of green islands and brown-backed reefs, which all at once seemed to reach out to encircle the ship. It had taken longer than most people had expected to reach the protection of this small group of isolated islands, but the deception in time and distance was only visual. Each of the islands was higher than one would have anticipated from its small area, with hills rising two or three hundred feet above the burnished blue sea.

Corbett said calmly, 'We'll anchor in two fathoms. Put out a stream anchor from aft to stop us swinging. It'll be a pretty tight fit in there.'

Trewin saw Mallory exchange a quick glance with the yeo-man. Corbett's casual remarks about the islands and the dangerously confined anchorage had obviously impressed them. But Trewin knew that Corbett was no longer giving facts from memory. He had left the bridge for the first time just ten minutes earlier, as the ship had crossed the ten-fathom line and settled on her final approach towards the centre of the islands. Trewin had heard him slam the chartroom door, and minutes later when he had returned to the bridge he had seen the circular shape of the big magnifying glass inside Corbett's breast pocket. Now, behind those expressionless eyes, he probably had a complete picture of the islands, imprinted there by a few minutes of desperate concentration.

A flock of white sea birds rose in unison from a nearby reef and circled angrily above the slow-moving gunboat, their shrill cries only helping to add to the tension. Behind the bridge the Oerlikons swung overboard to cover the nearest islands, and on the forecastle the anchor party huddled together as if suddenly conscious of their vulnerability.

The tallest hill on the centre island looked very green and cool in spite of the relentless sun, and Trewin stared with sudden longing at the wide sweep of trees which came right down the hillside to the water's edge to cover the narrow strip of beach in deep shadow.

Two more weed-covered reefs parted across the bows, and Trewin saw the proposed anchorage opening up like a small lagoon. There would be little room to manœuvre, but the choice was a good one. He knew that the leaking fuel would stand little chance of spreading much beyond the protective rocks and sandbars, and any searching aircraft would have to fly very near to spot the tell-tale stain around the camouflaged hull. Provided their luck held, the wide slick of oil which had marked their passage for the past few miles would be carried away by the current, and it might be some time before some extra diligent pilot became suspicious.

Corbett said, 'Tell Hammond to stand by!'

Trewin climbed up beside him and lifted his hand towards the bows. The men around the cable were intent on their work, and Hammond was shading his eyes to look up at the bridge. Around the upperdeck gunners and look-outs watched the land as Corbett guided his ship towards the tiny bay.

At first Trewin imagined it was a shadow on the water or a strange trick of light. He blinked to clear his vision and looked again. Behind him a voice said, 'Four fathoms, sir.'

Trewin glanced quickly at Corbett but he was still staring ahead, his features composed and impassive. When he looked forward again he knew he was not mistaken. He swung round. 'Full astern together! Emergency!'

It seemed to take an age before anyone moved or passed his order to the wheelhouse, and all the time the dark, rust-coloured shape loomed nearer to the *Porcupine*'s probing stem.

Corbett leaned forward. 'What is it? What's happening?' For a few seconds he sounded startled, even unnerved.

Trewin felt the churning screws dragging at the hull and kept his eyes fixed on the jagged, rust-covered wreck which lay directly across the ship's path within feet of the surface. The distance became constant, and then as the screws took hold the ship began to move reluctantly astern.

He said tightly, 'There's a wreck right ahead, sir.' Without moving his eyes from it he added, 'Stop together.' The back-wash from the screws churned up a surrounding froth of sand and disturbed weed, as well as a strong stench of leaking fuel to remind him of the gunboat's hidden wounds.

Corbett replied thickly, 'Thank you.' He was looking over the screen, but it was obvious to Trewin that he still saw nothing of the wreck which in seconds would have torn out the *Porcupine*'s bottom like cardboard.

Trewin did not wait. 'Slow ahead together. Port fifteen.'

With her rounded flank almost brushing the submerged hulk the ship swung into the undisturbed calm of the anchorage, and as she slipped past Trewin found himself staring down through the clear water at the listing, shattered wreck which had tried so hard to claim a companion for her lonely vigil.

Corbett said, 'I'll take her now, Trewin.' He seemed controlled once more.

Trewin stepped down beside the table and peered at the chart. Mallory whispered savagely, 'It's not marked, see for yourself! D'you think I'd have kept quiet about a thing like that, for God's sake?'

Trewin felt the sweat running freely down his spine. He replied, 'It was probably missed when they surveyed the place last.' His voice sounded brittle.

Mallory stared at him. 'That doesn't explain why *he* missed it.' He waited for an answer, then added stubbornly, 'Well? What the hell is the matter with him?'

Trewin said, 'It was covered in weed.'

'Well, you saw it!' There was defiance in Mallory's eyes. 'I'm not satisfied that . . .'

Trewin faced him. He could feel his hands shaking from both shock and anger, but he could not stop himself. 'I don't give a bloody damn whether you're satisfied or not! I've already warned you once! This is the last time, see?'

Corbett called, 'Slow astern together! Let go!' There was an answering splash from forward and the fast rumble of cable. Then he said, 'Tell Mr. Tweedie to carry on aft with stern moorings and then lower the boats. I want the ship camouflaged within the hour.' He seemed to become aware of the tension behind him he added coldly, 'when you are ready, gentlemen!'

The telegraphs clanged once more, and below decks Nimmo and his sweating staff stared up at the demanding dials with relief.

Trewin made himself walk around the upperdeck to make sure the shore party knew what to do and then returned to the bridge. As he ducked beneath the hastily rigged nets and painted awnings he saw that Corbett was waiting for him.

Corbett said directly, 'You were having an argument with Mallory!'

'I lost my temper, sir.'

Corbett removed his cap and sat down wearily on a flag locker. 'I know. I heard most of it.'

Trewin watched the nervous tick jerking at Corbett's face. 'Do you think I was hard on him?'

Corbett gave a short, bitter laugh. 'It is you I'm worried about, not *him*. I've been watching you, listening to you. You must get a hold on yourself!'

Trewin gritted his teeth. 'I'll be all right, sir.'

Corbett jumped to his feet. 'For God's sake, you've not understood a single word, have you? Didn't you see what just happened?' He looked around the deserted bridge, his face suddenly filled with anguish. 'I nearly ran her aground! Nearly wrecked her!' He did not seem to know what to do with his hands. 'But for you I'd have ripped the heart out of her!'

Corbett's agonised outburst had the effect of sobering Trewin's angry despair. He asked, 'Your eyes, sir. Are they worse?'

Corbett would not look at him. His head nodded violently, and Trewin saw him rubbing his knuckles against his face with something like madness. 'Like a curtain coming down! There used to be long periods when I thought things were all right. Then the gaps got shorter and shorter.' He was speaking very quickly. 'Just now it closed in! I couldn't see anything but blurred shapes!'

Trewin said, 'You've been too long on the bridge. In this sun with the additional strain . . .'

Corbett swung round, his pale eyes wide and staring. 'Don't talk like that, Trewin. I've been deluding *myself* enough, without your adding to it!'

'What do you want me to do, sir?'

Corbett took a deep breath as if to calm himself. 'I just want you to understand what this means to you, personally.'

'I think I do.' Trewin watched the motor boat returning loaded with palm fronds. 'I thought I could get this ship to safety, with or without your help. I know now that I was wrong. You've already proved that you are the one, the only one who can do it. If I had accepted your offer and taken command at Singapore, this ship would never have got beyond the Durian Strait. Right now we'd all have been sharing the same grave as the *Beaver*.'

Corbett was watching him unwinkingly. 'Don't undersell yourself, Trewin.'

'I'm not, sir. I've had experience of war, but this is something else again. This sort of thing calls for more than just guts and determination. It goes right back, deeper than maybe even you understand.' He looked past Corbett's intent face, seeing himself as if from the outside. 'Before the war, when I was trying to find some sort of life to suit me, it was all going on, and I didn't realise it. Then the war came, and because I was a part-time sailor I thought I knew all the questions, and most of the answers, too. But I was wrong, and I realise it now. Any man who has the will and the determination, courage if you like, can be taught to pull a trigger and stand his watch, even be led to oblivion if the time calls for it. But it takes something extra to mould a ship and men into one entity, to give them that reserve to *hold* them together when by all just rights they should be running like rabbits.' He dropped his gaze. 'So if my eyes are all you need, then you have them, sir.'

Corbett fumbled with his pockets. 'I shan't speak of it again, Trewin.' He held out his hand. 'But thank you.' He looked round the bridge and gave another short laugh. But it was no longer bitter. 'The *Porcupine* is a very lucky ship.' He picked his cap off the locker and walked towards the hatch. Then he paused and looked back at Trewin's grave face.

'What other gunboat has *two* captains, eh?'

*   *   *

Petty Officer Bill Dancy pushed his cap to the back of his head and looked across the flat water towards the anchored gunboat. Beneath his shoes the beach felt cool and damp, and he had a great desire to sit down with his back against one of the tall, salt-stained trees which hung over the gently lapping wavelets at the edge of the beach.

'That about does it.' He put his head on one side and stared critically at the ship's crude camouflage. Some of the men were putting final touches to it, but as far as aircraft were concerned the ship was as well hidden as she could be. Below the netting he could see the low hull, and felt strangely saddened by its dirty and unkempt appearance. Scars and unexplained dents, and round the howespipes there were long streaks of naked rust.

Ordinary Signalman Phelps was standing at his side, a heavy pair of binoculars slung around his neck. He said, 'D'you reckon we're goin' to get away from 'ere, P.O.?'

Dancy nodded slowly. 'Of course I do.' He turned his head as Trewin and three seamen appeared through the trees walking in a tight, silent group. The men carried shovels, and Trewin's face was grim.

Dancy said, 'They've buried him, then.' It was strange that he did not even recall the man's face. The marine bandsman who had died as the flying-boat's bomb had exploded had been brought ashore to be hidden inland in a crude grave with neither ceremony nor any of the usual rites.

Trewin stopped beside him and Dancy asked, 'All done, sir?'

'Yes. I made a note of the place as best I could, Buffer, and we put some stones on the top.' He stared at the dog-eared book in his hand. 'I read a few lines. It wasn't much.'

Dancy studied the shadows of strain around Trewin's eyes. 'Never mind, sir. He's none the worse for it.'

Trewin sighed and looked at the anchored ship. Corbett would be waiting to hear about it. It was obvious that he had wanted to bury the man himself, but as Trewin had pointed out, the islands were not so safe that the captain could leave the ship for more than a few minutes. He kept thinking about the man he had helped to bury. Then the embarrassed aftermath with the three sailors leaning on the shovels while he read from the ship's prayer book. They had not known the man. It was difficult to find the right sort of words.

Phelps said, 'Well, I'll be off to the top of the 'ill, sir. I'll come runnin' if I see a ship gettin' near.'

Dancy nodded. 'That's right, son. The whole island is only a mile and a half long, so you should get a good view all round.'

Trewin realised that Phelps was beside him and said quietly, 'I'm sorry I barked at you, Bunts. As a matter of fact, I do miss my pipe, so if you have a moment later on?'

The boy's face lit up. 'Sure, sir. No trouble at all.'

He walked away whistling, and Dancy said admiringly, 'God, to think I must have been like that once.'

Trewin smiled. 'I know. He's a good lad. I was wrong to fly at him because of my own worries.'

Dancy grinned broadly. 'Well, you said it, sir!'

'We'd better get back aboard.' He watched the dory being rowed slowly towards the beach. It made a thin clear channel through the thickening spread of oil, and there was a tell-tale black stain around the boat's small hull.

Dancy said, 'Pity we can't do something to stop that leak.'

'No chance of that.' Trewin shaded his eyes as a brightly coloured bird flashed between the trees like a fiery dart. 'The only way would be to beach her again, and there's no suitable sandbars around here. Apart from which, the captain would not allow it. The ship would be bloody helpless stuck on a wedge of mud!'

Dancy reached out slowly and took Trewin's arm. His face was still relaxed, there was even a smile on his lips, but his voice was tense and sharp. 'Keep talking to me, sir! Just stay as you are now!'

Trewin stared at him. 'What are you talking about?'

Dancy said, 'I saw something move in the trees behind you, sir.'

'Are you sure?' Trewin felt his spine go cold. 'Was it Phelps?' He was conscious of the sudden menace and the gentle, uninterrupted splash of oars from the dory.

Dancy's hand moved very casually until it rested on his holster. 'Not Phelps. He's gone the other way.'

Trewin stared across Dancy's shoulder. The three seamen were squatting by the water's edge talking together in low tones. They were unarmed, and he realised with sudden despair that he had left his own revolver aboard the ship.

Dancy slipped the flap of his holster and then said evenly, 'I think we're all right. They're making too much noise to have seen us.'

It was true. Trewin could hear the occasional crackle of dry brush and the rattle of loose stones as the advancing footsteps came nearer and nearer.

He snapped. 'You there, hit the beach!' The sailors stared at him and then threw themselves sideways on to the sand. Dancy whipped out his pistol and sprinted towards the trees and then dropped on one knee. The dory swung unsteadily below the beach as the oarsmen realised that something was happening, and from the gunboat's deck came the sharp bark of orders and the sound of running feet.

Trewin stood where he was but facing towards the steep

slope beyond the trees. Whoever it was would see him first, and while they reacted to what they saw Dancy would get a chance to use his pistol.

The petty officer moved first. Trewin saw him jam the revolver back in its holster and then start running towards the slope. He yelled, 'It's all right, sir! It looks like two of our chaps!'

Trewin shouted at the men beside him, 'Tell the ship! I'm going with the Buffer!'

Some more poor devils from Singapore, he thought. Probably soldiers who had managed to get this far only to have their ship shot from under them.

He burst through the bushes and stopped dead. Dancy was on his knees beside one of the figures his arm cradling his shoulders, while the second man stood leaning against a tree, his chest heaving from exertion, his shirt almost black with dried blood.

Dancy looked up his face dazed. 'This one is Lieutenant Hughes, sir!'

But Trewin was still looking at the other man. Despite the blood and filth on his clothes, the scratches on his unshaven face, he recognised Fairfax-Loring. He wanted to go to him, to help him down to the beach, but his limbs refused to move.

The admiral peered at him and said thickly, 'I knew it was you, for God's sake! I was afraid you'd weigh anchor before we could get here!' He pushed himself away from the tree and gasped, 'My Christ, when I saw you heading for the islands I thought I was going off my bloody head!'

The flag-lieutenant was staring up at the trees, his eyes wide and vacant. His mouth was moving in quick jerks, but no sounds emerged.

The admiral said, 'He's all in. Had a bad time of it.'

Trewin made himself ask, 'The *Prawn*, sir? What happened?

The admiral began to walk down the slope, his eyes fixed on the water and the small group of watching sailors. 'We were spotted by a Jap aircraft the second day out. We tried everything. Dodged about the islands and nearly ran into a bloody destroyer in the Berhala Strait.' He pushed the hair from his eyes. 'Then, just as we were crossing open water towards these islands we were picked up by a fast patrol boat.' He shrugged and grimaced. 'By God, she was damn fast all right!'

They had reached the water's edge now, and the sailors by the beached dory were staring at the admiral as if reading their own fate in his words.

Fairfax-Loring continued, 'They raked the *Prawn* from stem to stern, and then, just as I thought it was all over, the four-inch gun managed to land a brick right on the bastard! It was too damn dark to see, but it was a direct hit right enough. She went limping off like a bloody sick dog!'

Trewin asked harshly, 'Where is *Prawn* now, sir?'

The admiral shrugged. 'Back there over on the north side of the island somewhere.'

Dancy watched the flag-lieutenant being lowered into the dory and then said, 'Are you wounded, sir?'

Fairfax-Loring glared at him. 'Never mind about me! I've got a job to do!'

Trewin said, 'I'll go over to the other side of the island and see what I can do!'

'You'll get aboard your ship with me, Trewin!' The admiral's eyes were red rimmed and angry. 'The *Prawn* is a write-off, any decisions must be made right here and at once!' He threw his legs over the boat's gunwale, adding, 'The passengers are safe enough. They were all battened below during the action.' He shuddered. 'Just as well for them. It was a living hell on deck!'

Trewin followed him into the crowded boat, his brain still reeling from the admiral's words. Seeing Fairfax-Loring had been bad enough. To know that Clare and the others were somewhere on the other side of that green hill, helpless and without hope, was like the climax to a nightmare.

The boat bumped alongside, but he was only partly aware of the men leaping down to assist the flag-lieutenant aboard, of the anxious questions and the faces which stared down from the guardrails.

Fairfax-Loring watched Hughes being carried towards the sick bay. 'Poor chap. No stamina. He's been raving since the attack.'

As Corbett hurried down from the bridge he added shortly, 'I am glad to see you. I was beginning to give up hope altogether.'

Corbett shot Trewin a questioning glance, but the admiral said firmly, 'For God's sake take me to your quarters. I need a drink!'

Hammond joined Trewin at the rail, his face tight with anxiety. 'I just heard. What are we going to do?'

Trewin looked at him. 'I'm going to find out.' He lifted his eyes to the bridge. '*Right now!*'

He found Fairfax-Loring sitting behind Corbett's desk, a dressing gown around his broad shoulders, and one hand thrust into the front of his shirt like a sling. Corbett was by an open scuttle, his face troubled and grave.

Trewin said, 'I'd like to ask what we're going to do to help *Prawn*, sir?' He purposely avoided the admiral's angry stare.

Corbett replied quietly, 'It seems that she is in a bad way.'

Fairfax-Loring winced and moved his arm up and down. 'It's like this, my boy. As I've just told the captain, there is not much we *can* do. The *Prawn* is an old ship, and this fresh damage would slow her down even more.'

Trewin faced him coldly. 'Then she's not a complete write-off, sir?'

The admiral frowned. 'Well, she can get steam up obviously, or I wouldn't be here!'

Trewin turned to Corbett. 'I'd like permission to take the motor boat around the island at once, sir. I think it essential that we keep together.'

'Very well.' Corbett did not look at the admiral. 'You realise of course that if we are discovered here in the meantime we may sail without you?' There was pain in his eyes. 'But if you think you *should* go . . .'

The admiral shouted, 'What the hell are you talking about? Even if *Prawn* does eventually sail she can't keep up with you!

Two ships in company would be asking for disaster!'

Corbett looked at him coolly. 'Are you ordering me to keep Trewin here, sir?'

'I'm not ordering you to do any damn thing! But that Jap patrol boat was only damaged, she'll be screaming for help and will bring the whole search party down on our ears if we sit here!'

Corbett nodded. 'I can see that, although it is obvious that *Prawn*'s gunners managed to knock out the enemy's W/T before she could send a signal for assistance.' His tone was mild. 'Otherwise we would have been attacked *before* we reached here, eh?'

To Trewin he said shortly, 'Go at once. But remember this. I will have to sail as soon as it is dark.' He followed Trewin into the sunlight and continued quietly, 'Take care, Trewin. Take *good* care!'

Trewin paused at the ladder. 'I will.'

'When I weigh anchor I will take *Porcupine* up and around the island before I head to the south again, Trewin.' Corbett was watching him intently. 'If *Prawn* can sail she can come out and meet me. But send a messenger back in the motor boat as soon as you know what is happening.' He looked meaningly at the cabin hatch. 'The admiral is evidently keen on leaving her behind.'

As the motor boat headed away from the gangway Trewin looked back and saw Corbett staring after it. Then as they chugged between the reefs the *Porcupine* was hidden from view and the motor boat had the islands to itself.

*   *   *

The *Prawn* was so well camouflaged with palm fronds that Trewin almost passed her hiding place. She was very close inshore with her anchors embedded on the beach itself, while her square stern was moored to a long outcrop of jagged rock which stuck out from the tree-covered beach like a stone breakwater.

It was all so unreal that as the boat glided gently towards the sand neither Trewin nor Dancy or any of the boat's crew said a word.

At first the concealed gunboat appeared like a deserted wreck, her hull showing all the new traces of combat, her upperworks pitted with splinter holes and blackened by fire. Then as the motor boat drew closer they saw figures running down from the hillside and others wading into the sea itself to greet them.

The keel grated ashore and Trewin staggered dazedly on to the sand, his ears ringing with cries and shouts of excitement as women and children, hobbling soldiers and smoke-stained seamen pushed round his little party, slapping his shoulders, calling his name, or just staring at him through tears of surprise and fresh hope.

He saw Lieutenant Adair with one arm strapped in splints and a reddened bandage around his head striding to meet him, his tired features split into a great grin of welcome.

Trewin said, 'Thank God you're all right!'

Adair nodded, 'Never imagined we'd meet like this old boy,'

Trewin looked at the top of the narrow beach. There was a long line of sandy graves, and he asked quietly, 'All yours?'

Adair wiped his face with his good hand. 'Yes. Including my number one. He was killed outright.' He looked at Trewin as if he still could not believe it. 'So the admiral sent you to help us, eh?' He shook his head. 'I never thought he'd get to you in time.'

Trewin thought of Fairfax-Loring's words and replied, 'Yes, he sent me.' The lie came easier than he expected. 'Corbett is sailing as soon as it gets dark. Can you be ready by then?'

Adair shrugged. 'I guess so. We've been patching and plugging all day. We were holed so many times that I had to jettison more coal, so I've had my chaps hacking down trees for the bloody boilers.' He grinned, but the strain was stark in his eyes. 'That's the advantage of my old kettle!'

Trewin looked at the savage scars along the gunboat's bridge. 'It must have been bad.'

'It was. I had to let the Jap boat get right up to me before I could pot her with the old four-inch. But before that happened I lost fifteen men killed. I suppose I should have surrendered with all those poor devils crammed below.' He looked away. 'But after getting so far, I thought, what the hell!'

Trewin turned his mind away from Hammond's report of the butchered nurses. Surrender would not have helped. He said, 'I'll send my boat back with a message for Corbett. I shall stay here and give you a hand, if I may?'

Adair studied him carefully. 'I'd appreciate that. So would the others.' He looked over Trewin's shoulder. 'She's over there, waiting to see you.' He smiled briefly and walked back towards his ship.

Dancy said quietly, 'I'll tell the boat's crew what to say, sir. I'm staying here with you.' He did not wait for Trewin's reply but strode back down the beach where the *Porcupine*'s sailors were talking and laughing with about thirty children.

Trewin looked towards the trees. Clare Massey was standing quite still against a dead trunk, her arms hanging at her sides. She was wearing the same green dress as when he had put her aboard the *Prawn* and he could see the great stains of oil and what looked like blood on the skirt.

As she saw him looking at her she started to run. She did not stop until she was in his arms, and for a full minute they did not speak. When she did speak her voice seemed to come from far away. 'Oh, Ralph, I never thought I'd ever see you again. After we sailed one of the men told me that you would not be able to follow, that your ship was too damaged to move.' She clutched his shoulders, feeling him as if to reassure herself that this too was not just part of a mad dream. 'And you did not tell me! You let me go thinking it would be all right!'

Trewin said, 'I'm here now, Clare. That's all that matters.'

She lifted her chin and looked into his face. 'Even when it was bad I hoped and prayed that you would be safe.'

He touched her hair. 'Thank God you were not hurt.'

She shuddered against him. 'We didn't see anything. It was terrible. All the lights went out and we could feel the ship being hit again and again. Some water started to come in, and we had to hold the children above us to keep them from drowning before they got the pumps started.'

Trewin held her tightly, seeing only too clearly what she must have endured. 'I wish I could have spared you that.'

She shook her head. 'I'm glad I was there, Ralph. I mean it. Now I shall know what it's like.' Her mouth quivered in a smile. 'When we came on deck and saw these islands I really did think I was dreaming.'

Trewin thought of the journey which still stretched ahead. Over three hundred miles. He said, 'We're not alone any more.'

Over her head he could see the departing boat and Dancy trying to drive the children back to the cover of the trees without much success. He saw Jacqui Laniel helping a wounded soldier into a patch of shade and asked, 'How is Corbett's wife? Is she safe?'

The girl nodded. 'But she's changed. I can't explain it, but she seems so different from before. She doesn't speak to anyone, but just stays quiet and keeps to herself, even amongst all these people.'

Trewin ran his arm around her shoulder and together they walked along the edge of the beach. 'I expect we've all changed,' he said slowly. 'Some of us for the better, I hope.'

She said, 'Will we be leaving soon?'

'Tonight.' He felt her go tense. 'But this time we will be keeping you company. So try not to think about it.'

She shook her head. 'It's not that, Ralph. It's just that it seems so soon now that we are together again.'

'I know.' He glanced at the battle-scarred ship. 'I wanted so much for you. To make things better again.'

She did not answer, but gripped his arm even tighter.

Trewin looked at the sky. There were a few low clouds, and he could feel a growing breeze on his face. At any other time the daylight would have dragged. Now, even his heart beats seemed to register the passing of time. But in spite of his anxiety he felt strangely content. Perhaps for the first time in his life.

16
The Common Enemy

Trewin paused on the crest of the great outcrop of rocks and looked down at the moored *Prawn*. He could feel the afternoon sun across his neck and shoulders, and the heat from the rock burned through his shoes like the top of a stove. He noticed that the boats alongside the ship's battered hull were rising and falling with extra vigour, and that the anchor cables and stern wires were no longer slack and motionless. One minute they were bar taut, the next dipping deep into the clear water as the ship stirred uneasily on a growing swell. He shaded his eyes and stared towards the hard horizon line. There was no haze any more and the sea's edge was marked with a border of deeper blue, and below in streak upon streak of shadow some far-off disturbance transmitted itself towards the islands in a regular procession of shallow rollers.

Trewin turned away from the sea and continued to climb towards the jutting spur of headland. The *Prawn* was as ready as she ever could be for the next part of her journey. There was nothing more that he or anyone else could do now.

He pushed through some dry scrub and stood looking down at the girl. She was sitting beside a deep pool of trapped water which had probably been thrown up from the rocks in some fierce gale, and which gave some hint of what the sea and wind could achive when they had a mind.

Her green dress lay drying beside the water, and she was wearing a towel wrapped beneath her arms like a sarong. She smiled at him. 'I have been waiting for you. It's cooler up here, and we can see the ship if you want to.' She tossed her hair across her bare shoulders and added, 'You look worn out. Why not have a bathe?'

Trewin was suddenly aware of the dust and weariness on his body, which was made all the more apparent by the girl's smooth skin and the inviting stillness of the pool.

She was watching him gravely. 'I have brought some food. We will have a picnic.'

Trewin said, 'You'll have to look the other way.'

'I shall lie here and watch the sky.' She laughed. 'I promise not to embarrass you.'

Trewin stripped off his clothes and lowered himself into the water. After the heat of the rocks and the airless confines of the *Prawn*'s hull, where he had been helping to supervise the stowage of timber for her boilers, it felt almost cold.

He heard her say, 'We could live here for ever. Just let the ship go without us and forget the outside world. I should like that.'

Trewin climbed from the pool and saw that she had brought a towel for him. He wrapped it round his waist and dropped on to the sand beside her. Her eyes were closed and he could see a small pulse beating at her throat. He took her hand and held it very gently. 'You wouldn't find me arguing with you on that point, Clare.'

'I find I can think about all which has happened now. But when I try to look ahead I get frightened. We seem to have lost everything from the past. And the future is all strange.' She lifted herself on one elbow and stared at him. 'Don't you think so?'

He nodded. 'Rather like a book waiting to be written. Or trying to think of a garden where there's only rough ground.' He smiled. 'Maybe it's better that way.'

She reached out and touched his shoulder, her fingers cool against the skin. 'Remember when we first met? A lot has changed since then.'

Trewin thought of his shame and his anger. But as her hand touched his scars he was conscious only of her nearness, of his desperate longing.

She dropped her hand and plucked at the sand between them. 'We will be parted soon, Ralph. That is the only future

I am sure about. I don't want to lose you again. I must have something to hold on to!'

Trewin put his hand on her shoulder and felt her tremble. The whole world seemed to be confined to this small shaded patch of sand and scrub and the gathering clouds which moved purposefully overhead. A hot breeze rippled the surface of the pool and he saw the blown sand settling in her dark hair. Beneath his hand her skin was warm and there were small flecks of perspiration across her forehead.

She said quietly, 'Please, Ralph. We must have this moment just for ourselves.'

She closed her eyes as he moved his hand to hold her breast, and as the towel dropped away she said, 'It's you I want. There's never been anyone else.'

For a moment longer he made himself lie quite still, looking at her perfect body, torturing himself with his longing. Then he ran his hand across her breasts and down over the softness of her thighs. She was moving her head from side to side, her lips parted as if in pain. But as he rose above her and his shadow covered her like a cloak she opened her eyes and looked directly into his face.

Trewin felt her hands reaching up for him, all at once insistent and demanding, their touch sweeping away his last control, so that he seemed to hear a great wind roaring in his ears as their bodies came together as one.

He thought he heard her cry out, but as she rose to meet and encircle him he forgot everything but their love, which by its power and desperation held the other world far at bay.

Later they lay without moving or speaking, their bodies whipped by the drifting sand beneath the wind-stirred palms which looked so black against the sky.

Trewin felt her lips move against his shoulder. 'Now we have something to remember if things get bad.'

He lifted her chin and studied her with great care. 'We can wait up here for a while longer.' He saw the bushes swaying in the wind and heard the distant murmur of surf against the beach. The weather was changing fast. It might be an ally, or a bad enemy.

He said, 'It's strange. I'm not afraid any more.'

She took his hand and laid it impulsively against her breast. 'Feel my heart, Ralph.' She turned her face away, but not before he had seen the sudden tears. 'I'm stupid to cry like this. But it is because I'm happy.'

A few drops of warm rain touched their bodies, but they stayed in each other's arms, neither wanting to let go, and each praying for the sun to stop its measured journey towards the horizon.

Far below them on the *Prawn*'s bridge Lieutenant Adair squinted at the sky and consulted his watch. Then he looked up at the headland and gave a small smile. To a petty officer he said, 'Call all hands. We'll get under way in thirty minutes.'

The man followed his gaze and asked, 'Shall I fetch 'em down from there, sir?'

Adair shook his head. 'They'll be here in time.' As the man walked away he added to himself, 'That's the least I can do.'

*   *   *

By the time the sun had dipped behind the nearest hill the *Prawn* was edging away from the protective rocks and butting her nose into the first ranks of unbroken rollers. The wind had increased, but the rain had shown no inclination to follow the first quick downpour. Far out towards the horizon the sea looked broken and angry, with small tufts of white curling from the crests of incoming rollers, and the troughs which opened beneath the gunboat's bows were already making themselves felt.

Trewin clung to the bridge rail and watched Adair as he sat in his chair, his splinted arm resting on the screen for support.

Adair said, 'It's going to be hard on the passengers. These little ships were not designed for deep waters.' He ducked as a burst of spray pattered over the screen. 'But with any kind of

273

luck we should be into the Banka Strait by midnight. There will be some shelter there.'

Trewin felt the old ship lift and plunge forward over the back of a long roller and saw the water creaming back over the forecastle. Without her camouflage the *Prawn*'s battle-scarred bridge and decks added to her appearance of forlorn frailty as she headed away from the island's small protection.

He stared back towards the headland. It was already curtained with bursting spray as the waves swept jubilantly amongst the reefs and leapt to claw at that little piece of jutting cliff which he had left such a short while ago. Even the beach where he had waited beside Clare for the motor boat to collect them was covered by the inrushing water, and he could see the tall trees swaying and quivering as the waves thundered inland to the foot of the hill itself.

Adair turned as a look-out reported, '*Porcupine*'s rounding the headland, sir!'

Trewin watched the familiar shape turning end on as she butted into the swirling crisscross of waves, a shaded signal lamp flickering across the narrowing distance between them.

'Signal, sir. "Nice to have you around again." '

Adair showed his teeth. 'Acknowledge. Make to *Porcupine*, "We are sending your first lieutenant across by liferaft." ' He grinned, 'And tell them "Thanks for dropping by!" ' '

He turned and looked at Trewin. 'Sorry about the raft. But it's too dangerous to lower a boat. You won't even get your feet wet if you're lucky.'

Trewin climbed down the swaying ladder and stood beside the guardrail as the waiting seamen manhandled the liferaft alongside and paid out a line in readiness to drift him across the water where *Porcupine* had already moved to receive him. He looked around the spray-washed decks. Apart from the gunners, they were stripped for action and deserted. It was hard to imagine that beneath his feet were crammed all those people he had seen on the beach. People who were solely dependent on Adair and the battered little ship around them. He recalled his words to Clare as if he had just spoken them aloud. 'Don't try to see me when I leave. Just remember that I shall be thinking of you all the time.'

A rating shouted, 'It's now or never, sir!' He was actually grinning.

Trewin clambered down to the raft and felt it fall away beneath him as the seamen paid out the line. The raft lifted and dipped in great, painful swoops, and he caught sight of Adair watching him through his glasses. A gaunt shadow against the darkening sky holding the binoculars in his one good hand.

When he turned his head again, the *Porcupine* was swaying above him like a grey cliff, and he saw Hammond and Dancy with the men by the rail and others staring down at him from the guns.

He waited for the right second and then jumped, his legs kicking at air as the raft was hauled rapidly away. Even before he was properly aboard he heard the clang of telegraphs and saw the spray flying back from the stem as the ship gathered way towards the open sea.

He touched Hammond's arm as he reached for the bridge ladder. 'She's safe and well, Sub. So you can stop worrying.'

Hammond did not seem to be able to speak. He just smiled and then walked quickly along the tilting deck.

Corbett was seated on his chair, his body shrouded in a black oilskin. He peered at Trewin and nodded briefly. 'Good show.' Then he settled down in his chair and stared over the screen, apparently indifferent to the spray which ran down his face like tropical rain.

Phelps stepped on to the gratings. ' 'Ere's an oilskin, sir.' He held it out for Trewin, his body swaying easily in spite of the motion. 'By the way, sir. I fixed yer pipe.' He grinned. 'Nice to 'ave you back.'

Trewin smiled and hauled himself to the bridge wing where he managed to wedge his body against a flag locker. When he looked astern he saw the *Prawn*'s blunt shape swaying dizzily from side to side, a long banner of smoke streaming from her funnel as she swung on to the other ship's wake. Behind him he heard Phelps whistling a little tune and wondered how he managed to stay so cheerful.

Phelps readjusted the signal halyards and glanced at Trewin's back with a small, secret smile on his freckled face. He was glad he had mended the first lieutenant's pipe. Apart from anything else, it helped to ease the guilt from his uncomplicated mind. Briefly he wondered what Trewin would have said if he had known that he was still on the top of the hill with his powerful binoculars when he had met the girl by the pool.

Masters growled, 'Quit makin' that row, Ginger! You're like a cat with a sore arse!'

But Phelps was unmoved. He had a secret, and in a ship of this size, that was hard to come by.

*　　　*　　　*

In spite of the deep swell and a steadily rising wind the two ships somehow managed to maintain their southerly course towards Banka Island. The motion aboard the *Porcupine* was both savage and frightening as Corbett used every trick he knew to hold his ship on her corkscrewing track, and the fear of being discovered by the enemy seemed to fade in the face of the sea's probing anger.

Trewin clung to his corner of the bridge wing and watched the water come surging back over the bows to thunder around the superstructure and leave the forward gun isolated on its small steel island. It was bad enough heading into the long, dark-sided rollers, but when they began to turn around Banka Island into the Strait they would have a diagonal attack to contend with, and the danger of capsizing would have to be considered if the weather persisted in worsening.

The silence from the radio room added to the sense of complete isolation. No warnings, no messages of guidance from some far-off friendly weather station. It was as if the whole world was in the grip of the enemy forces and the moment the ships touched any part of it they would be destroyed.

Once, just before darkness finally blotted out the misty horizon, he saw the mountains of Sumatra far to the south, aloof and unreachable, as if suspended above the sea, and he wondered grimly if the Japs were already there too and if there were other refugees from Singapore hiding and dying in the jungles, fugitives already forgotten by the world they had abandoned.

He gripped the wet steel and watched a long hummock of water as it rolled out of the gloom on either side of the bows. Just before it reached the stem its smooth crest curled and broke into a sharp-edged wave, as if caught in a strong wind, and then crashed across the forecastle with a booming roar of triumph. He felt the ship shudder, and watched fascinated as the whole of the foredeck became buried beneath the onslaught of water and the leaping white spray as it burst above the bridge and stung his face like hail.

After what seemed like minutes the ship pulled herself wearily above the surface, the water streaming in rivers from decks and guns and draining noisily from the scuppers as she lifted her bows before crashing down again into the greedy trough beyond.

Every piece of the bridge seemed to be squeaking and groaning in protest, and above the hiss and boom of the sea Trewin heard the steady clank of pumps as they too fought their battles from within. Some of the fuel oil had leaked into the bilges, and no doubt the pumps were unwillingly adding to the trail which still floated astern, defying even the fury of the sea.

If only they could increase speed, but Trewin knew it was impossible. The *Prawn* was holding her own in spite of the crazy rolls of her gaunt superstructure and masts, but only just. And to maintain her six knots in this weather her stokers must have sacrificed the very last standards of safety. Down in the tiny boiler room her men would have their work cut out to avoid being thrown bodily into the demanding furnaces as they struggled to maintain steam and answer Adair's needs.

Corbett asked sharply, 'Is it time to turn, Pilot?'

Mallory was clinging to his table, his head and shoulders beneath the hood, his buttocks and legs soaked with spray as he fought to work out the ship's approximate position while the world went mad around him.

'Five minutes, sir!' His voice was muffled. 'Then alter course to two three zero!'

Corbett shouted, 'Good.' He settled down in his reeling chair and wiped his face with a sodden towel. 'Banka Island must be about three miles ahead. We will run down the north-west coast as close inshore as we can.'

Trewin lifted his glasses and stared beyond the distorted spectres of broken wavetops. Corbett was doing the right thing. No enemy destroyer would risk being caught near the great mass of Banka Island with its treacherous shallows and eager reefs. The gunboats' shallow draught and the weather were their only true allies, he thought.

A voice called hoarsely, 'Land, sir! Dead ahead!'

Trewin squinted through his glasses, and before the lenses were again shrouded in spray he saw the darker shadow which stretched away on either bow, a solid link between the tossing water and the racing clouds above.

Corbett snapped, 'Stand by to alter course! To Masters he added, 'Signal the *Prawn,* Yeoman!'

Masters wrapped his arms around Phelps' slim body and held him against the bridge wing as the boy trained his shaded lamp astern for that one brief message. It was dangerous to show a light, no matter how well it was concealed. But the danger of *Prawn* running headlong on to the shore was far more serious. Adair's small bridge lacked even *Porcupine*'s scanty protection, and Trewin imagined that watchkeeping in this sea must be like clinging to a half-submerged rock.

Corbett watched Masters and the signalman reel back together in an untidy heap and then ordered, 'Carry on, Number One!'

Trewin gripped the voice-pipes. 'Starboard fifteen!' He tried not to think of the straining rudders and Nimmo's hasty repairs. 'Midships!' He peered at the blurred figures on the luminous compass repeater. 'Steady! Steer two three zero!' He heard Unwin's voice from the wheelhouse, followed by a shouted obscenity as one of his telegraphsmen stumbled and fell headlong on the tilting deck.

The *Porcupine* swayed alarmingly on the surging crisscross of rollers and hung suspended over a deep trough. She seemed unwilling to right herself, and as the water lifted and thundered along her submerged sidedeck Trewin heard Dancy yelling at his damage control party to put more lashings on the motor boat.

'Breakers on the port beam, sir!' The look-out's voice was neither surprised nor fearful. Like the rest of the men, he was too bruised, too stunned by the weather and the dreadful pitching to have any emotion left.

Corbett grunted. 'Good. That'll be Bulu Bay. The entrance to the Strait is about twenty miles ahead. It will be more sheltered once we reach there.'

Trewin rubbed his eyes and then cursed as he was hurled against the voice-pipes. His body felt as if he had been at sea for months. Even the matter-of-fact tone Corbett had used did not disguise the reality that the worst part of the voyage was still ahead. The Strait was one hundred miles long and sometimes only ten miles in width. Perhaps Corbett no longer cared. He was trying to do what he had promised, but his words and actions seemed automatic and without feeling.

He looked round as another figure lurched on to the bridge and pulled himself towards the chart table. Trewin realised that he had forgotten completely about Fairfax-Loring, or perhaps he too had forgotten how to care.

The admiral was wearing an oilskin, but his bared head was streaming with blown spray, and in the small chart light his eyes looked angry and wild. He shouted, 'Where are we?' He pushed Mallory aside and thrust his head down to the chart. Then he climbed up beside Corbett and said, 'For God's sake, can't we get a move on?'

Corbett's face was hidden in the upturned collar of his coat.

'In three hours we will be turning around the headland and into the Strait, sir. By daylight we should have reached the narrows, and with luck I hope we can shelter behind some small islands there.' He ducked below the screen as a solid sheet of bursting spray hissed above his head and swept across the look-outs behind him. Then he said calmly, 'Another night like this one and I think we will be all right.'

The admiral wiped his streaming face with his hand. 'That bloody *Prawn*! She's holding us back, just as I said she would!'

Corbett shrugged. 'Unless you want me to keep going in daylight, I don't see that she makes much difference, sir.' There was no hiding the contempt in Corbett's voice.

The admiral said suddenly, 'There may be Japs on Banka.'

'There may.' Corbett's mind seemed to be elsewhere. 'But I should think it more likely they'll be dealing first with Sumatra, eh?'

Fairfax-Loring dragged his heavy body across the awnings, still keeping one arm tucked inside his oilskin, and Trewin wondered if he had allowed Baker, the sick-berth attendant, to treat his injury yet. In his heart Trewin tried to find some sort of pity and understanding for the admiral. After all, he was probably more valuable to the Japs as a prisoner than the small victory of sinking the two gunboats.

Masters shouted, '*Prawn*'s signalling, sir!'

The admiral whirled round, his head jutting forward as he followed the petty officer's arm. 'The bloody fool! What the hell does he think he's doing?'

But Trewin did not listen to him. He was watching the faint, stabbing light as it rose and fell in the darkness astern, and he could feel something like fear growing with each painful flash.

Masters said gruffly, 'Hull leaking badly. Previous repairs not standing up to sea. Must reduce speed immediately.'

No one spoke for several minutes, and Trewin imagined that he could hear a note of savage triumph in the chorus of sea and wind which buffeted the bridge without mercy.

Corbett said slowly, 'Acknowledge, Yeoman.'

The admiral was leaning towards him. 'That settles it! We shall *have* to leave them behind!'

Corbett ignored him. 'Make to *Prawn*, "Can you maintain speed until we enter Strait?"'

The admiral asked harshly, 'What good will that do? There are still one hundred miles to go before we can see any hope of getting through.'

Corbett touched his arm and slid from the chair. 'If you will excuse me, sir.' He walked past the admiral, his slight figure somehow retaining its balance while the deck swayed from one impossible angle to the next.

Masters said at length, '*Prawn* says she will try, sir.'

Corbett sounded satisfied. 'Good. Now tell *Prawn* that we will continue as before, but will reduce to four knots as soon as we alter course.'

He looked at Trewin. 'We may be able to help with repairs once we find shelter.'

The admiral stepped between them, his voice lowered so that the others would not hear. 'I'll go along with you, Corbett, but only just so far! I feel as worried as anyone about those people in *Prawn*, but for the most part they are civilians, and lucky to have got this far under the circumstances!'

Trewin clenched his firsts so hard that the pain helped to steady his mind against the admiral's words. Any pity he might have felt for the man had gone completely. The admiral was the man who was responsible for many of those civilians even being here in the first place, and but for the *Porcupine*'s arrival at the Seven Islands would be over there now sharing their misery and fear while the little gunboat tried to carry them to safety.

Corbett merely said, 'I don't think we should rely too much on luck, sir.' He walked back to his chair. 'For *any* of us.'

The admiral looked as if he was going to follow him but said, 'I shall go below. I'm still a bit weak.' He glared round the bridge, as if expecting someone to comment. 'But call me if the weather gets any worse.'

Mallory peered at the ravages done by the spray to his chart and muttered, 'He won't need to be told! If the weather does break he'll have the bloody sea in his flaming cabin!'

Trewin dragged his eyes from the darkness behind the bridge. He could picture the frightened women below the *Prawn*'s decks, the whimpering children and the air of helplessness as the waves pounded against the hull and fought to break into their last refuge.

Corbett said, 'Tell the cook to get something hot for the men to drink. It might take their minds off things for a while.'

Trewin stared at him. How could Corbett find the time to remember all these small details? Was it determination or hard self-discipline? Or was he just saying anything he could think of in order to delay some inevitable decision?

He looked at the leaping spray and listened to the labouring beats of the engines. It was as if they had never been intended to get away, and all the past sufferings and disappointments were linked to some final disaster.

There no longer seemed to be any point in planning and calculating. Time and distance were meaningless. There was just the ship and the endless, destructive cruelty of her common enemy.

*　　　*　　　*

The daylight was slow in making an appearance. There was no dawn at all, just a sudden transition from night to a searing pewter brightness which made the men on the bridge look at each other as if surprised to find that nothing had changed from the previous day.

Below the shelter of Banka Island the motion was certainly easier, but like Trewin the look-outs and gunners were now too tired and bruised by their vigil to notice or draw comfort from the change. Far out on the opposite beam it was possible to see what might be the mainland of Sumatra. Or it could have been part of the wavering sea mist which jingled with the flying spray to make a long, unbroken curtain below the skudding clouds.

Trewin's eyes felt red-raw and his tongue seemed to have swollen to twice its size. He heard Mallory remark bleakly, 'Looks like a drop of rain about. That's *all* we need now!'

Corbett stretched his legs and readjusted his collar. 'Could do worse. Now give me a course for those islands. They must be about five miles away surely?'

Trewin looked over the rear of the bridge and felt his heart sink. The *Prawn* was farther astern and her black funnel-smoke hung close to her wake, as if the strength had gone out of her.

Corbett said vaguely, 'She's holding up quite well. Good show.'

'New course is one four zero, sir.'

Corbett turned his head, and Trewin heard his stubbled chin rasp against the upturned collar. 'Good, bring her round, Trewin. In thirty minutes we should be in very shallow water. It shoals to less than two fathoms between the islands. No ship is going to come sniffing after us in there, eh?'

Trewin gave his helm orders and then leaned heavily on the table as Mallory folded away the oilskin hood. The islands were just some more useless humps of land, like small pieces which had broken away from the main mass of Banka far back in time, when the world was still changing. Who could ever have believed they would be put to use like this?

Corbett watched the ship's wake turn away in a shallow curve. Then he said, 'Reduce speed again, Trewin. We will let the *Prawn* go in first.' He saw Trewin watching him and added quietly, 'They'll be feeling low enough as it is, without seeing us vanish amongst these islets without them.'

As the small cluster of islands separated from the dark mainland behind them the *Prawn* drew alongside, and after what seemed like an age, began to force ahead. In the misty daylight she showed all the scars of her battle with the sea, and as she lifted and plunged across each cruising wave the men on the *Porcupine* saw the great patches of bare rust where the pounding water had stripped away the paint like skin. She had lost both her boats and the guardrails were buckled in several places and hanging dejectedly overboard.

Trewin moved his glasses down her length, feeling her pain as if it was his own. He saw Adair in the forepart of his bridge, staring ahead, his shoulders hunched behind the glass screen like a man too dulled and exhausted even to move his head.

But her ensign still made a patch of jaunty colour from the gaff, and as the ship moved slowly into the lead Trewin saw one of the gunners waving back at them.

Corbett said absently, 'Now *there* is a ship. Not worth her weight in scrap to some people, but I'll stake my life that Adair would say differently.'

The islets opened up on either side of the other gunboat, and as she turned to swing around the first green hump it seemed from the *Porcupine*'s bridge as if she was being swallowed up by the land itself.

Hammond appeared at the hatch ladder, his eyes seeking the captain. 'Permission to send the hands to breakfast, sir?'

Corbett eyed him sadly. 'Breakfast or dinner, Sub. Call it what you like. Just get them fed, eh?'

They all froze as a look-out yelled, 'Aircraft, sir! Bearing green nine oh!'

Trewin left for the voice-pipes but Corbett snapped, 'Stay where you are! Any increase of speed now might attract attention!'

Every glass and gun-muzzle lifted and settled on the slow-moving shape, and only those down amidst the thundering engines were unaware of that steady, hateful sound as it crossed the turbulent water like a taunt.

'Another flyin' boat, sir!' It was Tweedie's voice over the bridge speaker. A pause, then, 'It's flyin' due south towards Sumatra.' They heard him curse. 'He's turnin' slightly now.'

Trewin watched the distant aircraft swinging on to a new course as if it was controlled by invisible wires. Now it was flying parallel with the ship about five miles clear.

His eyes throbbed with the effort of staring at that small black outline. He must see us! What the hell is he playing at?'

Tweedie again. 'He's turnin', sir!' Even over the speaker his relief was obvious. 'Headin' south again!'

Corbett snapped, 'Full ahead together!'

Trewin heard Masters groan, 'Gawd! Look at our bloody oil slick! Any fool will see it!'

Corbett remarked, 'He may have missed us this time. Or he might just be trying to put us off while he calls up assistance.' He rubbed his chin thoughtfully. 'Well, we shall soon know, one way or the other!' Then he said, 'Take the con, Trewin. I'm going to have a wash and shave before we drop anchor.'

He walked across the bridge, but as he passed the chart table he cannoned into the voice-pipes and almost fell. He hurried down the hatch ladder without a word, nor did he look back.

Trewin climbed on to the gratings as Mallory murmured, 'Hell, you'd think he was bloody well blind!'

Trewin watched the narrow gap between the islets and imagined Corbett locking himself in his cabin alone with his dreadful secret. What a time and a place for it to happen to him. To *us*.

He saw the anchor party mustering by the four-inch gun and tried to close his mind completely, as Corbett had done. 'Slow ahead together. Stand by to rig camouflage.'

He tilted his cap to shade his eyes from the glare as the ship glided slowly above a carpet of white sand. After all, he thought, the pursuer had always been able to call every move. The man on the run had no choice at all but to keep running and hold on to his hope for survival.

17

The Man Who Was Afraid

All through the day until late in the afternoon the two ships lay in their cramped hiding place between the small cluster of islets, the *Porcupine* at her anchors, and *Prawn* lashed snugly alongside. The threat of rain seemed to have departed, and by midday the sky was clear. Both ships were pinned down by the sun again, so that in the confines of their anchorage the relentless heat seemed to come from all angles, smashing them down with its power.

All the *Porcupine*'s engineering staff had gone aboard the *Prawn* within minutes of mooring, and in spite of the heat and the primitive conditions had worked without a break to help repair the little gunboat's storm damage. The passengers meantime were transferred to the *Porcupine*, where instead of taking advantage of rest and shelter, they worked beside the men whenever and wherever possible.

It was hard to see them, particularly the women, as the ones who had surged aboard at Singapore while enemy bombers had painted the skies red above the burning city at their backs. All pretence and normal individuality had been stripped away in their common fight for survival. The smart dresses had been replaced with oddments of sailor's clothing or improvised from scraps they had managed to salvage from the storm. Their nearness to disaster had given them a strange strength, and there were no longer any tears or bitter recriminations.

Trewin had seen Adair sitting on his bridge dictating orders and instructions to his petty officers while a tall girl dressed in a seaman's jersey and little else lathered and shaved him, her tanned features set in grim concentration. Adair had seen Trewin staring up at him and had lifted his splintered arm in salute. 'It pays to be wounded!' was all he had said.

Although look-outs had been posted on the nearby hills, there had been no further reports of enemy aircraft. Only once, halfway through the afternoon, had there been any sign of danger. A fast-moving warship, probably a destroyer, was sighted far out across the Strait heading south towards the narrows, her low shape almost lost in the great wash from her raked bows. The repair work had not even been halted for that.

Maybe Corbett had realised the uselessness of calling the men to their action stations, Trewin decided. Most of the seamen were completely spent. Even the anti-aircraft gunners slumped or lay at their stations, too weary to drag themselves from the glaring sunlight which shone through the camouflage netting and threw strange, hard shadows across the decks, as if both ships were entrapped inside one huge mesh.

Trewin stopped on the battery deck and leaned wearily against the guardrail. Below him the other ship was still alive with scurrying figures, stokers carrying lengths of metal, and army engineers, with freshly cut timber for shoring up a sagging bulkhead. But the pace was slower. It moved in time with the sun, as if both measured the minutes of decision.

He saw Corbett conferring with Adair on the *Prawn*'s quarterdeck, his neat figure dwarfed by the other's gangling shoulders. Corbett looked serious but very calm, with little outward sign of what he must be thinking.

Trewin thought back to that morning. He had been aboard the other ship helping to shepherd the dazed passengers across the narrow gap to the comparative spaciousness of the *Porcupine*'s upperdeck. He had seen Clare assisting an elderly woman over the swaying crevasse between the hulls and had waved to her. They had held each other's eyes for just a few seconds, but in that time Trewin had felt the same sense of peace and belonging, which for such a small moment held everything else from his mind. Then he had climbed down to the *Prawn*'s wardroom to make sure there were none of the refugees left aboard. Before he had been able to stop himself he had seen Corbett standing amidst the litter of sea-stained furniture, his body picked out in stars of sunlight which filtered through the countless splinter holes on both sides of the wardroom. He had had his back to the door, and opposite him, her face upturned as she crouched on an empty ammunition case, was his wife.

Mildred Corbett had changed almost beyond recognition. Her fair hair was uncombed and disordered and her dress, which was torn in several places, barely covered her shoulders. Trewin could recall the emptiness of her voice, the alien dullness of her eyes.

'I did not want to see you, Greville.' She had tried to shrug, but even that had seemed too much of an effort. 'But I've had so much time to think and remember. Too much time. At first I *wanted* the ship to sink, but as things went on I felt I had to see you again. Just to tell you.' She had dropped her head, and Trewin had seen tears splash on her oil-stained arms. He had seen too the change which had come over Corbett. Although his back was to the door, Trewin had been able to see the slow clenching and unclenching of his hands, as if he was holding himself still by physical effort.

She continued dully, 'All my life I've tried to hurt you, Greville. The more you tried to make things work out for both of us, the worse I behaved.' She had looked up, her eyes suddenly alive and desperate. 'But I never meant Martin to die!'

Corbett had spoken very quietly. 'I know.'

'You loved him so much, didn't you?'

Corbett had thrust his hands in his pockets. 'I always loved him. Just as much as if he had been my own son.'

Trewin had wanted to get away, but Corbett's words had held him motionless by the door.

'You knew?' Her eyes had been streaming with tears. 'All this time, and you never said anything?'

'There was nothing to say.'

She had spread her hands. 'And I've done nothing but *hurt* you! When you left the Navy because of my brother I should have stood by you, shared your pain, too.' Again the gesture of hopelessness. 'Now we've lost everything, and all because of me!'

Corbett had laid his cap on the ammunition case and had seated himself beside her. 'That is where you are wrong, my dear.' Corbett had reached out to touch her face, the gesture nervous but gentle. 'I need you now.' As she had flung herself against his chest Corbett had added very quickly, 'Perhaps more than you will ever know.'

Now, as Trewin watched him from the upperdeck he could see none of the pain and the unhappiness he had witnessed in those few minutes by the open door.

As if realising that Trewin was looking at him, Corbett nodded briskly to Adair and then strode towards the gangway. When he arrived on the battery deck his features were strangely determined.

He said, 'Officers' conference, Trewin. Go and get them at once.' He sniffed the air. 'I still think the rain will come. It might be of some use.'

It did not take more than a few minutes to gather the officers in Corbett's cabin. They had been sitting or lying in the wardroom, too weary to speak or eat.

Corbett seated himself at his desk and touched his fingertips together. 'I've been over the *Prawn*, gentlemen. She is ready to sail when we are. I think she can get her six knots again, so we won't waste any more time, eh?' He glanced around their lined faces. 'In ten minutes you can start moving the passengers back aboard *Prawn*.'

Hammond asked quickly, 'Wouldn't it be better if we kept them all with us, sir?' He swallowed hard under Corbett's flat stare. 'We can manage more than twice *Prawn*'s speed, and I'm sure we could squeeze them in easily enough.' At his side Tweedie nodded ponderously.

'I'm afraid not, Sub. If we were attacked we could not expect to fight with all those people aboard. It would be slaughter. No, this way we have one good ship instead of *two* cripples, eh?' He laughed shortly. 'Adair tells me he is ready to try for the last leg of the voyage. And I'm sure you've seen enough of the local scenery?'

Trewin watched him with cold amazement. Corbett seemed actually cheerful. And his eyes, apart from a noticeable redness, looked strangely clear and bright.

Corbett looked round. 'Right then. I intend to sail in two hours. We can't wait for complete darkness. We must clear the Strait before dawn at the latest. That destroyer was no doubt searching for us. It probably never occurred to the enemy that we might still be hanging around here. We wouldn't have either, but for *Prawn*.' He smiled. 'So it's an ill wind, eh?'

They all rose from their chairs but Corbett held up his hand. 'Remember this, gentlemen. Just in case we are called upon to face the enemy in battle.' He walked slowly round his desk and stared thoughtfully at the leather-bound books by the scuttle. 'In the life of every ship, perhaps only once in a lifetime, there is a moment of decision which must overshadow all else which has ever happened to her. To justify the years, the past mistakes, and the genuine beliefs of all those men who have served her, that decision must be taken without hesitation, with no considerations of personal gain or even survival.' His pale eyes moved slowly across their faces. 'If we are called, it will be very soon now. I am sure I shall not have to ask for your best, for, as captain I must take it as a right and not a privilege of rank.'

He became brisk once more. 'Now call the hands and carry out my instructions.' He watched them file out of his cabin and then said to Trewin, 'I must inform the admiral of my intentions, eh?'

'Is that wise, sir?' Trewin saw Corbett slip the magnifying glass into his pocket. 'He might wish to overrule you.'

Corbett patted his pockets and stared at his empty desk. 'I will tell him my intentions, Trewin.' He smiled shortly. '*Not* my method!'

*   *   *

In accordance with Corbett's instructions both ships left their hiding place, and hugging the Banka coastline headed for the final challenge of the Strait. As the sun moved towards the distant mountains of Sumatra and the nearby hills changed from dark green to a darker purple, the first anxiety of sailing gave way to relief.

Every hour put another six miles behind them, each turn of the screws carried them nearer and nearer to safety.

Trewin rested his elbows on the port screen and trained his glasses on the undulating hills. The sky was clear and filled with small, bright stars, and in the strange, private world of the powerful lenses the hills looked like part of an untroubled desert.

He thought momentarily of the actual time of sailing from those last islets. Just as every man had been occupied in stripping away the camouflage and letting go the mooring wires a narrow native fishing boat had coasted towards them, quite unseen by the look-outs until the last moment.

Corbett had rapped, 'Cover that boat! Shoot if they try and escape!' Then as the machine-guns had swung threateningly towards the upturned faces of the fishermen he had added, 'Tell Hammond to go and speak with them. They may be of some help.'

They had all watched Hammond climb aboard the boat, which had seemed little more than a hollow log and two crude outriggers. The surprise and caution on the native faces had soon given way to grins and loud laughter as Hammond had stumbled to question and translate with his limited vocabulary. The natives had offered him a sack of fresh coconuts and some smoked fish wrapped in leaves, but Corbett had shouted down to him, 'Give them money, Sub! All that you've got available!' To the bridge at large he had added, 'We can't rely on loyalty and love too much at this point. Singapore dollars might make 'em think twice about reporting our comings and goings, eh?'

Hammond had climbed back aboard, red-faced, but quite pleased with himself. 'They say the Japs are already on Banka.

But as far as I can make out they are on the other side of the island. We'll be safe enough to stay inshore on this side, sir.'

Corbett had nodded 'Good. So even if our brown friends want to sell our whereabouts to higher bidders, they'll have a long way to go.'

Trewin felt the edge of the screen grate painfully against his chin and realised that his head had fallen forward in a doze. He shook himself roughly and wished there was a cold wind or another fall of rain to keep him awake. He turned and peered down into the bridge, seeing the shadowy figures with a sudden sense of alarm.

He snapped, 'Come on then! Move your feet! Wake yourselves, you idle lot!' He heard someone cursing him and grinned in spite of his strained nerves. The idea of the ship steaming straight into some hidden enemy with all her watchkeepers asleep was enough to make anyone sweat.

He heard Corbett mutter, 'Must you make such a damn row, Number One?'

'I thought you were asleep, sir.' He saw Corbett's face pale against the black water beyond the screen.

'I was. But not any more!' Corbett wriggled in his chair. 'A few more hours, Trewin. When do we alter course again?'

Mallory's voice sounded drowsy, as if he was half drunk. 'Fifteen minutes, sir. Course will be, er, one one zero.'

'You see?' Corbett yawned. 'We're through the narrows. I knew we were doing the right thing to take our time.' He became brisk. 'By dawn we'll be well round the southern side of Banka.' His eyes flashed in the gloom. 'In the Java Sea!'

Trewin nodded. All those miles. Twisting and turning, hiding and running. When they had started, the idea of reaching the Java Sea had seemed too remote to be taken seriously. Now it was just a matter of hours away, and the thought of failure too terrible to face.

Corbett said suddenly, 'I want you to go to the chart room and get some sleep, Trewin. But first pass the word for our people to turn in at their stations. They can do an hour on and an hour off. That should help. Heaven knows, they deserve it.'

Trewin asked, 'Is that wise, sir? It might take several minutes to wake them up again.'

Corbett laughed. 'I think we're all right for a while.' He dropped his voice. 'Tomorrow is the testing time. Nobody saw that destroyer return down the Strait. She, or others, may still be waiting and searching for us. If so, I want our people to be as alert as humanly possible.'

'And you, sir?'

'I shall sleep later, Trewin.' He added dryly, 'And do stop fussing! It unnerves me!'

Trewin walked down to the chart room and threw himself on the leather-topped bench seat. He lay on his back with his hands behind his head, half listening to the familiar shipboard noises, the steady sluice of water against the hull.

At dawn they would anchor and rig camouflage for the last time. Then under cover of darkness they would head out to sea once more. The next time the anchor rattled down on its rusty cable would be amongst friends. The voyage over. With a smile on his lips he fell instantly asleep.

*　　　*　　　*

The scream of alarm bells hurled Trewin from the bench and he was up and running for the bridge hatch, his brain still too shocked to record the stampeding figures around him and the tannoy's metallic chant, 'Action stations! Action stations!'

He thought he had been asleep for only a few minutes, but as he thrust his body through the hatch and on to the upper bridge he saw that the sky had changed to pale grey and where there had once been stars there were closely knitted clouds and the first heavy drops of rain across his upturned face.

Corbett was on his feet, his glasses trained towards the starboard bow as he snapped, 'Full ahead together! Maximum revolutions!'

The voice-pipes were chattering on every side, and from the foredeck came the sharp click of a breech-block.

Corbett did not lower his glasses. 'Destroyer, Number One! At green four five!'

Trewin snatched his glasses and peered across the long stretch of open water. At the corner of his eye he could see the small inset and the islands behind which they had intended to shelter for the last stop of the journey. But his mind only recorded the distant patch of white foam, the wafer-thin outline of the enemy ship.

Tweedie's voice intoned, 'Range one double oh! Target's course is three zero zero!'

Trewin wiped the sweat from his forehead. She was only five miles clear. He looked at Corbett. 'Has she seen us?'

'Unlikely.' His voice was clipped. 'We've got Banka behind us.'

The deck was trembling violently as the *Porcupine* worked up to her maximum speed, so that she seemed to be planing across the unbroken water.

Corbett snapped, 'Starboard ten!'

Trewin stared at him. 'We'll pass the islands, sir! It'll be full daylight in a few minutes!'

'Midships! Steer one two zero!' Corbett pursed his lips as he watched the far-off streak of white. 'The captain'll be asleep if he doesn't see us soon!'

Trewin looked past Corbett's rigid figure and saw the *Prawn*'s shadowy outline close inshore, still moving very slowly and dropping rapidly astern.

Corbett said, 'This will give *Prawn* time to get amongst the islands, Trewin. The enemy will be too busy gaping at us to notice her.'

'Target's altering course, sir! Steering approximately three five zero! Speed twenty plus!' Tweedie sounded totally absorbed as if on an exercise.

Corbett spoke very softly. 'There is another inlet about five miles along the coast, Trewin. We'll make for that. It's sheltered and very shallow. The destroyer will lose her keel if she tries to follow us.'

Trewin asked tightly, 'What about *Prawn*, sir?'

'I've already told Adair what to do. I rather thought the enemy would hang around here just in case we came this way.' He eyed Trewin calmly. 'You see, I think the Japs are only looking for *one* gunboat. Whenever we have been sighted we have been separated, remember?' He studied Trewin's grim features and continued patiently, 'Adair will lie amongst the islands under camouflage as planned. As soon as it is dark he will head south for Java. It'll be up to him from that moment.' He lifted his glasses again. 'But he'll need help before that. And time. I intend to give as much time as I can!'

The islands loomed out of the half light and seemed to brush against the ship's flank as she surged past, her long, white bow-wave streaming away to wash noisily across an outcrop of sand and into the trees beyond.

Corbett said, 'Port ten! Steer zero nine zero!'

The deck canted as the helm went over, and Trewin heard the water thundering hard against the exposed bilges as the gunboat swung slightly away from the enemy warship.

There were two sharp flashes, followed almost at once by the shriek of shells overhead. One ploughed into the sea, and the other burst savagely amongst the trees on the nearest islet.

'Well, now they know!' Corbett sounded more relieved than anxious. 'Port fifteen!'

There were more flashes, and two columns of water soared skywards within fifty yards of the starboard quarter.

Mallory called hoarsely, 'Bring her round to oh four five, sir! It's about four miles to the inlet!'

'Very good. Tell the coxswain!' Corbett was watching the enemy with all his concentration.

The hatch cover was flung open and Trewin saw the admiral dragging himself on to the bridge, his eyes white below his heavy brows.

Corbett said, 'Enemy destroyer, sir! But her shooting's very poor so far.'

Fairfax-Loring clung to the table and peered astern. 'Where's the *Prawn*?'

Mallory replied, 'She's dropped back into the islands, sir.'

The admiral staggered on to the gratings beside Corbett and shouted, 'You wouldn't listen, would you?' He waved his free arm. 'You see, we had to leave her in the end, just as I told you we would!'

He ducked as another salvo screamed above the bridge and exploded somewhere in the shallows far abeam. He appeared to get a grip on himself. 'Or did you intend to use her as a red herring from the start?'

Corbett snapped his fingers impatiently. 'Half ahead together!' He was staring at the mass of land which rose above the bows like a cliff.

More shells followed the *Porcupine* as she swerved between the sandbars, but as the land moved out on either beam and the depth gauge registered less than two fathoms the bombardment ceased, and within half an hour of first sighting the destroyer she dropped anchor.

It was then, as the rain began to fall in earnest, that Corbett faced the admiral and said calmly, 'I should have told you, sir. I intend that *Prawn* should sail as soon as it is dark. She will head south, and by dawn tomorrow will be out of reach of surface attack.' He watched the admiral thoughtfully. 'In the meantime that destroyer will be waiting here for us to come out.' He gave the smallest hint of a smile. 'So you see, in a way we are the red herring, as you so aptly put it!'

The admiral shook himself, as if he imagined he was enduring some impossible nightmare. 'You're mad, Corbett! You don't know what you're saying!'

'I sent our boats over to *Prawn*, sir. And as much food and water as I could spare.' Corbett was waiting, his eyes following the admiral's agitation with cold indifference. 'If I can give Adair a few hours, I believe he and his passengers will be safe.'

Trewin broke in quietly, 'Shall I rig the camouflage, sir?'

'Not this time, Number one.' Corbett looked around the bridge, his face quite impassive. 'If the enemy have any planes, and they come searching, I want them to see the ship.' His tone hardened. 'Just this ship do you understand?'

Trewin saluted. 'Aye, aye, sir.'

The admiral swayed and gripped the table for support. Then he said harshly, 'I want all officers on the bridge immediately!'

Trewin looked at Corbett, who said coolly, 'See to it!'

Fairfax-Loring strode to the bridge wing and stood staring at the overhanging slab of cliff which, in spite of the watery sunlight, still held the ship in deep shadow.

The officers gathered uncertainly beside Trewin, while Corbett seated himself in his chair.

Then the admiral turned and said very slowly, 'You have all heard what has happened by now, gentlemen.' His tone was grave, and something in it reminded Trewin of the Fairfax-Loring he had seen and despised in the deserted bunker at Singapore.

He continued, 'It is therefore my unhappy duty to take steps to put right what has occurred. I must blame myself in many ways for all this. My trust was perhaps too blind, my choice for authority too biased by past connections.' He sighed heavily. 'But my duty is clear.' He looked at Corbett. 'I am relieving you of your command as of now. As soon as it is dark we will return to the islands and sail with *Prawn* as arranged. The enemy will go after the slower ship, but as I said earlier, we cannot hope to save every refugee from this unhappy affair!' He turned to Trewin. 'You will assume command.'

Trewin replied evenly, 'I agree with the captain, sir. You will have to replace me also.' He was surprised just how calm he felt. Or was it some sort of infectious madness? As if in a dream he heard Mallory mutter, 'And before you ask, it goes for me too, *sir*!'

Trewin turned and stared at the unsmiling Australian. But Mallory merely shrugged, as if he no longer understood either.

The admiral swallowed his anger and said stiffly, 'I will not humiliate you, Hammond, by asking for your loyalty. I know your father. His shame would be more than I could stand.'

Tweedie stepped forward, and everyone turned to watch him. 'You 'aven't asked me, sir?' He shuffled his feet and then said firmly, 'But rather than 'umiliate you any more than necessary, by makin' you address a ranker like meself, let me say that I want to stay alive as much as most.' He scowled and thrust out his blue chin. 'But I don't want no one callin' me a bloody coward, see?' He lapsed into silence and looked at his feet.

The admiral looked at each face in turn, his eyes blazing with anger and disdain. 'Then, *gentlemen*, I will assume command myself, in spite of my injuries, and take the ship to Java.' He paused meaningly. 'I don't think I have to tell you what will happen to you there?'

Corbett said calmly, 'I think you've not questioned *all* the officers, sir?'

The admiral swung round as his flag-lieutenant, supported by Baker, the sick-berth attendant, and Petty Officer Dancy appeared at the top of the hatch.

Hughes' thin face was very pale, but as he stared at his admiral his eyes lit up with some last desperate strength. 'Tell them what happened when *Prawn* was attacked, sir!' His voice was shrill and unnatural, and Dancy had to grip him with both hands to stop him falling. Hughes shouted, *'Prawn's* Number One was killed in the first attack!'

The admiral rasped, 'You were too frightened to see anything! So hold your stupid tongue!'

Hughes' head lolled. 'Frightened, yes! But not so scared that I didn't see you strip that officer of his shirt and put it on yourself!' Spittle was running from his mouth, but no one moved as he shouted wildly, 'You wore a dead man's shirt so that you could pretend to be wounded and hide below with the poor bloody women!' He was sobbing now. 'You bastard! You rotten dishonest, cowardly bastard!'

Corbett lifted one hand. 'Take that officer below, Baker!' He looked at Fairfax-Loring, his face sad. 'Do you wish to say anything more to my officers, sir?'

The bridge look-outs and signalmen were pushing forward

298

at the rear of the bridge, and the small group of officers fell back as the admiral removed his arm from inside the blood-stained shirt and stared at it with something like horror.

Dancy murmured in disgust, 'I should have shot him when he came down the beach.'

The admiral looked round, his eyes pleading. 'I had to save myself, don't you see? I'm more important than this ship, or those people on the *Prawn*! Can't you *see* that?'

No one replied to his outburst and he shouted, 'You're the ones who are wrong!'

Corbett's eyes were devoid of pity. 'We shall see, sir. When the opportunity arises to have me court-martialled, then you will know that my decision was right. If I was wrong, then it won't matter anyway.' He looked at Trewin. 'Please escort the admiral to his quarters.' Then he turned his back and walked to his chair.

The admiral seemed to sense the hostility around him mirrored on the unshaven faces and in the angry eyes of the watching men. He looked once at Corbett's back and said brokenly, 'I could forget all that you've done, if you'll only do as I say.'

Trewin touched his arm. 'I think you'd better go below, sir. Too many people have listened to you in the past. Nobody is ever going to *need* you again.'

For the first time he thought he saw fear in the admiral's eyes, and in those few seconds he had a stark picture of the man so terrified for his own safety that he was prepared to hide behind the blood of a dead man.

He swung round and said harshly, 'You go with the admiral, Pilot! He makes me feel unclean!'

Long after Fairfax-Loring had left the bridge nobody moved or spoke. Then Corbett looked at Trewin and said quietly, 'It's a strange thing. You wait for years to destroy the man who has ruined your life. But it's not really important, is it? When it comes, you merely feel ashamed. For him, and by him.'

As the bridge party moved slowly towards the ladders Trewin glanced along the full length of the ship. He could see the narrow entrance to the inlet and the hard line of the horizon stretching from wall to wall, like water in a great dam.

Corbett was right, he thought. It was not important any more. The past was over. And the future? He stared at the empty strip of horizon and felt strangely moved. Like the horizon, it seemed for ever out of reach.

18

A Mind of Her Own

Trewin pushed open Corbett's door and stepped over the low coaming. 'Ship ready to proceed, sir.' The simple formality seemed to hang in the humid air, and he was conscious of the steady, drumming rain across the deck above and the gurgle of water running down the superstructure and wet planking. The rain had gone on all day, while the ship tugged at her anchor in a sluggish current, penned in on either side by the great walls of the inlet. As the time for sailing drew near the rain had increased, so that through the open scuttle Trewin could see the nearest cliff running with countless muddy streams and small avalanches of displaced stones and uprooted bushes.

Corbett stood up and stared emptily at the scuttle. 'There's no sense in prolonging it.'

He looked alert and neat in his fresh whites, and there was no sign on his face to show the agony of mind he must be enduring. With Trewin at his heels he had been right round the ship, through every compartment and flat, pausing here and there to speak to some individual sailor, or to examine a particular section which took his attention.

Trewin said, 'I'm glad this waiting is over. I couldn't take much more.'

'It's always the worst part.' Corbett picked up his cap and placed it carefully on his head.

Trewin noticed with surprise that it was his best cap.

Corbett saw his glance and said simply, 'No point in doing things by half, eh?' But he did not smile.

Together they climbed up to the bridge and pulled on the thick, damp oilskins. The humidity brought Trewin into an immediate sweat, but without an oilskin he knew he would be unable to think, for the rain was heavier than he had expected and without relief.

Corbett looked around the open bridge, nodding to Masters and the signalmen. 'Ring down stand by.'

Trewin felt a tightness in his throat and suddenly longed for a drink. He heard the telegraph's remorseless reply and the sudden increase in vibration around him.

Corbett said, 'I want every spare man either on ammunition parties or damage control.' He looked at Masters. 'You can send one of the signalmen.'

Phelps spoke up nervously, 'I'll stay here, Yeo.'

Masters gestured to the other signalman and replied with a grin, 'Suit yourself, fire-eater! I 'ope you've got yer Jap sword with you!

Trewin gripped the voice-pipes hard and listened to the clank of incoming cable, steady and final above the roar of falling rain. Then faintly, 'Anchor's aweigh, sir!'

Corbett said, 'Slow ahead port, half astern starboard!'

Beside the voice-pipes Trewin saw the rain-soaked cliff begin to swing away as the ship turned slowly in her own length. When he looked towards the entrance of the inlet he could no longer see the open sea or the waiting horizon. The rain hung across the gap like a steel fence or the inside of a giant water-fall.

'Stop together!' Corbett looked up at the sky. 'Slow ahead together!'

A tremble ran through the deck plating, and somewhere far below there was a dull thud as some last watertight door was clipped home.

Corbett lifted himself on to his chair and reached for the bridge handset. The ship was moving very slowly with the stream, the channel widening almost imperceptibly as they slipped towards the entrance. He cleared his throat and pressed the button.

'This is the captain speaking,' His voice echoed around the upperdeck where the men already at their action stations crouched to avoid the rain, their faces now turned towards the bridge. 'We are putting to sea in order to draw the enemy away from the *Prawn*'s departure point.'

Trewin heard a hatch grate open, and when he looked over the screen he saw Nimmo staring up from his private world of noise and machinery, his eyes squinting in the downpour as he listened to Corbett's steady voice.

'There are three hours to darkness. Within that time we must endeavour to draw the enemy to the east, so that the *Prawn* may have the chance she so richly deserves.' He paused, and Trewin saw his face moving with emotion.

'I know that you all hoped we might escape without further danger. You deserved to attain that, as you have all done more than any captain could have wished. I know you will do your best.' He was about to replace the handset. Then he added, 'God bless you.'

Trewin watched him, feeling the men around him and the ship around them.

Corbett said suddenly, 'Hoist battle ensigns!'

He gestured towards the land, and Trewin saw a small group of motionless natives watching as they moved past.

'Not much of an audience, eh?' Corbett tugged the cap down over his forehead and turned as first one then another of the big ensigns crept up to each masthead.

Phelps made fast the halyard and muttered, 'Gawd, they're big!' His eyes followed the great ensign above his head. It looked very bright and clear against the dull clouds.

Above the rear of the bridge the rangefinder turned slightly behind its steel plating, and Trewin saw Tweedie standing to get a better look at the streaming flags. Poor Tweedie, he thought vaguely. Bungalow and retirement had been his final goals in life. If he lived after today nothing would ever be the same. He had spoken out against the authority he had served and helped to fashion. He was now standing to watch a small, tired river gunboat sail to face an enemy whose power they could only guess at.

'Port ten! Midships!' Corbett twisted in the chair, the rain bouncing from his shoulders and making the oilskin shine like glass. 'As soon as we break cover I shall turn hard to port and keep close inshore amongst the shallows.' He looked hard at Mallory. 'You'll earn your keep today, Pilot. For the next three hours it will be up to you to guide us from one piece of shelter to the next, right?'

Mallory met his eyes calmly. 'The next group of offshore islets are twenty miles along the coast, sir.'

'Good.' Corbett nodded. 'They will do for a start!'

Trewin swallowed hard. Do for a start! In three hours it might all be over.

When he raised his head he saw that the channel had widened right out on either beam, with the low swell from the open sea already sweeping lazily to greet them.

Every glass was trained above the screen as the *Porcupine*'s bows lifted contemptuously above the disturbed backwash of tide and river, but in the torrential rain it was impossible to see more than a cable's length in any direction.

'Port fifteen! Steady!' Corbett craned slightly forward and rested his binoculars against the screen.

Unwin's voice echoed up the brass tube. 'Steady, sir. Course oh nine oh.'

Several men glanced astern as the ship's small wash boiled away in a wide curve and the inlet faded into the rain. They were probably thinking of the *Prawn* and that every swing of the screws was taking them further to the east. Away from safety. Away from hope.

Then, as if the sea and sky had been waiting for just this moment, the rain faltered, and as the last of its downpour trickled noisily through the bridge scuppers the sun began to break through. It was a strange sunlight, which painted the sea like bronze and followed the departing rain until it touched the distant cliffs, so that the haze looked like steam rising from some subterranean fire.

Tweedie's voice shattered the sudden silence. 'Warship, sir! Bearing green one three oh! Range one double oh!'

Trewin ran across the gratings, his glasses pressed to his eyes, his mind empty as he stared back across the swaying screen. Then he saw it. The small low hull, the twin funnels almost overlapping as the destroyer completed a shallow turn and headed towards the shore.

Corbett snapped his fingers. 'Recognition manual! Lively there!'

Masters said thickly, '*Akikaze* Class, sir. Four four-point-sevens. Thirty-four knots.' He closed the book with a snap. There was nothing else which needed to be said.

'Full ahead together! Inform the chief that we have sighted the enemy!' Corbett swivelled round in his chair and peered back at the other ship. 'She'll be within accurate range in a few minutes.'

Tweedie's voice moved around the bridge like a threat. 'Target's course is now oh four five! Speed twenty plus!'

Corbett said, 'Four guns to our two. We must get him to draw nearer.'

Phelps jumped, 'He's opened fire, sir!'

The muffled explosion reached the *Porcupine* almost simultaneously with the sharp whine of a shell overhead. The waterspout rose ahead of the gunboat, between her and the shore.

'Port ten!' Corbett swayed slightly as the ship tilted to the rudders. 'We must keep him astern if we can. He can only bring one gun to bear then.'

Another bang and another waterspout, some eighty feet from the port bow.

Tweedie sounded tense. 'Target's range is oh nine two!'

Corbett picked up the handset. 'Open fire with "X" gun!'

Trewin craned round the funnel as the aft gun lurched back on its mounting, a long orange flash darting from the muzzle like a tongue. He saw the gunners ducking and grappling with the next shell and heard the shout, 'Ready, sir!' The gun cracked again, and he felt the pain probing at his ears as the shell ripped back at the overtaking destroyer which now seemed almost in line astern.

A giant column of water burst above the bridge and cascaded down over the screen, blinding and choking, and as Trewin staggered against the chart table he heard the ring and clash of splinters, the sharp cries from the deck below.

Tweedie sounded very calm. 'Up two hundred! Shoot!'

'Starboard ten!' Corbett did not look round.

Trewin felt the broken glass beneath his shoes and realised that the starboard screen had been shattered to fragments. There were some bright-edged holes in the funnel, but when he leaned over the wing he saw Hammond beside 'A' gun giving him a thumbs up.

'New course for the islets is oh seven five, sir!' Mallory stared at a drop of blood on the back of his hand, and then dabbed his forehead with his fingers. 'Bloody hell!'

Corbett sounded detached. 'I'm going to turn to starboard. We must bring "A" gun to bear.' He snatched the handset. 'Now listen, Guns, I want . . .' He waited as the aft gun cracked out again, the shockwave searing across the bridge like a hot wind. 'I want you to get a straddle if you can. We must hold him off until we can find some shelter.'

He did not wait for an answer. 'Starboard fifteen!'

With the screws at full speed the gunboat seemed to sway right over, and for a stark moment Trewin saw his own reflection staring back from the sea alongside before the boiling wave from the stem surged over it, cutting it aside in a bank of flying spray.

Both guns fired together, the recoil shaking at the bridge foundations, the twin explosions making men cry out and clasp their ears while the cordite smoke drifted around them, acrid and blinding.

Tweedie's voice was magnified and distorted with excitement. 'A hit! Jesus, a *hit*!'

Trewin tried to hold his glasses still and saw the destroyer leap wildly into focus, her towering bow-wave making a white moustache beneath her stem as she charged in pursuit. But at one side of her bridge, just below the wheelhouse, was a bright orange light, and as the deck swung beneath his feet he caught sight of the smoke drifting back to join that from her twin funnels, the final evidence of a direct hit.

Corbett shouted, 'Hard aport!' He sounded stiff with concentration as he brought his ship swinging back drunkenly to her original course.

But for those few, jubilant moments she had exposed herself to the enemy gunners. Not just a smoke-shrouded, end-on picture in their rangefinder, but her whole length.

Trewin felt the shell explode, but heard nothing. One minute he was clinging to the voice-pipes and the next he had his face pressed to the gratings, with someone else struggling across his spine. Water was falling around him, stifling him with salt and the foul taste of burned cordite. He could feel the ship still turning, the power of her racing propellers transmitting through the water and steel to strike against his chest like frantic heartbeats.

Pressing his hands on the warm plating he forced himself upright, and as his hearing slowly returned he heard the uninterrupted bark of gunfire and distant shouts which seemed to come from far away.

Mallory thrust his face close against his and yelled, 'Direct hit below the bridge!'

Corbett had apparently fallen from his chair, but as Trewin moved to reach him he staggered to his feet and snapped, 'Tell the chief to make smoke!' He shook his head sharply from side to side and then said, 'Get below, Number One. See what has to be done.'

Trewin nodded dumbly and clawed his way towards the ladder. For a moment he thought his legs would give way and he stood clinging to the rail, his eyes smarting in the gunsmoke as he peered down at the men who were running along the exposed sidedeck. He saw Dancy carrying a long axe and others with red fire extinguishers. Savagely he thrust himself down the ladder, and all but fell to the deck as he realised that the steel rungs had been severed as if by giant shears. The enemy shell had ploughed straight through the chartroom and across to the opposite side before exploding inside the radio room.

As he pushed past the crouching men he could see the sunlight through wide patterns of splinter holes, and beyond the buckled bulkhead of the radio room there was a steady glow of fire.

He shouted, 'Get those extinguishers up there, Buffer!' He stood aside as more men staggered by to seize the door, only to fall back cursing as they laid their hands on the hot metal clips.

Trewin tried to think, but his mind seemed too crowded with noise and confusion. Men were shouting and swearing, and from above he heard Tweedie's voice again, flat and impersonal 'Range oh seven oh!'

The hull gave another great lurch, and the confined passageway filled with blown smoke and the stench of burning paintwork. Above the din someone was screaming. It went on and on, in the same terrible note, so that some of the men appeared too shocked and sickened to move.

Dancy snarled, 'Get back!' He swung the axe against the clips, and as the door burst open he waded forward, his sturdy figure soaked instantly by the extinguishers as he stood framed in the rectangle of leaping flames.

Leading Telegraphist Laird was rolling and kicking below the remains of the smashed transmitter. He had no hands, and his blackened face was contorted in a mask of agony as he fought to escape the spreading fires. He saw Dancy and screamed, 'Me mate! 'E's back there!' He screamed again, and Trewin saw his blood spurt across Dancy's legs in a bright fountain.

Dancy shut his ears to Laird's cries and protests and hauled him bodily into the passageway. He gasped, 'Get those fires out, lads!' To Trewin he added thickly, 'Telegraphist Mears is done for. He's plastered across the bloody bulkhead like jam!' He retched and said fiercely, 'Where's the S.B.A., for God's sake?'

Trewin found his voice again. 'Let these men carry on here. They seem to be holding it now.' He pulled Dancy towards the ladder. 'We'll get aft!'

Like two drunks they swayed and staggered down the ladder and on to the other sidedeck. Nimmo's engineers were certainly complying with Corbett's order, and the sky was completely hidden beyond the dense smoke which poured back from the funnel and spread across the sea astern in an unmoving, choking fog. 'X' gun had fallen silent, and Trewin heard the gunners coughing behind their blinded sights, and someone else yelling, 'Stretcher party down aft!'

As they reached the end of the superstructure Trewin and Dancy stared down with sick horror at the crater which spread across the small quarterdeck almost from side to side. There was no fire here, but as he peered down at the ragged-edged hole Trewin saw the faint gleam of water.

Dancy muttered, 'My God! We can't take much more of this!'

Something crawled from the smoke and made its way towards the sidedeck. Trewin gritted his teeth, holding back the nausea as he watched it.

'Get that man below, Buffer!'

Dancy ran across the deck and caught the crawling figure as it rolled on to its side. He looked up at Trewin, his eyes shining. 'He's dead, thank God!' He lowered the corpse to the deck. 'How did he stay alive so long?' He looked away. 'His face has gone!'

Baker and his stretcher party came aft at the run, and Trewin shouted. 'There's another man by the guardrail! I think he's still alive!'

Baker skidded to a halt, and Trewin saw the blood-splashes across his white jacket. Like a butcher, he thought dully. He made another effort, 'Are you managing, Baker?'

The man looked remarkably calm. He nodded. 'We're doing what we can, sir. I can only drug and bandage them.' He stared at the mutilated corpse by his feet and wiped his face with the back of his hand. 'Even a real doctor couldn't do much here.'

They ducked as another shell burst on the opposite beam, sending a small tidal wave of spray leaping up and over the battery deck.

'They're shooting blind now, thank God!' Dancy spoke between his teeth. A smoking shell-splinter clattered by his side and with a grunt he kicked it over the edge of the hull.

Trewin looked forward and tried not to remember how far they were from those next islands. Not that it mattered. The ship had altered course so many times to avoid the enemy's shells, distance meant nothing.

But the screws were still beating the water into a mane of froth below the counter, and above the greasy smoke he could see the shadowy outline of the ensign. *Porcupine* was dying, but she was not giving in easily.

A stoker petty officer ran through the smoke and stopped when he saw Trewin. 'No real damage below, sir! Just a few plates down aft, but the pumps can cope for a bit!' He wiped his streaming face. 'I've counted seven dead an' wounded, so far!'

There was a sharp crack followed instantly by one thunderous explosion. The petty officer's face twisted in agony, but before he could cry out he was picked up bodily and hurled against Trewin.

Dancy shouted, 'The bridge! That one hit the bridge!'

Trewin dropped the dead man on the deck. One jagged splinter had caught the petty officer directly in the back, ripping him almost in half.

Trewin kept his eyes on the new pall of smoke above the battery deck and refused to think of his own fate. But for the petty officer's shield he would have taken the splinter in his stomach.

He dragged himself up the ladder, shutting his ears to the screams around him, ignoring the headless corpse which stayed strapped in an Oerlikon, its hands still training the gun towards the enemy.

The starboard wing of the bridge had vanished in a trail of splintered planking and long strips of torn metal. The steel was folded and buckled like tinfoil in a great heat, and as he staggered across the bridge Trewin almost fell on top of Masters, the yeoman. Phelps rose from beneath his upended flag locker, shaking himself like a dog, apparently unhurt. He saw Trewin staring at him and tried to grin. Then he looked around the smoke-filled bridge, seeing it for the first time. His gaze fell on Masters, and with a quick cry he bent down and tried to lever the man away from the gaping hole above the leaping water.

Trewin found Corbett clinging to the back of his chair, one hand reaching out towards the voice-pipes. He saw Trewin and gasped, 'The wheelhouse! Is it intact?' He coughed and then added, 'I'm all right, Number One! I think someone must have broken the blast for me!'

Trewin shouted, 'Wheelhouse!'

Unwin sounded near and very relieved. 'All correct down here, sir! Both engines still full ahead, steady on oh eight oh!' He added, 'I thought you was all done for up there! There was bleedin' smoke comin' down the tube!'

Trewin looked down as something touched his shoe. It was Mallory. He was lying on his back, his eyes very wide, and for a moment Trewin thought he was dead. But the hand moved and gripped his leg, as if quite independent of its owner. Trewin dropped beside him and tried to push his arm under his shoulders. Mallory's eyes moved slightly but refused to focus on his face.

He said tightly, 'Don't move me, for Christ's sake! My back's busted!' He moved his mouth and then whispered, 'I always knew the Pommies'd do for me!' His teeth clamped suddenly on his lip, and Trewin saw blood running down his chin. Mallory said, 'Sorry we never got time to know each other.' He reached up and patted Trewin's shoulder, the tired movement bringing his hard features out in a rash of sweat. Then the hand dropped and his eyes became suddenly blank and disinterested.

Trewin stood up and looked at Corbett. 'Dead.'

Two shells exploded through the smoke, throwing up two tall waterspouts and hammering the hull with more splinters.

From aft came a yell, 'Heads below! The mainmast is going!'

The funnel smoke was too dense to see from the bridge, but Trewin heard the crash of timber and the scrape and screech of trailing stays as the severed mast pitched overboard. He

311

heard axes, too, and Dancy's voice carrying like a trumpet as he urged his men to hack the wreckage away.

Corbett looked up at the other flag above the bridge and said, 'We can't reach those islands! The destroyer must have hauled off to use another gun on us!' He stared at Trewin, his eyes blazing. 'We can't run any more!'

Trewin became aware for the first time of someone sobbing. When he looked beyond the splintered chart table he saw Phelps on his knees rocking from side to side as he stared wretchedly at the yeoman.

One of the look-outs touched his arm and said, ' 'Ere, Ginger, leave 'im. There's nowt you can do for 'im.'

But Phelps stayed down beside Masters' body, his eyes running with tears. 'I couldn't stop the bleeding! I tried, but it kept comin'!'

Trewin pulled Phelps to his feet as the look-out threw an oilskin across the dead yeoman. 'Easy, boy! You did your best.'

Phelps said between sobs, ' 'E kept lookin' at me. I know 'e wanted to tell me somethin'.' He dropped his head. 'But I couldn't do nothin' for 'im.'

Corbett said quietly, 'Masters was a good yeoman, Phelps. I expect he was trying to tell you that it's your turn to take charge now.' He watched the boy's tortured face. 'So just remember what he taught you, eh?' He looked at Trewin across the signalman's head. 'This isn't doing any good, is it?'

A shell ripped through the halyards and brought the last big ensign floating down towards the bridge like a shroud. As it touched the blood-spattered gratings Phelps seemed to come alive again. With sudden determination he picked up the flag, and without another glance at Masters, began to splice one of the broken halyards for it.

Trewin replied harshly, 'The Jap doesn't have to worry, does he? He just follows our oil slick and keeps firing into the smoke.' He looked astern, his eyes angry. 'And our gunners can't see a bloody thing!'

Corbett regarded him calmly. 'I know. It also means that we will be useless as far as *Prawn* is concerned. We can't survive for another hour, let alone until darkness.' He gripped the torn steel with both hands. 'We just can't run any more, Trewin. You know that now, don't you?' His eyes were searching. 'Well?'

Trewin did not even flinch as another shell exploded somewhere abeam. His body and mind seemed past care and beyond feeling. *What are we saying? Why are we always pretending?*

He looked around the scarred bridge, at the bodies covered with their oilskins. From beneath one he could see Mallory's hand, stiff and pointing, like a condemnation. And aft, beyond the screen, past the dead Oerlikon gunner and riddled funnel, where was the ship Corbett loved so dearly? The battery deck was pitted with holes, and right aft, where the men by 'X' gun still stared helplessly at the smoke, the stump of the mainmast seemed to mock him like a splintered lance.

Corbett reached out and gripped his wrist. In the distorted light his face looked lined, but strangely peaceful. 'It has to be your decision, too, Trewin. If it is to be done, it must be done perfectly.' For a moment a shaft of despair crossed his pale eyes. 'Poor old girl. She doesn't deserve this!'

He looked away and then said harshly, 'Warn the guns. Prepare to fire at about red four five. Tell Tweedie yourself.' He gestured towards the tangled mess of severed wiring beside the two bodies. 'Communications have all gone.' He climbed on to his chair and stared ahead towards the empty, inviting horizon. To port the long beach of Banka was still shrouded in mist and looked very remote.

Trewin tore his eyes away and climbed quickly up the short ladder to the spotting position abaft the bridge. He found Tweedie and his two ratings behind the steel shield and said, 'We're going to turn. You'll have to lay both guns right on the bastard. There'll be no second chance!' He saw that Tweedie's arm was wrapped in a crude bandage and asked, 'Are you all right? Shall I send for the first aid party?'

Tweedie swung slightly on his metal seat and scowled. 'I can manage!' He touched the rangefinder. 'God, I'll smash a couple into the sod when I see 'im!' He picked his handset, but as Trewin climbed down the ladder he added gruffly, 'But thanks all the same! You done quite well for an amateur!' Surprisingly, he grinned. 'If ever you gets to 'Ampshire you can come an' stay with me an' the old woman, if you like.' He turned his back and snapped, 'Attention all guns!' He was lost again in his own world, which he shared with no one.

Trewin found Corbett crouching over the chart, his magnifying glass held inches above it. He said, 'Shallows to port, Trewin. Barely two fathoms.' He rubbed his chin. 'But it deepens out in the next half-mile.' He met Trewin's questioning stare. 'It'll have to be *now*.'

Trewin looked up at the ensign. It must have been the last thing Mallory saw on this world, he thought.

Corbett moved to the voice-pipes. 'Cox'n, this is the captain. In fifteen seconds I am going hard astarboard, right?' Unwin's voice was lost in another sharp explosion. Some splinters clanged against the bridge, and from below a man cried out like a wounded animal. Corbett continued in the same flat tone. 'Whatever you see or hear, I want you to hold the course and the speed I give you.' His voice hardened. '*No matter what!*'

He turned and looked back at the writhing smoke, 'He's lying back there, just biding his time. He knows we can't reach the islands. He's just got to keep firing into the smoke beyond our trail of oil. Sooner or later he'll hit the vital spot.' His lips curled bitterly. 'If we give him the chance!'

He glanced again at Trewin. 'I'll not forget this.' He did not explain what he meant, but pulled himself forward against the remains of the screen.

Then he said firmly, 'Hard astarboard! Stand by to engage!'

Broken woodwork and glass cascaded over the bridge deck as the ship responded immediately to the rudders and swung crazily across her own backwash. A freak down-draught plunged the bridge into semi-darkness, and the slipping, struggling men fell choking and coughing in the dense oily smoke, while their bodies angled further and still further against the madly tilting decks.

Corbett shouted, 'Stop the starboard engine! Get her *round*!'

The bridge structure quivered from top to bottom as the starboard screw raced impotently in the air before falling silent in its protective tunnel, and all the time the ship was plunging round, her remaining mast reaching across the boiling bow-wave, her gunners clinging to any solid thing to stop themselves from being hurled to the mercy of the sea.

Corbett pulled himself towards the compass repeater and called, 'Midships! Full ahead starboard!' He peered down at the spray-dappled glass, heedless of the din around him or the demoniac shriek of shells overhead. 'Steady! Meet her, man!'

Unwin sounded as if he was knocked breathless. 'Steady, sir! Course two four five!'

Corbett began to claw his way back to the screen. 'Steer two six oh!' He did not wait for an acknowledgement, but held tightly to the teak rail below the splintered glass and watched intently while the ship swayed through another roll and then stayed upright.

Trewin stood by his side staring with smarting eyes at the writhing wall of smoke which parted across the bows and billowed back around the bridge. It was like tearing through a long tunnel, and apart from the razor-back bow-wave which lifted almost as high as the gun mounting, the sea was hidden, as was the sky.

He yelled, 'We'll see her soon!'

Corbett licked his lips. 'He's still firing! Hear those shells!' He turned with a strange expression of defiance and excitement on his face. 'He didn't see us turn!'

Trewin peered forward and saw Hammond crouched beside his gun crew, a handkerchief tied across his nose and mouth. The smoke was streaming around the gunshield, so that it looked as if the mounting and gunners were standing in space.

A look-out shouted wildly, 'Look, sir! Fine to port!' He was pointing, unable to find the right words any more.

At first Trewin could see nothing. Merely a slight thinning of smoke as the *Porcupine* raced to the final limit of her own screen.

Then the destroyer fired again, and he saw the brief orange flash above a darker patch in the swirling smoke. As the dying sunlight dipped to greet them and the gunboat's forecastle pushed out above a patch of clear blue water, Trewin saw the other ship less than two cables away.

He was thrown back from the screen as Hammond's gun recoiled, and when he looked again he saw the shell strike home almost on the destroyer's waterline. The two ships tore towards each other, and Trewin judged that the enemy would pass down the port beam with not much room to spare.

Corbett was shouting, 'Hit him! *Shoot*, lads!'

'X' gun fired at an extreme angle, so that its shell ripped past the *Porcupine*'s bridge wing, flinging back the machine-gunner with its shockwave before exploding with a blinding flash below the enemy's forecastle.

From somewhere aft on the destroyer's low hull a single gun fired in reply. It was probably the first shot from that gun, and for that reason its crew were the best prepared for the *Porcupine*'s sudden appearance. The shell slammed into the port side of the bridge structure, so that Trewin felt the explosion through his feet and legs, as if he had been kicked in the spine.

Corbett seized his arm, his face contorted through the smoke. 'We can't stop her now, Trewin!' He swung away as a voice shouted, 'Wheel's jammed, sir! No answer from helm!'

'Are you hit, Cox'n?' Corbett cupped his hands above the voice-pipe.

Unwin's answer was clear even over the surge of water and the dogged explosions from both guns. 'No, sir! But the wheel won't answer!'

Corbett said brokenly, 'We must steer from aft, Trewin!' But as he looked across the voice-pipes Trewin saw the misery and defeat in his face.

Above the screen he could see the destroyer's topmast, the patch of colour from her battle flag. It would soon be over now. The last gesture of defiance had failed. Within the next few minutes the destroyer would swing away and pound them to scrap, without quarter, without pity.

Phelps almost fell across the gratings as he pulled at Trewin's arm. 'Sir! We're *turnin'*!' His voice broke in a shriek. 'Look! We're headin' for the destroyer!'

Trewin gripped the rail, his brain stunned by the sick madness of battle. For a moment longer he thought the other ship was already swinging inwards to smash into the gunboat's punctured hull and roll her under the impetus of her charge. But Phelps was right. The *Porcupine* was turning, and with her maximum speed still making the screws race, the rudders were wrenching her round, so that her blunt bows were already pointing directly at the destroyer's high, raked stem.

A man screamed, 'She'll cut us in half!' But nobody heeded his words.

From the wheelhouse Trewin heard Unwin shout in despair, 'I can't shift it, sir! The rudders is hard over!'

Corbett stood upright against the screen, both hands firmly on the rail. He seemed suddenly to relax, so that Trewin watched him instead of facing the charging force of destruction across the bows.

Corbett said, 'We failed her, Trewin. So she's taking her own revenge!'

Trewin looked towards the enemy. She was so close that he could see the depth markings on her stem, the frantic figures running away from the forward gun, and the gesticulating officers on her high bridge.

The *Porcupine* was across those bows now, a diagonal barrier of solid steel, which would smash the destroyer's stem to fragments before it sliced into her own vitals and drove her down for the last time.

Corbett said. 'She's got her helm down!' He sounded as if he no longer knew what to expect. 'She's trying to turn!'

Across the narrowing gap they could hear the scream of power as the destroyer's thirty thousand horsepower roared against the rudder and threw her into a last, desperate turn.

Trewin tore his eyes away and swung on the shocked, mesmerised men behind him. 'Open fire! *Shoot*, you bastards!'

He pulled the seaman away from the starboard machine-gun and pressed his thumb down on the trigger.

The destroyer seemed above and around them, a swaying wall of grey steel with her deck slanting down towards them as she swung away like a mad thing. Away from the *Porcupine*'s maddened charge, away from that final embrace.

Trewin kept his thumb on the trigger, seeing nothing but the steel deck alive with flying sparks as his bullets raked across it, cutting through a group of running seamen and tossing them aside like bloody rags.

He saw a line of tracer lifting from the destroyer's main-deck, watched it lift so very slowly before it plunged down to flay the *Porcupine*'s reeling hull like a steel whip. It was like fighting a duel with that last enemy gunner to keep his head when his own ship was swaying over like a beast gone mad. Trewin followed the ship across his jerking sights, ignoring the crash and whine of bullets around him, the sudden cries and the wild yells of the *Porcupine*'s gunners. He knew it was Phelps by his side, his hands guiding the long ammunition belt, but his mind held nothing but that line of tracer and the small stabbing spurts of flame.

As if in a nightmare he heard Unwin yell, 'Helm's answerin', sir! Comin' back on course now!'

Then he forgot even that miracle as the destoyer's bows appeared to lift, shudder, slide forward and then plough into a great welter of bursting spray and sand.

Dimly he remembered Corbett saying about the shallows. In his desperation to avoid the *Porcupine*'s challenge, the other captain must have forgotten the nearness of danger below his racing keel. He saw the froth shooting helplessly from the destroyer's screws and heard the grinding crash of metal being buckled and prised apart by the force of the grounding. The tracer had stopped, and the enemy's decks were alive with running men, some of whom scattered and fell to another burst of automatic fire from aft. When Trewin looked over the rail he saw Sergeant Pitt striding along the battery deck, a Bren cradled on his hip as he fired continuously across the widening gap of churned, discoloured water.

Sweating, and bleeding from a cut across his cheek, Hammond ran up the bridge ladder and threw his arm around Trewin's neck. 'We did it!' He was weeping with delirious excitement. 'We *did* it!'

They both turned as Phelps said, 'The captain, sir! He's been hit!'

With the gunboat already swinging back into her smoke-screen, the stranded destroyer was lost within minutes, her menace gone.

Trewin knelt beside Corbett and lifted him against the side of the bridge. Corbett opened his eyes as Trewin unbuttoned the oilskin he had worn throughout the action. Then he looked past Trewin towards Hammond and the men of the bridge party who crowded round behind him.

Trewin stared at the blood on Corbett's chest and at another clotted wound below his ribs. 'Get Baker on the double!' He tried not to meet Corbett's eyes. Then he said, 'You were already wounded, sir.' He eased his arm behind Corbett's shoulders, holding him away from the vibrating steel. 'Why didn't you tell me?'

Corbett smiled. 'We were all too busy, Trewin.'

Petty Officer Dancy pushed through the silent men, a wad of dressing in his hands. As he placed the pad across Corbett's chest he said quietly, 'The admiral's been wounded, sir.' He tried to smile. 'He really has this time.'

Corbett looked up at the flag and said wearily, 'I'd forgotten about him.'

Trewin said, 'The *Prawn* will be safe now. We pulled it off.' He felt his eyes smarting with despair and pride. 'You were right about the *Porcupine*, sir. She's a mind of her own.'

Corbett smiled. 'Help me up, Trewin. Into my chair.'

Trewin saw Baker watching him. He gave a small shrug.

Very carefully, with Hammond and Phelps beside him, he lifted Corbett on to the same scarred and chipped chair. The move must have been a torment of pain, but Corbett said,

'Thank you. I can see her better now.' Then in an almost normal tone he added, 'Reduce speed. She's taken enough for one day.' He grimaced and then said, 'Alter course. Steer due south.' His fingers gripped the dressing into a bright red ball against his chest. 'There's nothing ahead of us now except Java. The end of the voyage!'

Tweedie had climbed down from the rangefinder, and Trewin saw Nimmo too in his filthy overalls, and Petty Officer Kane carrying a Bren beneath his arm.

They were all looking at their ship, the battered, listing but defiant gunboat which had drawn them together and had held them so in the face of final disaster.

Corbett said suddenly, 'This would have been the last one for me anyway.' He sounded very tired. 'But the darkness is here at last, thank God.'

Trewin saw the men look away. The bridge was still bronzed in the strange sunlight, and the horizon stood out clear and sharp below the last of the clouds.

Trewin said quietly, 'Yes, sir. It's dark now. You can rest.'

Unwin's voice echoed amongst the silent, smoke-grimed figures. 'Course one eight oh, sir! Steady as you go!'

Corbett's hand dropped against the chair and his head lolled slightly in time with the ship's easy movement.

Trewin stood back and removed his cap. It was over.

Dancy was the first to break the silence. 'This is something none of us'll forget. The mistakes and the failures.' He dropped his eyes. 'And the shame.'

Trewin nodded. 'There *was* shame, Buffer.' He let his eyes move along the splintered decks, the grotesque holes in the plating, and back over the straight, unbroken line of the *Porcupine*'s wake. 'And there was glory, too. . . .'